THE BATTLE WAS THEIRS!

Hawk's Shadow, tossing his young son into the air, told boisterously of the chase, the fight, and the victory. Blake, very tired and excited by the talk, dropped down by the fire and took a bowl of stew in eager hands.

Abruptly, Hawk's Shadow stopped talking. The lodge was still except for the gurgling of Little Chief and the rain outside. Looking around questioningly, Blake found all their eyes on him in the dim light. Seeing him looking, they looked away. Then he felt a movement behind him and, very softly, a small voice said, "Why do you sit on my blankets?"

"My God!" he whispered and leapt up, almost stumbling into the fire.

What he had done, coming into the lodge and sitting down on the edge of the blankets that Shy Fawn lay wrapped in, was a kind of marriage proposal. Had he sat there without thinking? Or was this something he really wanted without quite knowing?

FRANCES CASEY KERNS

This
Land
Is
Mine

WARNER BOOKS

A Warner Communications Company

WARNER BOOKS EDITION

Library of Congress Catalog Card Number: 74-9990

ISBN 0-446-82704-5

This Warner Books Edition is published by
arrangement with Thomas Y. Crowell Company

Cover art by Ben Wohlberg

Warner Books, Inc., 75 Rockefeller Plaza, New York, N.Y. 10019

 A Warner Communications Company

Printed in the United States of America

Not associated with Warner Press, Inc. of Anderson, Indiana

First Printing: May 1976

Reissued: May, 1978

10 9 8 7 6

FOR ALAN
who brought home the germ of the idea
and always
FOR JACK

The Camas Valley, western Montana

1. eastern pass
2. trail to buffalo country (3.)
4. western pass
5. Camas Post
6. Darkwater River
7. Medicine Rock Creek
8. the Medicine Rock
9. village of Medicine Rock
10. Blake's valley
11. Never Summer mountain
12. north fork of Medicine Rock Creek
13. Hamilton ranch
14. Harmony City
15. Clark's Fork
    trail running west (16.) to the Clearwater River
    and east (17.) to buffalo country
18. Camas Prairie
19. Pass crossed by Medicine Rock men to ambush the Blackfeet
20. Continental Divide
21. Divide bounding Camas Valley on the west

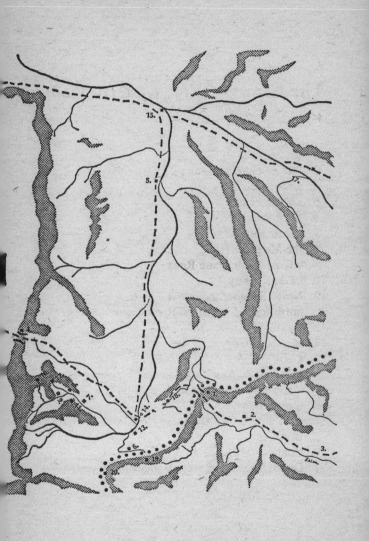

BOOK ONE

I

BLAKE WOKE, or half-woke, conscious enough to be too aware of the pain. He had, it seemed, been trying to hide from the pain for a long, long time. He ached all over, but the pain was centered in his head and great throbbing waves spread out from that center, engulfing him. Matters were not helped by the fact that he was now being moved —carried? He tried to struggle away from what seemed a large number of hands but that only made the pain worse. He chanced opening his eyes and the light of a fire hit them like a blow. The people bending above him had dark beardless faces, black hair . . . . Were they Indians? Where was he? What had happened? How had this come to be?

They had put him down and someone was prodding at him. He opened his eyes again, a little. The young man who wanted his attention said, in sign language, "You will be better. Good strong medicine."

It was night. There was a big clear sky, the stars pushed back by the firelight. Men and women and children were hurrying around him. One of the men had a drum and he began to beat on it. Blake groaned and turned his face away, trying to sink so deeply into the robes on which he lay that he needn't be aware of anything.

There was snow, hard-packed around the fire, and the silhouettes of lodges stood up at the edges of the light. A dog came and sniffed at him and Blake shrank away, his body breaking out in a light sweat, a sweat brought about by the pain and by fear. This was an Indian village. The people moving purposefully about him were Indians and they were making ready for some sort of ceremony. Some of them had rattles made of strings of deer hoofs or of a few rocks in a rawhide covering. They began to shake the rattles in time with the drum beats and in time with the throbbing waves that emanated from his head. And now the pain, the drumming, the rattling, the just-begun chanting were accompanied by nausea rising within him. He was a prisoner. They were going to kill him in some horrible, ritualized way. They were mountain Indians— Flathead? Nez Perce? Coeur d'Alene? Cayuse? What the hell did it matter? Except that the tortures of the mountain tribes were not likely to be so sadistic, so drawn-out as those of, say, the Blackfeet. But was that really any consolation?

An old man was bending over him, a hideous, toothless old man who wafted the smells of rancid grease and other things. Chanting, he drew off the robe that covered Blake. The cold air struck his naked body jarringly. The old man began, horribly, to howl like a wolf. Thinking was impossible now. All Blake could hope for was that it would end soon so that he need not try to think. He wanted only to close his eyes, to slip into unconsciousness, into death, without knowing any more of it.

The old man touched him about the head, body, arms, and legs with something cold and clammy and withdrew a little to dance, still howling. Blake tried weakly to pull up the robes on which he lay, to cover himself. It seemed important beyond all reason that he not die exposed like this. But the young man, the one who had made sign to him, snatched the edge of the robe from his groping hands, muttering something with sharp urgency. Blake caught only the word "No!" The noise, the cold, the pain would drive him mad. He lapsed a little, his senses refusing to see or hear so well, protecting him to a degree from what he could not bear.

He wondered vaguely, disinterestedly, how he had known the meaning of the word "no," spoken as it had been in the young brave's own language, and how he had known the meaning of the signs made to him earlier: "You will be better. Good strong medicine." Blake might

12

have smiled if he had had strength for smiling. That was a trick, of course. Indians liked to try to deceive their captives. It was an intrinsic part of the torture. He would not be taken in. Lying here, with freezing now added to the rest of it, he was expected to shout insults and bold claims at them until he was dead. He would disappoint them, bring ridicule on himself by not trying to do that, but he wanted what strength there was for trying to be oblivious. They considered the insults, the bravado as the manly way to die, the way of dying that brought merit to a captive in their land . . . . How did he know these things?

He could not have learned them as a boy in the mountains of western Pennsylvania. The few Indians still left there lived in specified reserves, most of their old ways and their pride gone. They had taken no white captives for a long time. He had not learned sign language and customs of torture as a teamster with the freight line over the Alleghenies, nor as a surveyor's helper, nor on the schooner *Lydia*. He had had nothing to do with any Indians during those obscene, guilty, beautiful years in New Orleans. During the months he had worked around the St. Louis waterfront, there had been an Indian now and then, but not like these. These people were in their element, lords of their land, masters of themselves and of him, but how had he come here? How did he understand?

The old man, howling mightily, came close to him again, knelt down and began gently blowing into his ear. It was too much. Blake sank gratefully into unconsciousness.

When he again became unwillingly cognizant of his surroundings, they seemed to consist of unbearable heat. He lay on robes, in darkness, breathing steamy air, his aching body running with sweat. But they were not burning him alive, not yet. The ground beneath him was cool. He sought it weakly, hungrily. An imperious hand stopped his movements, a woman's hard, work-worn hand, and she spoke to him harshly, ordering him to lie still. Light from a fire came to him momentarily through some temporary opening and there was a great hissing sound. The light gleamed again, briefly, and was gone. Fresh steam came into his nostrils.

He remembered having measles when he was a little

boy, he and one of his cousins in the same bed, feverish, half-delirious in the midst of July heat, and how their grandmother had kept a fire going in the room and had made them stay wrapped stiflingly in quilts until they were thoroughly "broke out." "Stay still, Blake," she had ordered in the same sharp tones this other woman used. "It's for your own good."

Gasping in the smothering cloud of fresh steam, he was aware amid the pain and heat that there was chanting, drumming, and rattling outside where the brief light had come from and that the old man was beside him again, first howling, then breathing foully on his head. What seemed hours later, he was again aware of movement. They were wrapping him in the sweat-soaked robes, carrying him out again into the night. What next? God, let it be over soon!

They moved away from the fire swiftly, the howling old monster walking beside him. He heard the sound of running water. "No!" he said and it was only a feeble whisper. "Please . . . ."

It was true. They were, in their own particular, ghastly way, trying to make him well. For what reason? So they could more satisfyingly torture him to death? But what did it matter? He would surely be dead in a moment now.

They stripped away the robes. The icy air stung his hot body brutally. The old man howled with renewed fervor . . . . How did he know this was supposed to be a cure? They could hardly have devised a worse torture, but how had he come to know things about the ways of these Indians?

Rough, strong, well-meaning hands seized him, lowering him toward the frigid water where a hole had been broken, near the edge of the stream, in the thin spring ice. Blake cried out weakly, hopelessly. The water came over him with a grinding shock and he fell at last into complete oblivion.

Blake Westfall had come up from New Orleans to St. Louis working on a riverboat, a hot, dirty job in the engine room, he the only white among a crew of blacks, stripped to the waist in the heat, feeding the fire. He had come to the New Orleans waterfront in desperation, run-

14

ning, seeking a ship to take him away, anywhere. The only ship putting out to sea that night had a full crew. He had no money. The mate of the river steamer looked askance at the good clothes he wore, then shrugged with a grim, mean little smile.

"How do you feel about gettin' your hands dirty, boy? One of my roustabouts died this mornin'. You anxious enough to leave this town to *work* your way to St. Louis?"

Blake had no interest in St. Louis. He had thought fleetingly in time past that when the time for his escape should present itself, he might work his way to France. His French was very good now. He could find some kind of work there, in another country, try to make sense of his life and become reconciled to living with himself. Etienne St. Croix had died finally and the only boat leaving New Orleans that night was the river streamer bound for St. Louis.

Blake's hands, that had held little more than a pen for two years now, blistered badly on the shovel handles. One of the crew members, with a kind of rough, considerate tolerance, wrapped them for him in some greasy rags. Blake worked doggedly, hardly knowing if it was day or night in the reeking, stifling darkness.

"I don't pay," the mate told him shortly, "till we're back in New Orleans. This here's no one-way business. My roustabouts signed on for a round trip."

"I didn't sign anything," Blake said, looking bleakly up at the docks and warehouses of the St. Louis waterfront.

The mate grunted scornfully and made a derisive gesture of dismissal. "You got a cargo to help unload. Get on with it."

With darkness, Blake slipped away from the boat and into the city. St. Louis was almost as old and diverse as New Orleans, though not so large or cosmopolitan. For many years, it had been the jumping-off place to the unknown west, existing under several flags, attracting many and varied people. As Blake walked the streets, hungry, with no destination, he recalled that William Clark still lived here, the William Clark of the Lewis and Clark Expedition, sent out near the beginning of the century by President Jefferson to see how far it might be to the western ocean and if there was a water route, to begin mapping the northern part of the United States' newly purchased Louisiana Territory. That he remembered and not much more. He had no interest in St. Louis. An old town it might be, but comparing its atmosphere to that of the life he had been leading recently, he noticed only the roughness, the harshness, the feeling of hurry and transience of the place. He overheard some French, mostly dialects strange to him, some Spanish of which he understood only a little. Even the English he heard had a rough, different, frontier sound. It was the fall of 1840. Blake Westfall was twenty-one years old, alone, bewildered, hungry, broke.

In the damp, cold dawn, shivering in his light southern clothing, he came to an old man limping behind a broom in front of a warehouse.

"You lookin' for work, boy?"

"Yessir, I am."

The old man looked him over with sharp blue eyes, the good but now worn and filthy clothes, the stocky frame, dark brown hair, open, unhappy face, uneasy green eyes.

"What can you do?"

"I can sweep," Blake said with a small tentative smile.

"Anything else?"

"I've been a clerk, a sailor, a teamster, a surveyor . . . ."

"Clerk, huh? Higgins is lookin' for a clerk. You know anything about buffler hides?"

"Buffalo? No."

"Can you learn?"

"Probably."

"Hungry, ain't you? Come on in here. I got some coffee an' stuff."

His name was Henry Melton and he had a little room in a rear corner of the warehouse, partitioned off with packing cases, barely large enough for a dirty, rumpled cot and a rusty, decrepit stove. The whole place had a pungent, particularly unpleasant smell about it.

"Hides and furs," Henry explained the smell and the stacked bales in passing.

He gave Blake coffee so strong and bitter it must have been brewed at least three times. It tasted of the odor that seemed to permeate everything, but Blake took the hot

16

cup and drank greedily. Henry fried pieces of fat side meat in old, sputtering grease.

"Wisht this was buffler meat," he said restlessly. "This child would surely like to taste some fat cow again." His blue eyes took on a strange look as though they were seeing far beyond the cold, dirty room. "You ever eat buffler?"

Blake said he hadn't, but he knew it wouldn't have mattered what he said or if he said nothing. The old man was launched upon recollections and tales of the hunt and the trail, oblivious to everything else.

"I first come west in '18," he said. "Come from back in Kentucky. First I was in the war. You wouldn't remember. It was one of them wars we had with the Britishers. Fought under Bromleigh, a good man. He was killed up on the lakes. I got out to the mountains and went to work for the RMF—Rocky Mountain Fur Company, that was—Tom Fitzpatrick, Jim Bridger, Jed Smith, the Sublette brothers, I knowed all of 'em, worked with 'em, as fine a bunch of ole hosses as ever crossed the mountains. I seen comp'nies come an' go; seen the beaver go, too. Hell, it ain't nothin' now like it was then. Buffler robes! Waugh!" He spat on the floor.

Blake squeezed past him to turn the sizzling pork. Henry had forgotten it.

"Beaver goin', a lot of them good ole boys gone an' Henry Melton still around, takin' care of a goddam warehouse full of buffler robes. Why, I seen the day when one good beaver plew'd fetch a half dozen buffler robes, but then them fancy Jehus used to want beaver hats decided beaver wasn' good enough for 'em, got to have silk now; least that's how I've heard it. Silk! Waugh!" He spat again and went on wistfully, "But it's just as well, I reckon. Beaver's mostly gone now, except for a few places maybe, like the Bayou Salade. Never went down in that part of the country much myself. That's part of the Platte, South Platte. The stompin' grounds I always liked best was to the north, Powder River, the Yellowstone, Three Forks, and over acrost the Divide on the Green, the Snake, some down the Clearwater an' Clark's Fork, though that country was supposed to be Hudson's Bay territory. There was one time—I was workin' for Ameri-

17

can Fur then—that woulda been about '29 or '30—I led a brigade down along some of them rivers, right by Hall an' Spokane House both, right under them Britishers' noses."

He went into lengthy detail about that season. Blake speared a piece of meat on the knife he had been using to turn it, held it up to let some of the grease drain off and offered it to the old man.

"Pork eaters!" spat Henry contemptuously, but he took the meat absently, not bothering with the knife.

"I never thought I'd end up like this, takin' care of buffler hides an' wipin' Bill Higgins' nose. This here's a two-bit outfit. Higgins' never been farther west than the west side of town."

He chewed pensively. The meat was tough and he had no teeth.

"No, I always figgered to die in the mountains. Would have, too, if I'da had good sense, ten years ago while it was still real good country, place where a feller could live an' die like a real man . . . . The beaver's most gone now, army's out there tryin' to tame the Injuns, comp'nies goin' broke an' pullin' stakes, workin' out of posts now, what's left of 'em. I hear they may not even have a rendezvous this year. But the worst of it is all them *people* goin' out: goddam missionaries, even farmers, ruinin' the country. If them redskins had a lick of sense, they'd quit fightin' each other an' git together an' kill ever' last one of them greenhorns. Ole trappers'd help 'em an' that's God's truth. This coon'd help . . . .

"I got the rheumatiz. Comes of wadin' around in cold water so much. Ever'body works in the mountains gits it, one time or another. But I was aimin' to stay out there with Ole Gabe—that's Jim Bridger. Him and some others was talkin' about buildin' 'em a fort an' tradin' post. I thought I could make myself useful. Then I got word my brother'd died—back in Kentucky, that was. It was a year from the time he died till I got the word, but so far as I knowed, that left just me of all my family, except for my ole mother an' this here word said she wanted to see me. I went back there an' she died pretty soon after. Lord God! It was a good thing for me she did. I couldn' stand that country, all settled up, neighbors here an' neighbors

18

yonder, so close together a feller can't breathe. I started back west an' this here was as fur as I got."

He stopped, his wrinkled old face bleak. His eyes came back from far distances and looked down at his greasy fingers.

"I'll git there though, one day," he said, looking up at Blake, his blue eyes snapping defiance. "This ole coon ain't fixin' to die in no *town*." He spat again, explosively, as a door slammed.

"That's Bill," he said a little dully. "You can tell him you're lookin' for work. He won't want to pay you nothin' hardly, but even he ought to be able to see you look like you need a job. Them was once right fancy duds you're wearin'. You must be hard up, hangin' round a place like this. But this whole goddam town's full of pork-eatin' greenhorns. I swear, I don't know what the country's comin' to."

Bill Higgins was a dapper, fussy man in his thirties with small, stingy eyes. He quickly established that Blake knew nothing about the business, that he was broke and a little desperate, and hired him for what Blake knew, even for St. Louis, must be a ridiculously low wage. It was the off season, Higgins explained, trying to make them both believe he was simply doing the boy a favor.

In this off season, Blake and old Henry Melton were the only employees. Blake did a clerk's job. He also did everything else around the warehouse and office, including Henry's work when the old man felt too "stove up" to do it himself. Higgins allowed Blake to keep a cot in the warehouse which he could, at night, carry into the office for sleeping. Bill strove to convince the boy that this allowance was made strictly as a result of his innate generosity, but it also gave him a watchman in the office—he had an inordinate fear of thieves and robbers—and an additional excuse for paying so little. Higgins was, Henry proclaimed at least once daily, "so tight his farts whistled." Blake didn't much care what his wages or his work were. His mind and feelings seemed dazed, a little numb, and he did not try to change that. He badly needed respite from thinking, trying to understand what had happened to him, what he had done.

It was a long bleak winter. Thinking back on it, Blake

19

remembered little more than damp coldness, always permeated by the heavy smell of baled hides and by old Henry's talk. Often, he did not really listen to the old man. It didn't matter to Henry whether he listened or not.

One day in March, returning from an errand, he found Henry tilted back in a rickety old chair against an outside wall of the warehouse, somewhat sheltered from a chilly, straying breeze, soaking up the weak sun.

"Bring yourself a chair out," the old man said absently, rousing himself a little. He had been looking out over the roilly river, seeing other places, other times. "Bill's gone home for his dinner. Ain't nothin' has to be done right now."

Blake had scarcely noticed until this moment that it was beginning to be spring. Weeds along the wall were showing green. Sparrows and river birds flew about with revived energy. The sun's meager warmth in this place of shelter made him feel sleepy and relaxed.

"What you figger to do with yourself, boy?" Henry asked drowsily out of the silence, startling him a little. "You seem a bright enough child, got yourself some book learnin' an' such. You aimin' to keep on clerkin' for Bill the rest of your life?"

Blake was faintly surprised by the realization that he had been here four months. The days had melted together with a cold, weary sameness and he had almost lost track of them.

"I don't know, Henry," he said with a slight feeling of irritation. "Something will come along, I guess."

Impatiently, Henry gummed off a chew of tobacco.

"That ain't the way a man does, hoss, just set around an' wait for somethin'."

"It's what I always have done," Blake said slowly, and, looking back, he reflected that it had netted him a rather strange life.

"Well, it ain't the way to do," Henry declared firmly. "The way a man does, he goes on out an' meets things, goes more 'n halfway if he's got any grit in his guts. That way, he's got a little somethin' to say about what happens to him."

Blake yawned a little nervously, trying to call back the

20

relaxation of a few moments before. He said disinterestedly, "Well, what do you think I ought to do?"

"Waugh!" Henry spat. "Now, how would I know about that? I don't know what a feller with book learnin' an' fancy ways ought to do with hisself. Far as I go, all such as that's a bunch of foolishness, though there's some dudes seems to set a mighty lot of store by it. It seems to me like anybody young an' strong like you are ought to be headin' west. God knows it's not the country it used to be, but still it's all that's left that's worth two hoots in hell. *I'm* aimin' to git back out there.

"You got any notion what this kind of weather'd be like in the mountains, ice startin' to break up in the streams, birds comin' back, stuff gittin' green, deer an' elk startin' to move, trappin' still good some places, an' the buffler . . . ."

Blake stretched. "It sounds nice, Henry. I'd better get back to work before I fall asleep."

"You ain't answered my question," Henry said a little querulously, coming back to his present surroundings.

Blake stood up. "I tell you what," he said with a touch of tolerant fondness, "when you go west, I'll go with you."

Higgins' off season was ended. He hired a strapping, not-very-bright boy of fifteen to help with the warehouse work. The boy came cheap. More people began to come in, buyers and traders, and very occasionally, someone from "up the river," from the West. Henry kept these men talking for as long as he could manage, trying to catch up on the news, reliving the old days. Usually they invited him to go out somewhere with them, to be treated to a few drinks. After these excursions Henry always came back to his warehouse corner glum and morose, to lie on his cot muttering curses and vituperations until he finally slept.

One day toward the end of the month as Blake worked alone with the door to the musty little office propped open and the breeze bringing in smells of the river and of spring, a tall, gaunt, gray-haired man came in.

"Good morning, young man. My name is Elijah Prewitt. I am a minister of the gospel. I'm told there's someone here who knows a good deal about the West. You wouldn't be the one I'm looking for, I suppose."

"No, sir. It's Henry Melton you want. If you'd like to sit down, I'll go find him."

He pushed aside the order forms on which he had been working with some relief. He had been ordering trade goods which Bill Higgins' customers could barter with the Indians and he was finding the difference between what was paid for the goods and the value received for them in buffalo robes and other furs rather appalling. When he had mentioned this to Higgins, his employer had said blandly, "You have no idea, Westfall, of the expenses involved in the carrying trade. I'll be lucky to have a shirt left on my back by fall." Blake thought he had a fair notion of the expenses. After all, it was he, not Higgins, who kept the books. When he casually mentioned the great disparity in prices to Henry, the old man snorted, gesturing the idea away. "Injuns! What do you mean not gittin' their money's worth? Some people God put on earth to be made use of, if you can call 'em people. What if they don't git nothin' but a pot or a few beads for a buffler hide? You tell me what the thing cost 'em in the first place. Not a blessed thing but some sweat an' maybe a little powder an' lead is all. What do you know about tradin', young-un?"

He found Henry now and the old man limped after him back to the office. Elijah Prewitt introduced himself again, seeming to feel some doubt now about whatever it was he had in mind. After an instant's hesitation, Henry shook the proffered hand, looking dubious. Blake brought Henry the chair from behind Higgins' desk and went back to his books and figures.

"Mr. Melton, I understand you know something of the west."

" 'Bout all there is," said Henry coolly.

"Well, yes," agreed Prewitt a little awkwardly. "You see, I'm the leader of a party, a group of missionaries, teachers, and settlers, bound for the Oregon country to work among the savages. We arrived in St. Louis on Monday—"

"Farmers!" Henry spat. "Be the ruination of that country. Preacher, that country's meant for hunters an'

22

trappers an' that's all. Ain't meant for nothin' else, ain't fit for nothin' else. Can't feed only so many. Too many out there already. You an' your folks'll starve if you ain't scalped first. You got to know about country like that, how to live off of it. You know anything atall about Injuns?"

"We've studied and learned all we can," said the other pompously. "We're being sent by our church board, you see, to bring Christianity to the Indians, to civilize them, so that the country *will* be safe for all the—"

Henry made a rude sound. "They're savages, I'll grant you that, but they're all right the way they are. Civilize, hell!"

"I *beg* your pardon."

"Indians ain't made nor meant to be civilized. Now you looky here. You're a preacher. Don't you know about how God made ever'thing? Well, them things He made wasn' made for bein' changed, not a goddam one of 'em, not even Injuns."

Elijah Prewitt got jerkily to his feet. Glancing at him, Blake couldn't help thinking of Ichabod Crane in Washington Irving's story.

"I must assume then, Mr. Melton," he said sourly, "that you're not the man I'm looking for. I'd been given to understand that you might . . . . Well, perhaps you might be able to suggest someone else. We need a guide, you see, as far as a place called Fort Hall, someone who knows the country, what they call the Oregon Trail. Perhaps you could suggest a younger man, one who would not feel so—ah—strongly as you seem to about our calling."

Blake glanced curiously, covertly at the old man. Painfully, Henry sat up a little straighter in his chair. Expressions followed one another across his wrinkled face, anger, thoughtfulness, than a kind of hope. His blue eyes grew clear and shrewd.

"How many people you got?"

His fingers absently sought out his plug of tobacco; he gnawed off a chew and, still absently, offered the plug to the minister, who shook his head, looking slightly revolted.

"Eight families counting my own, some livestock. Some

23

of the party has already gone on up the Missouri by boat to wait for us at a town called Westport."

"You're takin' women," said Henry. The statement was a mixture of incredulity and resignation.

"Nine women," affirmed Mr. Prewitt proudly, "including my young daughter, and we have four children, three of them mine. Most of the people going out are young couples newly married, fine, strong people, ready for sacrifice and toil in the Lord's work."

Henry said adamantly. "That ain't no country for white women an' children, nor for white men either, if they ain't suited to it."

"Mr. Melton," the other said earnestly, "the chief reason for our going is that we may bring light into a dark, savage world. We know there will be hardships, but someone must make a beginning. Another reason, and only a secondary one, you understand, is that we may help to *make* that a country for white women and children."

Looking unimpressed, scornful, Henry said, "How many wagons you figger to have?"

Mr. Prewitt, seeming to fold joint by joint, eased back into his chair. "About a dozen I should think. We have a good deal of freight besides our personal belongings, books, stoves, nails, and much else that is needed. Our church has had missionaries in that field for two years now so that the board has a good idea of what is most needed. Considerable thought and expense have gone into this—ah—expedition. We are also carrying farming tools and we have a small herd of cattle, some sheep, pigs, and chickens."

"Waugh!" breathed Henry and spat. It might have been an exclamation of admiration or incredulity, but Blake thought it was more likely disdain. Henry said, "Whyn't you join up with another train? I hear there's plenty goin' these days."

The minister looked uneasy. "The only other that I know of just now, Mr. Melton, is another—uh—church group, another denomination, you understand. We feel it would be best not to attempt to travel so far with them. Not to gossip, you know, but I have heard many rumors

24

about what a contentious group they are. We don't need added problems."

"What about the army? They say there's bunches of them goin' out ever' so often."

"We prefer to make our own party. It's my understanding that some of the army people are quite—rough, crude, you see. I can't see any reason for exposing ourselves, our women and children, to that sort."

"You don't think the Injuns is goin' to be rough, crude?"

"Mr. Melton—" Prewitt leaned forward, an earnest light on his long face—"those poor heathen souls have not had the opportunity of learning about proper Christian ways. Each and every one of the adults in our party has felt a definite call to this work, this mission field. Some of us, myself included, have waited as much as ten years for the time to be right, for the Lord to be willing that we should go. I have been a teacher as well as a minister while waiting. We have a young doctor among us, farmers, mechanics, another teacher. It is a wonderful opportunity the Lord has laid before us, and a mighty responsibility. He intends that the savages and that country should be brought into His fold and we are fortunate indeed to be chosen to help, in our small ways, in so great a work. We are determined to travel on our own, if we possibly can, in order to commune with each other and with the Lord, to savor—you might say—our chosen state, to pray and think about our duties to come. We do not need the disturbance and worldly distractions of having to contend with a group of military men. They and many other parties, I understand, do such things as traveling through the Sabbath, just to give you an example of what we would be expected to put up with if we were to join with others."

Henry grunted. His jaws worked and he looked out the open door, over the river.

Prewitt said uneasily, "Do you think there are not enough of us to be safe in the crossing?"

"Any of your bunch been west before?"

"No, but we are all willing—"

Henry stopped him with a grunt, still looking off into far distances.

"There are enough of us to take care of driving the wagons and handling the stock. What we are looking for is a guide and perhaps another man or two to help with the camping and so forth, people who know the country, the watering places, you know, and something about dealing with the Indian tribes we must pass among. I was told you are such a man, but I didn't know you were—uh —handicapped; your limp, I mean, the stiffness of joint that seems to trouble you."

"I can travel," Henry said coldly. "When did you want to start?"

"Why, as soon as possible. As I've told you, some of our group is at Westport now, buying wagons and supplies. I'm told there'll be another boat the day after tomorrow that can carry the rest of us up the Missouri that far."

Henry brought his old, bright eyes back into the room. "If I was to take you on," he said with slow deliberation, "I would be in charge from the jump-off at Westport till we got to Fort Hall."

Prewitt nodded a little hesitantly. "Yes, of course, in matters concerning travel . . . ."

"The only way for greenhorns to go west is to have a leader an' to do like he tells 'em, always. You could have a mighty lot of trouble. It ain't goin' to be no easy job. Now then, Reverend, I ain't what you might call a churchy man. My mama was a good, God-fearin' woman. I was raised right but I been away from that kind of thing a long time. It might be you wouldn' like my way, but if I was to take on this job, what I say goes."

"I understand that in matters of travel—"

"In matters of anything," Henry said shortly. "You ain't goin' to know or understand or like, sometimes, about things I do. Like if we was to have a party of Pawnees come round beggin' an' threatenin' an' I say for you people to do some certain thing, there won't be no time to talk it over an' pray about it. You'll just have to by God do like I tell you or end up scalped, maybe."

Prewitt shifted uneasily. "I see," he said censoriously.

"Now what I would do is try to find another good man or two to help me out some, an' it just might be we could git you through, if you'll listen an' mind what I say. I can tell you don't like what I'm sayin' to you right now so you better look around an' see can you find some other ole coon willin' to risk his liver gittin' a bunch of pure greenhorns to the mountains. But I don't think you'll find one. They're hard to come by. Them as can have stayed out yonder; them as couldn' make it has come back an' gone to farmin' or some other god-awful thing, like me with this puny job here. Them as is just passin' through here has got their own to travel with an' they ain't lookin' to shepherdin' no missionaries. You're right, I got some stiff joints, but I reckon I can ride a horse, an' I know I can still think an' talk an' figger things about as good as the next, an' I want to get back out there. I want to go bad enough that I'll even try to play nursemaid, though I don't hold with none of this that you're aimin' to try to do. But I can tell you one thing certain: You better not try to set foot much past Westport without somebody knows what he's doin', for you won't last on the road. Now I expect you'll want to think an' pray on this, but you just keep in mind that if I go, I'm boss. That's all there is to it. What was you figgerin' to pay?"

They talked for a time about money and supplies and the Reverend Mr. Prewitt unfolded to his feet.

"You're right, Mr. Melton, I must pray about it. If you're going to be here late this afternoon, I'll come back and tell you what the Lord makes known."

"Yeah," Henry said absently, "lemme know what He has to say."

He did not get up or say any more in parting as the minister left. Blake wrote figures on his tally sheet.

"Well?" demanded Henry after a long silence. Blake looked up, meeting the sharp blue eyes questioningly. Henry's face was almost glowing. He said impatiently, "You got your gatherin's together? You ready to go to the mountains?"

"Me?"

"You said you'd go with me, didn' you? Here while-back, settin' out yonder by that wall?"

"But I was just—"

"You said, that day, you'd just wait till somethin' come

27

along. Well? Ain't it come? You want to scrabble for Bill Higgins till your liver rots? I swear, boy, you aggravate the very devil out of me!"

"Henry, I don't know anything about that kind of thing. I'd be just another greenhorn—"

"Damn right, but I know you some. I believe you got some sense, sometimes, know when to pay attention to them as knows what they're talkin' about. Now, are you comin'? You told me once you'd been a teamster. You might be that much help. I'll lay you odds that most of them church people ain't never drove much more'n a buggy, an' that on good roads in good weather. Can you see, at a crossin', say the Platte, with the water high an' some Sioux or Pawnee right behind? Waugh!" He smiled grimly.

"Maybe I can see them," Blake said stubbornly, "but I can't see me. They probably could handle that kind of thing a lot better than I could."

"All right," said Henry angrily, "but I trust you—a little. At a crossin' like that, I don't believe you'd just run off to pray on me. Great God, Blake! Don't you even want to see what that country's like out there? Don't you never wonder about the other side of the hill?"

"If I went," he said slowly, "what would I do there?"

"How the hell am I supposed to know that? You could take you a piece of paper, I guess, an' write down numbers with your left hand the way you do; that's about all I've seen that you're good for. If you didn' like it, I expect you'd find a way back. If you was to want to stay, maybe you an' me could do us some independent trappin', tradin' with the Injuns if they ain't made too Christian for it." He spat. "Yessir, boy, with me doin' the thinkin' an' you doin' like you're told, we might just make out all right for a while. That's the way to do it these days, independent. It don't pay to be nobody's comp'ny man no more, never did much. I figger to buy some trappin' gear with some of that money Preacher Prewitt mentioned. He said half in advance, you heard that. It's a hell of a lot cheaper to buy the stuff here than to wait an' buy it out yonder, an' you got a lot more an' better stuff to pick from. I might even talk a little business with Bill Higgins."

Abruptly, Blake found he wanted to go. It would be

hard, unaccustomed work, helping the missionaries get west, then trapping or whatever he found to do once there, but it would be a new and different way of life, a diversion. What could he lose besides maybe a year of time? When he came back to the States, the memories of New Orleans would be dimmer, easier to live with, less painful. He said, "But you don't want those people going out there. Why are you—"

"They're goin'," Henry said grimly. "If I don't take 'em, they'll go some other way, some time. I need the money they'll pay to git my outfit, an' even greenhorns to travel with might be better than nobody atall. A man or two can't cross that country by theirselves."

"What if, after he's prayed about it, Mr. Prewitt decides to look for someone else?"

Henry snorted. "You think he ain't already done that? You think he's goin' to come first to a ole stove-up coon like me? He's looked around. I been hearin' about him lookin' for several days now. They want to go right now, without waitin' around. Yessir, the Lord's fixin' to tell him, if He ain't already done it, that I'm the last one. Ain't nobody else around here now wantin' to git out yonder bad enough to take on his job. An' if he was to find somebody else, then you ought to go to that man an' offer to pay *him,* was he willin' to let you go along. Great God, boy! If I was your age again an' strong . . . ."

II

BLAKE ROUSED SLOWLY, consciousness returning in waves of increasing awareness. He was afraid to open his eyes. The pain in his head was not as bad as it once had been, but it was there still and it might spring on him viciously if he became fully awake. The pain was not the only thing that might be waiting to spring; he knew that only dimly, too weak, too lethargic to try to think of what else there might be. He was aware of other pains now, separate from the one in his head. His chest ached and breathing was hard, and his right leg throbbed with a pulsing ache. Trying experimentally to move the leg a little, he found that he could not. Was it bound or . . . ?

Then memory came back, of that other time when he had been conscious, the Indians, the drums and rattles, the howling, capering old medicine man, the sweating, the icy water. And now what? Perhaps his leg was tied somehow, but he lay on robes, was covered by them, and he was near a fire. Its light struck his closed eyelids. He was too drowsy, too weak to be afraid now. Whatever they had in mind would simply have to happen and he didn't much care what it might be. Still, if he didn't open his eyes, they would not know he was awake yet. It was an easy enough thing to do, not opening his eyes. The lids were very heavy and he had never known such utter weariness.

Drifting in and out of consciousness, eyes closed, he ascertained a number of things about his surroundings. He was inside a lodge. There was a fire and there were

30

some women. They were cooking something. Indian women always had something cooking. The men and children, the women too, ate when they were hungry, not at any specified time of day, so there was always a pot on the fire. He could hear the women moving about, talking and laughing quietly together, smell the cooking meat with perhaps some roots thrown into the pot to make a stew. He heard someone stirring the pot once and she made an appreciative sound, indicating that the food was going to be good. A baby, a very small one, made little sounds of hunger or discomfort and one of the women went and took it up. She made soft, proud sounds to it, laughing a little.

Moving very gingerly, keeping his hand under the robe, Blake touched the outer pole-and-skin wall of the lodge. He had thought he was near it because there was a little cold draft on his cheek. He fought down a need to cough and was aware that his body under the robes was naked. A dim notion had come into his mind that, lying against the wall, he might be able to slip out under it at night when his captors slept. Now he remembered resignedly that mountain Indians dug a depression to set their winter lodges in and piled dirt, then snow, around the lower walls for warmth. Getting out that way would be no simple matter. Besides, what could he do without clothing? It was winter out there or, at best, early spring, which in this country could be more brutal than winter. He had heard stories of men running and hiding from Indians through the mountains with no clothes. Some of those stories were true and some embellished to pass the time around an evening camp fire, but his account would not be added to them. He was too tired, his mind too heavy and dull now to think long of escape. Besides, bravery and daring had never been his strong suits. What were his strengths? He was a drifter with tides, a weak drifter, and that was about all . . . . All right. He didn't care now. He was too tired to care. The slight effort of cautiously moving his hand to touch the wall had been exhausting. He lapsed again into a drowsy semiconsciousness for what seemed a long while.

Then he heard someone, one of the women, throw down an armload of wood and he felt on his face the draft that had been created when she raised and then let fall the skin that covered the doorway. Outside the wall by which he lay, he heard the soft sound of moccasined feet on packed snow. The feet moved on around the corner of the lodge and a woman's voice called something. One of the women inside shouted an answer.

"We looked to your horses," she said. "They are all right if there is no more snow. There is plenty of bark."

"The snow is so long in leaving us this year," said the one outside.

"Don't worry about the horses. Go on and see to White Flower and the baby boy. Is he strong?"

"Yes, a good strong boy. He will make his father glad to come back from the hunting." She was moving away.

How do I know what they're saying? Blake thought listlessly, swallowing, desperately fighting down a cough. He had been dreaming, he remembered, of old Henry Melton and St. Louis. He had dreamed of many things in the past hours or days or months, however long he had been here, but he still could not think how this situation had come to be. He knew that it was winter or early spring. He and Henry and the missionary party had come west in the spring and somehow he knew that had been nearly a year ago, but how—

The cough burst from him uncontrollably, wracking his aching body. When the spasm passed, his eyes were open, watering profusely, and one of the women bent above him.

"You're awake!" she said, pleased.

Blake wiped at his streaming eyes, further weakened by the coughing so that it was all he could do to lift his hands.

"Your eyes are green," she said in mild wonder. "Look here, girls, he has green eyes."

They came and looked, two of them, while his eyes streamed and he gasped for difficult breath.

One of the others brought something hot and steamy in a bowl. She was a girl of perhaps fourteen. The first woman—perhaps she was middle-aged, it was hard to tell about Indian women—squatted down and thrust a short, strong arm under Blake's shoulders. He tried to struggle away. The smell of the food the girl had brought made nausea rise up hotly in him.

"You must eat," said the older woman firmly. "You have broken bones, your leg and your head. We have made a broth for you with things to make you strong again. Crooked Wolf has made good medicine for you. He says you have a strong spirit. All one night he made medicine for you and he said you would wake up and live again. That was three days ago. We were beginning to think that this time he might be wrong but we should have known better."

Blake did not understand all her words, but enough to catch the gist of what she said. She took the clay bowl the girl held and, seemingly with little effort of her left arm, drew him up like a child so that his head rested against her shoulder. She set the bowl on the ground and held some of the broth to his lips in a horn spoon, saying to the girl, "Go and tell Crooked Wolf his patient's come back," and to Blake she said in explanation, "He is a very old man now, Crooked Wolf, but his medicine is still strong. You can see that. But he is too old for going on the hunt. Open your mouth, Green Eyes, this is good broth."

He choked as she forced the thick hot liquid between his teeth. "No," he said pleadingly. "How—how long have I been here? What . . . ?" Then he realized he was speaking in English and she did not understand. He had learned to understand enough of several Indian languages in the past year to get by in trading, but when it came to talking to them, he still had to rely chiefly on sign language. He was too ineffably weary now to try to think of the right words or to lift his hands to make sign.

She kept poking the broth at him, holding him firmly, forcing his mouth open with the spoon. It was so hot it burned his mouth and he had to swallow. He had been sure he must begin retching with the first mouthful, but then it began to taste good. Its warmth spread through him, adding to his lethargic drowsiness.

The other girl had come again to stand above him. She was very young. She held a small baby who was hungrily nursing; in her free hand she held two otter skins which she had been in process of sewing with sinew and a bone awl. These people must need needles and pots and things, he thought automatically; there ought to be good trading here; the pelts the girl held looked prime.

She observed, "He has no strength at all now," and smiled kindly.

The older woman nodded; to Blake it seemed she might be gloating. "He has no more strength than the Little Chief there," she said, glancing fondly at the baby, "but he will eat and be strong again. I thought he might go on sleeping as if he were dead until there was no strength or spirit in him, but he is awake now, and eating. He will be well again." She thrust another spoonful of broth roughly between Blake's lips and said to him teasingly, "Look, Green Eyes, Little Rain has a lot of fresh warm milk. Maybe you will want some of that too, to make you strong. The Little Chief grows very fast on it."

Little Rain giggled shyly and the older woman laughed. Faint color rose up in Blake's white drained face.

"Yes!" cried the older woman, delighted. "Just thinking of it makes color come into his face, you see, Little Rain? I don't know how anyone can tell about a white man's health from his color, but it looks a little better this way. When he has swallowed all this broth, you can give him—"

Other people crowded into the lodge then, having followed the girl back, talking and laughing loudly. They were women and children except for one bent, emaciated old man. With horror, Blake recognized him, remembering the maddening, interminable howling, the beating of his aching body with a stick, the sweat lodge, the frigid stream.

"He lives now," announced the old man, obviously pleased with himself. His voice was faint and cracked. Perhaps, Blake thought grimly, he was hoarse from howling. Maybe he didn't have the strength or the voice to begin howling again.

Crooked Wolf put a trembling, clawlike hand on his face. "The fever is going from him. He will be well now."

And one of the women near the door called to someone outside, "The white man will be well again, Crooked Wolf says."

The woman thrust more broth at him. He had had enough now. If only they would leave him alone! He struggled weakly and the broth she held spilled down his face. He began to cough and when the paroxysm had passed his head fell limply against her shoulder. She still held him firmly.

"You see what you've done?" she scolded him good-naturedly, wiping roughly at his face and his streaming eyes.

"He still has some of the badness," Crooked Wolf said thoughtfully, tapping Blake's chest. "You hear the rattling and wheezing of his breath, and the coughing. At first, the badness was in his head where it was broken. I drove it from there, but it is still with him, in there, though it is weakening now."

"Will you dance again?" asked one of the older women.

Crooked Wolf looked speculative and Blake convulsively swallowed more broth. He could not live through another exorcism, but they would be offended, probably angry if he made any pleas or protests.

"I have done much," Crooked Wolf told his questioner and the lodge in general. "Five days ago, the young man brought this white man among us. 'Make him well,' Hawk's Shadow said to me. 'You can do it. You have the medicine.' Hawk's Shadow is a good boy, one of the old kind. His grandfather, Winter Thunder, my brother, would find him a good boy. Hawk's Shadow does not laugh at the old ways. See the cradle his woman puts his son in? It is a bark cradle of the old kind that few of our people will take the time to make anymore.

"I did not know if I could heal the white man. His head was broken, and his leg. He barely breathed and he had been almost frozen to death before they found him. But, to please Hawk's Shadow because Hawk's Shadow pleases me, I said that if he still breathed after two days I would try."

Crooked Wolf was a kind of warrior now, counting his coups. The women and children listened approvingly, making sounds of admiration. Blake could hardly hear their voices; his eyes closed heavily. Still there was another spoonful of broth and the strong arm, holding him half upright.

"Red Sky, chief of the Medicine Rock People, my nephew, said he should not live," the old man went on. "Red Sky's heart is not good toward any whites. In that, he is very much like his father, my brother Winter Thunder who has gone on now to another land. My heart is not good toward whites either, but I am an old man and it has long been my way to heal those who come or are brought to me. I said to Red Sky that I should try to heal this white man. We talked about it in a council. I said that maybe he had been sent to us for a reason we did not yet understand. Our young men found him almost dead, but he was not dead. Perhaps it was meant that he should live."

The shaky, cracked old voice was filled with pride and conviction. The old man's breath came hard, with a slight whistling sound.

"Sit here, old one," murmured one of the women, "on this good bearskin, and tell us the rest of it."

Crooked Wolf eased his old body down and went on earnestly, "We do not always know, at the time a thing happens, why it happens. Sometimes, we can only go on with what seems best and wait to see what will come . . . . Many years ago, Winter Thunder my brother, a great chief of our people, saw the vision that told him we should come here to this valley of the Medicine Rock to make our home each winter. He told his dream to me and we both knew it was strong medicine. Some others knew that, too, and came with us, away from the main band. Since that time, the spirits of all things good in earth and sky have looked on us well. We were living in this good valley when those first white men came among others of our people. We did not see them, but only heard talk of them. Then other whites came. After a time, there were many of them and we of the Medicine Rock knew it was not good. We kept away, only sometimes trading, when we could make a good bargain. Are we like those Cayuses and those Walla Wallas who let the whites turn their men into scratchers of the earth? Winter Thunder is dead now but I am still here, and there is his son Red Sky and my

36

son Many Bears and their sons Hawk's Shadow and Beaver Tooth who hold to the old ways, the good ways.

"We have not allowed the white man to come into the valley of the Medicine Rock. There are beaver in our streams. Our young men have not been made mad with the white man's burning drink. Our young women have not been traded away to become white men's women and it will not be so, so long as people of Winter Thunder's family, and mine, are left to remember.

"This white man that you see here, being held like a child by Owl Woman, is the first white ever to sleep in the valley of the Medicine Rock. I said to Red Sky in our council that since those young men, Hawk's Shadow and Beaver Tooth and the others, had been led to him while he still lived, maybe we should wait and see what else was meant to happen. Beaver Tooth and others wanted to kill him, and even Red Sky thought that might be best. But I said to them, 'What kind of glory would there be in killing one who is already dead? That is the kind of cowardice our enemies, the Blackfeet and others, might call bravery. It comes to me that he may have been found and brought here to test my medicine, so that I, and you, may know if it is still truly strong. I will see what I can do to make him well again. If he does not live, we will know it is not meant to be so. If he lives and we find he is a trouble to us, he can always be killed. This one man is not really our enemy, is he? Not yet. He has done nothing to make him an enemy. So let us wait and see what will come.'

"Sometimes, if a man lives after his head has been broken, he is mad. At least, it's that way among our people. I don't know how it is with whites. Once when we were hunting buffalo, I saw a young Flathead that that had happened to. He went about like a small child, wetting himself sometimes, talking crazy talk. The doctor who had tried to heal him had not done enough, maybe. His body grew well and strong, but his mind was different. Some said that it was good medicine to have one such as that around. I thought that might happen with this white man.

"I went away from our council and I fasted, waiting for a sign to tell me what I should do. My spirit-brother the

37

wolf came to me and said he would help, and together we made good medicine. The white man woke for a time. Some of the badness left him. What is left is here in his chest. If it does not leave him within a day or two, I will make medicine again for him. Now I will go back to my lodge. I make medicine now for my great-grandchild, the boy child of my grandson Beaver Tooth and of White Flower his woman. I am an old man now. My body is weak. It trembles. Last night, I had to help in the asking of favor for the hunt that our men left on before the dawn. When Shy Fawn came to call me just now, I was calling on the spirits of my medicine bundle, for bravery and strength and wisdom for Beaver Tooth's boy child who is with his mother in the birth lodge. He is strong. It seems as if he is meant to stay with us. Though my body is weak, my medicine is still strong. You see this white man here that I and my spirit-brother have given life. But I can only work for one thing at a time. The son of my grandson is more important to us than this white man, so, if he needs more help, he will have to wait for a time . . . . Owl Woman, have you made the broth as I told you?"

"Of course I have, uncle of my husband," she said fondly, a little reproachfully. "Won't you eat something now from our fire?"

"I am fasting," he said reprovingly. "You must know it is the only way to find the best medicine. What have you put in the broth?"

"I cooked the meat as you told me," she said patiently, "and put in the roots and herbs that Brown Leaf brought from your lodge, and toward the last I put in the elk's blood. See, he has eaten nearly all of it."

Blake, half conscious, began coughing again, his body wracked by spasms of coughing, then of retching.

"The badness is coming out!" cried Crooked Wolf exultantly, and the women and children murmured in wonder.

Finally, Owl Woman's strong arms laid the unconscious white man back on the robes. He breathed but faintly. They all listened to his breathing and agreed cheerfully that it was better, easier than it had been. Crooked Wolf went back to his lodge, helped solicitously by his daughter-in-law Brown Leaf. Owl Woman directed Little Rain, her own daughter-in-law who had put the baby back in his cradle, to bring another robe to cover the white man, and she told her daughter Shy Fawn to take away the robe soiled with his vomit and see what she could do about cleaning it up.

"I'm going to get some grease from Brown Leaf," she told them at the door. "She said she has some to spare. We're running low on everything. Eve, if the men make a good hunt, we will still need grease. No animal is fat at this time of year. I don't ever remember a spring so slow and late as this one."

"He's skinny," observed Little Rain judiciously as the two girls spread fresh robes around Blake, "and such a sickly color. His eyes were strange. Did you see them? I never knew there could be green eyes. How would you like to have one like this for your husband?"

They giggled. Shy Fawn picked up the soiled robe gingerly and brought it close to the fire along with a pot of clay to use for the cleaning.

"I don't see any badness here," she said thoughtfully, daringly, "only broth."

"Shhh!" said Little Rain, glancing around warily, and they both giggled guiltily.

In his own lodge, the weak, half-starved old Crooked Wolf sought visions that would bring good medicine for the son of his grandson. In Red Sky's lodge where Shy Fawn scrubbed at the robe, Blake, unconscious, lived again in the past of last year's spring.

Henry Melton had not lived to reach Fort Hall. He died not far west of Fort Laramie, while they were crossing South Pass, on a day of burning sun and searing wind, toward the end of June.

"He had somethin' like a fit an' fell off his horse," reported Emmett Price, coming to find Blake where he trailed in choking dust behind the missionaries' small disconsolate herd of cattle. "Dr. Simmons says he's dyin'."

So many people have died, Blake thought desolately, urging his drooping horse toward the head of the train. Alec Douglas had died; Etienne St. Croix had died; now Henry. How much did Blake himself, his association with those people, have to do with it?

39

They had laid the old man on a saddle blanket in the meager shade of a rock and some sagebrush. His body seemed, all at once, fearfully shrunken. His voice was weak but his blue eyes were clear.

"You been seein' the mountains?" he demanded as Blake came up. "You can fair see 'em now. Them to the south, we used to say was Mexican territory, but nobody seems right sure now who that country belongs to. Them to the north is the Wind Rivers. The next water you come to will be runnin' west. You wait an' see if it ain't . . . . You figger to go on with MacPheirson, don't you? He'll help see these crazy people gits through. He's all right, for a Hudson's Bay man. It's lucky we come acrost him."

"We'll go on with him," Blake said, "and after that, we'll—"

"I want you to have that gear we bought back in Missouri. Sell it if that's what you want to do. Prewitt was here a while ago, wantin' to pray over me. I told him that stuff is yours an' that the money still comin' to me at the end of the line at Hall belongs to you."

"Henry—"

"Now don't start in with a bunch of goddam nonsense talk. I've got as far as I'm goin' an' that's all there is to it. I hope you'll stay an' trap a while or somethin', git to know the country some if you can hang onto your scalp long enough. If it was back ten year ago, I could turn you over to some good partisan I knowed an' feel easy about you."

"I'm all right—"

"All right, hell! You're still as green as buffler grass. Nearly drownded the other day crossin' the Sweetwater, didn' you? An' the Sweetwater not even high, not hardly enough water for a seasoned ole coon to get wet in."

Henry gazed wistfully at the distant mountains, standing up hazily to the north.

"We're west of the Divide now," he said dreamily and he died.

They buried him there in that high, harsh dry land. Tom Spier, the young minister, read the Bible and prayed for Henry's soul, which, Blake knew, the missionaries already felt certain was beyond help or hope. They sang "Rock of Ages," those who felt like it, their voices sounding small and lost in the great empty openness. The missionaries wanted to mark the grave but Connall Mac-Pheirson told them bluntly how stupid that would be. Some roving Indian band would come along and dig it up, he said. And then he went on coolly, "We've got three hours till sundown. The nearest water's about four hours away at the rate these God-forsaken wagons can travel. We'll be moving."

Mrs. Prewitt objected querulously, "It's not Christian to rush around that way when Death's just been among us."

"In this country," Connall said, looking kindly at her tired, contentious face, "it usually pays, ma'am, to think of the living first. Henry was a good old man, but he's gone. There's nothing we can do to help." He turned to Blake who stood there, feeling helpless, angry, lost. "You ride on ahead some with Jesse Harris yonder. The two of you pick out a camp before it's completely dark."

Blake knew that MacPheirson's sending him on ahead with Harris was a kindness. He had been Henry's friend and Connall was giving him a chance to get away from the train where the people seemed to spend most of their sapped energy in bickering and fault-finding. Certainly he had not been singled out for his scouting abilities. In this high, relatively flat country of sagebrush, rocks, and sameness, he did not doubt that, out of sight of the train's dust and with the sun now being covered by fast-moving afternoon storm clouds, he would be completely lost. That needn't worry him, though, so long as he kept Jesse in sight.

Jesse Harris was a strange, mixed kind of man. One thing Blake was learning about this western country was that the people were likely to be that way, mixtures of one kind or another, only it was more noticeable in Jesse. Henry had known him, or at least knew his reputation, as he knew of anyone who had spent any amount of time in the mountains, and Jesse Harris had been in the country for ten or fifteen years, since his boyhood. He was a physical mixture of white, Negro, and Cherokee, the best tracker in the country, Henry had thought.

Jesse had already been at Fort Laramie when the missionary party came in from the east and when Connall

41

MacPheirson's group came down from the northwest. Blake heard that Jesse had been trapping and trading more or less alone up in the Crow country through the past winter. Most whites, the other men told him, wouldn't go to sleep with Crows around, but Jesse had some way of getting along with them. One helpful thing to Jesse was that he had had a Crow wife when he had gone up into that country in the fall. He hadn't brought her down with him in the spring and there was a good deal of speculation around the fort as to whether they had split the blanket or she had simply died. Jesse was not saying. Blake had not heard him make a sound in the past few days. He was silent as they rode over ground that had begun to slope very gradually now toward where the low sun was hidden.

After some time, Jesse lifted his hand, pointing. Blake shaded his eyes, trying hard to see what the other was seeing. The sun had come out again, fiercely bright. Finally, he had to shake his head. He could see nothing different.

"Water," Jesse said simply. "We can camp there." And he turned his horse back toward the train.

Blake followed, rubbing his eyes, feeling embarrassed and totally inadequate. He doubted that he would ever again be sure of water seen from a distance. All the long way across the desert prairie, he had kept seeing sparkling blue lakes, surrounded by cool green trees—mirages. But surely there had been nothing more where Jesse had pointed than the same hot sagebrush country.

"I— couldn't see," he said diffidently.

There was a long silence and Jesse said, "Trees, far off. There's a little stream the Indians call Little Fox. Whites call it Fitz Gulch. It's not dry yet. Trees look good."

"I didn't see any trees," Blake said, wanting with a kind of desperation to have the man tell him it was all right, but Jesse was not talking anymore.

After a time, he drew his horse up sharply, holding up a hand for Blake to stop, too. A moment later, he grunted and they rode on. After what Blake judged to be at least a quarter mile more, he, too, saw the dust of an approaching rider. It must be all right, since Jesse kept on stolidly.

The rider was young Emmett Price, come out to meet them. Emmett's parents were the other older couple in the missionary party. They were laymen, going out to help teach farming to the converted Indians and to find some good, virgin Oregon country land for themselves. The hill farm they had worked back in Missouri had been a very poor one.

Emmett was a tall, lanky boy of seventeen or eighteen, with a long, serious face. His fair hair had been scorched by sun and wind to the color of old straw and his fair skin was burned red.

"I was right sorry about Mr. Melton," he said shyly to Blake, turning his horse to ride beside him. "I liked him a lot an' I didn' git a chance to say anything before . . . ."

Blake did not want to talk about Henry or about anything else, but he was relieved when the boy at least changed the subject.

"Did y'all find a campin' place?"

"Jesse did. It's about—five miles from here?" He looked to Jesse for confirmation, but there was no sign that Jesse had heard.

Emmett looked uneasily from one to the other. He was innately shy. Jesse made him uncomfortable and he had found through the past months that Blake, though only a few years older than himself, was hard to know. Still, he had to talk to somebody and he said ebulliently, "Ain't this country somethin'?"

"It's something all right," Blake said grimly. He was tired and sadness was heavy upon him. It didn't help to realize that the missionary party was not supposed to be chiefly his responsibility. He knew nothing.

All the way out, Emmett, unlike most of the others in the party, had shown only enthusiasm, had had nothing but questions and good things to say about their travels. Henry had taken to him instantly and they had spent a good deal of time talking, or rather Henry talked while Emmett listened eagerly. Emmett was, on the whole, the most capable of the missionary party. All the men did the best they could and even Henry admitted that the strength and staying power of the women was something of a marvel. Fired as they were with religious fervor, driven on by hope for the future even if it was as far away as heaven,

43

and by whatever it was in their various pasts that they were escaping, they had all shown an amazing amount of fortitude and stamina through heat and storms, Indian threats, wind and dust, river crossings, toiling with the difficulty of getting the wagons through, the debilitating sickness that Henry said came to every greenhorn when he came to where he had to drink alkali water. Their strength was especially remarkable when you considered that they spent so much of it in petty quarrels and in trying to show each other the real Christian way.

Emmett seemed to take no part in this constant, edifying warfare. He worked willingly at anything, was mostly quiet, and almost everyone liked him almost all the time. None of the party approved of the time he spent with Henry and Blake. They could hardly prohibit him during the day, but at night, when he often came to the separate fire they usually kept, he was summoned back to the fold, sooner or later, by a harsh reproving voice. Seemingly, Emmett could ignore their bickerings and insecurities and see the good in them, and he saw only good in this hard, desolate country.

He said now, reaching for just the right words, "No, I mean it's—pretty, in a kind of big, scary way. Them mountains we can see up there. Mr. MacPheirson told me they're more'n fifty miles away. Ain't that—somethin'? . . . An' we'll be *in* mountains soon. Some range is between us an' where we're goin' to meet them other people. We might even see some snow one day, here nearly at the first of July . . . ."

Blake couldn't think much beyond laboring with the heavy wagons when he thought of being in mountains.

Emmett went on warmly, "I wish I could see it all. Have you heard about that country they call Yellowstone, up north somewheres? All them hot boilin' springs an' things comin' out of the ground. Wouldn' that be somethin' to see?"

"Don't you think it sounds like part of hell?" Blake said perversely. "That's what Mr. Prewitt said it must be when the men back at the fort were talking about it."

Emmett's long face was perplexed. "Mr. Prewitt knows a lot more about that kind of thing than I do," he said slowly, refusing to be completely deflated, "but, to me, it don't seem like that. It seems like it must be a—a wonderful thing that God's put here on earth."

Blake was completely fed up with talk of heaven and hell, of what God meant and of who could come closest to a correct interpretation of that meaning. Now Henry was gone and he must keep on with these people to the end. He had been a fool to make the trip. Hadn't he had enough of God as a boy from his good, righteous grandparents and his aunt Millie? And now here he was, responsible for a bunch of fanatic missionaries. He found himself spitting into the dust, though he never chewed tobacco, couldn't stand the taste of it, and his mouth was so dry that there was almost nothing to spit. He smiled wearily. The next thing he knew, he'd be yelling "Waugh!" He said more kindly to Emmett, "There's no reason you can't see all the country, is there? You're here now."

The perplexity did not leave the boy's face. "Well, only that I've got to work at the mission, at least till things are started good. They'll need me. It's what I'm here for. The thing is, though . . . . They say that country out there where we'll build the mission is right in the shadow of some real high mountains. Now I don't mind farmin' an' all that, you understand, but I just can't hardly imagine lookin' up, say, from plowin' and seein' mountains like them yonder, only close up, an' not knowin' what's in 'em. Can you?"

"No," Blake said thoughtfully.

As a boy, he had had his share of farm work, more than his share because of who he was. His cousins found it easy to shift some of their own work onto him and to give him the blame if a thing was not done when or as their grandpa wanted it. No matter how he had tried, Blake could never be right or good enough. After a while, he went on trying not so much to be right or to earn a good word for himself, but only to get out briefly, now and then, from under the heavy, dragging, unending work and the critical, disapproving eyes. The mountains of western Pennsylvania were nothing like these mountains. Nowhere could they be seen for a distance of fifty miles, but they had had a strong attraction for him as a boy, particularly if there was a chance he could slip away from the farm and go wandering in them with Alec Douglas.

Almost anything would have been an attraction to him then . . . . How long had it been since he had looked on anything with Emmett's kind of eager enthusiasm? He felt very old.

"Mr. Melton said you'd be goin' trappin'," Emmett said softly, "you and him. Are you still goin' to?"

"Yes." Blake drew in a breath stinging with alkali dust and let it out slowly. "That is, if I can find anybody willing to teach me. Henry would have done it, but I don't know anybody else willing to spend the time and patience."

Emmett said helpfully, "Mr. MacPheirson might hire you. He was askin' if any of us is any good with figgers an' things. I told him Mr. Melton said you are. He said he needs a clerk. I wish I *could* do it, but it's about all I can do to write my name. Clerkin' ain't like just ridin' around and lookin' at the country the way I'd like to do, but you'd see a lot of it on the way to that post of his—what do they call it? Camas Post? It's way up north an' some west, he says. I guess if you was to go to work for him for a while, you might maybe come onto somethin' else you could do, if you wanted to."

"Maybe," Blake said slowly, still wishing he could have seen Jesse Harris' trees. Would he ever be able to?

"Hire you?" roared Connall MacPheirson and laughed loudly.

He was a red-haired giant of a man and often boisterous, but he sobered now to a broad smile, looking into the serious face that somehow seemed older than Henry Melton had said. "I've seen you work, lad. You're a good, strong, willing enough worker at what you can do, but you don't know a damn thing about this country or what's to be done here. *You* ought to pay *me,* was I to take you on."

Almost the same words Henry had said once. A slight flush rose in Blake's face and he said soberly, apologetically, "I don't have any money. I was told you might want a clerk."

"Aye, well, yes," said Connall, growing thoughtful. He had a bit of a brogue or a burr, left over from somewhere. He looked up at the sky, bright where the sun had gone down, and felt sad.

They would be at the rendezvous site by this time tomorrow. In former years, he reflected, a scouting party would have come out to meet them by now, whooping and shouting. The rendezvous had always been, more or less, an American affair, but the Hudson's Bay Company had been sending representatives for some years now, and the trappers had always been glad to see and do business with almost any other white men. For the past few years, though, rendezvous hadn't been the same, quieter, not nearly so much hell-raising, fewer trappers, fewer company representatives, fewer Indians. This year, Connall suspected, might be the last gathering of its kind. There had been some high old times at those gatherings and their passing was one more heavy weight added to the scale that weighed change. He took the cup Marie was offering him and drank off half the rum.

"Change *will* come," he said aloud, beginning to feel a little better after his momentary melancholy. "Aye, if a man is to be alive, he's going to see change. It's not the first time it's happened, and I'll manage it. For the matter of that, I'll be a little ahead of it, with my cattle and all."

Part of his business at Fort Laramie had been negotiations to buy a white-faced bull, which Henry had said was "a hell of a thing for somebody calls hisself a mountain man to be runnin' 'round the country doin'."

Connall sighed, drank again and came back to the immediate question. "As a clerk, yes, I need one. The last youngster I had went off to Montreal to work in the warehouse and marry some girl. I've noticed you're left-handed but Henry said it didn't seem to hold you back much, with writing and such. Are you a good clerk?—uh —what's your name again?"

"Blake Westfall. Yessir, I am."

"Well, now, that's your word, isn't it? And I've yet to have mine. Here's what we'll do. You work for me through this rendezvous, keeping track of trade goods and all that, doing all the writing and figuring, which are things I hate, and then we'll see about your going on to Camas. Are you under any sort of contract to the Reverend Prewitt and his people?"

"No, sir."

"Good. Though contracts don't mean what they ought

47

to to most people these days, I wouldn't like to be responsible for one being broken. You'll have some rum, then? Marie, get the lad a cup. Where is it you come from Blake?"

"Pennsylvania."

"Would you be Dutch then? Or a Quaker?"

"My father was German, I think—"

"You think?"

"He died before I was born. I was raised by my grandparents. They were English."

"English," said Connall a little disdainfully. "Well, I suppose they're all right. The English do pay the wages of many a Scot and Irishman and Frenchie in this country. It's the English own the H. B. Company, you know. But your father was German, you think. You wouldn't be Popish, would you?"

Blake was surprised. He had not heard the word Popish in a long time. It had not been used in Catholic New Orleans, but as a boy he had heard it often enough, in recrimination, threat, accusation: *"On top of all the rest of it, your father was Popish. Poor little Sarah went so far wrong. How could that happen to our girl when we tried so hard to show her the right ways? We'll make certain with you. You've got that man's eyes, his looks, that shameful left-handedness, but we'll do the best we can since God sees fit for us to have to raise you."*

He said now, carefully, "I'm not, but he was, my father."

"Well, I'm Popish," Connall said complacently. "Marie there, she is. Her mother was a Cree and her father a Frenchman, both good Catholics. Our religion's not looked on with much favor in this part of the mountains, but farther north there are more of us. We're not very good Catholics, that I'll admit, with no church to go to, no priest, but we do what we can. We send our kids east to school in Montreal when they're old enough. There's but one of them there so far; others too young. We've two more daughters at home besides the baby in the tent and another on the way. Please God, this one coming will be a boy. Daughters are all well and good, but five of them should be enough for any man. Will you have more rum?"

"Thank you, no, Mr. MacPheirson, I—"

"You needn't call me that, but I'll ask you not to call me Mac as so many do. Half the Scots and Irishmen in the world are called Mac and I've never cared to be lumped in like that. Neither do I like to be called Red. You can call me Connall if you like, and you can leave off the sir too. In this country if one man respects another that other will know it without a lot of titles and frills. It's a good country, but hard. It does away with a good many unnecessaries, if you take my meaning."

Blake nodded, liking the man. "I won't drink any more now. I should go and see if their stock is all right."

"Aye, you'd better do that soon. We could have them thieving Crows skulking around any time now."

"Only—I was wondering—about leaving Mr. Prewitt and his people to work for you through the rendezvous. They may not be happy about that."

"Yes, I can see they mightn't be, but there'll be others there willing to help them with what they need, ones that can't help to handle my trade. From what Henry told me, you've agreed to go with them as far as Fort Hall. As you know, I'm going there myself, along with whatever trappers I pick up to work for H. B. The missionaries will have to go to rendezvous and wait until we're ready to leave, unless they're fools enough to think of crossing that country without a seasoned guide, which I don't doubt they are. I've had a talk with the Reverend Prewitt about it, tried to tell him something about what to expect at rendezvous, to soften the blow, so to speak, but there's not going to be anything about it that will make them happy. I've seen missionaries at other rendezvous, shocked to distraction. They're so concerned about souls that they can't or won't realize how little these men have in the way of—you might say of diversion—through all the rest of the time."

He had been filling a pipe and when it was ready Marie held up a small stick from the fire to light it.

"As to your adding to their unhappiness, you must please yourself about that. But you do understand that I can't set any value on your work until I've seen it."

"Yes."

"Well, then, think about it until tomorrow, if you like,

and then let me know what you've decided. It's quite a responsibility for you, having these people on your hands, green as you are, and it speaks well for you that you're concerned. I don't want you getting any notions, no matter what they say, of trying to go on to Hall without the rest of us. You'll have to have help with that. Once they're there, that's as much as they were promised . . . . I'll tell you another thing, lad, that a man learns from this country, and that's to look to his own interests when the time is right for it. There's hardly a man I know who wouldn't give his life for a friend, or even for a stranger if there was need, but you must learn to decide when there really is need, and you must take care of yourself so that need does not come for your friends. And that applies in smaller things. If you want to stay out here and work, you'd best take what's offered, if there *is* an offer. You don't know anything about trapping. Other jobs are hard to come by in this country. That's not to say I can pay you much if I do take you on."

"I'll think about it." Blake had stood up but he said, "How long have you been out here?"

Connall shrugged, smiling. "I was born in the mountains. My father was factor for a time at the old Rocky Mountain House. My mother was French, her father worked at Fort Vancouver. She died when I was born."

Blake found himself wondering if Connall's parents had ever been truly married; if Connall and Marie had had any such formalities. He disliked himself for such thoughts. What did a thing like that matter? It made him seem as bigoted and sanctimonious as Mr. Prewitt and the others, as his grandparents and Aunt Millie.

"I was born in 1809," Connall was going on readily. "My father was with the old Northwest Company for a time and then he went to war, that was the war the English had with you people, the last one, you know. I never did understand why he bothered with it. When he came back, he went to work for H. B. Not too many years after that, the companies merged. While my father was at war, I was in Edinburgh, living with some of his people. I went to school for a time. There were some there that called me a breed bastard, things like that, I remember. I had no notion what the words meant at the time and they didn't

50

seem to bother the old man any. He was fond of me.

"We came back and I started learning to trap and trade. The old man died when I was thirteen, but I was already nearly on my own. After some years I got to be a partisan, and then, five years back, the company built a little new post up on the Camas and I was made factor. It's a good country up there, if you don't mind hard winters, a place I'd like to stay no matter what happens with the company or in this argument over who the land really belongs to."

Blake did not want to go, but he kept thinking guiltily of Emmett left alone to guard the stock. He had to take time to ask, "It belongs to the Indians, doesn't it?"

"Well, it does and it doesn't," Connall said thoughtfully. "An Indian doesn't own land, you see, not to have a title deed and so on. One Indian alone, or one family of them could hardly imagine *owning* land. To them, some certain parcel of land, a big parcel, belongs to a tribe or band, to the people all together. But what I was talking about was the argument between Mother England and Uncle Sam. Once that's settled, there'll be a lot more whites coming out to this country. There are already more of them than I'd like to see, but when they want this land, they'll take it. It may belong to the Indians by right of being on it first, but right has never much mattered when a stronger person wants something a weaker one has got. That's the way it is."

"Will you take up land?"

"Aye, I will, as soon as I can. I already have, for the matter of that, except for knowing who to go to to have the papers drawn up, which government."

Blake shifted his feet, looking away.

"You don't think that's right, do you?" Connall said easily. "Well, I'll tell you another thing you'll learn if you stay here long, this one more thing and then you'd best get to your livestock. My new bull is out there too, you know. He's already serviced two missionary cows that I know of. There ought to be some usage tax or something I could put on a thing like that . . . . But what I'm saying is that I think you must learn to take things as they are, and that includes people. Some things are just hard, cold facts and you can't make more than that of them. You

51

know what's been done with a lot of the Indians back east. They've been moved into the middle of a no-man's land, foreign to them, with reservations set up by the Great White Father and other big fat important know-nothings who've never set eyes on those Indians, their land or the land they've been moved to, who never will and who don't give a damn about it. It's sad, perhaps, but it's a truth, a fact, and maybe it's not altogether bad. It will happen here. I hope the day is a long time coming to this country, but come it will. The strong always triumph, and that's another fact, whether they're strong in muscle, in numbers, in money, or in just going strongly after what they want. It will always be that way; it always has been. . . . Some day, if we go together, I'll tell you about H. B.'s Indian policies. I think they're better, for the most part, than what the Americans have done so far. You'll have a look at American dealings at rendezvous. It's my belief that if England gets the Oregon country, the Indians might fare better, in some ways, than they will under the United States, but I doubt England will have it. She's spreading herself thin these days and it's a lusty young country you come from, lad, out to grab off all of everything she can. I read more and more often in the papers —year-old ones we get here—the words 'Manifest Destiny.' People believe in it and it's the belief in a thing that counts, not the right of it. If a man believes enough, he'll *make* the thing right, at least in his own eyes . . . . And now goodnight to you. See you look well to that bull of mine."

III

THE RENDEZVOUS had one redeeming aspect for Mr. Prewitt and his party. Except for the time at Fort Laramie, it was their first "resting Sabbath" in almost three months, since leaving Westport. Oblivious to grumbling and threats of retribution from on high, Henry had kept them moving on the road, maintaining adamantly that it made no sense wasting time like that, laying off one day out of seven; no partisan worth his salt would stand for it. A thing like that was only asking for trouble, sitting around waiting for Indians to think up things, using up your supplies to no purpose.

"God *tells* us we must rest on the Sabbath, and worship," one of the women had said righteously.

"You folks just go on ahead an' rest then, ma'am," Henry had replied with deceptive gentleness. "You rest Sundays an' any other days you feel minded to. Me an' the boy yonder'll be goin' on to the mountains."

But they had a real Sabbath—as real as surroundings would permit—near the rendezvous site.

For the missionaries, the gathering was a foretaste of hell. Almost everything horrified them, the drinking, gambling, swearing, "trafficking in women," all of it; and at the same time the mountain men and Indians who had been participants in past rendezvous lamented sadly the mild tameness of this one. To a man, the whites were courteous to the missionaries and considerate of their feelings and convictions. Most of these men had not been back to the States for years, but they had a deeply ingrained respect for white women and for religion. Factors and partisans invited members of the Prewitt party to dine with them, giving instructions that liquor be held back until the guests had gone, that language be kept fit for ladies, that guns not be cleaned nor trading done in their presence. The missionaries went, with obvious condescension, where they were invited, and stayed awake half the night afterward to enumerate the evils they had seen and heard.

Their camp was set up a little apart from any of the others. They would have liked it to be farther but safety would not allow more distance. There was a bend of the river in front of their camp. Connall MacPheirson's Hudson's Bay outfit was on one side of them and a group of tough, independent trappers, mostly up from the south and west, camped on their other side. These two groups felt that they were watching over their greenhorn charges benignly, while the missionaries usually felt only outrage. Sometimes, late at night, one of their unwelcome fellow campers passed by their tents, singing or swearing loudly. Once a Canuck of MacPheirson's party, quite drunk, rode his pony through Mrs. Prewitt's cookfire and one of the independents had brought his Indian girl right through their camp on his eager way to his own.

The Indians—Crow, Nez Perce, Flathead, Snake and others—were strung out in camps on the flats across the river. When any of them appeared in the missionary camp, many of those come to bring light to the savages were apt to disappear into their tents.

One morning Blake had come upon two young women of the party by the edge of the river. They had come down for water and were now afraid to walk back to their tent because two young Snake boys were cavorting about the camp on horseback.

"Those are *Indians*," pointed out one of the women. "They're drunk and you're no more a gentleman than they are. There's not a gentleman here—not anywhere."

Gesturing for them to walk ahead of him, he picked up their buckets of water. "I thought that's what you came here for," Black couldn't help saying. "I guess," he added musingly, "they aren't so much different from the ones you're going to teach."

One of the girls, Mr. Prewitt's daughter Charity, turned on him with blazing eyes. *"Our* Indians are waiting for the word of God. They will *not* be drunken heathens."

Mr. Prewitt and the others had many willing hands of various shades to help prepare a place for Sunday worship. They cleared the brush out of a little willow grove and built a makeshift pulpit, and they held services all day. Most of the whites attended, for a part of the time. It was a new thing for this part of the country, a church service. They liked lifting their voices in the old hymns from childhood memory and hearing the familiar, almost forgotten words of chastisement and exhortation from Bible and minister. Some, to the missionaries' joy, were even "saved"—for that day, or a part of it.

The Indians showed great interest. They came in large groups and sat on their horses or on the ground, a little apart, watching and listening with great solemnity. The ritual and sobriety impressed them mightily. Some expressed interest in knowing more about this white man's medicine, but the missionaries, strangely, showed little inclination to talk with them. It wouldn't work well, they said, having to use an interpreter. Besides, these were not the savages they had been sent to rescue. They would wait until they got to those and had learned their language, at least enough of it to make certain they understood their teachings properly.

At a distance, far enough away not to be a distraction, horse races, a shooting match, and other things went on through the hot, dusty day. Men drifted back and forth, from one diversion to another, most of them with heavy heads that still ached from the previous night. Connall and others had asked that there not be too much drinking, trading, and such on this day, in deference to the church people, but it was only a request and by no means an order. No one could have enforced such a command.

Blake walked alone by the river, far enough away from human sounds so that the harvest flies' dinning was the loudest thing he could hear. It wasn't such a bad place, he thought. He was tired and glad to be this much alone, but then Connall came riding down from his camp.

"Get a horse and come with me," he said, looking harried.

"What's happened?"

"I told that fool man to keep his camp guarded. Didn't you hear me telling him again this very morning?"

"I thought he had."

"Aye, but the guards needed to slip away for a bit to services and I've just been told that Big Cloud's thieving bunch of Snakes have taken every holy thing they could lay hands on. Come on! They'll be leaving the country."

Connall was still muttering imprecations as they rode across the river. He shrugged and said, "Stealing's not the same to them as it is to us. Most of them wouldn't steal from their own, but when it comes to another tribe, or to whites, they look at it differently, as a kind of game."

"Who told you they took the things?"

"A Crow told me. Crows and Snakes are not my Indians, but everyone seems to think of these missionaries as *my* whites. I can't think how I get into such things . . . . This Crow also told me some Blackfeet have come in in the night, not many, but more are supposed to be on their way, coming to destroy the Flatheads, they claim. They're always just on the point of destroying somebody, those Blackfeet. The trouble is that they very nearly do it sometimes. If you do any trading with them, see you be careful."

At the Snake camp, Blake watched in a silence that was near to awe as Connall maneuvered for what he wanted. He, Blake, had done most of Connall's trading with whites during the past few days and had not had much time to observe Connall's or anyone else's dealings with the Indians. When they learned what Connall had come about, the heads of the camp grew extremely solemn, threatening, it seemed to Blake. He inferred from signs that they claimed to have no knowledge of the missing goods. Connall indicated curtly that he did not quite believe this. One of the men then recalled that some Crows had been in the camp. He said you could never trust those Crows; that perhaps they had taken the missionaries' goods and left some of them in the Snake camp just to make trouble. Connall said that he expected the goods to be found and returned, well before sundown, that perhaps then some of Big Cloud's people would care to stop at his own camp to talk trading. They reminded him that they were not Hudson's Bay Indians, but said they had a few pelts left, would he look at them now? Connall shook his head coolly and took the reins of his horse from Blake. He said he was angry now and disappointed in the Snakes, that he could not look at their furs and think of trading until his heart was good again.

"That must not be easy," Blake said softly when they were away from the camp, "facing them when they look like that. Would they kill you?"

Connall snorted. "I suppose they might, if they thought they could get away with it. Not many men here would ride in and accuse strange Indians like that with no one to back them up but one pork-eater. I've never been much afraid of Indians. I don't know why because I've had some close scrapes, one time and another, but they know I'm not afraid. I'm fine with them, mostly, as long as I can look them in the eye. It just takes being able to think as they think and I've had practice there."

"Are they really so much different? Do they think all that differently?"

"Of course they're different, lad," he said impatiently. "I've seen from the first what you are. You're one of these 'noble savage' people, aren't you? Thinking one human's as good as another and just the same under the skin. I don't know if there's a prayer of hope for the likes of you."

By the time the missionaries came back from the willow grove for their cold supper, most of their goods had been returned and Connall had had to do some trading which was less beneficial to the Company and to himself than his dealings with Indians usually were.

The next morning when Blake came to work at the trading tent, Connall was still petulant and irritable.

"Don't come in here," he ordered curtly. "If you think you're going to work for me, you've got to get out and look around and try to learn what you can. The rest of those Blackfeet came in last night. There'll be a lot of bluffing and showing off today. You ought to see what goes on. Also, some of the brigades will be leaving tomorrow; things are nearly over. This is likely to be the last rendezvous ever held, lad. Go on out and take it in; see if you've got something more than ink in your veins

. . . . No, wait! First find Jacques and send him here. I'd better go with you. You're apt to be scalped out there on your own."

There was a kind of parade all through the morning. Various groups of Indians, carefully and ceremonially dressed and painted for war, rode hellbent through all the camps, yelling wildly, shoting off their muskets, displaying feats of horsemanship. Behind them, on foot or on horses, came their women and children, also yelling, beating on trade kettles, shaking rattles, many of them as skilled as the men in such things as standing up on their mounts or flinging themselves from one side of a horse to the other, under its neck, at a full gallop. There were dogs everywhere, all barking furiously amid the other noise. Some of the trappers joined in the display. Connall, watching, seemed cheered.

The missionaries cowered in their tents, peeking out now and then when danger seemed most imminent, trembling. Glancing around apprehensively during one volley of shooting, Blake found Emmett Price on a horse beside his.

"A feller could git killed," Emmett observed mildly with a slightly shaky grin, "but, man! can't they ride! I never saw anything could come close to it."

A young brave stopped to talk briefly with Connall.

"Red Elk says the Flatheads are having a big game over at their place," he reported. "Come on, both of you."

At the Flathead camp, they were fed from a great community pot. The game, a hand game where small pieces of polished bone were passed from hand to hand among a team and their whereabouts guessed at by the other team, had already begun. It was very noisy, having a kind of ritual chant and banging on the ground to accompany it, and there were the shouted comments of all the players and observers, plus the ubiquitous barking of many dogs. Connall, in the midst of the game, was as vociferous as any of the others. These were some of his own Indians, their home ground being not far north of Camas Post. Blake saw him lose a knife and two or three other small articles. The action was a little hard to follow through the noise and dust and shifting of players. One of the other companies sent over a barrel of drastically cut American whiskey, ready for trading with the winners, and the men who brought it eagerly joined the hand game.

A young Indian with a scar all across one cheek tapped Blake and Emmett, indicating that they should join the play.

"I can't," Emmett said, meeting the man's eyes apologetically. "It's gamblin'."

He seemed to accept Emmett's refusal good-humoredly, but kept staring at Blake, who had also shaken his head. Awkwardly, Blake tried to say, in the rudimentary sign language he had just begun to learn, that he had nothing to wager. The Indian grunted, indicating the bright cotton shirt he had purchased from Connall's stock.

"Come on!" Connall yelled. "What kind of trader are you going to make if you don't make friends? If you lose the shirt, we'll take another out of your wages."

He lost the shirt to Cutface and everyone laughed. Then Cutface indicated that he wanted Blake to put up his horse.

It was not much of a horse, really, but Henry had chosen it for him. He didn't want to lose it.

"Many ponies have new owners here today," Cutface pointed out reasonably with Connall as a willing translator.

Blake shook his head.

"Have a little faith in yourself, lad," Connall urged gleefully. "All you have to do is keep things from showing in your face. Just don't always look so guilty."

Cutface had made a peremptory gesture behind him and a young girl came up, looking shyly through her lashes at Blake.

"Ah, now," Connall breathed with anticipation. "Cutface says he doesn't think much of black ponies, but this is his offer: you put up the horse, he wagers the girl. Is that fair or not?"

Blake was shaking his head vehemently, the others all laughing again.

"Does he not like women?"

"Careful that you don't damage diplomatic relations," cautioned Connall with a broad grin.

"Well, what the hell am I supposed to—"

He was saved from further embarrassment by two riders, passing through the camp like a whirlwind, yelling that the Blackfeet were challenging to races. The whole Flathead camp, along with their guests and what was left of the barrel of whiskey, moved to the race course that had been marked off some distance down the river.

"I guess I ought to go back," Emmett said uneasily some time during the course of the afternoon.

"Me, too," agreed Connall easily. "Jacques is probably drunk and giving away my goods by now, if there's anyone around to give them to."

Connall refilled his gourd at someone else's whiskey keg. There was a sad feeling here, under all the gaiety, and he was doing his best to shake it, a feeling of ending, of finality. He said to the boys above the noise of the crowd, "Have you ever heard a harvest fly still carrying on like mad the way they do, when the first snow's already begun to fall? That's what we all remind me of at this gathering. Look on it well, lads. I think it'll not happen again." He drank deeply, a little desperately. "And maybe I'm an old man, with all these premonitions and such. Hell! You can't be an old man at thirty-two. *I* can't. It's only the feeling of change that I have. I ought to know by now that when one thing ends, another begins, sometimes something better."

He felt better as the day drew on toward sundown. The Coeur d'Alenes and Flatheads were going to have a dance, just to show the contingent of Blackfeet that they were prepared. "They've come to destroy us, have they?" they were saying disdainfully

"Go back to camp," Connall said to Blake. "See that things are all right with Prewitt's flock. Then you and Jacques bring some things over here for trading. Tell Marie where I am if you see her. I've been looking around for her but she doesn't take so much to this kind of thing as most Indian women do. Tell Mr. Prewitt he ought to be over here learning things, and you can tell him, too, that we'll be leaving early on the day after tomorrow." He stood up a little unsteadily. "And bring along some rum. I've had about all of this watered-down American whiskey I can stand."

Emmett's parents and the others of the band were outraged that the boy had spent most of the day away from their supervision and protection. They had been terribly worried about him, they said, but too afraid to risk searching for him. Imperturbably, Emmett went about doing some camp chores, saying little, but when Blake and Jacques had loaded some goods on pack horses, he was there, ready to go back with them.

It was a warm still night, with just a faint touch of chill in the breeze down from the mountains, presaging the early high-country autumn. Blake felt relaxed and good; he had had just about the right amount to drink. He would have liked to go away somewhere and sleep, or perhaps just lie, looking up at the sky. The flats were pleasant to cross with the stars shining warm and near. He had little relish for returning to the frenetic noise and activity of an Indian camp. One thing he was learning was that, in this huge, lonely country, it was a rare thing for a man, a white man, at any rate, to be truly alone.

"Do you think they can be farmers?" Emmett asked earnestly, startling him a little.

"I don't know, Emmett. Maybe. Some time."

The boy sighed. "They'd be better off, I know, settled some place, but it's sort of like one time I saw a wild horse caught. It was never the same thing after that."

Connall, hardly able to stand now, seemed to have lost none of his sharpness as a trader. He told Blake to go away until he was sent for.

"This is the way I got started." he said almost defiantly, "trading in Indian camps. It's a damn relief to get out of a post now and again and back under the sky."

Blake and Emmett sat in the shadows, holding the reins of their horses, watching the dance. It was a wild, seemingly disorganized affair and several other things went on in conjunction with it, a counting of coups by young braves from several bands, sporadic trading, and a number of fights. The pugilistic participants, whatever their skin color, were too drunk to do each other much serious damage, except that one trapper shot another in the thigh. The injured man's friends carried him contritely to the missionary doctor.

Toward midnight, Blake went to tell Connall he was leaving.

"Pack up this stuff and take it with you," said his employer. "I don't know where Jacques has gone off to. You'll notice a good bit of peltry changed hands at the races today. Some of it came from the Blackfeet and I think we've wound up with the best of it. You sleep in the trading tent tonight. Jacques and the rest of us are too drunk."

Blake turned at a touch on his arm to look into the eyes of the Flathead girl who had been offered as a wager earlier. She smiled at him boldly now, pointing with interest to his own eyes. Connall laughed boisterously.

"Give her something, so long as it's not too expensive and then go with her. She likes your eyes. I'll watch the goods till you come back. Good God! don't tell me you don't want to go with her. Surely you know that's partly what a rendezvous is for."

She chose a string of little hawking bells. Blake stood, feeling the heat rising in his face, waiting for her to choose something more, but she seemed to feel the bells were sufficient payment.

At Fort Hall, the missionaries were met by a small group of whites already established near where the new mission was to be and by some Indian parishioners. Mr. Prewitt refused to pay Blake any part of the rest of the money he had agreed upon with Henry Melton. He said the boy had not kept his end of the bargain because he was not a seasoned guide and had worked for Connall through the rendezvous. Blake put up no argument, though Connall was furious. There were the traps and other gear Henry had bought in St. Louis, he had those things. If he needed cash or other goods, he could sell or trade for them, so long as Henry's gear lasted. All he cared about having now was some distance between himself and the missionaries. Since that brief time with the Indian girl, their nearness had made him more uncomfortable and irritable than ever. It was like being a little boy again and feeling that his grandparents were omniscient, their sharp, critical eyes able to see into his mind. And that night, or bit of a night, with the girl, had brought New Orleans again into the front of his mind along with the questioning and torment such thoughts always meant. "If a thing brings pleasure to the body," his grandfather had once said, seeming to be embarrassed by the very word body, "it's a sinful thing." Grandpa had had a tight hard mouth and small parsimonious eyes but, to Blake as a boy, it had seemed that God must look something like that. He was a boy no longer and he was struggling to win free of the strictures of his boyhood but the criticism that had engendered such painful self-doubt was still very much with him and then there was New Orleans . . . . How far would he have to run?

Some Flatheads and Nez Perce had ridden with Connall's party to Fort Hall, and they rode with them still, across the Snake and north, everyone heading home. It was a party of respectable size, and a good thing, for they kept hearing rumors that there were bands of Blackfeet still roaming west of the mountains, eager for trouble.

"Whites have had a good lot to do with this," Connall said irritably, "they've persuaded a lot of Indians to move just because it's convenient for trade. For instance, they've got nearly the whole Oglala Sioux nation living around Fort Laramie now, a place that never was Sioux country. They've upset the balance. It used to be nearly enough for the Blackfeet that these mountain Indians came out to their country once or twice a year to hunt buffalo. They could do plenty of exterminating then."

But they had little trouble and Blake began to be taken by the country. It was huge and varied, from the empty, dry Snake River badlands to the high mountains, still showing patches and fields of snow at the beginning of August; from burning sagebrush flats to thick, dark, cool, evergreen forests; from deep twisting canyons with tortured, brawling streams in their bottoms to placid little lakes, sparkling demurely in the sun; from vast distances to closed-in, eerie-feeling encapsulations in heavy fog. It seemed to Blake that the air had a different feel here, whether it was the soft, whimsical breeze just after sunrise, wind stinging with alkali dust and underlaid with pine scent in mid-afternoon, the fresh wet air after a shower, or the first really cold wind of the season that struck into their faces as they crossed the last high pass before coming down into the Camas Valley. The air had a feeling of vastness. It had passed over great, unknown distances and would go on that way forever. It had a feeling of complete indifference to the small insignificance that was Man, and that was somehow soothing. No matter who you are, it seemed to say, or who you're not; no matter what you have or have not done, it's all one to me; I'll just go on, being the same. What else really matters?

Once or twice when he was awake at night, he had a brief delusion that the silhouettes of the mountains leaned, ever so slightly, toward him, in a gesture of comfort and reassurance. What are all these things, they seemed to be asking, that you've worried and agonized over for so long? And Blake smiled a little, relaxing. They were not leaning, of course. They would never give a damn, and somehow that uncaring, dependable indifference was more of a comfort than anything he had ever known.

The Camas was a beautiful valley where their trail came down into it, about halfway along its course from high mountains to the south, running between two great ranges on its way to join Clark's Fork. At the point where they reached it, the river was quiet and wide, running close to one side of the valley where sheer, low cliffs rose up. On the river's other side was meadowland, dotted with little groves of willow and cottonwood. Back where the valley's sides steepened, the dense evergreen woods began. The grass of the meadows was dry and browning now, but it was sprinkled over with the colored patterns of frenetically blooming late summer flowers. In the still, clean air, the mountains were vivid, seeming nearer than they were. One of the men pointed out a peak, higher than others around it, up the valley to the south and told Blake it was called Never Summer. He liked the sound of that and stood looking at the peak until sunlight, shimmering off a snow field, made his eyes uncertain of what they were seeing.

"What's that one?" he asked dreamily, turning slowly to pick out a mountain across the valley in the eastern range.

"Huh? Hell, I don't know. The Divide runs along that range for a ways, Continental Divide, but not much is named that I know of. You think we got nothin' to do around here but name mountains? God, there's a million of 'em. I just know Never Summer because it's special some way to some of the Indians around here. Come on an' git busy. You're some pork-eatin' greenhorn, standin' there lookin' at mountains with your mouth nearly hangin' open."

They came down to Camas Post on a cool, clear afternoon in August. They were met by a small, noisy welcoming party. Connall's daughters who had been left at home, aged about three and five, rode their own ponies like accomplished horsewomen. There was firing of muskets from the new arrivals and from the welcomers, much shouting and barking of dogs.

The post consisted of a small fort with warehouses and a few shops built around the inside of its walls. There was room for all the post's engagees and their families to live inside if they had to, but there were several small cabins outside the walls. Connall's cabin had two rooms. He and Marie were very proud of it. There were a few pieces of sturdy, handmade furniture and a lovely, simple crucifix hung on the wall above the bed.

"I shot the bear two years ago, just there by the gate," Connall said matter-of-factly, indicating a grizzly skin.

He had a small barn and a fair-sized rail fenced enclosure for his cattle. Two young halfbreed boys took the little herd out into the meadows every day that weather permitted and a guard was kept on them and on the horses at night. If trouble threatened, the animals, too, had to be brought into the fort's enclosure.

"The Indians around here don't make me any trouble," Connall said. "I trust any of them I know, so long as I can look them in the eye, but a man's a fool to take chances when he's not got to. There's enough in living that has to be left to chance as it is. The thing about the Indians is, they're like children. Not many of them will stop to think anything out. They just blow around and change with the wind, and you never know, until you've listened to them for half a day, what bee they may have in their bonnets. But anyway, the cattle. They've not been much but trouble up to now. It's a fine thing to have meat and milk for ourselves, but that's all they've done for us so far. One day, there'll be a power of people using the

Oregon Trail and it's my plan to drive stock down to Laramie or Hall to sell to those people and to the army, maybe beginning next year."

"It seems awfully far," Blake said. He was thinking he might never want to go that near to civilization again and with what satisfaction old Henry would grin if he could know those thoughts.

"Of course it's far," Connall snapped impatiently, "and you've got not one whit of imagination, not to mention foresight. Can't you think how hungry those poor travelers are going to be for the taste of some beef and milk? And how they'll be needing fresh horses after toiling all that way?"

"I don't want them to come. I wouldn't want any part of anything that might encourage them."

"For the sake of the Lord!" Connall spluttered in disgust. Then he laughed. "Is it that you've got it in your head now that what you want and what you do can stop them? Were you there, by any chance, when the Red Sea was held back?"

Blake found the warehouse stock and the books and papers relating to it in a deplorable state.

"It's all there," Connall said a little defensively, "all the figures and information you'll ever need. Is it too much to ask that a clerk be able to look for a thing, now and then, among a few little papers?"

"Where will I find the price, then, that you want to charge for these blankets?"

Connall dug his big strong fingers into his red beard, frowning. Then his face cleared. "It's in that ledger, of course, listed with nightshirts. Where else would you put blankets?"

It was a busy time at the post, with trappers and Indians coming in for supplies for the fall hunt. Hudson's Bay had never encouraged white trappers so much as the American companies had done. They preferred to have the Indians do most of the trapping, then trade their furs, either at posts or with itinerant traders. The Canadian company prided itself on giving a fair and reasonable exchange and on not trading much in whiskey, except where the proximity of American traders seemed to make it a necessary staple. It seemed to Blake that there was a great deal of rationalization and adjustment of morals necessary in this business, but he went about learning all he could. After all, he had not come to the mountains to revolutionize trading and morality. What difference did any of it make, so long as the parties concerned came out of their transactions with, more or less, what they wanted. Still, the difference between what the company and Connall paid for goods and what the Indians, and even the trappers, paid for them appalled him. But all things considered, he felt lucky to be here, to be seeing all of it. He kept hearing from the trappers how things were changing in the mountains and how Camas Post was in one of the few areas left that was pretty much as all the country had been once. Most of the beaver had been trapped out of some of this country and there wasn't much demand for beaver anymore, but there were other good furs to be had and the immigrant trails were still far away.

Connall was busy with his own affairs as well as with those of Hudson's Bay. At Fort Laramie, he had acquired some wagon parts and, cursing happily, he went about completing the construction of the wagon so that he could haul wild hay. He put two half-wild Indian ponies into harness, and only his great, exuberant strength kept the whole affair from being smashed beyond recovery. He had got some seed at Fort Hall and was planning his grain field for the following year. When his farm work had let up a little, he took a few men and went out to pay courtesy visits to the Indians within a two or three hundred mile radius, to smoke and eat with them, to listen to their boasting and do his own, to hear about the hunting and trading, to find if their hearts were good toward Hudson's Bay. While he was away, Marie gave birth to their sixth daughter.

"I hear you've got some traps and gear of your own," a newly arrived trapper said in careful English to Blake.

He was a tall-dark-haired Frenchman named Paul Micheau, with troubled dark eyes and a whimsical smile that never seemed able to spread farther than his mouth.

"You and I can make an agreement, maybe. I can rent that gear from you for the fall hunt. You won't be needing it, will you? What will you take for the use of it?"

Blake had heard talk of Micheau, that he had been to Montreal that summer, that he was a wise, well-educated man who could have been factor of a post far more important than Camas if he were willing to stay in one place and if it were not for his excessive drinking.

"Paul's a sick man at times, when it comes to the drink," Connall had said regretfully.

And old Mote Stanley, a tough, cantankerous little man whom they called "Banty," but not to his face, said sourly, "Paul's weak is what he is. Any man's got the right to be blind drunk once in a while, but Paul can't quit so long as there's anything left to drink or anything left to get it with. Back at rendezvous in '36, I seen him lose the best bunch of plews I ever hope to lay eyes on an' come out with nothin' in the world but a hangover an' his fiddle, no traps, no horse, no clothes, no nothin'."

"Ah, well," said Connall a little unctuously, puffing on his pipe, "the wind favors a shorn lamb."

"Wind, hell!" spat the old man. "I know how he got outfitted that year, an' some other years too. The soft ones like you makes nothin' but trouble for the rest of us. We try to make our own way, work our livers out, an' you smooth things out for the weak ones like Micheau."

"We've all got our weaknesses, Mote. Paul's a canny man. There's not anyone I'd rather be out with than Paul —when he's sober."

"It's a grub stake I ask for," Paul said now to Blake. "Do you understand? Usually, the man who provides the gear gets half the goods."

"Half seems like a lot when I wouldn't be doing any work."

"You're an innocent child. How will you ever make your fortune if you think like that?"

"If you're here, and if you'll let me go out with you in the spring, you can use the gear for the fall."

"Why are you not going out now, if you want to go?"

"Because I'm supposed to get Connall's books and things straightened out."

Paul nodded, smiling his limited smile. "For a short time, I was a clerk here. Connall also wanted me to make hay and build a fence. But, listen, you're not much of a business man. Surely you must have heard I'm not one to be trusted with your worldly goods."

"They didn't cost me anything and they're no good to me when I don't know what to do with them. Can I go with you in the spring?"

A young trapper named Ellis Williams came in then, to collect supplies he had ordered. Paul went outside, smoking a pipe in the shade of a wall. Williams stayed for a while, trying to impress Blake with stories. Most of them had to do with his prowess with Indian women. Blake was dubious and unimpressed. One thing he had learned quickly was not to believe most of the stories men told, or at least to take them with a grain or two of salt.

When Williams finally left, Paul Micheau came quietly back into the trading room and laid a worn case on the counter.

"My fiddle," he said simply. "You can keep it till your gear comes back."

Paul's fiddle had become a kind of legend in the country, the fiddle and how Paul always managed somehow to hang onto it or get it back when it had been stolen or traded away for whiskey and other necessities.

"You'll need it for company while you're out," Blake said. "It wouldn't be much good to me."

"I'm offering you what's called collateral. Do you play a little then?"

"Very little. Not for a long time. I'll get the things together for you as soon as I can. But go ahead and keep the fiddle."

"This is a fine instrument and I think you are not a very bright boy. Maybe I will not come back with your gear. Maybe I will change my mind about taking you out before spring. You must not trust people."

A young Indian boy, one of those who lived around the post, came sidling into the room and picked up a pot that had been left lying on the counter. In French, which most of the Indians here understood fairly well, Blake asked him what he had in mind. Grinning a little abashedly, the boy shook his head, put down the pot, and left silently. Paul Micheau was staring at Blake.

"You speak New Orleans French," he said, trying to

approximate the dialect. "The boy hardly understood you."

"I'm trying to do better," Blake said in English.

"How long were you there? Such a beautiful city! I have a sister living there."

Paul still spoke in French, but Blake refused to change from English again. Suppose Paul's sister knew of the St. Croix and, somehow, of . . . .

"Not long," he said evasively. "If you want to stay here and look after things for a few minutes, I'll get the gear for you."

"But take the fiddle," Paul insisted. "I'm going to have an Indian girl for company. Let me hear you play some time. I don't know anyone else who can. Did you learn in New Orleans?"

"I learned, a little, when I was a boy, from a Scotsman."

And that, too, all the time he had spent with Alec Douglas, had been forbidden, but it was far safer ground than New Orleans.

Someone else came in then and Paul went away, taking his fiddle. In the evening, as Blake sat outside by a small fire, he came back and thrust the instrument into his hands. Embarrassed, Blake found that he could not even hold it comfortably, but he tried to recall and to play a bit of a reel Alec had used to like. He played very badly and the wailing sounded even more pathetic in the great empty quietness of the valley.

"Sorry," he mumbled, flushing as he offered the instrument to Paul who looked pained. "I told you I can't."

Paul held the fiddle with a gentle, familiar ease, and began to play. In a few moments, everyone within hearing had gathered round him. He played for hours, looking more and more morose as the evening passed, while his listeners grew gay and garrulous. They danced, the white men taking turns in partnering the Indian and half-breed women in white folk dances.

There was a little boy, Jacques' son, a half-breed child about three years old, chubby and grinning, who stood at the edge of the firelight for a long time, bouncing deliriously with the rhythms. Blake, leaning on an elbow

70

near the fire, took a large piece of bark from a log and some charcoal from the fire to sketch him. It had been years since he had done any drawing, but it happened now almost without his being conscious of what he was doing, a kind of reflex out of his relaxation and his enjoyment of the evening.

"What's that you're doin'?" one of the men asked and then they all crowded around him.

The little boy, on being told that this was his likeness, stared at Blake with awed, frightened eyes. He offered the picture to the child, wanting to be free again of their attention. The boy drew back his hand as though it might be burned, but his mother took the bark with a kind of reverence.

"Who taught you to draw?" asked Paul as he was putting away his fiddle. He insisted on speaking to Blake in the cultured French he treasured so highly.

"No one," Blake said, wishing he had not done the sketch and drawn attention to himself. He wanted simply to be there, unnoticed.

"I know," Paul said, smiling, "that it was not the same one who taught you to play the fiddle."

As a matter of fact, it had been, in a way. Alec Douglas was the only person who had ever encouraged his drawing. From Blake's earliest memory he had had a desire, a compulsion to try to put things down as he saw them. His grandparents had said it was a sinful waste of time, an indication of the innate evil in him, which they were trying so hard to root out, that he should think of spending time in such ways. Very early, he had grown painfully self-conscious and guilty about it, but still, the need to draw and sketch would not leave him, and Alec Douglas, who had a way of looking at things from directions Blake could hardly think of, had said, "The devil, my foot! You ought to be an artist. A portrait painter can do right well for himself these days, in a city."

Alec himself had once been an artist of sorts, a carver of tombstones and an artisan in other stonework. That kind of work was not much in demand after he came to live in that particular part of Pennsylvania. He had a little farm and sometimes he had some smithwork at the new mines. He was not much liked or trusted by most of his neighbors and he was considered a scourge by Blake's grandparents, who railed at the boy almost constantly for sneaking off to spend time—or waste it—with Alec, a nonbeliever, full of wickedness. And Alec, calmly, said things like, "They're so bent on seeing hell, they'll never recognize heaven."

Sometimes Alec carved someone's tombstone and sometimes he did a little stonework just to please himself. He urged Blake to help with these things as the boy grew older. "You lay it out for me," he would say eagerly. "I can carve anything, only I need someone who can plan it in his mind first, see it all before it's begun so that everything will come out just right. It'll be good practice for you and a help to me. When you're grown, you might find work of this kind."

It was a great, guilty satisfaction, working with Alec like that, and thinking about the work.

Alec owned several books and that helped in setting his family apart from most of the rest of the community. Children should learn to read and write, they believed, but the only book necessary and right to have in one's home was the Bible. One day, when Blake had slipped away from home to help Alec with a tombstone, he showed him a picture in one of the books, a picture of a castle.

"Just look at the stonework there," he said exultantly. "If I could have been a workman on some grand thing like that . . . ."

Blake, wondering uneasily if it was not somehow sinful to show so much enthusiasm, couldn't help catching some of it.

"You could build one now, maybe," he said diffidently. "I could try to help you."

Alec smiled. "Ah, son, we're not all meant to live in castles, nor to build them. But a castle, you see, doesn't have to be like this one here in the picture. It can be a thing of the mind, do you understand? If I carve a good tombstone, one where I can be proud of the work, for old Mr. Thomas, then it's a kind of castle for me, in a small way. If we just do what we *can* do, the *best* we can, or something that makes us feel happy, properly fulfilled.

. . . But you don't understand, do you? Never mind. The understanding will come. Only just try to forget about the devil and such rot."

"Can you make maps?" Paul Micheau was asking him now.

"I never tried. I've helped some with surveying work, but I never did any of the drawing."

"Can you hold a picture of the country very well in your mind?"

"I've never really tried, but—I don't think so."

"Then you'd better start trying to map it out on paper. Anyone who goes out in this country needs to know just where he is all the time. You could be separated from people you're with, then what would you do? That's the first thing you'd better work on if you want to go out with me in the spring. Get everyone who comes in here to tell you all he can about the country and make yourself maps. Most people who last in the mountains can see a place once or be told about it and they have it. If you can't do that, then you'd better find another way of remembering."

He worked on maps in spare moments. The other men contributed to his knowledge in a condescending way, laughing at him. They knew that maps were only for such as the army or greenhorns, but Blake took what he could get from them and tried not to notice their scorn. He enjoyed the planning and logistics involved in the drawing and perhaps he was learning.

He liked Paul Micheau very much and yet he was relieved when Paul left for the fall hunting. His insistence on always speaking French kept Blake a little uneasy, though Paul had not mentioned New Orleans again.

On a day in late October, when there was a cold, blustery wind with a few flakes of snow in it, and Connall, puffing his pipe, had just strolled through the warehouse, saying comfortably that no more visitors were likely at Camas Post for several weeks, three men came riding down the valley. One of them was Jesse Harris, one was a Spokane named Blue Feather, and the third was Emmett Price.

"I don't like what they're doin' at the mission," Emmett told Blake uneasily. "They expect ever'thing to be changed overnight, for them Indians to just turn into

73

white Christians, right now. Maybe I've got the wrong notions—they're sure I have—but I couldn' stay. I guess it's a weakness in me. I can't see that even the Lord's work, most of it, can be done that fast."

Blake was glad to see him. He said, "So now you're seeing the country."

"Some of it. I hoped Mr. MacPheirson might have some work for me. It sure has been a silent trip. Jesse and Blue Feather travels mighty quiet."

"I don't know about work," Connall told him. "Blake can handle most of the greenhorn chores."

"Yessir," Emmett agreed humbly. "I kind of hoped I could go out an' do some trappin', maybe in the spring. I know it's diff'rent around here, but I used to be pretty good at trappin', back in Missouri. First, though, I got to earn myself some gear an' what I am really, is a farmer. I got to thinkin' about that bull you got, an' about the rest of the cattle you told us you had. Ridin' in, I seen your meader, where you been hayin' . . . ."

Connall's eyes had lighted and they went into a long discussion about the possibilities of the land. Emmett had his job.

At the end of February, time for the spring hunt, Blake and Emmett went out with four other trappers, assuring Connall they would be back by the time work in their separate spheres should grow heavy with the season. Their companions and teachers were Jesse Harris, the silent white-Negro-Cherokee; Paul Micheau; old Mote Stanley; and Ellis Williams, the dapper, braggart ladies' man, who turned out to be a careless coward.

Paul and Mote were in charge of the group and it was usually split into two teams working up the valleys, each team taking the tributary streams on one side, meeting every few days to compare notes and lay plans.

When they came to an Indian village, they usually went in in a body, with Paul handling most of the trading. Mote disliked Indians, admitting that they had their uses but that he never wanted to do with them in groups, refusing to try to learn their languages or even to talk sign unless he had to. Strangely enough, Jesse seemed to have an aversion to most of them too, and Ellis Williams' attitude was one of pure condescension which an Indian could spot a mile away and begin to resent. Emmett was liked by the Indians, as he was by everyone, and at most camps he had to be extricated from a herd of children before the traders could leave. This did little to raise the braves' respect for him, but they seemed to look on him with a kindly tolerance; after all, what could one expect from a white-eyes? Blake, it developed, had an affinity for picking up their languages. He did not speak the languages with much facility yet, but he understood more than anyone had expected him to so soon and he utilized Connall's and Paul's advice about reading faces.

"Just because they look a little different," Paul had told him, "doesn't mean they don't have expressions that give them away, when they're about to agree to a bargain, when something makes them angry and so on."

"Also," Connall had said, disgusted because he felt Blake had muffed some trading with Cayuses at the post, "it doesn't mean they can't read *your* expression. You're a canny enough lad, at times, but you've got to quit giving everything away in your face."

As they worked through the country, it became Blake's private opinion that he might, some day, make a trader, but that he wouldn't stand a chance as a trapper. It was a miserable life. This was a very bad spring, with severe cold and heavy, violent storms lasting far longer into the season than usual. He could not imagine how anyone could *want* to go into the icy water to set and retrieve traps, or to handle the incredibly stinking bait, or to skin out the catches and handle the stiff frozen pelts, or any of it. His facility with map drawing and Indian languages won him nothing from his camp mates. To him, no matter which group he was with, fell the hard, repetitive chores, caring for the pelts, keeping the fire, doing most of the cooking, watching over the horses and gear. After all, he was still a pork-eater, a greenhorn. What did he think they had brought him along for?

Emmett, with his customary docility and never-flagging eagerness, was taken immediately under the wing of old Mote, who saw great hope for the boy, while volubly allowing that Blake was arrogant and stubborn and probably beyond hope or help.

They had not been much concerned about hostile Indians for the first two or three weeks. Who, with any sense, would be trying to move around in weather like this? Then they heard, from some Nez Perce, that a marauding Blackfoot party had come over the mountains. Moving with a little more caution, they crossed over from the Salmon into the upper Camas Valley, some seventy-five miles south of the post, agreeing to work the tributary streams back toward the fort and to stop there for a few days of respite from the weather if it had not relented by that time.

"No villages between here and there," Paul said. "Just work on down. Maybe we won't see you again until we all get to the post."

"What about them what-do-you-call-'ems up that big side valley," said Mote. "Them Medicine Rocks?"

"We won't bother them. They don't want whites in there and Connall says it's best not to stir them up. When they want trading, they come down to Camas."

"Them's virgin streams they're holdin' up there," Ellis Williams complained righteously. "Hardly ever had a trap in 'em. No Injuns got any business hoggin' things that way. When they go out east huntin' this year, I don't give a damn what Connall or anybody says, I'm goin' to trap that valley."

"Plews wouldn' be worth a goddam that time of year," Mote said disgustedly.

"I don't give a shit if they're worth anything," snapped Ellis. "The thing is, *we're* here now an' redskins got to be kep' in their places."

"Well, you can ride along with Paul an' Blake the rest of the time," Mote said coldly. "I don't believe I'll need you with me. Somebody can't foller orders from his partisan with all this bellyachin's liable to try to put *me* in my place, an' I don't hardly believe that'd do."

Blake, Paul, and Ellis took the east side of the valley, working against the heavy odds of snow and cold. Paul cursed, in French, with a kind of matter-of-fact acceptance; Ellis very nearly whined; and Blake for the most part kept silent, wondering why he had ever thought he wanted to be a trapper and if old Henry Melton was laughing somewhere. Three days after they had separated from Mote's group, another blizzard struck.

IV

BLAKE WOKE AGAIN in Red Sky's lodge. It was different this time. He was waking from sound, restful sleep, not struggling with consciousness, and there was little pain, only a great feeling of weakness and, with it, relaxation, a lethargic well-being. The lodge was silent. The whole village seemed to be quiet. He looked around, at ease. The fire burned low, a pot steaming gently at its edge. There was no one there but himself, not even the baby he remembered. The skins that covered the door were fastened aside and sunlight on the packed, trampled, melting snow outside hurt his eyes.

He remembered all of it now with fair clarity, how he had come to the west and decided to try to be a trapper. He remembered that last blizzard, how he and Paul and Ellis Williams had found a good overhang to shelter under, up on the side of a low cliff above a stream they called Darkwater. They had hurried desperately with making camp. Darkness came on with driving snow and a wild, howling wind before they were finished. They peeled bark for the hungry horses and tied them in a thin willow grove along the little creek. They hauled their packs up under the overhang and cut brush and branches to try to add what they could to its shelter. The fire would be hard, perhaps impossible to keep going through the night. They ate some jerky, complaining a little, loudly, above the noise of the storm.

"You go down with the horses, Ellis," Paul said placidly, digging into the bottom of a pack. "When you think you're about frozen, come back and wake Blake."

"Good God, Paul! There ain't any need of a guard in this weather."

"There's always need of a guard."

"Well, shit, what about you? When's your turn?"

"I'll have a turn. Right now, I'm a partisan, which means I give the orders." From the pack, he drew out the rum he had been saving.

"Means you git drunk," said Ellis sullenly.

"That, too, perhaps, if I'm lucky. Go on down. It feels to me as if there are Blackfeet around."

Muttering rebelliously, Ellis got his rifle and a buffalo robe to wrap himself in.

Blake had never seen anyone drink as Paul Micheau did. There was no ritual involved, seemingly no pleasure. He drank as much as his throat would accept, paused and drank again, waiting doggedly for results. Often, in the evenings, he had smoked a pipe, but not tonight; he only drank.

They had wrapped themselves in their robes and neither of them spoke for a long time. Then, across the edge of the weak, wavering firelight, Paul offered him the bottle. Blake tried not to seem to notice how its contents had diminished. He drank a little and returned it. He was cold and hungry, a little in awe of this man, and he himself had never cared much for rum.

"I hate storms," Paul said musingly in his beautiful French, "particularly spring storms. I can only stand so many of them, then I begin to think too much, closed up somewhere like this with nothing to do."

Then he began to talk earnestly, quietly, so that Blake sometimes missed words under the noise of the wind. Paul's family had been of the minor nobility in France. His parents had fled the country when they were very young, escaping most of the horror of the Revolution. All their children had been born in Canada. They had no money and little left in the way of status, but they still had family pride and it was painfully outraged when the boy Paul ran away to join a group of voyageurs in the far northwest country. His mother, in particular, had hoped

78

that Paul, her fourth son, born late in her life, would be a priest.

"I'm a black sheep to them," he said quietly. "My older brothers have died and my parents are very old now. They're unhappy and bitter and bewildered. This country still seems to be a new and puzzling thing to them, though it's been more than fifty years since they left France. I'd like to make them happier if I knew how, them and those others. Sometimes, I decide to go back and stay near my parents until they die, but I always find I can't. It's as if I never knew them and they never knew me. What does one do with responsibilities he never asked for and can't cope with?" He shrugged, wanting no answer from the other. "One runs away."

He drank, peered speculatively at the bottle, drank again and lay down. After a time, Blake slept uneasily.

When he woke, he felt a kind of foreboding over everything. The wind seemed to have died down a little. The fire was nothing more than a few embers. He could hear two people snoring. So Ellis had come back and gone to sleep without waking him. That was not like Ellis, too considerate. Probably in the morning, he would tell Paul that Blake had refused to go out. Well, he wasn't going to worry about it now. Let the damn Blackfeet have the damn horses.

From where he lay, he pushed branches into what was left of the fire, hoping they would catch. They did, but he found irritably that he could not drop back into sleep. Probably the most part of what was wrong was that he was cold, but he couldn't stop thinking of the three of them there, asleep, with Blackfeet maybe, near by. Sleep was gone and, muttering, he got up and found his rifle.

It was a funny thing about snow, how it seemed capable of making its own light. The sky was still close and heavy with clouds but the wind was not so steady now, and when it let up from time to time, Blake found he could see a little after his eyes adjusted from the firelight.

He slid down the low cliff. There was a deep drift at the bottom. He could make out the silhouettes of willow trunks around him, but no horses. Perhaps he was mistaken about exactly where they had been left. He moved carefully through the scattered grove, not worried yet, thinking he ought to go back and wake Paul, wondering if anything could wake Paul for the next few hours.

The wind rose gustily and he stood still, waiting for the time when he could see again. It did not come. Suppose he was right about where the horses had been? Then they had been stolen. He began to feel afraid, and then foolish. Probably, he had missed the horses somehow. This was exactly what the others would expect of a greenhorn, wandering around in the middle of a blizzard, perhaps in the middle of a Blackfoot raid—lost.

He turned and began groping his way back toward camp. Of course the horses were where they had been left. If Blackfeet had taken them, they would have taken everything else, including three scalps. He was wrong about the exact spot where the horses had been, that's all. It wouldn't be the first time. He wondered then why he hadn't heard any of them whickering when he came down. Horses almost always noticed the presence of any person or animal with some sound.

Finally, he began to admit that he truly was lost. It made him angry. He moved carefully, telling himself levelly that he would find his way and the others need not know about this. He would have to see light from the fire. Even he could not miss that. He would climb up and wake them. They would have to be told that the horses were gone.

. . . . And that was as far as his memory would go. Evidently, these people, these Indians who had been trying to make him well, had taken the horses and had taken him too. He stirred, squirmed in embarrassment. He was truly a fool and, no doubt, this was the end of his trapping and trading ventures. So what was he going to do about getting out of this?

He sat up. A jarring bolt of pain struck through his head and dizziness all but overcame him. Weakly, he hung onto the edge of the robe on which he lay until the pain and dizziness passed with a sickening slowness. He still had no clothes and his right leg was enclosed in rough, heavy splints, bound on with strips of skin.

The Medicine Rock People, that's what the old medicine man had called them. All right. He knew where the valley of Medicine Rock Creek lay in relation to the Camas and the fort and to the mountain called Never Summer. The valley lay right at the foot of the mountain and it was a long way to walk back to Camas Post. These people had been kind to him, in their almost-lethal way. Was it possible he could get a horse from them? Or maybe they still meant to kill him as soon as he was strong enough to be a proper captive. And what had happened to Paul and Ellis? How long ago had he been brought here?

A little yellow dog came whirling into the lodge, barking wildly. It leapt onto the robes where he lay and licked Blake's face with tremendous enthusiasm. While he tried shakily to save himself from its frantic show of affection, the dog was followed by a wide-eyed little girl of perhaps eight.

"Lie down, Green Eyes!" she ordered staunchly, a little out of breath. "We are your guards, this dog and I. He is named Protector Of The Camp and he is very brave."

"And what are you named?" he asked soberly, drawing the robe around him, still sitting up.

"I am named Cricket now. Perhaps I'll have a better name one day. Chief Red Sky is my father."

"Where is he? Where's everyone else?"

"The women are up a little way on the side of Never Summer, digging kouse. The men are looking to the horses and doing other things. It's past the time when we should be ready to go to the buffalo plains. Spring is a long time coming this year. Are you hungry?"

"Yes."

She came closer, looking at him critically. "I will give you some food. You look very sickly still."

As she was bringing the food, two boys, a little older than she, came in.

"Who told you to feed the prisoner?" demanded one of them menacingly.

"He is only just able to sit up by himself," said Cricket reasonably. "I thought we would not let him starve to death after all this."

"What do women know?" said the smaller of the boys with tolerant scorn. He was Cricket's brother Smiling Fox, small and quick and wiry, with a most expressive face, a good study, Blake thought, for learning about Indian moods and emotions.

The food tasted good, though it was almost more than he could manage, in his weakened state, to hold the bowl, eat and fend off Protector Of The Camp.

"He must be guarded well," said the other boy importantly. He was called Buffalo Calf and, to Blake, he seemed as big as one as he moved ponderously to take up a war club and hold it ready. "What kind of guard are you, Cricket, with no weapon?"

"What can he do?" she asked, giggling. "He has no clothes and he's very weak."

"Who knows what a white might try to do?" said her brother darkly.

"Why do we call them whites?" wondered the little girl. "See, he is not white at all, but a sick pink color, and I never knew anyone who lived had green eyes."

"Maybe they'll change color when he's well again," said Smiling Fox a little uneasily. "Do you see that he eats with his spoon in his left hand?"

"Some of our people do that," she said. "Half Moon does and he's not a good warrior or a good hunter either."

"If he's going to be well," said Buffalo Calf belligerently, "it's time he did something to earn his food. What can you do?" he demanded of Blake, looking at him with great fierceness. "I suppose you will be somebody's slave. It's been a long time since there have been any slaves in this village. You should belong to my grandfather Crooked Wolf, since he's the one who saved your life."

"No!" Cricket said hotly. "It was Hawk's Shadow who kept him from being killed in the first place and asked Crooked Wolf to make him well."

"I think they'll let him go," said Smiling Fox. "Red Sky my father told his friends he could come back if he lived."

"My friends?" Blake said. "Was someone here?"

They looked at him, then at each other. Though he had spoken before, they seemed to realize suddenly that he understood most of what they said. Smiling Fox said finally, shyly, "Two whites came. They thought you would die if they carried you with them. They thought you would die anyway. They gave some gifts to my father and went away."

"How long have I been here?"

"Seven days," said the boy, "maybe eight. Your friends came a day or two after you were brought here, just before Crooked Wolf made medicine for you."

"He's a prisoner," Buffalo Calf reminded his cousin sternly. "A prisoner has no right to ask questions or know anything."

"He cried out as loudly as he could," recalled Cricket relentlessly, "when they put him into the stream to drive out the badness."

"Yes," agreed Smiling Fox with his clever little smile. "He's no danger to us."

"Danger!" scoffed Buffalo Calf. "Nothing living is a danger to the People of the Medicine Rock. Didn't we drive away those Blackfeet?"

"You didn't," reminded Cricket. "It was Hawk's Shadow and Beaver Tooth and the others. You're no warrior yet."

"Be quiet, girl," he ordered pompously. "And give me some food. I'm hungry."

She obeyed readily, but with a pert, complacent expression.

Buffalo Calf relinquished the war club to Smiling Fox who held it casually.

"How did I come to be here?" Blake asked, putting down his bowl which Protector Of The Camp attacked voraciously.

"You were captured," said Smiling Fox matter-of-factly. "Some Blackfeet were sneaking around and our men were chasing them. Those Blackfeet stole your horses from by the Darkwater and our men followed them and got the horses back. They got three Blackfoot scalps too. They came back by the Darkwater to see what else might be there and they found you, lying at the foot of a bank with your head and your leg broken and almost frozen in the storm. Maybe you have a strong spirit watching over you that they didn't take your scalp and leave the rest of you."

"Probably we will still take it," said Buffalo Calf comfortably, around a mouthful of food.

"Where are the horses?" asked Blake.

"With our herd. They are ours now. Didn't we take them from the Blackfeet?"

"Then how did my friends get here?"

"They were with other whites that didn't come into the valley. Red Sky my father would let only two come in. Whites are bad medicine."

"No more questions," ordered Buffalo Calf peremptorily. "What will you do, Green Eyes, to pay us back for your life? We've been left to guard you. You must make it worth our bother."

"*I* was left," said Cricket. "No one told you boys to come in here."

"Will you let me go out in the sun?" Blake asked. "It would feel good."

"What if we do? What will you do then?"

"I could tell you about—about the rest of the world, things you haven't seen."

"Every year our people go to the buffalo plains," sneered Buffalo Calf, "and often to the Salmon for fishing. We know the Flathead country and the Snake country. That is no kind of payment for what's been done for you."

"Maybe it is," said Smiling Fox thoughtfully. "Maybe he knows about those boats I have heard talk of, those that go on the rivers with smoke and noise and no one to paddle them. There must be a mighty spirit in those boats."

"I'll draw one for you," Blake said, "if I can go out in the sun."

He wrapped himself shakily in the robe and stood up with their help. His ankle was terribly sore and swollen and could bear little weight, but he was feeling a kind of desperation to be outside again.

"Whites are very weak," observed Buffalo Calf smugly as they helped him make his slow painful way through the door.

"Especially if they have green eyes and eat with their left hands," supplemented Cricket with a giggle.

She threw a robe on the ground and Blake collapsed on it, coughing. The ground was cold and damp with melting snow, but the sun was a hot, bright, wonderful thing. It was a long time before he could fully open his eyes in the light. They brought him charcoal and a large, tattered piece of elk hide and watched with a mixture of suspicion and wonder as he sketched a steamboat.

"In what part does its spirit live?" asked Smiling Fox softly, studying the drawing with great care.

"It has no spirit," Blake said. "Wood is burned inside to make water boil. The steam from the water—"

"How is the boat not burned up?"

"Because they—"

He broke off, looking up as the sunlight was crossed by shadows. Two men stood above him. They must have looked, a few years ago, much as the two boys looked now, one rather slight, quick and wiry, with sharp eyes that saw everything, the other large and heavy and unusually handsome.

"What are you doing with our prisoner?" growled the larger one.

"He's showing us the riverboat," said Smiling Fox, holding up the drawing.

The two young men looked at the sketch, frowning.

"I am Hawk's Shadow, son of Red Sky," announced the smaller one. "Does the sun make you strong?"

"It's good," Blake said.

"Where did you learn our language?"

"At Camas Post and at some villages."

"If he is strong," said the other, Beaver Tooth, belligerently, "then it is time he began to behave like a man."

"I'm told," Blake said awkwardly, "that you saved my life. I'm grateful."

"A man does not want to owe his life to another," Hawk's Shadow said soberly. "You should get up now and fight for it. If you win, maybe there will no longer be any debt."

Blake shuddered inwardly at the eager looks on all their faces. There was nothing for him to do but try.

Beaver Tooth flung away the piece of hide. "You will make no more of these markings. We do not want such things in our village." He picked up a large, heavy stick. Protector Of The Camp began to bark.

"You don't need a stick, Beaver Tooth," Hawk's Shadow said mildly. "Look. He can't stand by himself."

85

"He'd better try. If he's a man at all, it's time he began to show it."

The faintest of smiles was showing around Hawk's Shadow's eyes and Blake realized dismally that this was, somehow, a kind of game in which they were supposed to try out bluffs on one another. With Beaver Tooth, though, it seemed to be another story. His heavy face was mean and menacing. Grasping a pole at the side of the lodge, Blake dragged himself to his feet and stood there, swaying a little, trying to look calm and unfrightened.

Beaver Tooth hit him heavily across the shoulders with the stick. He fell, clutching at the robe. With them all looking on speculatively, he struggled again to stand up. When he was on his feet, Hawk's Shadow took the stick.

"Kill him," said Beaver Tooth coolly. "He is a waster of our food."

To Blake's dull surprise, Hawk's Shadow held out the stick, offering it to him.

"Use it for walking," he said carelessly. "It's better than leaning on children." And to Cricket his sister, he said, "Find him something more to wear. He does not make a good buffalo; his robe keeps falling off. And get me something to eat."

Beaver Tooth, scowling in disgust, went away. Blake dropped back to the ground, trembling with weakness. There was silence while Hawk's Shadow ate. When he had finished, he said to the children, "I will guard your prisoner for a while." He turned to Blake. "Can you walk now, for a little way?"

Slowly, painfully, Blake followed him through the village. Snow still lay deep in places, making his awkward steps treacherous. Hawk's Shadow walked here, as he walked in any terrain, with deceptive ease and carelessness. Distracted with pain and with trying to put his good foot in the right places, Blake wondered a little what he ought to expect at the end of this walk, but by the time they reached it, he was too exhausted to care much about what was going to come next.

They came to the edge of a stand of pines on a low bank above the creek. It was a sunny spot. The needles were warm and dry on the surface. Hawk's Shadow had brought two robes. He threw them on the ground and lay

86

down on one, shading his eyes to look up into the bright spring sky.

"I was hunting yesterday and this morning," he said lazily as Blake tried to settle himself comfortably. "I shot only one deer and it's a poor thing, tough and scrawny. We make ready now to go on our spring hunting and gathering and it's past time. The storms have been a long time leaving us. Look up there at Never Summer. I have seen twice ten winters and never so much snow as this on the mountain."

The mountain bulked heavily above the valley, a vagrant wind pulling streamers of snow off one of its great shoulders. Blake looked at it obediently and closed his eyes again. It was quiet here except for the quiet voice. He was tired and growing drowsy.

"We will come, after a time, to the buffalo country east of the mountains," Hawk's Shadow said and he sighed. "First there are many things to be done. The women must stop and stop along the way to gather roots and berries. My father and others say to me that I am too impatient for the hunting, that it's all I care about, and they are right. Game has been scarce here all the winter. I want to get to the buffalo . . . .

"Which horse was yours? the black? I thought so. He's a poor animal. His feed has been better since he came here but still I don't know if he will last on the journey."

Blake was not sure he had understood him. "Journey?"

"To the buffalo country," said Hawk's Shadow carelessly.

"I don't think I can ride," he said uneasily.

"Of course you can ride. Don't be a weakling."

"If I can ride, I have to go back to the post."

"No one can ride there with you. We will be leaving. Blackfeet may come, though probably not. If they did, they would like finding you riding alone. You are not so wise even as a Blackfoot. Neither are you so wise as a Snake or a Crow I think . . . . I thought you would come with us on the hunt. It will be a slow journey because of the women always having to stop. You will have time to rest and heal."

"My friends might be looking for me."

"Your friends thought you were dying when they were

87

here. That shows how much whites know about powerful medicine. I have asked Red Sky my father. He says you can come if you want to. I think you should come so that you can tell me about some things."

"What things?"

"Things like the boat you made with marks on that piece of hide. I have heard about such things that whites have and I don't understand about them. Most of them, I don't believe. People like to make stories. I don't want those things but I should know something about them, maybe. Some day, I may have to be chief of the Medicine Rock People as my father is chief now. If that time comes, I should be able to answer some of the questions the People ask, to tell them why these new things coming into our country are not good. It is better to hunt than to sit in council and argue, but a chief must do that. Beaver Tooth would like to be chief when the older ones are gone, but he would not be a good one. He can hardly find game on his own and he is too concerned with things that do not matter much, things such as telling people what they want to hear instead of what is good for them . . . .

"I would like to know why the guns our people get in trade do not shoot nearly so well as those the whites have. You could tell me about that. Maybe you could teach me some of the whites' talk so that if I must talk with them some day, they cannot say things I will not understand. I hope you can speak the whites' language better than you speak ours. What is your name?"

"Blake Westfall."

Hawk's Shadow lifted himself on an elbow and looked intently into his face, his lips carefully forming the words.

"It does not have a very good sound. What does it mean?"

Blake had looked back at him. Now he let his eyes close again. "It's—just a name."

"But what does it *mean?*"

"Whites have at least two names," he said, groping for the foreign words in his drowsiness. "The last name is the name of their father, his last name, and the first is the name the parents choose for the child. The names don't have meanings like Hawk's Shadow. They're just—names."

"The women have these meaningless names too?"

"Yes. Long ago, I think they had meanings, but people have forgotten them."

Hawk's Shadow was puzzled and irritated. "What were your parents' names?"

"My father's was Eric Westfall and my mother's was Sarah Blake—until she married. Then it was Sarah Westfall—"

"Why?"

"Because when a woman marries, she takes the last name of her husband."

"That's reasonable I suppose, for whites. But perhaps you don't know the answers to the questions I will want to ask."

"Maybe not."

Hawk's Shadow shifted discontentedly. "You could look at me when I'm talking to you. You could try to answer those questions as they come into my mind, couldn't you?"

"I could try."

He seemed mollified. "I can teach you things that are very worthwhile. I think you know nothing about tracking and hunting. If you did, I think we would not have found you as we did."

"That's true."

"What about caring for horses?"

"I know a little about horses," he said a little defensively. He wanted to close his eyes again, to be left alone, to sleep.

"Do you want to learn the things I could teach you?"

"I suppose I ought to."

"I think you may be lazy . . . . How can whites live and call themselves men without knowing the things you need to know? What do you know about?"

"Adding and subtracting," Blake said drowsily, in English.

"What does that mean?" demanded the other with ruthless interest.

He shifted back to the proper language. "Writing numbers."

"Can you read those talking papers?"

Blake had to open his eyes at the tone. There was

89

eager excitement in Hawk's Shadow's mobile face as he said, "Make one and tell me what it says."

"Can't I sleep for a while first? I'm very tired."

Hawk's Shadow said sternly, "When we found you, half frozen and with your head broken, Beaver Tooth and the others would have taken your scalp but I stopped them. Have you no pride? Don't you feel any debt to me? I have never seen one of those talking papers."

Blake sighed. "Bring something to write on and something to write with. How long will I have to pay this debt?"

Hawk's Shadow grinned happily. "A life is a long thing to pay for," he said complacently and, unwillingly, Blake answered his smile.

Preparations for the beginning of the journey were long and noisy. While they went forward slowly, Blake had a little time to think about where he was, recalling the maps he had drawn to set the country in his mind.

Medicine Rock Creek was a good-sized stream and it and the upper Camas River drained all the area around the mountain called Never Summer. The upper Camas came around from a steep, narrow valley on the south side of the mountain. Medicine Rock Creek came out of a short twisting canyon to join the river, but above that canyon it drained the valley, a beautiful mountain park. It was one of those small, relatively open spaces that occur fairly often but always unexpectedly in the rugged high country, meadow land, dotted with trees and small groves and here and there a low, grassy rise. It was higher than most of the river valleys where other Indian villages were located, but sheltered and protected and growing beautiful now with the grass greening as it came out from under the snow and myriads of wild flowers holding up their eager, varicolored faces to the sun. The Medicine Rock People liked to boast that their horses rarely had to eat bark, though their valley was higher than most permanent camps. The horses, in normal winters, could paw and trample away the snow and find plenty of good grass, dried on the stem.

The valley walls were steep and sheer. Never Summer and the high ridge that connected the peak to the main range lay along one side of it; the other was flanked by a high, rugged, almost even-topped ridge, so steep that, in many places, no trees could find footholds on its sides. The People kept a guard or two always watching the canyon entrance to the valley and they needed little else in the way of protection.

The great Medicine Rock itself stood just at the head of the canyon where the small North Fork came to join the main stream of the creek. It was a gigantic boulder, standing somber and imperturbable at the forks of the brawling creek. The village lay perhaps a mile above this place and, on the night before the long journey was to begin, the People went down to the rock for a council and ceremony. They arrived solemnly, just before sunset. Blake thought the big rock looked brooding, a little sinister even with the sun's rays still on it, but the Indians felt only friendliness emanating from it. It was their own special good omen, their strong medicine, and the men, sitting in a council circle while the women and children, and Blake, kept a little apart and listened, recounted again the old story of Winter Thunder and of how the People had come to the valley.

Those who became the Medicine Rock People had once lived beyond the great range of mountains to the west. Long ago—some time around 1780 as nearly as Blake could ever figure it—when Winter Thunder was a young boy, he had been led to this valley during a long time of wandering and, in the midst of a crashing winter storm of sleet and lightning, he had come up through the canyon. As he stepped into the valley, the sun came out, with thunder still crashing above the mountains, and brightness fell on the wet, somber rock. Spirits spoke to the Indian boy, who only then knew that his name was to be Winter Thunder. He stayed there, fasting, seeing visions, listening well to the voices that spoke to him. After a time, he went on to explore the valley, but it was simply a perfunctory action. He already knew what a good place it would be.

That had been a time of trouble and dissension for the band to which those who would become the Medicine Rock People belonged. The use of horses was a new thing to them then and it was causing great upheavals. In some ways, they were stronger and more prosperous than they had ever been. They could more easily join together with their friends to fight their enemies. They were trading more widely than had ever been possible without horses, and many of them, rather than relying on salmon fishing as their chief source of sustenance, were beginning to go east of the Divide to the Buffalo plains for hunting each year. They were picking up many things and many ways from far-flung tribes, and not all the newness was good.

Many of the people of the large band, including its chief, pointed out Winter Thunder's extreme youth when he came back to them with his visions and accounts of the valley to which he had been led, but the boy's family and others listened, took up the dream, and came with him. They held staunchly to what they knew to be good in the old ways, at the same time admitting the practicability and desirability of innovations such as horses and buffalo. The horses they bred began to be sought after in trade and in war by all who saw or heard of them. The whole People went every year to the buffalo plains, the camas prairie, the fishing places, but they came back, always, to winter in the valley of the Medicine Rock and to hold it inviolate to outsiders.

Winter Thunder had lived a long, brave life, a good and wise chief, and he had told the People many times that the whites were the greatest danger ever to come into the mountains. "They will keep coming," he had said. Our people cannot stop them. We can only hold this valley. It is ours. Here, we can be as we have been, as we are meant to be. Don't let the young men be tempted. What is happening to some of the tribes and bands is like a bear being led to a pit. He is a proud, mighty animal until he falls in. Then he is a thing only to be laughed at and poked with sticks."

"And you," said Red Sky, son of Winter Thunder, now scornfully to his people as they sat in the shadows by the Medicine Rock, "you know these old words and the wisdom of my father, yet you pant like dogs after things the white-eyes have. You wait to be led to the pit."

"If all their things and their ways are bad," said young Beaver Tooth brazenly, sullenly, "why is this one allowed to stay among us, even to sit in our council?" He glared at where Blake sat, well away from the council and the firelight.

Red Sky frowned at his nephew. He was a big, sober man of fifty, feeling his load of responsibility grow heavier with the years.

"This is a plan of Hawk's Shadow my son," he said heavily. They had talked about it before and Red Sky, obviously, had never thought very highly of it. The young men had to be given a chance, now and then, to try out their own ideas and Hawk's Shadow was his son, who sometime pleased him and made him proud. The chief was uneasy about the white man's being there and about his own ambivalent feelings, and Beaver Tooth was too young to be speaking at this time in the council talk. He said patiently, "Hawk's Shadow thinks to learn something of the white-eyes in this way, so that we may know the pit is there and not come to it. We cannot prevent the things we don't know about."

"I have the same plan," Beaver Tooth said shortly. "It has been in my mind for some time, but my plan does not include feeding and caring for a white and giving him clothing and other things. I would go down to what they call Camas Post to see their things and their ways. I would bring back what it is good for us to have. Some of those things we could use."

"You're only a boy," said his father, the bulky Many Bears, in a warning rumble. He was embarrassed that his son was talking this way in council, before the older men had finished.

"Hawk's Shadow is younger than I," Beaver Tooth said, unabashed. "I'm older now than Winter Thunder was when he led the People to this place."

The others shifted, muttering at the audacity of the comparison.

"Did I not take two Blackfoot scalps this spring?" demanded Beaver Tooth righteously, "the first scalps taken by any of our people in a long time? Perhaps we grow weak and a little cowardly from only protecting our valley and keeping away from the new things."

"My grandson," said old Crooked Wolf warningly in his cracked voice, "we will have no more talk like that, of cowardice and weakness. That is not talk of our people.

You forget yourself. The clothing and other things that have been given to that white come from Red Sky's family. If Red Sky believes it may be wise to let Hawk's Shadow do this thing, then we know he has thought well on it and made the decision that seems best to him. Be quiet now, until older, wiser men speak, those whose tongues do not run away with them. Then you will tell us again about the taking of the scalps."

By the time it was his proper turn to talk, Beaver Tooth seemed to have got over sulking at the rebuff. He made a long, involved, picturesque job of telling how he and some of the other young men, riding back from hunting, had crossed the trail of the Blackfeet, followed them and come to battle, surely saving the Medicine Rock People from attack. Three Blackfeet had been killed—here the scalps were displayed again for the admiration of all —and the rest of the wary party had run away like frightened women, leaving many horses.

Beaver Tooth redeemed himself with this recounting. The older men were proud of his talking. Things were as they should be again.

It was then Hawk's Shadow's turn at oratory because it was he who had taken the third scalp, but he passed lightly over the skirmish with the Blackfeet, saying that Beaver Tooth had told of it well. Hawk's Shadow preferred to talk about his prowess as a hunter, how he had found game through this past bad season and what he would do when they finally got to the buffalo plains. Most of the older men were dissatisfied with Hawk's Shadow's performance; it left something to be desired, and they glanced at each other in some concern. This was Red Sky's son, the grandson of Winter Thunder. He was, beyond question, a very good hunter, but he ought to make a better showing for himself in council.

The whole band, with Crooked Wolf and Red Sky as their spokesmen, asked for the help, guidance, and protection of all things good in earth and sky. They asked that roots, berries, buffalo, and all other game be plentiful, that good health be granted to the People of the Medicine Rock, with destruction for their enemies. They reminded the Powers of things they had done in past seasons, what good and true People they had been. They spoke to their medicine bundles and danced, and in the morning they began the journey.

Blake was glad that he had been taken under Hawk's Shadow's guidance and could ride out with him and a few other young men, chosen as scouts. He would not have liked going in the midst of the main body of the camp, which was a melee of shouting women and children, barking dogs and protesting horses. Anyway, he was not wanted there. Owl Woman had told him, during the interminable preparations, that he certainly must ride out with the scouts because he was only in the way of the women. He had attempted to help her with her packing and that had been cause for hilarity among the whole village.

He was not certain yet what his feelings were about this trip, but he was too weak and lame to do much in the way of rebellion, even if he had wanted to. He felt a mild interest in and curiosity about these people and about the journey, reminding himself that he was a drifter with tides who should take what came and see what he could do with it. One thing of which he *was* certain was that he was tired of being called a greenhorn. The Medicine Rock People didn't have that particular word in their language, but they had several others, just as descriptive and even less complimentary.

"He is Hawk's Shadow's pet," Beaver Tooth said derisively as their small group rode out into the valley of the Camas. "It is as if Hawk's Shadow has become attached to a silly dog or some such thing. Perhaps he will teach him tricks."

"His ways are different from ours," Hawk's Shadow answered calmly, "but I think he may be able to learn."

It took several days getting to the camas prairie, their first important stopping place, where the women would dig and dry camas roots. They found deer and other game on the way. Blake was in awe of the bow and arrow prowess of the young men with whom he rode. A few of them had muskets and they were not very successful with those, but with arrows it seemed they could bring down anything at any distance.

"What's wrong with those guns?" Hawk's Shadow asked Blake privately.

"I think they're not very good guns," Blake said, "but why do any of you need them when you can shoot like that with a bow?"

"Half Moon and Storm Coming Out Of The East and a few others have been to Camas Post and traded for them. They paid well and they should have some good from those guns. Also, our enemies have them and so they say we should have them too. They say they are supposed to shoot farther and better than a bow . . . . Maybe it is partly that we don't know the right way to use them. You see Half Moon there, with his flat, crooked nose. That is because the first time he shot his gun, he put the end of it against his nose to make it steady."

Blake winced, though he could not help smiling, and Hawk's Shadow frowned, saying soberly, "These are the things whites do to us. They make us look like fools and we don't know how they do it or why."

Several other groups had reached the camas grounds before them. The women went to work with great gusto and everyone visited. Blake had never heard so much talking in his life. A good deal of it was about the whites in the area, which meant anywhere west of the Divide and north of Great Salt Lake. He heard some strange and interesting interpretations of the missionaries' religious teachings. The general consensus at the camas grounds seemed to be that while these were funny, often ridiculous people, they might have some ways and some goods that were good medicine, that perhaps the people who had been here a long while might withhold final judgment for a little time yet, to see if they could find out anything that might prove useful to them. As each new group came in, Blake was, briefly, a center of interest and curiosity, but then attention and conversation moved on to more important things.

He could not walk yet without pain and weakness and so was forced to stay near the camps most of the time. He tried again, tentatively, to offer help to the indefatigable women, because he was bored and tired of doing nothing, and received only ridicule in return for his offer. The men, when they were not out hunting or scouting or simply riding over the country, talked and ate, boasted and gambled or slept amid the noise. Blake, lying a little apart in a shady spot, wished fleetingly that he had something to read. Somehow the thought, in these surroundings, made him smile, a little wistfully. Storm Coming Out Of The East was passing by and Blake asked to borrow a knife so that he could whittle on a stick. After a while, he found that he was making a snake.

"Why don't you make something useful?" demanded Beaver Tooth, stopping indolently to look over his shoulder. "Our people are the finest makers of bows and tools that there are. What is that? A child's toy."

"Maybe it's white medicine," said Shy Fawn curiously, stopping as she carried water. "Why don't you leave him alone?"

Later, he gave the snake to Smiling Fox, who seemed pleased with it.

"I've never seen a snake like this."

"It's a kind that lives far away, in the east."

"We have some stories about snakes," said the boy. "Do your people have stories like that? and about how the world was made and the creatures in it?"

"Yes. Most of them have been written down in books."

"Talking papers? What good is that? We tell our stories by a fire at night. Who would want them from a paper, so that only one man at a time could see what they say?"

"One man could read them aloud and share them that way."

Shy Fawn was there again, bringing them food. Turning to leave, she said over her shoulder, "Maybe it is that whites can't remember things as our people can and they have to have those talking papers to remember for them." She smiled the little, clever smile that was a characteristic of all Red Sky's children, and hurried away.

"She thinks she knows so many things," said Smiling Fox irritably. "My other sisters who have husbands now behave better than Shy Fawn and Cricket do. Little Rain, the wife of Hawk's Shadow, has a sharp tongue too. Sometimes it's not good to live in our lodge. In the old days, I think, women did not talk so much."

Blake smiled, looking away from the earnest, pensive young face.

Smiling Fox said, "Will you make another animal I've never seen before?"

97

He nodded readily, having thought of an alligator.

When they had been at the camas grounds for several days, word was brought that two white men were riding in with a party of Flatheads. They were Connall and Paul, and they greeted Blake uproariously, having felt certain he was dead. They had come with trade goods.

"So you're in with the Medicine Rocks," said Connall, pleased. "I'd like to get hold of some of their horses. Talk to them about it, will you? And what sort of furs have they got?"

"I can't talk to them," Blake said. "Most of them don't want to trade."

"Of course they want to trade, lad. Every man wants to better his life."

"They seem to like things the way they are, and who's to say which kind of life is better? Isn't that up to the people living it?"

"He's become a missionary in reverse," Paul said, smiling.

"He's always had odd notions," said Connall shortly. "He's one of these people who's apt to begin raving about the noble savage. I've seen it coming from the first. Well, if you won't help us with the Medicine Rocks, at least tally up this stuff we're getting from the others. It belongs to Hudson's Bay."

That night Blake went with them to where they were camped. It was strangely, beautifully quiet at this little distance from the bustling Indian camps. Paul gave him a pipeful of tobacco—Connall hadn't brought any rum—and they told him about the night the Blackfeet had come.

Ellis Williams had admitted finally, under old Mote Stanley's intensive questioning, that he had suspected Indians were in the neighborhood of their camp on the Darkwater.

"He was scared and he crawled in there where you and Paul were holed up," Connall cried, still incredulous about it. "Before he could decide what he ought to do next, he went to sleep. The man's a fool! Anyone with the guard, the responsibility for other people and my goods who would do an idiot thing like that! He's not with the company anymore."

98

Evidently, Blake's getting lost and being more or less captured, Paul's drunkenness that night, could be passed over more lightly than what Ellis had done. Blake thought again that mountain morality could be a strange thing, but he was relieved not to be reminded of his own ignorance and did not pursue the subject.

"We found Mote and the others," Paul said, "or they found us the next day and we rode some of the pack horses. We'd cached our things, up there on the Darkwater. Jesse Harris looked around and got a pretty good notion of what had happened to you, though I don't know how he managed it, the way it had been blowing and drifting. We went up the Medicine Rock and they let Mote and me come into the village. Both of us thought you wouldn't live through the night. It seemed the only thing we could do was leave you there. You surely would have died if we'd moved you any more."

"I had medical treatment," Blake said dryly. "I think I must have been very strong and healthy to have lived through it."

"Well, you don't look any too strong now," said Connall. "That ankle bothers you a good bit, doesn't it? Several of my cows have calved. We'll give you good milk and meat back at the post, have you in shape again before you know it. You can ride all right, can't you? We'll be wanting to leave early in the morning."

"I'm not going back."

"What?"

"I'm going with Red Sky's people to the buffalo country."

"Good God! Why?"

"I just—want to; to see what it's like."

Connall glowered. "I suppose you've got yourself a woman."

"No."

"You owe me a job of work."

"I've worked for you almost a year."

"I've not got the time to keep those goddam books in order."

"I'm sorry, Connall. I just—want to know about other things."

After a little silence, Connall offered, "I'll send you down to Vancouver later in the summer."

"I don't want to see Vancouver."

"And I suppose you're collecting bits of flowers and things in little bags like that botanical greenhorn that was here one year," Connall said derisively. "*He* got himself killed seven different ways by a bunch of Bloods."

"You've lived with Indians," Blake pointed out mildly. "Almost everyone out here has."

"Yes, for trading and such sensible things. Are you going to do any trading?"

"I haven't got any goods."

"And I suppose you expect me to set you up?"

"No. I just want to know—what they're like."

"Good Lord, lad, they're savages. That's all."

Blake might have pointed out that Connall's wife was a half savage, that his daughters were quarter-breeds, but he said mildly, "I don't suppose you've brought any books with you."

"Books! Now why in hell would I have books on a trading expedition?"

"I've got one," Paul said quietly. "You can borrow it if you like."

"Borrow it!" sneered Connall. "You talk as if you think he'll be coming back."

The book was tattered and dirty, written in French, a small book of philosophy. It didn't much matter to Blake what it was. He said to Connall, "Could you let me have some tobacco?"

"What have you got to offer for it?" Connall asked coldly.

"Somebody has my traps and things still."

"I have them," Paul said. "You can put his tobacco on my account."

"Accounts!" Connall muttered. "All I ever hear from any of you is accounts!"

He went to a pack, his own, not one of trade goods, and took out a sack of good, uncut tobacco, his fierce eyes daring them to notice.

Blake went back to Red Sky's lodge and found the chief sitting before it with Many Bears and some other older men.

"I've brought you this," he said diffidently and dropped the sack of tobacco before Red Sky.

Red Sky picked it up gingerly, hefting it in his hand, peering at it in the firelight.

"What is it?"

"Only tobacco."

"From those white traders?"

"Yes."

He loosed the string, poured a little into his hand, and sniffed it.

"It does not look different. Why do you bring it to me?"

Blake shifted uneasily. He was miserable under their eyes, wanting the chief simply to accept the small gift and his admiration and gratitude. "A few days ago, I heard you say you needed tobacco. I—I bring it because your family has been kind to me and because I want to go with you on the buffalo hunt."

"We are not kind to you," Red Sky said severely. "When a man is sick it is no kindness to take him in and give him food. Somehow, Hawk's Shadow my son likes you. This is no kindness. There is no need to bring me gifts."

"It gives me pleasure to bring the tobaco,' he said, looking at the ground, feeling his face flush.

The chief grunted and turned away. Blake left, completely abashed. He had gone only a little way into the darkness when someone touched his arm.

"It's Shy Fawn," the girl said softly. "Maybe you don't understand that you've made things hard for my father."

"How have I?" he asked, hurt, sounding angry.

"He does not want you to tell him he is kind. He's a chief. Of course he is a kind and generous man. You have brought a gift and he does not want to like you."

"It's a very small gift. All of you have cared for me and—"

"Another thing is that the tobacco came from the white traders. He needs tobacco, but he does not like having it from them."

"I thought the tobacco would be enough like any other tobacco so that that wouldn't matter so much. Should I go and take it back? Will he throw it in the fire?"

She giggled. "Of course not. That would be a stupid waste. He and the others will be smoking some of it now, saying it is not so good as what they are used to. Do you want to go close and listen to what they are saying?"

"No," he said quickly.

"That's right," she agreed. "You would walk on a stick or something and they would catch us both. I have to go now, with more stones for the camas pit. Remember, though, not to tell chiefs they are kind. Some day you will tell me about that strange, ugly animal you made for Smiling Fox, about where it lives and things like that. He told me a little of what you said but I didn't believe him. There are no animals like that nor places such as he told about. He got angry and wouldn't tell me any more of it. That boy is a brat and growing too big for his moccasins. Goodnight, Green Eyes. No more kind chiefs."

V

FINALLY, THEY LEFT the camas prairie. Now the Medicine Rock People traveled with contingents from other tribes, other bands, a long, slow train, stretching out across a valley or moving up a winding mountain trail. They stopped often and for varying periods of time, so that the women could dig roots, gather fruits and berries, dry and pack them. The men, eager as they all were to get to the buffalo country, complained at the interminable delays, but the berries and roots must be harvested when and where they were ready. They were necessary staples of the winter's food supply.

"You have to have a name," Hawk's Shadow said to Blake as they rode along one day.

Blake had been practicing archery under his tutor's critical eye and they were now rejoining a small group of other young men. Hawk's Shadow was irritated that Blake must use his left hand but, aside from that, the shooting had gone rather well. He went on, "Green Eyes is no proper name for a man and we can't call you that white name you told me once. It is not very pleasant to say and it means nothing. How do you want to be called?"

Blake thought about it. "Straight Arrow?" he hazarded a little wistfully and the others laughed.

"Broken Head," suggested Storm Coming Out Of The East more practically.

"Shadow Of Hawk's Shadow," said Half Moon.

Beaver Tooth scowled. It did not please him that the

others were coming to accept the white man who was in a sense Hawk's Shadow's white man.

They were into the high mountains now, near to the Divide. It was often cold and stormy and the traveling was hard. One evening as they looked to their horses, Blake found that his black, like many of the others, had sore, broken hoofs. He went to Owl Woman and got a large piece of rawhide from her. He cut it up and bound it round the horse's feet.

"That is not a good thing to do," Hawk's Shadow pointed out patiently. "He will slip and fall."

"But his hoofs won't be cut up so much."

"What kind of thinking is that? If a horse falls on you, you won't care if it has sore feet or not. It's always been so with our horses, having their feet cut up on this journey. It's a hard thing for them, but it can't be helped. Many of them die, crossing the mountains, or we have to leave them behind, sometimes the best ones, but you would not be losing much if you were to lose that black."

He looked proudly at his own favorite, a small, tough paint stallion.

"You ought to get yourself some good horses," he advised Blake. "That black is too big. His wind is not very good."

"How would I do that?"

"Well, if you had something to trade . . . or you would catch some wild ones or take some from somebody else. Anyway, you'd better take those things off that horse's feet."

"I want to try it this way for a few days."

Hawk's Shadow and Storm Coming Out Of The East looked at each other resignedly and Storm said, "Maybe we should name him Horse Moccasins."

"Do you want to come with me to see something?" Hawk's Shadow asked later that evening.

"Yes. What?"

"I'm going to catch an eagle if all things are willing. We need feathers for our war dress and other things. Tonight, I go away up to the crags to do what is necessary for such a thing. If the signs seem right, I will build the trap. You can come up there in the morning to see how it's done. Get food from Owl Woman or Little Rain or

Shy Fawn to bring with you. These people move so slowly; we will catch up with them easily. Do you think you can find me tomorrow?"

Blake was not at all certain, but he did find him, or rather the black horse found Hawk's Shadow's horse, in the edge of some low, twisted trees, just at timberline. Hawk's Shadow had dug a pit in the rocky ground higher up and covered it with brush.

"You wait down there in the trees," he said with a quiet excitement. "It may be a long time. Take my bow and things."

"You're not going to shoot the eagle?"

"I told you, I will catch him. Why would I have dug this pit if I were going to shoot him? White men do not catch eagles?"

"Not that I know of."

"It's not an easy thing. Only a few of my people can do it."

"Have you done it before?"

"A few times. It is one way, maybe, that I am a little like Winter Thunder my grandfather. He was a great eagle-catcher. See, I have killed this good big rabbit. She will look good, I think, to the eagle. There he is up there. Do you see?"

Blake made the bird out, a dark spot flashing through sunlight.

Hawk's Shadow stripped off his long buckskin shirt and leggings and gave them to Blake, along with his bow and quiver. A small stone knife hung round his neck on a thong with a large blue-green stone. The knife, he had told Blake, had been made long ago by Winter Thunder and given to him by Red Sky when Hawk's Shadow rode in his first war party. The stone he had got in trade from a Snake who had won it from a member of some tribe far to the south. It had been found by the original owner, they said, with the hole already in it for the thong to pass through that was very strong medicine. He climbed into the pit, crouching there and pulling the brush over him. Blake laid the rabbit on top of the brush.

"Take everything and go away now," Hawk's Shadow said softly. "See that you don't disturb the eagle. I think this will be a good day."

Blake went down into the edge of the trees. He sat in the thin, fierce sunlight for a while, until it grew too hot, then moved into a skimpy shadow.

The eagle circled about, seemingly aimlessly, in and out of his view. He thought it must know about the rabbit and, probably, about the two men on the mountain, but it seemed proud, disdainful of them.

Lying a little tensely on the hard, stony ground, he remembered times from his boyhood when he had gone into the hills and woods with Alec Douglas. Alec had known the names of trees and plants and some things about the habits of birds and animals. He did not much like hunting and he told Blake he wished the rest of the community did not feel it so necessary to wipe out all the wolves. He talked, sometimes, about the balance of nature.

Alec had been killed in a wood-cutting accident when Blake was fifteen. Blake went numbly to the house when he heard about the accident; he hadn't wanted to go there again, but had felt he must and, looking briefly down at his friend's face, he had known with an aching surge the finality of death and the true meaning of being alone. Mrs. Douglas and her children, all of them older than Blake, had been kind to him, and thoughtful in the midst of their own sorrow. They said he should stay for the funeral, that Alec would have liked having him there. He could not bear the house and the people. As long as he could remember, there had been Alec to come to when he could. Alec's hand, occasionally touching his head, had been almost the only touch of gentleness he had known. Now what?

He ran from the house, from the Douglas farm, from the county. He never saw it again. His first job was as a swamper for a teamster freighting across the Alleghenies. The man was stupid and cruel, cursing the boy more than the mules, striking him often until one day Blake took a bullwhip in his hands and with fiery eyes dared the man to take it away from him. Things, outside things, were easier for him after that.

Later, he worked with a surveyor for a time, carrying his equipment, keeping his camp, learning what he could. As time passed, he found he was asking himself more and

106

more often, Who am I? Is there anywhere that I really belong?

His grandparents had objected with such violent righteousness to everything he seemed to be. He had tried hard as a little boy to be what they wanted, but that seemed beyond attainment. He could *not* be good. Nothing he did pleased them. He tried to use his right hand rather than his left, he tried to keep his green eyes lowered, so that they would not offend, he tried to pray and to be right, just now and then. He knew, thinking back on it when he had been away from home for a year or so, that it didn't matter. Nothing he could have done would ever have pleased them. It wasn't really faults in him so much as their determination to see evil and wrongness in him that must be destroyed. They were old, poor, ignorant, soured people who had truly believed they were doing what was best for him and his soul. Realizing those things, though, did little to relieve the guilt and uncertainty, the self-doubt that lay heavily upon his mind.

When the surveyor no longer needed him, he found work on the Philadelphia waterfront where there were uses for the writing and ciphering that had always come so easily to him. Eventually, he got a berth on the schooner *Lydia* to the West Indies, working as the lowest class sailor while the boat was at sea and as a clerk when she was taking on or discharging cargo.

Finally, he became clerk to a Carolina plantation owner. The man owned boats and warehouses in addition to his land. Blake found the life incredibly easy, even though he was allowed to live only on the edges of it. It had been three years since he had run away from Alec Douglas' house. The questions of who and what and why he was tormented him no less. It seemed to him that he had never been allowed anywhere but on the edges of things. Alec had been a good friend, but Blake had been only a peripheral thing for Alec. The grandparents and Aunt Millie had shared things, been close in their harsh, ascetic ways, had loved his cousins, he had been an outsider. There had been no closeness with the people he had worked for and with. Some had liked him well enough, some had not, but he had never really known them.

Mostly, they couldn't even seem to remember his name. He began to think that perhaps it was a basic part of himself, to be a little apart from others, only touching the edges of their lives and relationships, an onlooker. All right. If that was how it had to be . . . . He was trying now to accept and be reconciled to what he was beginning to believe himself to be.

He knew very little about his parents, only that his mother had been "a young, pure saint on earth till she was ruined by that man." The wickedness of "that man," his father, so far as Blake could understand it, lay in the fact that he was not the one the parents would have chosen for their daughter to marry, he had been a stranger come to work in the new mines, unknown to them, foreign, a Catholic, and other such onerous things. Sarah had married against their wishes and her father had told her never to come into his house again. But Eric Westfall had been killed in the mines before his son was born and Sarah, ill and alone, had had no choice but to beg to be taken back. There was nowhere else to go. She, too, had died before her boy was a year old and to the diligent, martyred grandparents had fallen the task of bringing him up, of ridding him, "root and branch," of whatever wickedness and evil he had inherited.

By the time he went to live in Carolina, Blake had begun to believe, with what seemed to him great daring and temerity, that he had never been altogether bad, that there was something of good and of bad in every person. For the lonely, bewildered boy, it was an earth-shaking idea and surely no one had ever thought such a thing out for himself before. He began to grow less frightened by the audacity of the thought that, perhaps, there was hope for him after all, that life could be better, that he could find the answers to at least some of his inner questions.

And then Etienne and Celese St. Croix came to the Carolina plantation and he was flung violently back into bewilderment and uncertainty, into a life that was a terrible, fascinating morass of good and evil, where he felt powerless and ill and sometimes almost unbearably happy, where, in his weakness and indecision, he might still be if Etienne had not died.

Blake roused himself on the mountain side, in the

shadow of the gnarled bush that had stayed there, trying to grow, for perhaps as much as a century, trying to be the tree it had been meant to be. There was complete silence except for the eagle's screaming. It had come nearer and suddenly it plummeted down toward Hawk's Shadow's rabbit.

Blake had to make a conscious effort to be still, not to leap to his feet. He was gripped by a strange, wild excitement and lay there trembling, his fists clenched. The bird looked tremendously big and powerful.

It struck the rabbit and there was a wild flurry in the brush beneath. Hawk's Shadow had the eagle by its feet. They screamed together, the Indian and the eagle, one cry as wild and defiant as the other.

Blake was standing now, not knowing he had risen, breathing hard. The struggle seemed long. Hawk's Shadow, holding desperately to the wildly beating bird, clawed his way and was dragged up out of the shallow pit. Finally, when Blake had reached the place and stood there breathless, he got a hand free somehow, seized the eagle's fierce head and, with a mighty effort, broke its neck.

Hawk's Shadow cried out as the eagle died, one single, wordless sound of triumph, and then he was silent and utterly still for a moment. Gently, he laid the huge bird on the ground and stood again, looking into the sky. Blake looked away from his eyes. They were awesome with a mixture of wonder and wild exultation.

"You did it," he said. His lips formed the words but there was no sound. "You really did it!"

Hawk's Shadow, turned away from the white man, made a brief song to the eagle spirit, then took the bird's skin and feathers and the other things he wanted. Finally, he stood up, holding out his bleeding, lacerated hands and Blake looked at them, nodding with respect and admiration.

"What food have you brought?" Hawk's Shadow asked. He spoke casually, but his voice was lowered, his eyes still full of awe.

Blake told him softly.

"There are bighorn sheep on the peak over there. I'd rather have the meat of one of them. Let's go and see if you can shoot one."

The bighorn were canny animals and hard to come close to. Hawk's Shadow stayed on one side of the ridge, just within their view, keeping their attention while Blake, by a long circuitous route, came up on their other side. He shot a young ewe. It was not a very good shot, but it crippled her. In her fear and pain, she ran toward where Hawk's Shadow was and he rushed down and killed her. It was growing dark by then.

"How is it," Hawk's Shadow wondered, "that a white can come to be a grown man and shoot so badly? How have you made your meat all this time? With a gun?"

Blake had been feeling rather proud of the shot. The ewe was almost the first live thing he had hit with an arrow. As they dressed the meat and made their camp, he told Hawk's Shadow about the tame herds of cattle, hogs, sheep, and fowls that white men kept for their meat.

"What kind of life is that?" said the other disdainfully. "Do all white men live like women? Where is the joy in such a life?"

Blake made no answer and after a while he said, "I wish you had chosen a ram to shoot at. His horns would have been good to have. Still, this ewe will be more tender."

While the meat cooked, they sat by the fire and Hawk's Shadow recounted with ritual solemnity his catching of the eagle, then he said quietly, "Now you."

Blake smiled. "It was bad shooting," he said softly, "an accident that I hit the sheep."

"That is not the way to do it . . . Maybe you will want to be named Killer Of Bighorn now."

"No."

"Well, we'll think of something." He laughed, testing the meat. "A name is a very important thing. When we were boys, we called Beaver Tooth 'He who Pisses Into The Wind' for a time. He was not pleased with that name."

Blake laughed.

"And," said Hawk's Shadow, "my woman Little Rain, with her sharp tongue, has given me a new name that is being passed around among the people. She has called me Limber Lance. Is that showing respect for one who may be a chief one day? It is not true, you understand, only that girl's strange sense of fun. Some day I will beat her and see if she finds *that* funny. We have the Little Chief who proves it's not true and there will be other babies . . . . Have you no woman somewhere?"

"No."

"You might have one of ours. My sister Shy Fawn will be of an age soon, though there are those who would make better wives. My father might not like her to go to a white-eyes and besides, she will probably be the woman of Storm Coming Out Of The East. But you should have some woman. They are mostly alike . . . . Now we will wrestle."

"What?"

"It will be better to do it before we eat. I'd rather have a race but you have run enough today with your leg as it is, so we will wrestle."

"Why?"

"Because it is a good thing to do. I think you know nothing of having fun. We will see how strong we are against one another."

"You're stronger. I'll hurt my ankle."

"Are you afraid of pain?"

"I don't like it. I can't see any point in looking for it deliberately."

Hawk's Shadow stared at him in the firelight. "Never say you are afraid. A *man* does not say a thing like that."

"What if it's true?"

"It's not true if you are truly a man."

"Listen, Hawk's Shadow," he said slowly, "there are different kinds of people. Every person is a little different from every other person. We don't all think alike."

"But you have a chance now to learn the right ways," and he flung himself on Blake with a joyous cry.

Blake had never been a weakling. He was strongly built and taller than Hawk's Shadow. He would have been heavier if he had not lost so much weight recently. But, his illness aside, he would have stood little chance against the Indian's steel-wire strength and years of experience at this sort of thing. Besides, he refused to take it seriously. They grappled for a little while and then, just when Hawk's Shadow was struggling earnestly to pin his arms, he got a hand free and tickled him. Hawk's Shadow gave a grunt, a short burst of laughter, and drew away from him, staring, his face a mixture of outrage and incredulity.

"That was a boy's trick!" he cried, furious.

"You were hurting my ankle," Blake said, sitting up. "I told you I didn't want to wrestle. We both knew you'd win."

"If we are friends, you will try to be a man."

Blake said hotly, "If we're friends, you'll stop always telling me what to do and think. I don't try to make you a different person than you are."

"Because I am a right kind of person," Hawk's Shadow said sullenly. "You know nothing and I only try to show you how things should be."

They ate in silence and lay down to sleep. Hawk's Shadow was still angry, outraged. Blake was sorry but he would not give in this time. Through the years, he had grown stubborn about allowing himself to be what he was and in sometimes demanding that allowance from others.

A stick cracked in the fire; otherwise, it was utterly silent. In the camps, Blake had longed for silence. Now, he found it made him a little uneasy. Out of the darkness, Hawk's Shadow said softly, "I will tell you a thing. I will say it to you because you will not understand. It will not surprise you, maybe, as it would surprise any of my people if they knew.

"When I was a boy"—he spoke slowly, painfully it seemed, and all the anger was gone from his voice—"and I went out, when it was my time to see visions and seek a medicine spirit, I—I saw nothing . . . . I tried very hard. I fasted until I was almost dead. I rode and I walked in the mountains until there were no moccasins left on my feet. I fell down from weariness and sometimes I slept, but nothing came to me. I have seen no spirits nor talked with any, ever, in my life."

There was a long silence. Blake shivered, knowing what an awful thing this must be for his friend. The medicine dreams, liaison with the spirit world, were an incredibly vital part of life for all of them, particularly for braves and warriors, for one who might some day be a chief.

Hawk's Shadow said, "My father came and found me. If he had not come, I would have died there because I could see nothing and no one would speak to me. I had gone out on my wandering with great hopes and my father had great hopes for me. I am the grandson of Winter Thunder . . . . Beaver Tooth had gone out in the summer before and had seen mighty medicine. Crooked Wolf said he might be trained as a medicine man. Storm Coming Out Of The East and Half Moon and the others had gone out and had come back to dance in the guardian spirit dance, to tell of what they had seen and heard, but I . . . . saw nothing.

"So Red Sky my father came and found me. I was sleeping as the dead and he carried me back to the village on his horse. When I was strong again, it was the time for another guardian spirit dance. A band from the west was visiting us and it was to be a great celebration. All their eyes looked at me and said, 'What has the grandson of Winter Thunder seen?' And I—I made a story . . . . I said there had been a hawk, I have always felt friendly to hawks, and I said he had come to me while I waited on the mountain, to be my spirit brother. I had no things for a medicine bundle and I told them that the hawk had said to me that I should come back to that place when I was strong again, to find those things . . . . I went out later and I made a medicine bundle with things I hoped would be good, but those things were not given to me," he cried in utter torment. "I had to get them myself.

"When I go to hunt as I hunted the eagle today, no spirits come to me. Sometimes, still, I fast until I am nearly dead, waiting for something to come. Somehow, I am not pleasing to Them and I think that I would be better dead if I cannot make this right. I have wanted to tell Crooked Wolf or my father or someone these things, but when I come back to them, they look at me and say, 'What have you seen?' and they look at me as if I am going to tell them something and I—begin to make another story . . . . How can I be a chief of my people when I have seen nothing and heard nothing?"

Blake said slowly, "Maybe it's like that for some of the others."

"How?"

"Maybe they make stories too, and find the things themselves for their medicine bundles."

113

"You are a crazy white man," he said wearily, without rancor. "I knew you would have some crazy notion and no understanding. You told me before that whites need not see visions or have spirit brothers. You have no understanding of such a thing. Of course the others are not like this. There is something wrong with me, but I can't find out what it is. I have good fortune often, and sometimes I'm tempted to think it comes from me rather than from the spirits. That must be a thing that no one has ever thought before . . . . Sometimes I have hunted without doing any of the things that are necessary to have a good hunt, to see what would happen. Sometimes the hunting has been good, sometimes bad, as it is when I do those things. I wonder then if I am being watched over by a very bad and a very strong spirit who makes me not do those necessary things to tempt and taunt the other spirits but, if that is true, why does *he* not speak to me and make himself known? Then perhaps I could fight the bad spirit, if he is there. I could tell Crooked Wolf and ask him to make medicine for me."

Blake thought bitterly that religion, by whatever name it was called, seemed to serve chiefly to tie people up in knots of guilt and misery and self-doubt. He could think of nothing to say, though he longed to be helpful somehow.

Hawk's Shadow lay back on his blanket, wanting and expecting nothing from the other. He had had the release of finally making the awful admisssion and he could ask for nothing more. After a while, he slept.

Blake did not want to think deeply about anything. He had tried to forswear that sort of thinking when he went to live in New Orleans, but the silence here was so vast and there was nothing to distract the thoughts.

We make most of our own tortures, he thought reluctantly, all of us do that. And somehow, in whatever twisted way, each person must have some importance to himself. It's better to think oneself very bad than to feel that one is nothing at all. The pain and guilt at least set one apart . . . . Hawk's Shadow can't believe that anyone else could be making up medicine dreams and maybe a part of the reason is that, if he could believe that, it would make him seem to himself less different, less set apart, less important in this perverse, fearsome way that's a part of what he's convinced he is . . . . People *are* different and, on the other hand, they're not different at all . . . .

He got up restlessly and walked a little way into darkness, away from the glimmer of the dying fire. He sat on a rock and looked into the great night sky and it seemed he could hear, faintly, in the stillness that seemed to wrap him now, comfortingly, a humming that could be the throbbing, pulsing, cosmic life of the universe.

He listened for a long time, scarcely breathing. The questions were still there, deep in his mind, buzzing and flitting like tormenting flies, Who am I? What am I? And in the faintly humming stillness a voice that was not a voice at all, but a great presence, a great, quiet, sure knowledge all around him, seemed to be saying, Is it really such a big thing? Must you know it all at once? Does it really matter at this moment? Only *be*.

He sat rigid, waiting for something more. Finally, he relaxed, smiling faintly. More? Wasn't that enough? Would anything ever be enough? . . . But the silence no longer oppressed him. He felt a great peace within himself. He was only pleasantly tired now, relaxed. He limped back to his place near the fire and slept.

When he woke in the morning, he could not quite remember what he had understood with such clarity in the night, but the peace was still with him. They breakfasted on more of the ewe's meat. Hawk's Shadow, remembering his confession, was shy and quiet when he first woke, but then he began to chide Blake for his fire building and to be himself again. Blake ate. The meat was good. He did not mind the chiding.

They came down the eastern side of the mountains to heat and dust and no buffalo. There were ceremonials, dances, and councils to bring the game. The Walla Wallas said that next year they would persuade one of their missionaries to come with them because the missionaries had strong medicine and talked with the Great Spirit in the sky who was, perhaps, very powerful in bringing buffalo.

Hawk's Shadow and others questioned Blake about the medicine of the white man's prayer and the talking papers that told stories of the Great Spirit, but Blake said he knew nothing. When he had left home after Alec Douglas' death, Blake had decided, with trepidations that were nearly a physical trembling of fear, that he would have no more to do with God. He had tried to please Him, personified by his grandfather, but it could not be done. Alec was dead, did that not prove with awful finality that he, Blake, was to be alone, never one of the Chosen? Perhaps he would be utterly destroyed for such wickedness, but he was through with God. He was not destroyed. Apprehensions about his temerity stayed with him, but they lessened gradually. He began to believe himself free. If he had not believed before hearing Hawk's Shadow's story that night on the mountain, he was certainly convinced after it that these people had enough problems dealing with their own beliefs without trying to reconcile others with them. He would not discuss the missionaries and their teachings.

Waiting, searching for the buffalo, the men spent their time in hunting antelope and other game, in a few skirmishes with bands of Blackfeet and Crow, in the making and trading of goods, in horse racing and other games, in evenings of coup-counting and trying to impress one another. The women had new skins to dress, trade goods to work on, the never-ending chores of food preparation and camp work. They visited among themselves, constantly busy, always talking.

Little Rain's family was there. They were Palouses and Hawk's Shadow said they had fine horses, almost as fine as those of some of the Medicine Rock People. He said also that their presence made his wife harder than ever to keep in her place. He said that probably he should take another wife, then she would know that she was not so important. She said pertly that she agreed; it was an excellent idea. It would mean that her work and the nuisance of putting up with such a husband would be cut in half, and she offered to find a woman who would make him a good second wife. Hawk's Shadow scowled, Little Rain laughed, and they went away together into the brush by the river.

"You should have a woman," Storm Coming Out Of The East told Blake solicitously. "They can be a bother sometimes but, other times, they can be good to have. I

116

have had one wife but she died. One day I will take another. I am told that some white men pay well for women. We don't sell our young women the way some of those tribes do. The young ones are for our own men and those of our friends. Mostly, they're easier to train and they work better."

Blake was trying to get a drawing of an antelope to come out right, but he could not satisfactorily catch the grace and movement of the animal that were there, even when it stood still. Today he had watched as some of the men lured antelope within bowshot by waving pieces of bright-colored cloth.

"It is good to chase them too," they had told him, "but they're faster than horses if we can't head them. This way is fun, something different. Those antelope want to know about things. They come close to see about these pieces of cloth."

Blake had been a little sorry to see them killed. He had been even sorrier, some days earlier, when a large band of hunters had fired the grass and brush over a wide area to chase out game for shooting.

"What's wrong with you?" Hawk's Shadow had demanded then. "You look as if you think this is not a good thing."

"Why can't we just find the game and shoot it? It will take this stuff a long time to grow back and, before it does, the soil will wash away."

"Why would we care about that? There is plenty of grass, plenty of trees, plenty of soil. There are many people to be fed and this is a good way to get a lot of game. Besides, it's fun this way sometimes."

"It doesn't seem very—sporting," Blake said lamely. He could not find a native equivalent for the word and had to use the English.

"What is that word?" asked Hawk's Shadow carelessly, fitting an arrow to his bowstring.

"Never mind. I guess it doesn't matter."

He worked now on the drawing of the antelope while Storm Coming Out Of The East watched him and persisted, "When are you going to start getting together some goods so you can afford a woman? You could trade those drawings, maybe."

117

The people did like his pictures. They liked watching him make them and he gave them away in exchange for paints and for materials to put paints on. Sometimes they drew for him, their stylized, primitive, geometric figures and symbolic spirit representations. They said, with grudging admiration, that his drawings seemed almost alive and some of them were a little frightened, muttering that he was trying to capture spirits and imprison them on skin or bark, but many overcame their misgivings and he usually had several willing portrait-sitters, mostly young men who found hours to spend on their paint, their hair, their accouterments and their horses, prior to a painting session.

Some whites came to the camps from an American post to trade. When they heard there was a white man with the Indians, they sent for Blake, to find out if he was with Hudson's Bay and whatever else they could. Their company was little known to most of these mountain Indians and the traders were little acquainted with the languages. They asked Blake to help them in translation and trading. He refused.

They had brought a good deal of whiskey and there was trouble all the time they were there. A Yakima killed his brother in a drunken rage and there were fights and bad feelings throughout the camps. Red Sky tried to keep his people apart from all of it, but Beaver Tooth and a few other young men went to the traders' camp. They had some pelts and a few horses they were willing to trade to whites for things they needed. Many Bears, Beaver Tooth's father, suggested casually that Blake go along with them to see that they got their goods' worth, but Beaver Tooth made it quite clear that he could handle matters.

As the story came to them later, Beaver Tooth had done well, trading for some guns and ammunition, clothing and kettles, but, as he was ready to leave, the whites' interpreter, a Bannock, had asked if he would not try some whiskey. Beaver Tooth, saying to his companions that this was a matter they ought to look into if they were ever to be able to judge it properly, had a drink and so did the men with him, then they had another . . . . They came back to the Medicine Rock camp sick and staggering, wild with laughter, threats, and songs.

In the morning, they were miserable and Red Sky regaled their throbbing heads for a long, painful time. They had retraded the guns and cloth and kettles for what the chief called "white man's stupid water."

After the traders had gone, there was trouble with some Snakes who resented these other tribes' getting in on the American trade, but then scouts brought word that buffalo were being sighted and most enmities were put aside.

Crossing the plains with Henry Melton and the missionaries, Blake had seen buffalo. They had killed a few. The chase had been exciting and the meat good. Old Henry's delight had been a pleasure to see, but Blake had not dreamed that anything like this Indian hunt could exist. When word came in that there were buffalo, the excitement was a palpable thing, like the feeling of a thunderstorm in the air. Everyone ran around in a wild, seemingly aimless way, but they were making ready and the noise of dogs and horses and people was deafening. A band of Coeur d'Alenes had held an especially satisfying buffalo dance the night before and they claimed loudly that it was responsible for bringing the buffalo but the others were oblivious to their boasting. The buffalo had come, there would be ample time later for deciding why it had happened.

All the men rode out to the east of the camps scattering over the plains. Blake thought that the buffalo must know for miles they were coming, but he was enjoying himself, perhaps as much as any of the others, feeling a driving excitement that he would have considered childish a short time ago, reveling in it.

The group he rode with, Hawk's Shadow, Beaver Tooth, Storm Coming Out Of The East, Half Moon, and three or four others, saw a small herd that first day. They managed to kill only two. By nightfall, they were well separated from the other groups of hunters. They built their fire and made medicine to the buffalo for the next day's hunting. Since they were hunting, they could eat only a few ritual parts of the meat they had made that day, but it was sufficient for a good feast. They sent one

119

grumbling young boy back to the main camp with some meat and with word to the women to move the camp nearer to where they judged the game would be the next day. Blake took what he could in their ceremonies, completely caught up now in the fever of the hunt and all its ritual.

In the morning, long before dawn, Hawk's Shadow woke him.

"Get up, Green Eyes! Can't you hear the moving?"

"No."

"Listen to the ground."

"I don't hear anything," he said wistfully, having listened.

Hawk's Shadow sighed. "Come on! I'll show them to you. Even you will be able to see buffalo today."

He led Blake well away from the others, for Hawk's Shadow preferred hunting alone when he could. They came up over a long swell of ground and looked out, against the rising sun, over a wide, shallow valley. The main herd was there, thousands of buffalo, it seemed to Blake, some still lying down in the long, browning grass, some drinking, some rolling luxuriously, some grazing, some moving around, swinging their great shaggy heads lazily.

"God!" he breathed. Hawk's Shadow glared at him, signaling silence.

They looked to their weapons, Hawk's Shadow's lips moving in a soundless song to the buffalo.

There was a yell, far off to their left, and riders swept down on the herd. They let their own horses run. The world seemed made up then of great running animals, the heavy thudding of their hoofs, the dust they raised, their bawling, their great swinging heads. Blake had been warned that neither he nor his horse were trained for this kind of hunting, but as he lost sight of Hawk's Shadow, he forgot the counsel, he forgot everything. He was swept by a violent, all-pervading lust that eclipsed everything, a feeling that he would have found disconcerting and appalling had someone tried to tell him of it, a lust to kill one of these great, shaggy, ugly, magnificent animals.

He fumbled an arrow to his bowstring with a hand that shook with pure, wild animal ecstasy. It took a good,

120

strong shot to stop a buffalo and an arrow rarely killed one. They had to be finished off with a spear. Buffalo killing was one instance where whites' muskets and rifles were a great boon, but he must try what he could do. He had no thought for guiding his black horse or for making a sensible choice of animals for a shot. The young cows made the best meat, but he wanted to kill a big bull and he shot at one. He saw the arrow strike but it was far from being a death blow and he fitted another arrow, not knowing he was yelling as wildly as Hawk's Shadow or any of the others.

It seemed to him they had been running like this since the beginning of the world. Sweat poured down his face and his nearly naked body. The horse, dodging horns, stumbling, heaved painfully under him. Blake's breath rasped in his throat. It hurt from the dust and from shouting. The wild elation, the terrible lusting excitement were almost more than he could bear. Suddenly he realized he was holding his last arrow.

The realization seemed to rouse him, make him more aware than he had been of his surroundings, to still his inner feelings a little. He started. There was a man on the ground a little ahead of him and over to his right. The man was standing up, waving an arm while a great bull, wounded, stumbling, lowered its head to charge.

It was Hawk's Shadow there on the ground. Blake could not say, later, when they asked him to tell about it, how he and the exhausted horse got through the frenetically running buffalo, but he came to where Hawk's Shadow was and the young brave, his body running with sweat and blood, caught the horse and Blake's hand and flung himself up with a desperate effort.

If Blake had been wiser in the ways of buffalo, or if the horse had not been so exhausted, they might have got away unscathed—the bull was badly wounded, dying—but its horns caught the black in the flank. The horse's momentum carried it and its riders a little distance.

Most of the herd had passed now. Blake and Hawk's Shadow jumped free of the stumbling horse and dodged the final fringe of running, maddened animals. They stood still in growing silence. Finally they looked at each other briefly.

Hawk's Shadow had managed somehow to hold onto his spear. He looked at it as if in surprise, then ran to the fallen bull. The bull was not dead. It had sunk to its knees and, as he came up, it moved its head, still automatically making the gestures of a charge. Hawk's Shadow killed it, plunging his spear into its throat with a great, terrible strength.

A flood of blood gushed out into the trampled ground and Hawk's Shadow, kneeling, drank. Without knowing what he did, Blake dropped to his knees beside him. The blood was hot and salty. He was very thirsty.

They stood up together, slowly, and were silent again for a time. Blake shivered as the sweat began to dry on his body. He was aware now of their harsh breathing, of the rumble of the buffalo, running. Scattered around them on the prairie were several shaggy bodies, dead or dying. Blake could not believe how low the sun still was in the eastern sky. He turned to Hawk's Shadow.

"Are you hurt much?"

There was a gash down his arm from shoulder to elbow; his face, all the front of his body, were covered with blood. Hawk's Shadow moved his head slowly, dazedly, swinging it a little as had the bull.

"He was hard to kill," he said softly, looking at the bull. "I shot him many times and he was dead without knowing it. He would not fall. My horse fell and then he ran away from me. This bull will not make very good meat but he was a good buffalo."

He looked back at Blake, pushing the soaked hair out of his eyes. "You have paid me now for saving you from the Blackfeet."

Blake was surprised, embarrassed. "I didn't—"

"Where is your horse? Is he dead?"

They found the black where it lay quivering and groaning, its side ripped open.

"He was a good buffalo horse and we did not even know," Hawk's Shadow said gently. "I will kill him now so that he will not have this pain."

"If I had a gun—"

"No. It's my life he helped to save. I won't hurt him."

He put his hand on the horse's head. It rolled its eyes up at him.

"Horse," he said softly, "the horse of my friend, you who wore moccasins over the mountains so that your feet were not cut up, the buffalo bull has hurt you while you saved me from his horns. I will help you now to go more quickly where you will not feel the pain of this hurt. It will be a good place and you will understand that I do this only to help you."

He killed the animal with his spear. It did not even quiver.

Hawk's Shadow stepped back slowly. "The women will come up soon," he said wearily. "We will do the first part of the dressing out now so that these buffalo are ready for them. Then, when we have found more horses, we will go after the herd."

Blake did as he was directed with the skinning and dressing. It was hot, heavy, distasteful work. He was exhausted, his ankle paining him badly now. Some other men joined them, also covered with blood. The women and children, chattering and shouting with their own excitement, came up and he was glad to leave the work to them.

He eluded Hawk's Shadow and walked away into the prairie, awed and bewildered by the great turbulence of feelings that had been within him. He did not want to follow the buffalo anymore today. Surely he could not bear again those wild feelings that had come with the sunrise. He was not ashamed of the feelings, not quite, but they were awesome and terrible. Just what were the elements that made a man a savage?

At the bottom of a shelving bank, he found a pool in an almost-dry stream where he could wash off the blood. Under some scraggly willows, he lay down in scant coolness. Some of the people riding around the country today might not be friendly if they were to find him, but he could not worry about that now. He was too exhausted, too drained.

When he found the Medicine Rock camp that evening, darkness had fallen; the moon hung big and heavy above the prairie. The People welcomed him quietly, asking no questions. The women already had what seemed prodigious amounts of meat cut into strips and laid on drying

123

racks. In the firelight, they were sedulously scraping skins. Big pots bubbled and steamed on the fires. The men, surfeited with food and weariness, lay or sat about, talking quietly of the day and of their plans for tomorrow.

Owl Woman and the girls pressed Blake with food. He took it only out of courtesy, not feeling hungry, but as he began to eat, he found he was ravenous. He thought wistfully that it would be very good to have some coffee. When they went back west of the mountains, he would have to find ways of earning something now and then. He wanted to buy some coffee, some cloth clothing to replace his stiff, scratchy deer and elkskin clothes, to order some books; but there was time for all that.

He noticed Red Sky make a gesture to Smiling Fox and the boy got up and left the fire. Little Rain offered Blake more meat and he refused, drowsily, then he looked up as Hawk's Shadow stood above him.

"My father wants you to come with us."

He got up stiffly and followed them. Smiling Fox had led up a little paint mare and was holding her, a little distance from the camp.

"This horse," said Red Sky solemnly, "is a good little horse. I have owned her father and her mother. Her brother is my own buffalo horse, fast and strong and sure. She is from a good family of horses."

He stopped, seeming to expect something from Blake.

"She's—a fine horse," Blake said uncertainly.

Tentatively, he put out his hand. The mare snuffled and flung her head.

"She will get used to you," Hawk's Shadow said softly.

"She has dropped two fine colts in two springs," Red Sky was continuing. "Now she has been bred to a stallion of my friend Three Moccasins, the father of Little Rain. Next spring, if all things are favorable, she will bear another good colt. We have made good medicine so that it will be a spotted colt. You can see the paint marks on her rump."

Blake looked at them, not knowing what to say.

"You can start a fine herd with this mare," Red Sky told him.

"You are—a good friend," Blake said, his voice not

quite steady. "I have done nothing to deserve such friendship, or this mare."

"This morning," Red Sky said quietly and with great dignity, "you saved the life of my son Hawk's Shadow. You are my son now, as he is. We will not speak of friendship."

"But . . . . it was the black horse who—"

Red Sky smiled gravely. "We can do nothing now to show our gratitude to the black horse. It was you who guided him to Hawk's Shadow when he needed help. Why is it that you do not wish to talk about the good things you have done? Do you not know that when you talk about such things, it makes you want to do more of them? That is good medicine . . . . I have called this mare West Wind. You will give her another name if this does not please you. As for you, perhaps we may call you He Who Is Brave Without Wanting To Be. Take the mare back now, Smiling Fox, to the herd. We must be up very early in the morning."

Later, Smiling Fox came to where Blake lay in his robes, under the great sky.

"My father says there will be a ceremony for your adoption into our band. You will be my brother, and Hawk's Shadow's. How will it be, I wonder, to have a white brother?"

"Strange, perhaps," Blake said softly. "Your father, all of you, are very—good to me."

"Will you make us a picture of the bull trying to kill Hawk's Shadow?"

"Yes. Some day."

"Tomorrow?"

"No. In the winter, maybe, when we are—home again in the valley of the Medicine Rock."

"No other band has its own white man," Smiling Fox said with pride.

He brought his own blanket and lay down near Blake to sleep.

VI

THE HUNTING LASTED until the buffalo went farther afield than the People cared to follow. They began to move back west then. There were feastings, races, councils, some intermarriage. The women worked endlessly. They were an amazement to Blake. Even small, frail-looking Shy Fawn, whom her people called scrawny and laughed at, could work almost endlessly, often at tasks that took a great deal of strength and endurance. By next year, the girl would be of an age for wifehood, and Storm Coming Out Of The East, whom everyone assumed would be her husband, declared himself pleased enough with the way things were developing.

"There's not much there to keep a man warm on winter nights, but she works well enough and probably she will fatten up. Anyway, she makes good moccasins."

She did indeed. She had made a pair for Blake, as she made them for all the people of Red Sky's lodge, and Storm had just traded an elk skin for a pair for himself.

There had been a little trouble, now and then, with bands of Snakes and Crows, nothing too serious, just enough, the People seemed to feel, to keep life interesting. When they were well on their way home, up above the Three Forks, they began to be harassed by Blackfeet. Several bands, traveling together, made one big night camp for a while then, with the lodges set up in a large circle, the horses corralled inside and a heavy guard.

Nevertheless, Blackfeet crept up one night, to the back of a lodge, and killed two young Cayuse women. A great

126

war party went after them. There were only about twenty of the Blackfeet. They were caught, most of them, killed brutally and with relish. Blake had ridden with the party; but he found he could not stay when the slaughter began.

"You took no scalps," Hawk's Shadow pointed out with raised eyebrows.

"No."

"I think you don't like war."

"You're right."

"They killed those women," Hawk's Shadow said reasonably. "They have been our enemies since the world began, those Blackfeet. Why did you not help us?"

"You were already five to one. You didn't need me."

"They would have done the same to us."

"Does that make it right?"

"What is right? Things are the way they are. Blackfeet are enemies. You should have helped us."

"How? By shooting arrows into dead bodies as the rest of you were doing?"

"We collected most of those arrows and theirs, too. There was no waste. You are not a man. You are not even a woman. None of our women would run away as you did."

"I don't give a damn what—" In his anger, he was speaking in English. He tried to control himself, "I've told you before, people don't always think the same way. I don't like killing people. Sometimes it has to be done, maybe, but do you have to—enjoy it so much?"

"There are many bad things in living. When we make them pay for killing those women, that is a good thing, for us. Blackfeet would have killed you in the storm that time, if we had not driven them away."

"But they didn't."

Hawk's Shadow said impatiently, "A man can eat or not, as he chooses. All he has to do is get the food, put it in his mouth, chew, and swallow. If he starves to death, should he say it just didn't happen, the eating? Whose fault is it?"

"What kind of reasoning is that?"

"I can't say," said Hawk's Shadow in disgust. "To me, it sounds like some of yours. Red Sky my father and I are disappointed with how you have behaved. Come now and hear the council. Perhaps it will be good for you. You can have a close look at the Blackfoot scalps we have taken. Maybe they can begin to make your blood run as it ought to."

West Wind was a fine little mare. When they were ready to cross the high, rough country, Blake made rawhide shoes for her and, this time, a few of the other young men did the same for their favorite horses. The journey back was not so slow as the one going east had been, but it was long enough and, by the time they had crossed over again to the country where the waters flowed west, summer was well advanced.

"One day," said Hawk's Shadow as they rode along a trail high above a roaring little stream, "I will go again to that country to the south. That is a strange country, with steam and hot water coming out of the ground all around, and many bad smells. Some of that water is good medicine. There is much game and fine stone there for making arrowheads and things. Do you want to come with me when I go?"

"Yes."

"Snakes and Crows call it part of their country. There could be trouble. Maybe we will go when the People are safe back in the Valley again. Maybe this will be a long autumn and the weather will be good."

"Hawk's Shadow," Blake said slowly, "I've been trying to think of a way of making some money."

"What is this?"

"It's a thing whites use for trading."

"Why not just trade?"

Blake wished that so much explanation was not always necessary. "Because— It is a kind of trading. There are some things I want to get and I—"

"What things? You have clothes and food and a good horse. You will have more."

"But I can't do things the way you do. I'll never be able to hunt and get enough skins to trade for the things I want. I can't make bows and tools. I—"

"Be patient, Green Eyes, You will learn the right things."

"Not for a long time, if ever. There are some things I'd like to have now, things I miss."

"White man's things."

"Yes," he admitted with some reluctance.

"What are they?"

"Coffee, for one thing. It's something to drink."

"Stupid water?"

"No, just something I like. I'd like some books—"

"Why?"

"Because I like reading. It's going to be a long winter."

"You will do what we do in the winter. There is always hunting to be done, things to be made, much sleeping. You need to find yourself a woman."

"If I found one, how could I give presents to her father? I have nothing to give."

"Presents are not always necessary. Such things can be arranged sometimes. I have heard of a man from a band of Nez Perce over on the Salmon who has ten daughters and no sons. They say he is paying young men to come and take those girls away."

"I think I'll go down and work for Connall MacPheirson for a while, until the fall trapping is over."

"The Red-haired One at Camas Post? Why?"

"I've told you, I want some things. He'll give me goods or money as pay for working for him."

"I thought we would go to that strange stinking country."

"I'd rather go there with you, but I think I'd better work a while first."

"You will always be a white man," Hawk's Shadow said sadly.

"I guess I will," Blake said with equal regret.

After a long silence, Hawk's Shadow said, "You could trap, couldn't you? I don't know much about white men's traps, but I could show you where the animals are and how to get them. Together, we might get a lot of skins."

"Your father and most of the others wouldn't like that, would they?"

"It would not mean more whites coming into the Medicine Rock. That would not be changed. We would not have to do the trapping in the Valley, even. None of the people would have to go down to Camas Post if you were our trader. We might get some things like—those iron skinning knives are good, iron for arrowheads. Little Rain is wanting kettles and beads and bells like she has seen, belonging to women from other bands. She wants very loudly. You might take some horses to trade for traps to begin with. I have heard that the Red-haired One wants horses. Those Flathead ones he has are not much good . . . . Beaver Tooth has been saying for a long time he will be a trapper and have white things, but I think he is too lazy, only full of talk . . . . We could trap and trade if we went into that country to the south. We could take Little Rain with us to keep our camp and take care of the skins."

"You could talk to Red Sky about it, but—"

"Oh, no! It's your plan. You would be the one to talk to him."

"I think I'd better just go down to the post and work for a while."

They camped again at a camas meadow. The roots were at an even better stage of growth now than they had been earlier in the year and the women made a plentiful harvest.

When they were back again in the valley of the Medicine Rock, camp-making took a long time. This was a permanent camp, one which must withstand the winter. Blake helped with the cutting of lodge poles and other work suitable for men. He would go soon, but he did not much want to.

One morning he rode up to look at the horse herd. There was no need to keep a guard on them now, little chance that any of them would want to find their way out of the valley, that anyone would get in to try to steal them, but he had turned West Wind loose when they first came back and he wanted to see how she was faring. Also, he found it pleasant to get away from the bustling, noisy village for a little while.

The grass, sparkling with early dew, was long and lush where the travel-weary horses had not been at it. It was starred and dotted with flowers. He saw a buck watching him from the shade of some alders, with curiosity and no fear. The sun was hot, but Never Summer carried fresh snow on his shoulders. Blake thought it must be the beginning of August now, but he had no idea of day or date.

He found the horses, scattered over a particularly nice

130

meadow where a small stream came down from the north side of the valley to join the Medicine Rock. They pretended to be wild and skittish as he rode among them. West Wind looked fine. He let his mount drink at the little tributary stream and saw the tracks of a cougar in the sandy mud. He didn't really expect to see the cat. The tracks looked to be several hours old, but, almost idly, he turned his horse up the little stream, following the tracks. Having crossed the meadow and entered an evergreen wood, he found that his horse must walk in the stream to get up it. Very occasionally, he saw a paw print of the cougar's on the bank, but it was almost too steep for a horse to climb. He watched the branches above him with great care. There were roaring little falls and rapids so swift and rough that he had to lead the horse around them on the steep, needle-slippery bank. He kept climbing.

He had come more than a mile, he thought, from where the little stream joined Medicine Rock Creek, when, working his way around a final, gushing fall, he stopped and stood still, holding his reins.

He was above the little stream, where it had made itself a deep cut. Before him lay a perfect little cirque, an amphitheater hanging, as it were, up on the side of the main valley. The floor of the little park was meadowland, with scattered trees, its center taken up by the most beautiful little lake he had ever seen. The sides of the valley rose, gently at first, heavily timbered, then they grew steep and precipitous all around except for the way he had come up, where one side fell away steeply.

Blake turned to look behind him. He could not see, from here, the meadow where the horses grazed, but he could look over a large part of the Medicine Rock Valley, all the way down to where the creek joined the Camas. Up the valley, he could see heights of the great western range that lay between the drainages of the Camas and the Salmon. Across the Medicine Rock Valley, Never Summer stood up in the clear air so that it seemed that, by leaning out a little, he could have touched the snow sparkling in the sun. In a straight line, he thought the peak must be eight or ten miles away, but he could *feel* it there, close to him, without really looking at it.

131

The gray horse he had borrowed from Hawk's Shadow nudged impatiently at Blake's shoulder. He turned to it and removed its saddle and bridle. The horse began to graze eagerly, moving slowly down into the little valley, toward the lake.

Bemusedly, Blake walked into the valley, around the lake, looking out often over the larger valley and the surrounding peaks and ridges, set for him like a picture in the frame of the little amphitheater's open side. Blake had never before known the feeling of being the first to see anything. The Medicine Rock People certainly must know about this hanging valley, but he wanted to believe they had missed it somehow, that he was the first human being ever to set foot in it, to see its beauty and to look out from it at the big rugged country beyond. It was an awesome, beautiful feeling.

The meadow was heavy with wild hay. A doe with her spring fawn watched him almost calmly from the trees at the other side of the lake. At the edge of the water, he found the paw print of a bear, a black, he thought, not a grizzly. No sign of the cougar. Two jays flew around, squabbling with each other and asking what he was doing here. A dark squirrel chattered at him from a low branch.

A small stream fed in at the head of the lake. Blake followed it up through thick woods and found where a large spring contributed most of its volume, coming quietly out of the mossy side of the steep ridge. Around the spring were several dark mossy boulders. They reminded Blake of the Medicine Rock, except that none was nearly so large.

Distracted with quiet joy, hardly thinking what he did, he went back down to the edge of the trees above the lake and sat for a long time, simply looking.

There was a little rise at one side of where the stream came into the lake, dotted with a scattering of big pines. You could put a cabin there, on that rise. And then what? Well, you could sit in the door of that cabin and—just look at Never Summer and the rest of it. You could sit, reading by a fire at night and feel that you were the only person in the world, your own world . . . . There was enough game within easy distance to keep a man well supplied for a lot of years if he didn't abuse it. You could keep several horses up here and they would winter well on the wild hay, with the thick woods for shelter . . . . What else? Because he knew, sadly, that that would not be quite enough, that he would eventually grow restless and dissatisfied . . . . He would think about it, try to come up with some ideas of how he could spend time here in ways that would make him feel worthwhile in addition to being happy. In the meantime, he decided, he would not ask Hawk's Shadow or any of the others if they knew this place. He would not mention it to them at all. He would keep it for himself.

He watched an eagle, circling and gliding out over the valley of the Medicine Rock, before it disappeared into the trees over on the shoulder of Never Summer. Thin wispy clouds draped momentarily around the peak and blew away. Blake felt small and inadequate. It was not a bad feeling, but he wished he could make a song to the mountain. After a while, he slept for a little, his breath slowly, peacefully drawing in the pine-scented air. The gray horse dozed by the edge of the lake.

Connall said petulantly that he was not glad to see him —not surprised, but certainly not glad—though he did have a bit of paperwork that needed doing. He demanded to know if Blake was not finished with playing games.

"I've been learning things," Blake answered calmly. "Was it playing games when you lived with Indians?"

"Certainly not. *I* was building up trade. Here, take the pipe . . . . I must say you look fit to stand the winter now. You're almost as brown as one of your Medicine Rock friends. What do you want here? besides to get my books in order."

"You said once that you were thinking of taking stock down to sell on the immigrant trail."

"Aye, I've got a few horses for that purpose now. And there are my own cattle. I've made an agreement with McCandless down at Hall. Emmett and some others will be making a drive down there in the spring."

"I might be able to get some more horses for you, and some robes and other trade goods."

"You might, eh? Well then, go ahead."

"And I'd like to work for H. B. through the fall. I

133

could go to the Flatheads for you, and to the other tribes if you like. Not as a trapper, you know, but trading with them for the Company."

"You've always had a fine amount of nerve. Is it that you think you'll be taking my job now?"

"I'm not much good at trapping, but I can—"

"I'll say you're not, falling down a bank in a storm, getting yourself killed. How do I know you wouldn't lose yourself and my goods into the bargain?"

"You don't, I guess."

"Well, Paul's gone off somewhere, the California country I'm told, and God knows when or if he'll come back. I have a great deal to do here at the post . . . . Suppose I were to take you on this way. How permanent would it be?"

"I want to go back to the Medicine Rock when the season's over."

"Blake, for God's sake, be reasonable!"

"If I go to the buffalo country again, I'll do all the trading I can for the Company. I saw a lot of goods changing hands east of the Divide and none of them went to Hudson's Bay."

"I have never heard the like of gall! You're naught but a greenhorn still."

"Aye, but I'm canny."

Connall laughed in spite of himself, and made Blake come out to look at his stock.

In spare moments while he was at the fort, Blake read everything he could find. There was not much but it was a great deal more than he had had in the past several months. He made out a small order for some books of his own. Connall said triumphantly, "You'll never last for long away from civilization."

Blake went out that fall to the Flatheads, the Coeur d'Alenes, the Walla Wallas, the Spokanes, and others. He had with him two young Flatheads and a Palouse half-breed. To his delight, he found that he could now lay the country out in his mind, with no more need for drawing maps.

The trading went well. Most of the Indians in that part of the country had hearts that were good toward Hudson's Bay. Many of them remembered Blake, or had heard of him as the Medicine Rocks' white man. Though some did not agree with Red Sky's policies, they had great respect for the chief and his reputation.

Blake found that some of the Indians, mostly those living near to the missions, made him uncomfortable and sad. They were what the Medicine Rock People and others called contemptuously "white man People," eager to be almost fawningly friendly and to adopt white ways. He passed within a few miles of the newly established mission at the edge of the Blue Mountains and heard a great deal of talk about the missionaries and what they were doing, but he did not pay a visit to the Reverend Mr. Prewitt, not being interested and doubting his welcome.

In the course of his trading, he acquired for himself two more good horses, a young stallion and a mare.

"What do you want with them?" Connall demanded critically when he had come back to the post. "I've never seen the like of droopy, hang-dog animals as these Indian ponies are. Scraggly, too. If you're going to try to be a horse man, why don't you find yourself something with a little spirit?"

"Have you seen how they can last on a long, hard journey?"

"Aye, well . . . . I'll give you a bull calf for the roan. It's my final offer."

Blake took his horses, laden with goods that were his own, and went back to the Medicine Rock. He would come back to the post early in the spring to pick up goods for the trading. Snow lay deep up the Camas Valley. It was a slow trip. Blake traveled alone, careful, but at ease.

Hawk's Shadow had killed a grizzly. He had a scar down one cheek to show for it, and a new, proud story to tell by the fire. It would be a good winter, they all thought, if the signs held. There was plenty of food in the village and no one had been very sick yet. They accepted Blake's return to the valley casually. Red Sky and some of the older men frowned a little over the goods he had brought, but Owl Woman was very pleased with the kettles and scraping knives and the young men examined the traps with interest.

"I don't want to change anything," Blake tried to explain to the chief. "I thought these things I have brought might make things easier for the People."

"Hawk's Shadow has said to me that you and he want to trap and I know some of the other young ones want to try this, but you cannot trap in the valley. I have told them so. The spirit people showed this place to Winter Thunder. They said we should take from it what we need. They did not mean trapping for skins to trade to the white-eyes."

Blake nodded. "I meant the traps for other places."

"That is a good stallion you have brought. I think you got him from White Water's band."

"How did you know?"

"From the look of him. Perhaps you do know something of horses. What will you do now?"

"I'd like to stay here most of the time, if I can."

Red Sky's eyes showed surprise. "You are my son. Would I tell you you cannot stay?"

Blake turned away, pretending to look closely at the roan stallion, but his eyes were blurred.

"We'll go to the Yellowstone country now that you're back," Hawk's Shadow announced that evening.

"I thought there would be too much snow for traveling over the mountains."

"*I* will think of such things as that. Why must you always argue? We'll use snowshoes instead of horses. Perhaps you cannot make such a journey. Do you want to see it, or not?"

"Yes, I want to, but—"

"I must get these things done, Green Eyes, if I am to do them. If I have to be a chief one day, I may have no more time for wandering over the country."

Three of the other young men went with them. They were away most of the winter. It was a fabulous, incredible country of hot springs and geysers, cracks in the earth, a big, beautiful lake, great stone cliffs of many colors. Blake was awed by it. He would have liked more time for exploring. He wished, a little, that it were not necessary to hunt and trap, to keep alert for enemies, but only to look at the country.

In odd moments, he thought of the little valley. He had

been thinking of it like that all these months and, in his mind, it was *his* valley now. He had wanted to go there as soon as he got back to the Medicine Rock, but the snow was deep and climbing up there would have been hard. Besides, he wanted to go back alone, and there had been no chance for that. It was there, waiting peaceful and secure, his valley, a lovely quiet picture to take out of his mind and look at.

When they returned to the Medicine Rock, they found the village in mourning. Crooked Wolf had died. The winter had taken some others, babies and old ones, but Crooked Wolf was most particularly missed by all the People. He had been a sure, steady influence all down the years, the brother of Winter Thunder, interpreting the world for them. Red Sky looked tired, a little lost, older.

"Will Beaver Tooth be medicine man now?" Blake asked Hawk's Shadow uneasily.

"No. Many Bears. Beaver Tooth does not really want to be a medicine man. It can be a dangerous job for a man who is not equal to it. Beaver Tooth wants to be chief. He thinks a chief can win everything for himself with nothing but talk."

Blake went back to Camas Post for the goods and pack horses with which Connall was supplying him for the spring trade. Connall and Marie had had a seventh daughter. Connall asked pathetically that the Lord have mercy on him, while he held the baby lovingly in his big awkward hands and she reached up toward his red beard.

Blake met his people and other bands at the camas grounds, traded away the goods he had and went back to the post for more.

"You've not done badly with this batch of goods," Connall said grudgingly. "No doubt you'll be robbed crossing the mountains."

"It's easy, trading," Blake said quietly. "I give them fair trade. They know I do."

He was finding that English came a little hard for him now.

Connall said angrily, "If you're saying I don't give them fair trade, I tell you know that I've never cheated anyone in my life."

"I'm only saying it's not necessary to have quite such a

137

wide margin of profit. I think I've done better, setting my own prices than using what the Company suggests. The People—trust me."

"Ah, lad, there's no hope for you. Can't you see that some are put on earth to supply things and others to make use of them?"

"But they're all people, Connall. If you're going to begin talking about God-given rights, haven't they got the right to be treated fairly?"

"Blake, that's a bunch of idealistic rot. What do you mean by 'fair' anyway? It's one thing for one man and something else entirely for another. Every man has the right, the duty, maybe, to do the best he can for himself."

"What do you mean by 'best'?"

Connall made a gesture of disgust. "Just go on living in your dreams, lad, for as long as you can. Who am I to wake you up? We'll not talk about it anymore. All you do is make me angry. You can't listen to reason . . . .

"Emmett's come back from the south. They're expecting a great lot of settlers through at Hall this year. He'll go down again in the fall to bring up oxen and horses that have been lamed on the trail. We'll care for them here over the winter and take them down in the spring to sell again."

"You'll be a wealthy man one day."

"Aye, well, I doubt that. I don't even know what country it is I'm living in. I wish England and the States would go to war over the boundary, or whatever it is they're going to do. A man can't find much in the way of peace of mind and security when countries are dealing over his land with diplomacy. It's a wearisome thing."

Several young men had come down with Blake to the post from the camas prairie. Only one of them was of the Medicine Rock—Beaver Tooth. There had been a long council about his coming. Beaver Tooth had maintained it was his duty to look the situation over. Almost all that the Medicine Rock People had on which to base their thinking, he said, was hearsay. For the time being, at least, whites in the country were a fact. They had been a fact for a long while and more were coming. Should not someone responsible go and see them and their things so

138

that he could bring the People an absolutely factual report? Should the people of the Medicine Rock be left behind all others, ignorant?

No thinking young man who cared about his people, Beaver Tooth said, could just go on ignoring what was happening in the land. Whether they wanted them or not, white men and their ways were coming more and more among them. Did Red Sky not have one living in his very lodge? Red Sky said mildly that this one was enough, that Blake could tell them what they wanted to know. Beaver Tooth made a grand gesture of dismissal and contempt for what Blake could tell them. Blake was not truly of the Medicine Rock. How could he see things as the People saw them? How could he properly answer their questions?

Red Sky, Many Bears, and some others said that Beaver Tooth should not go, but some of the people felt differently. The chief purpose of a council was that the men might reach agreement among themselves. Unwillingly, the reluctant ones had given in.

Beaver Tooth had kept talking eloquently, relentlessly, making this seem like a kind of sacrifice he was making for the band. Hawk's Shadow, throwing a grin in Blake's direction, had said only that he already knew almost more than he could stand to know about whites and that he would not be willing to make a martyr of himself in such a way, not with the elk hunting as good as it was now.

Beaver Tooth stalked about the post, looking sober and important, taking in everything. Connall, looking for the Medicine Rock trade, flattered him. Beaver Tooth had taken some good skins in the spring and he traded for a musket, among other things. He sampled many of the white-eyes' things with an air of judicious disdain and spent a good deal of time in later councils condescendingly explaining the white man and his ways.

The buffalo were there before them when they got to the plains, but not in such numbers as last year. Many people said that white settlers, traveling west down on the Oregon Trail, were bad medicine for the buffalo and were keeping them away. They murmured and rumbled with threats and discontent that were, in great part, apprehension. There were rumors of attacks on the whites by Sioux

139

and others. There was not much trouble from the Black-feet that year. Many of their warriors had gone down the Oregon Trail to look and threaten.

Blake's trading went well. He traded not only the goods of Hudson's Bay for furs and robes, he exchanged Indian goods, getting things he or the People might want or that he knew he could trade with white trappers later. One evening as they looked over his things, Red Sky said to him in consternation, "I think you don't much enjoy this trading. Your face looks always so open. How can you take much pleasure from it when you do not try to fool the ones you trade with? Also, you need a woman to take care of those goods for you. A man should not always do all his packing and such."

After they had crossed the Divide on their way back west, when the Medicine Rock People had separated from most of the other bands with whom they had been travel-ing, some of their horses were stolen by a small party of Crows. A war party rode out joyously for retribution. Blake rode with them. One of his mares was among the stolen horses and Red Sky told him he must go.

They caught up with them where there was good cover for both sides and there was a battle that lasted all day, consisting more of shouted threats and brags than of shots with musket or arrow. Under cover of darkness, the Crows, being Crows, slipped away, abandoning the Medi-cine Rock horses and some of their own. No scalps were taken, though Blake was assured that some Crows had been killed and carried away by their fellows.

Half Moon was the only casualty among the People. He had taken a musket ball through his arm, not a very serious wound, so they went back to the camp in triumph.

It was the evening of the next day before they caught up with the village. They had had a long, hard ride, full of triumph and hilarity and bragging, and they were tired and hungry and well pleased with themselves. Just as they were coming up to the camp, a great, crashing mountain thunderstorm broke. They ordered the younger boys to see to the horses and ran for the lodges.

Hawk's Shadow, tossing his young son into the air, told boisterously of the chase, the fight, and the victory. Blake, very tired and excited by the talk, dropped down by the fire and took a bowl of stew in eager hands.

The people in Red Sky's lodge had gone to bed but Owl Woman, hearing the men's return, had got up and pulled the pot over the fire. She ladled out the stew to them, grumbling perfunctorily, glad they were all back safely.

Abruptly, Hawk's Shadow stopped talking. The lodge was still except for the gurgling of the Little Chief and the rain outside. Looking around questioningly, Blake found all their eyes on him in the dim light. Seeing him looking, they looked away. Then he felt a movement behind him and, very softly, a small voice said, "Why do you sit on my blankets?"

"My God!" he whispered and leapt up, almost stumbling into the fire.

Feeling his face flush hotly, he withdrew to the darkest corner, knowing they watched him, hearing the concealed laughter in Hawk's Shadow's voice as he placidly resumed his story.

What he had done, coming into the lodge and sitting down on the edge of the blankets that Shy Fawn lay wrapped in, was a kind of marriage proposal, a way of asking the girl if she would have him, and if she said, "Why do you sit on my blankets?" or words to that effect, it meant that she would. No one would broach the subject to him, he knew, but they would watch him and Shy Fawn and smile and wait, expecting him to go on with it. They would never believe he had sat there without thinking, only because he was tired and wet and cold and wanted to be near the fire. Had he? Maybe, without quite knowing he wanted to . . . . Anyway, the girl was promised to Storm Coming Out Of The East, wasn't she? And he had no business with a wife. Except for a few difficult moments when his body had become too much for him, he had tried to believe he was through with close relationships with women.

He found little pleasure in the rest of the trip, feeling awkward, observed. He left the People when they came to the Camas and went down the river with quite a respectable pack train, and he stayed there to help with the fall work.

Connall asked him to go up into what was undisputed Canadian territory to help with the escort of a train of goods from one of the larger posts. He wanted the goods at his own post before winter, ready for the spring trade.

Emmett went along, telling Blake about the Mormons who were now coming into the country far to the south. Connall planned to send horses and what cattle he could spare down to trade with them at Jim Bridger's fort in the spring.

"He might git one good year's tradin' out of them," Emmett said, "but I don't think it'll last much longer than that. From what I've heard an' seen, they're people that can take care of theirselves. Quick as they can, they'll have their own posts an' things. They had to leave the States because of some things they believe, mostly it seems to be about havin' more than one wife at a time."

Blake wanted no talk about wives. He said, "Do you know anything about Paul?"

"He's over at Spokane House, restin' up. I ain't seen him, heard he was there from some Cayuses. They say he's in bad shape—consumption, maybe. I guess he lost what little he had, drinkin' an' gamblin' down there with them Spanish where he's been at, only they say he's still got his fiddle."

When they got back to Camas, it was Christmas and Blake stayed for that. Then he went back to the Medicine Rock. He couldn't seem *not* to go now. It was a hard, slow trip in heavy snow.

He wanted to straight up to the little cirque valley without seeing anyone, but he knew it couldn't be like that. He opened his packs in the midst of a noisy welcome and waited as patiently as he could. He caught Hawk's Shadow smiling at him speculatively and looked away.

It was clear that Shy Fawn had not yet become the woman of Storm Coming Out Of The East. He wished she had. It would have saved him an awkward explanation that no one wanted to hear or would try to understand. While they looked over his goods, crowding into Red Sky's lodge, Blake went about as unobtrusively as he could, making up a pack that he could carry on his back. Hawk's Shadow followed him outside.

142

"I want to go away by myself for a few days," Blake said quickly, defensively.

"Do you go hunting?"

"No."

Hawk's Shadow peered at him in the dim light. It was snowing again.

"You are right when you have said, all those times, that we don't think the same. Maybe you will never make good reason to me. I think you don't make good reason to yourself."

"Can I use some snowshoes?"

"Why do you ask that? They're there, aren't they? I hope you won't be found by any Blackfeet. I have been hunting for five days before this and I would not like to have to go out again yet."

His little valley lay still and quiet under the pristine beauty of the snow. Blake stood at its edge for a long time, very still, reluctant to have even his own footprints disturb the deep, smooth whiteness. It was late afternoon, the sky heavy and dark with clouds, but snow light showed him a part of the little park in a dim, dreamlike way. Turning, he could see nothing, either below him or out toward the peaks. It was as if this place were not only a pocket in the mountainside, but in the clouds, the sky, as well. Never Summer stood there, just out of reach. He could feel the mountain's presence, majestic, unchanging, grandly indifferent. Slowly, he moved into the valley.

The lake was thickly frozen now. There were tracks around its edges. Blake did not study them. He needed no game yet and there was nothing here he would worry about. They were the tracks of animals, he knew, not people. He went up into the edge of the woods and began making himself a shelter. That night, he let himself, made himself think sanely about New Orleans.

Etienne St. Croix was a wealthy, a sophisticated, a much-respected, a fine man. His family had been in the Louisiana country for a long time, but Etienne was known in European circles as well, because of his money, his name, and his diplomatic services. In 1837, he had

143

been hurt in a riding accident, severely crippled, so that he had to retire to his town house in New Orleans and his plantation a few miles up the river. He was no longer able to walk or ride, but he still traveled when he could by boat, though friends and business acquaintances came to him at home, from many parts of the world.

He had been married, years before, to a Parisienne and there were two children, a son who lived on Martinique with a family of his own, and a young daughter in a convent school. Etienne's first wife had died while the daughter was still a baby.

A little more than a year before his accident, when Etienne was almost sixty, he had married Celeste, less than half his age and very beautiful. Her family owned a great deal of land in the tidewater country along the southeastern coast. It was a distant cousin of Celeste's for whom Blake was working in Carolina when he met them.

Celeste was restless and moody. They had an infant son, conceived before Etienne's accident, and she had insisted they come away from New Orleans, which she did not like very much, because there was a new epidemic of fever in the city and she wanted to get the child away. Etienne, though the trip sapped his strength, was willing and eager to make it. He was not ready simply to sit at home, waiting for all things to come to him there. Besides, he wanted to try to please his young wife. They made a long visit in Carolina.

Etienne had many business affairs and he wanted a secretary. In addition to business matters and correspondence with friends, he had decided to write his memoirs. He would begin with things he knew about his family before they had left France, work up through what he had known as a young man of the American and French revolutions, describe important and interesting people he had known, and recount the history of the Louisiana country from his own memory. He could not do much writing himself. It tired him too much, as did the research he wanted done for the book, to add to and verify his memories. Celeste's cousin, flattered and eager to please, allowed Etienne to offer Blake the position as his secretary and so the boy went to New Orleans.

It was a fabulous house to Blake, with beautiful gardens and a library the likes of which he had never quite imagined, with a music room and paintings from all over the world. Blake's awe and eagerness to know were refreshing and pleasing to the old man. It would have been hard to say which of them did most for the other. Blake became Etienne's secretary, his clerk, his valet, his legs and eyes and ears outside the house; and Etienne gave him access to the library and to his own mind, bringing a touch of reality, perhaps of cynicism, into Blake's thinking, taking some of the rough edges off his concepts of the world and of life.

Blake loved him. He had great respect for him, and admiration and appreciation. He was happy, fully caught up in an interesting, busy new world filled with more things, more ideas than he seemed capable of assimilating. And then one night, Celeste came to his room.

There was no talk that first time. Simply, he woke and she stood there, her dressing gown falling in a froth around her feet. He tried to protest and her mouth covered his, hot and wild, tearing him apart inside with battering, unthinking response. When she got up and left him, still without speaking, he lay trembling, sick with the wrong he had done Etienne and with wanting her to come back.

He locked his door after that, and lay tensely awake for most of several nights, not knowing what he was most afraid of.

One day she found him writing in the library, alone.

"Don't lock your door again," she said quietly, with a kind of casual, possessive imperiousness. "You can learn a great many things here and Etienne is not the only one who can teach you."

He stammered a protest, a kind of plea.

"How do you think it is for me," she demanded fiercely, "living with an old man who can do nothing manly anymore? Why shouldn't I find a little pleasure now and then if I can? If I come again and find your door locked, I'll tell him you've been trying to seduce me. Which of us do you think he's going to believe?"

She touched his cheek with a small, complacent smile, and it seemed to him that her fingers were tipped with fire.

"I could wish for someone better, more handsome, more knowledgeable, more experienced," she said coolly, disparagingly, "but you are here and so I will teach you what I want you to know, what will bring us both pleasure. Just be a good boy. I think you won't be sorry often."

And that same evening, as they sat late over some letters he was taking, Etienne said, "I want you to know, Blake, that you're a great comfort to me, very much like another son in many ways. You learn so quickly, so eagerly; it sometimes makes the world new again for me, watching you." He sighed. "Celeste is a fine, a beautiful, good woman, but she grows impatient at times, with me and with things as they are. And who can blame her? As things have turned out, she would have done better to have married someone else. Still, it helps me in everything to know I have you to depend on now. I don't know how I managed without you. You must never think of going away."

Blake bent his burning face over the papers before him, his throat tight.

It went on like that for more than two years. Blake, torn by attraction for the woman and concern for the man, would decide that, to save his own sanity and self-respect, if anything were left to save, he must go; Celeste, who seemed able to read his tortured mind, would tell, with calm, deliberate viciousness, the graphic stories she would relay to her husband if anything were done to upset the arrangement; and Etienne, with a seemingly guileless gratitude, would say how much he needed Blake's help, how he depended on him.

Celeste grew bold and careless and more cruel. She told her husband that she wanted to be accompanied on her carriage rides by Blake, rather than by her Negro maid, and Etienne agreed, saying it was an excellent idea. Did he know? He was far from blind or stupid about anything else. That possibility added to Blake's misery.

One day, she came upon him in the garden, playing with her little son. Etienne was sleeping nearby in a deck chair and Blake was drawing pictures for the boy. He did not know Celeste had come from the house until she touched his hair tenderly.

"Do you wish the child was yours? Perhaps I will have your son one day."

And she laughed softly, exultantly, at his paling face and the terror that rushed into his eyes.

Etienne asked him once if the possibility had ever occurred to him that he might marry the daughter, Yvonne, when she was finished with school.

"Don't look so troubled, Blake," he said, smiling gently. "It's only a thought I've had. It would please me to have you a legal member of my family. Actually, the idea was originally Celeste's. She, also, would be pleased."

Blake hated Celeste. Sometimes he hated Etienne, and always he hated himself and the tumult of feelings that seethed within him. Always, in the past, he had felt himself to be living only on the edges of other people's lives. Was this what it meant to be a part of something? He wanted to run, never to see them again, never to have to face himself, and yet he wanted what he had here, the books, the comforts, Etienne's trust and confidence, and yes, he wanted what he had from Celeste, the physical things; sometimes he wanted those things most of all.

He was less certain now than ever of who and what he was, and a sick self-loathing and contempt filled him. He slept badly and woke often, sweating, from nightmares.

And then Etienne was very ill.

"He's going to die soon," said Celeste with her smug, assured calm. "You can't marry me. You're not nearly my equal and perhaps I will want to find a suitable husband some day, but you can marry that little mouse Yvonne and be my business manager. We will have a very happy, cozy household."

And Etienne said faintly, "I know I can count on you to help Celeste. She will need one who has some understanding of the business."

He held weakly to Blake's hand and would not let go until he died.

While Celeste was at the Mass, Blake ran away to the waterfront and found the steamer just ready to cast off for St. Louis.

He lay cold and rigid in the buffalo robes. The little fire

he had had was only embers. Light snow, big wet flakes, fell silently on the boughs of his shelter.

And the great quietness said to him: It's over now. You were as much at fault as they. You need not have stayed, but you can't make any of it different. You can't change what they were, what you've been, or what you've done. Only be still, and know.

Know what? his mind cried out in agony. That's from the Bible: "Be still and know that I am God." I want no part of that anymore.

Know that this is a different world from New Orleans, that in some ways, you are a different person now. Only try to live so that you can be at peace with yourself. It won't always be so, but try. Let the past go. Accept that it has been and that now it is past.

Feeling weak and ill, he got up and walked to the edge of the woods. A small herd of elk was down by the lake, pawing snow away to get at the grass. They lifted their heads briefly to look in his direction, then went back to more important things.

The clouds were broken. A shaft of moonlight lay on the peak of Never Summer. Blake caught his breath in the great silence.

God is everywhere, the Quietness said to him. He is in all things, and all things in Him. He is not what your grandparents told you, or what anyone else has told you, or what you have read. Each person must find for himself the bit of God that is within that person. He is love and not vengeance. You begin to make your discovery of Him by starting to forgive yourself, by admitting that you are only human, and by learning to let yourself feel compassion.

He put his hands up to his face with a sound that was half fear, half aching, released joy. When he looked again, the clouds had closed, but he could feel the mountain. It seemed to him he could feel the world turning beneath him and hear again that quiet, steady, unchanging humming that was the existence of the universe. He felt ineffably small and unimportant, vital and safe.

At the village next morning, as Owl Woman gave him

food, she said, "You look as if you have been dreaming dreams."

"Yes," he said, thinking that probably they would understand better than any whites if he were ever to try to explain last night to them.

"Were they good medicine?"

"Yes."

"And now you are ready to talk to Red Sky?"

He looked up at her. "How did you know?"

"I know only that it's past time," she said shortly. "Just take the girl and don't think too much about what to give for her. Red Sky will not argue about it. She has not been pleasant to live with since you sat on her blankets. One moment she has been boasting because it happened, the next she has been sulking for fear you wouldn't come back. She is a good worker, though she is small, but she is a stubborn one, with a sharp tongue. I only hope you will be able to handle her . . . . When you go again to the post, you could bring me one of those very large kettles like Beaver Tooth brought to his mother Brown Leaf."

VII

RED SKY GAVE a feast. It was not simply to celebrate his daughter's being given to a husband. It was a chief's place to feast his people now and then and it was that time. The People took the ceremony of marriage casually, though the young men had a good deal to say to Blake. They spoke, as always, very exactly what they meant to say and he was uncomfortable at times, but it was the women who surprised him. They were most explicit in their jokes and advice, now that he was to have a woman. Hawk's Shadow seemed as pleased with this arrangement as he would ever seem pleased with anything Blake did. He was critical and teasing, but he smiled, watching Blake look diffidently at Shy Fawn in her fine, beautifully decorated clothes at the feast. Red Sky looked sober and concerned. Blake wished fervently that he knew some way of putting the chief's mind at ease, about this one thing, at least. Storm Coming Out Of The East did not seem at all disappointed or angry.

"Women are alike," he said carelessly, grinning at Blake, "but perhaps you do not know this yet. They all have the same parts. Some are thought to be better than others because they can work more and say less. I have never been really satisfied about Shy Fawn. She often speaks her mind when she ought to keep quiet and she is scrawny. A woman isn't much good if she may have to be given special care. Now I have waited too long, making up my mind, so I will just have to get another one."

Red Sky pointed out an empty lodge ring they could

150

use at one side of the village, a pit that sloped gradually to a depth of about three feet at its center. Blake cut the poles and set them, with difficulty, in the frozen ground. Shy Fawn did the rest.

"Now I have my own fire," she said with satisfaction as they sat beside it on the first evening after their lodge was finished. "Now I won't have to listen so often to Little Rain. My mother is one thing, and Little Rain is a good sister, but because she has the Little Chief and is Hawk's Shadow's wife, she thinks she knows everything. Her own people are not even of the Medicine Rock."

Blake was carving. He did not particularly want to be carving, but she was always busy with something and he doubted that he could ever achieve the Medicine Rock men's casual relaxation in the lodge while their wives worked endlessly. Her compulsively busy hands would not let him do nothing. He said "I'll go to Camas Post after a while, at the end of the winter. Do you want to come with me and live there while I work?"

"You are my husband," she said with a great and false meekness, not looking up from the buckskin shirt she was embroidering for him with porcupine quills.

"Do you think your father would mind very much if you went there for a while?"

"My father, too, knows that you are my husband." She flashed a look at him, all gentleness and submission, but with a mischievous smile around her lips and eyes.

"I think," he said, "that you are the one they should have called Smiling Fox."

"I am rightly named," she said with a faint reproof and a little pout before looking back to her work. "I am very quiet and very shy, always. I speak only when I am spoken to, and sometimes not then because I am so modest. I am here only to serve you, to keep your fire and your lodge, to sleep with you and please you and do as I am told. If you tell me to go and live with you at Camas Post, then I start to pack . . . . Do you think, my husband, that while we are there you could find some very bright red and blue cloths for me? You say that buckskin clothes are scratchy and I could make you some others. And, if I do that well and it pleases you, perhaps I could have . . . ."

151

He was laughing and, from the sound of her voice, knew that her smile had grown wider.

"Don't I do those things for you?" she asked mildly, "sleep with you and keep your fire and—"

"You do them very well," he said softly.

"So why do you wonder if my father will let me go with you?"

"I'd like him to be pleased and not to worry about you."

"I don't need anyone to worry about me, Blake."

"You're going to call me Blake, then?" he said, pleased and surprised.

"It's not a pleasant sound and you say it means nothing, but I will get used to it. I must call my husband something. I don't like Left Hand or Broken Head and you don't seem to like Green Eyes much. Anyway, it's the first word of English I know. Will you teach me others?"

"What do you want to know?"

"Well . . . . is there a word for saying you like to look at me? Surely you must like to because you are always doing it."

"Pretty," he said, smiling, "beautiful."

Looking at her slender litheness as she put wood on the fire, he found he could not help thinking of her mother Owl Woman, short, heavily muscled, with rough, hard hands and sagging breasts. The women's lives were so hard and she would never let him help her. "You will shame me," she would reprove him with unfeigned pain, "and yourself."

"I love you," he said now, softly, in her language. He had never said the words before. His throat was tight with joy.

"This is what a mother says to her child," she said, looking at him quizzically.

"No, it's not like that at all."

"You are strange," she said slowly, wonderingly. "Sometimes I feel afraid."

"Why?"

"Because I think I will never know who you are . . . . Blake, what is your medicine spirit?"

"I—don't know, Shy Fawn. I suppose I have none."

"You see?" she said tensely. "You *must* have a medicine spirit. Who watches over you? You make songs and prayers to no one. Who will keep you safe?"

"I try to keep myself safe."

Her large eyes, glancing up at him, were frightened. "That is not a good thing to say."

"I won't say it again."

There was a little silence and she said tentatively, "My own medicine spirit is the deer. Deer are not brave animals, but they are very useful and good. When you are hunting or must ride in a war party or such things, I will sing my song to the deer spirit for you. Other women do this for their husbands. It can be helpful."

"I will like that."

"But I wish you had your own spirit brother. It frightens me, thinking that you do not."

"Don't be frightened," he said gently. "We'll talk of other things . . . . Do you know what a cabin is?"

"No."

"It's a—a lodge, made of logs."

"Of logs? How can that be?"

"The logs are cut and fitted together and—"

"How do you carry these logs with you when you make a journey?"

"You don't. The cabin is built and it just—stays in the same place. The people who live in a cabin stay there most of the time. They don't make many journeys."

"Why? What do they do? How can they hunt buffalo and—"

"If we go down to Camas Post, you will see cabins and such things. The Red-haired One has a cabin, and a—a farm where he raises food for his family and his animals. He—"

"I don't understand this," she said a little wistfully, then dismissed the subject. "Tell me if there is a word in English for a man and a woman going to bed together. Would that not be a good thing to do?"

She put him off playfully, with her little smile, saying that she must straighten the robes on their bed of grass so that he would be comfortable, and taking a long time about it, glancing up at him with warm, liquid eyes. Finally, she lay in his arms, small and warm and lithe, her heart beating fiercely against him. At the last, her teeth

153

sank into his shoulder, bringing blood. Blake cried out, but he was scarcely aware of the pain in his shoulder. She laughed softly, exultantly, pressing herself against him.

Later, he said dreamily, "If we had a cabin, there would be a fireplace, a bed, chairs . . . ."

"I don't know these words," she said reprovingly and put her fingers on his lips. "Why do you talk, after the things we have been doing? Now is the time for sleeping."

They slept immediately, deeply.

They went down to the post in February. Connall and the others looked at them speculatively, with nods and knowing smiles. Shy Fawn grew subdued, puzzled, a little frightened. Blake tried to explain things to her and sometimes she questioned him, but, for the most part, she learned by intense observation. Marie tried to advise her but they knew little of each other's language, and Shy Fawn was uneasy, distrustful of the older woman.

They had a tiny room to live in, behind the warehouse office, and she seemed to feel trapped there, scarcely able to wait until she could get outside each morning. She had brought materials for weaving mats for the floor of their lodge and she chose cloth for them both and as presents for her family. She worked on those things. The weather was still very cold, but if there was even a glimmer of sunlight she sat outside, somewhat sheltered by a wall, to do her work. She said, apologetically, that candles smelled bad to her, that, in fact, the whole place had many strange and unpleasant smells.

Blake gave her needles and good sewing thread. She said that these things were very nice to have but that perhaps they made her work too easy, that maybe it was wrong to change things so much. She grew very quiet and thoughtful, rarely teasing or ridiculing him now, and he was eager for the time when most of the spring work should be finished so that they could go away again.

Mote Stanley and Emmett came in with a good catch of spring furs and Paul, accompanied by some Indians, had come over from Spokane House. Paul looked like a ghost, thin and white, often coughing blood. The three of them sat one evening in the office with Blake and Connall. Blake was working on the books. His eyes burned in the smoke-filled candlelight.

"So you're a squaw man now," old Mote said to him in a friendly tone.

Blake glanced up briefly. He hated the phrase.

"It's the only way for a young feller in these parts to do," Mote went on approvingly. "I been tellin' that to Emmett for a long time now. If a boy thinks he's got to wait for a white woman out here, his balls is liable to dry up an' drop off while he's waitin'. At least I hope they will. Any more whites comes into this country an' this child's got to find some place else to go . . . . There was one winter, a long time back, when I had me two Ute wives at onct . . . ."

He told them a long, rambling, reminiscent story of his life among the Utes.

"Some ways, I'm glad I don't need a woman the way I used to," he finished a little wistfully. "I ain't had a steady one for five or six years now, but if I was trappin' by myself, I'd damn well have one, to take care of the plews and keep my camp, if nothin' else. You won't find a white woman anywhere can dress pelts like a squaw can, nor one that's as ready for screwin' either. They're hot little bitches, ever' one of 'em."

"It's the life they have," Paul said thoughtfully. "The Indian girls grow up close to nature and they know how to take pleasure when they find it. They're not all bound up with a lot of ideas about the body's being a shameful thing. If my French wife could ever have felt like that, perhaps I could have stayed in Montreal."

He coughed, his fragile-looking face morose, and drank some rum. They had all glanced at him and then away. It was the first time he had ever mentioned having a French wife.

"I hadn't heard before that you've a wife, Paul," Connall said.

"Nearly ten years. A son and a daughter, too, though I've not seen them often. I married one of those times when I went back to the east, determined to stay. She thinks it's the worst thing that could happen to the children, seeing me, like looking on the devil. I don't know....

155

maybe she's right. I'd like to bring my boy out here to look around when he's older, but, I don't know, probably that would be wrong. This country, this way of living, gets in a man's blood. It can be a kind of sickness."

They were feeling a little uncomfortable and Emmett changed the subject, saying to Blake, "Will you be going east of the Divide again this year?"

"Yes."

"We've heard," Emmett said, "that the Americans are building a new fort at the Three Forks and some others around the country. They're going to station some troops there, they won't be just trading posts."

Blake frowned. "That's not going to do the hunting much good." He was finding that each time he came to the post English came harder for him, required more thought.

"They think they can keep the Blackfeet in hand."

Connall snorted. "That's funny. They may want to keep the Blackfeet from raiding the immigrant trail, but the more trouble there has been among the tribes themselves, the better the Americans have always liked it."

"Not just Americans," old Mote said belligerently. "H. B. has done its share of keepin' the Indians stirred up."

"An' they're sayin'," Emmett went on, "that there'll be hundreds of wagons comin' out this year."

Connall cursed and Mote said to him angrily, "I don't know what you're mutterin' about, Red. You're fixin' to make more money with your goddam stock raisin' than you've ever made with H. B."

"Listen, Mote," Connall said reasonably, sipping at his rum, "it happens I like this country. I like it a lot. No matter how much any of us would like to see it stay the way it was, it won't. It's already different. You're talking about looking for some place else to go. We'd all like that, maybe, but some time there won't *be* anywhere else, not like the old days. For myself, I'll be content to stay right here, and I've got to do what I can to—adjust."

Mote released a foul expletive and there was a little silence. Paul, after coughing again and pouring more rum, said, "Those Mormons. I hear it's a part of their religion that a man can have all the wives he can take care of."

156

"Heathens!" muttered Connall. "They ought to be strung up, every mother's son of them."

"Why?" Blake asked mildly, a little absently as he tried to interpret Connall's writing in the ledger. "Mote was just telling us about when he had two Ute wives."

"These are *white* women, lad! We can't have shameful carryings-on like that in this country."

"If it's wrong with white women, why is it right with Indians?"

"Oh, for God's sake boy!" cried Mote angrily. "Use some sense. There's nothin' the same about it. Indians ain't even people, really. Especially not the women."

Blake had run into this philosophy before. It made him furious.

"How can you say that? You've lived with them and you've just been saying you liked it. You—"

"I've had horses I *liked,* even a mule or two."

"Goddam it to hell—"

"Now, lad," Connall said soothingly, patronizingly, "you're a bit touchy, new husband that you are. Try to see the overall view."

"The hell with the overall view. You feel the same way he does and you—"

"You can't say how I feel," Connall said calmly. "I don't agree with Mote entirely, but it's an individual thing. I've lived with Marie now for more than ten years. She's a good woman, good wife, good mother. I'd miss her if anything were to happen, but be realistic, Blake. Marie, fine as she is, *is* an Indian, and I'm not. We'll never be or think anything like the same. That's how it is, and that's how it'll be, always, with even you and that little girl of yours. Unless, of course, you can go all the way and *be* an Indian yourself. A few whites have done that, almost, but they haven't been people I've liked knowing. I don't think you can do it."

"That's not what he's sayin'," said Emmett a little unexpectedly. "I think Blake just means we're all humans, it don't matter how we think about things."

Blake nodded but Emmett stopped him from speaking.

"Still, I don't think some things that might be all right for a Indian woman would be the same for a white one."

157

Mote grunted. "Blake's more'n half Indian already, looks like one, smells like one. How many scalps have you took, boy?"

"None," he said harshly. "I never will."

"Too good for that kind of thing, I guess," Mote said derisively. "Well, I've took some in my day an' I don't mind tellin' you, I've had me a good time doin' it."

"How can you say," Blake cried, "that Indians are on a par with horses and mules, when you've lived with them, taken scalps with them, done all the things they've done—"

"What's the difference?" demanded the old man complacently. "I'm still white."

"That's just it," said Emmett mildly. "You ought to know better."

"Ah," said Connall with satisfaction. "There it is. You're all saying the same thing. There *is* a difference."

"That's not what I meant," Blake said adamantly, but he could do no more with the argument. They were never going to change their ways of thinking because of anything he tried to say to them.

Paul said quietly, "I'll lay you a bet, Blake, that if you go on living with the Medicine Rock People or any other band, within three years you'll take at least one scalp. I would put up my fiddle."

"It's sinful to kill," Emmett said with quiet conviction. "We may live like they do, some ways, but—"

"What's sin at one time, for one man, may not be so in other circumstances," Paul said.

"Adultery's a sin," said old Mote firmly. "Blake don't seem to feel like he's damned for livin' with that little squaw. None of the rest of us has felt damned over that kind of thing, though we might have worried about it some if we'd wanted to live with a white woman out of wedlock. You can't do sin to an Indian, livin' with a woman or killin' a buck. We're white."

"That's the goddamnedest reasoning I ever heard!" Blake cried. He had stood up.

"You won't get away from it," Paul said sadly, quietly, "not here, not anywhere that there are different kinds of people."

"People!" Blake cried. "Can't any of you see that that's the whole thing? We're all people—"

"And not the same," Paul said gently, relentlessly.

"This is too deep for me," said Connall, standing up, stretching, so that his big hands lay flat against a beam. "I can't take in much of deep thinking at a time. It's enough for me just to know the way things are, the way they have to be. I'm going to bed, gentlemen."

They went back to the Medicine Rock after about six weeks. Riding up the Camas, Blake could almost see Shy Fawn changing, beginning to smile, becoming herself again. He would not let her ride behind him, but kept dropping back beside her, leading the roped-together pack horses himself.

"All right," she said finally, resignedly. "We'll ride like this, only not if anyone is coming, and not when we get to the Valley."

"Why not?"

"You know very well why not. You will shame me before my people. They will say I am not a good wife and that you are not a good husband . . . . Blake, will you go again to the post in the autumn?"

"Yes, I thhnk I'll have to. Why?"

She looked away, unhappily. "I think that if you were to ask me about going with you then, I might say I would like to stay in the village."

"I'm sorry you weren't happy there."

"You have talked before about being happy. It may be a wrong thing to talk of that, my husband. The good times come and we find pleasure in them, but to be always talking of being happy might tempt some evil . . . . It's a strange place, Camas Post. Sometimes when I was there, I could not tell who is Shy Fawn, daughter of Red Sky. Do you understand?"

"Yes."

"And is it like that for you? with the People?"

"Sometimes, and with whites, too."

She was silent and thoughtful for a time, then he felt her watching him and when he looked the little whimsical, vixen smile was on her face.

159

She said softly, "I would not want to go there in the autumn because I think your son ought to be born in the village."

"Ho!" cried Hawk's Shadow in the midst of noisy welcome. He held a new bow, made from the horn of bighorn sheep, aiming an arrow at Blake. "Get off the horse slowly. I will take him and all those goods. No white man comes into this valley."

"I am of the Medicine Rock," Blake replied soberly. It was an old game with them by now.

"No, not with those green eyes and all those white man things."

"I can make you a good trade for that bow."

"What will you trade? Do not move your left hand or my arrow finds your heart."

"The rifle. I've brought it for you."

"Any story to save your life, is that it? You know that we only get muskets in trade. Whites would not let you give me a good rifle."

"There's not much they can do about it, is there? Especially if you're going to kill me."

"Yes, this is a very sharp arrow. It would kill an elk, or even a buffalo. And I see you have stolen one of our women. What do you have to say about that?"

"I've brought her back."

Hawk's Shadow laughed then and lost the game.

Frantic preparations were under way for the spring journey, but Blake persuaded Shy Fawn to come with him to look at the little valley. She chattered all the way about the work she should be doing and he rather wished he hadn't insisted that she come, feeling certain she would not understand.

She stood beside him and looked over it, saying nothing. She knew that for some reason this place meant a great deal to him, but she saw only trees and grass and water. Those could be found in many places. She turned and found that he was looking up at Never Summer with a strange, quiet face that frightened her a little somehow. You could see the mountain from many places too. He was strange, her husband, and beyond knowing.

Blake, turning back to the valley, said softly, "I could build a cabin there, on that little rise."

"A cabin," she said slowly. "Like those at the post?"

"Something like."

"To stay in?"

"Yes. For us."

"So far from the village?"

He was savoring the quiet. "Your family and the others could come when they liked, and we could visit them."

"Surely, you do not think to stay here always? How would we get the things we need? It is a good little valley, to look at, but there is no camas here, no bitterroot, no kouse, no salmon, no buffalo . . . ."

"I could trade for those things."

"And what if the Blackfeet came? There would be no one here to help us fight them, or the Snakes or—"

She broke off, very troubled. Blake was feeling hurt and disappointed, and angry with himself for the feelings. Why should it mean anything in particular to her? He had wanted her to share his feelings, to understand, the way men and women sometimes understood one another in books, without even the necessity for talk. But, probably, that sort of thing happened only in books, and very rarely in life, even when two people came from the same kind of background.

Shy Fawn said softly, "If it is what you want, to live here in a cabin, then I will be with you. You are my husband." She was not smiling.

"We'll think more of it another time," he said contritely. "I only wanted to show you the place . . . . But since we're here, I'll just measure the foundation a little, maybe drive a few stakes . . . ."

He found he had a need now to leave some mark on the valley, something he could think of during the months away. She watched him for a time, moving around in the patchy snow, making careful measurements with an unknotted bridle, counting paces, catching his lower lip between his teeth when he concentrated hardest. Then she said meekly, "I will walk around a little and see what I can find."

It seemed to her that he did not hear the words or

161

know when she left. Well, that was not unusual. Men were often like that when they were thinking about a thing. Most of them did not seem able to think of more than one thing at a time.

When she came back, he was sitting on a log by the lake, drawing and figuring on a large piece of bark. She brought the bag of meat and camas cakes she had carried on her horse.

"There will be huckleberries on the hillside," she said, "and strawberries and some other things. Enough only for a few people, and not much to keep for the winter, but I saw the tracks of deer and elk. Some otter have a slide up there at the head of the lake. Did you see, Blake, that there are some boulders that look like the Medicine Rock, up there by the spring?"

He nodded absently, concentrating on his plans. She looked wistfully, thoughtfully at his bent head. Had he had some visions—something like Winter Thunder's, perhaps?—that told him to bring his family here? Perhaps those rocks meant something.

The buffalo hunting was good that year. The Medicine Rock People did not turn up the Camas on their way home, but crossed it and went on over the high range to the west, to fish in the streams of what had been their native country before Winter Thunder had led them across the mountains to live. They set up camp near the village of their old band and had many feasts along with the fishing.

Blake, as it turned out, had some natural abilities with spear and canoe. He enjoyed the fishing. Shy Fawn was very proud as she worked busily at the drying racks. He was concerned about her and couldn't seem to help showing it. She was small and her pregnancy, growing obvious now, was an inconvenience to her. She looked pale and drawn, but any indication of his solicitude embarrassed and angered her and brought ridicule on both of them.

"This is the natural way of a woman," Owl Woman his mother-in-law told Blake sternly. "You only make her work harder when you try to help. Is this not the way

162

with white women? If it isn't, how do they get their children?"

Blake's trading had gone well all through the summer. The people were kindly tolerant of him and his ways.

Little Rain bore Hawk's Shadow's daughter while they were at the fishing grounds, and Storm Coming Out Of The East took himself a wife from among the old band. A few old people and small children died before they got back to the Medicine Rock.

When the village was set up for the winter, Shy Fawn went to the birth lodge to live, waiting for her baby to be born. Blake went down to the fort to turn over the things that belonged to Hudson's Bay. Connall was in a haze of joy, almost distracted with it. Marie had borne him a son in the late summer, the first of his children to have inherited his red hair and blue eyes. Blake did not mention that he was to have a child of his own soon. He was pleased about it, but reluctant to talk of it with a white man.

When he returned to the village, his son had been born. Shy Fawn and the baby were still in the birth lodge. He was not allowed to see his wife yet and could only have a brief look at the baby, from a little distance.

"To me, he seems very ordinary," Hawk's Shadow said judiciously, a smile playing around his eyes. "Some of the people thought he would be born looking very white or some other strange thing. Shy Fawn told my mother that even she was afraid of what he might look like, but perhaps he is all right. Nothing special, you understand, in any way, but perhaps there is some hope for him, that he will be just an ordinary, right kind of person . . . . You can eat in our lodge while Shy Fawn is not with you."

"There's something I want to do," Blake said. "I'll be away for a while."

It was November now, but fine Indian summer weather. There would be some snow in the little valley, but that would make moving the logs easier, and it had not yet been severely cold long enough for the trees to freeze, so cutting would be all right.

"You've only just come back," Hawk's Shadow pointed out. "We need no meat."

Blake turned to Red Sky. "There is a little valley, up there on the side of the ridge, with a lake and—"

"I know the place."

"I'd like to build a cabin—"

And he tried again to explain a cabin, though, it turned out, Shy Fawn had already tried.

"If this is a thing you think you must do," Red Sky said dubiously.

"What I wanted to ask you is, is it all right with you, with the People, if I use that land?"

Red Sky frowned. "The land is not mine, nor anyone's, to give. The land is only there."

"I'm white," Blake reminded him reluctantly. "I didn't know if . . . ."

"You keep yourself a stranger," said the chief severely. "You are my son, the man of my daughter, the father of my grandson. Why will you hold yourself always apart from us? She tells me that you want to live up there, far from the village. I do not see reason in this. Perhaps you are not pleased with us, or perhaps you have had some direction that you have told no one of. Whatever it is, that little valley lies up there. It is not mine to give."

He had brought what tools he could get at the post, and he went up and began the work. Hawk's Shadow and some of the others came up to see what he was doing, to shake their heads and jeer. They would do nothing to help.

"When I put up the walls," he said to Hawk's Shadow, "I don't think I can do it alone. Will you help me then?"

"What kind of work would that be? Get your woman to help you. She thinks it is all right for you to do this white-eyes thing."

He cut the logs and dragged them to the rise, with the help of two very unwilling ponies. The weather held fine. He notched and dragged and hauled the foundation logs into place, feeling a great weariness and exultation. Using the horses, he got some of the wall logs into place and knew he could do no more alone, without a block and tackle. He had nothing suitable for making one now.

There was going to be a storm. He sat on the base of his wall and watched the clouds boiling and tumbling around Never Summer. It must be almost Christmastime now. He thought of the cabin, whole and snug, perhaps with a Christmas tree. His grandparents had said Christmas trees were pagan, heathenish, sinful, but the Douglases had always had one, and those in the St. Croix house had been so beautiful that they had been almost painful to look at. He smiled then, with a helpless little shrug, thinking of the explanation a Christmas tree would require here. Still, he might have one, one day, when the boy was old enough to enjoy it. Then he remembered that the boy, too, would not know about Christmas and trees to commemorate it.

He lowered his eyes from the stormy mountain and Shy Fawn was coming up over the edge of the valley, the baby on her back. He ran down to meet them, his face full of joy and consternation.

"I am well and strong now," she said happily, quickly, to still his words of concern. "There is talk that perhaps you don't want to live with me anymore, so I thought I would come and ask you."

"Of course I want to——"

"You've stayed away a long time . . . . So that's your cabin. It's not going to keep out much snow. What do you want to do? build a lodge here until it's finished?"

"I've been sleeping in a brush shelter, back there in the woods. The cabin can't be finished now. The winter's closing in. It'll have to wait."

"Will you come back to the village then?" She looked and sounded relieved.

"Yes. I was just about to get my things together and do that."

"Since we are here, the boy and I, we can stay this night."

"It's going to storm."

"Are we of the Medicine Rock afraid of a storm?"

They ate and sat reasonably warm in the shelter, a fire at its open side. Snow was falling heavily, sifted about by a faint icy breeze. She said shyly, "Blake? Do you think we've made a good boy?"

"I think he's a fine boy," he said softly.

The baby had been nursing. His small head drooped against her now as he began to fall asleep.

"I have noticed," she said hesitantly, "just in the past

165

few days . . . . his eyes seem to be turning green, like yours."

She held him up so that his drowsy eyes were in the firelight. Blake did not look at them for a moment. He had not thought of that happening, had wanted the boy to look, to be, all Indian.

"Are you sorry?" she asked timidly. "Some of the people say it is not a good thing."

He moved and took the baby from her awkwardly, feeling an unexpected surge of emotion that choked him a little.

"I'm not sorry. What have you called him?"

Shy Fawn was a little embarrassed. A man usually did not hold a baby until the child was old enough to take some notice, to be played with.

"I've called him Coyote," she said shyly. "It's only a name for a little while, the way babies have. You can give him another name whenever you like. It's just that sometimes he looks like a small coyote, peeking out of his robes, and he has a funny little smile, as if he thinks himself very clever . . . . Will you give him a white name? Maybe you will want to wait and see if he is going to stay with us. The first winter and summer are very hard for babies and sometimes . . . ."

Blake's arms had tightened convulsively. "He will stay."

"Don't say it so surely," she said fearfully. "Who can know about a thing like that? I wish Crooked Wolf were here to make medicine for him. Many Bears has done all the right things, I know, but Crooked Wolf was very special and . . . . Sometimes I have thought that maybe the medicine is not so important. Marie told me she doesn't believe it is, but now that I have this baby, I don't want to take chances or leave anything undone. You have heard the talk that a priest is coming to Camas Post next year?"

"Yes."

"A priest has very strong medicine, Marie said, stronger than ours and stronger than any of the other white missionaries'."

"Shy Fawn—"

"If the baby is with us still, in the spring, we could take him to the priest."

166

Her eyes were frightened, questioning, pleading.

"I suppose we could, if it's what you want."

"It's strange, Blake, the way I've been feeling. It frightens me. It's been like this since we went to the post. A woman should not say things like this to her husband, I know, but they are things I cannot tell to my mother or the others."

"What things?"

She was making a robe for the baby's carrying board. She had taken it out of a bag now to work on, trying to see the stitches in the dim, wavering firelight, not looking at him.

"Please don't do that," he said gently. "You'll ruin your eyes. Only tell me about these things."

She went on working. "I don't know how to tell. It is only that I feel afraid. It is as if there is a storm hanging over the world, not of clouds, of snow or rain, you understand. It is a feeling of badness that will happen and I can't know what it is or where it will come from or what to try to do to stop it."

"It was not a good thing that I took you to the post," he said contritely. "I'm sorry. Only try to live as the People have always lived, and not to be afraid."

"When I was a little girl, Crooked Wolf sometimes thought I might have a Gift. Women don't, usually, but some can be very good with medicine. He used to ask me often about my dreams and things like that, and he talked to my father about teaching me some of the secret things. Only then he said that I was too careless, that I laughed at too many things ever to learn well. I was glad because it's a heavy load to be that kind of person. Now, I wonder if I have done wrong, being so careless, if I have displeased my medicine spirits . . . . and you say you have none at all . . . . The Small Coyote must have them, fine strong ones."

"Please put away the work," he said tenderly. "Your eyes are red."

"If you gave him a white name, too, that might be good," she persisted, still refusing to look at him. "Wouldn't that make him more special to the spirits of the whites?"

167

He thought about it and said slowly, "I could call him Alec."

"What is that? Does it mean something?"

"It was the name of a man who was very kind to me when I was a boy."

"A relative?"

"No, a good friend."

"Alec," she said slowly. 'It has a better sound for saying than Blake." But still she was not smiling.

The baby was sleeping. She took him and wrapped him in small elkskin robes for the night.

"At the post," she said softly, with her face bent over the baby, "Marie said that if a white woman came who pleased you, even a little, you would send me away to my people and stay with her. Would you?"

"No."

"She said maybe all white men would do this, even the Red-haired One, even though she is half white and has been married to him by a priest. Marie says it's very important to be married by a priest. Is it?"

"For some people it is."

"Does it mean that if we were married by a priest and a white woman came who pleased you, you would not want so much to go away from me and live with her?"

"I'd never want to do that, Shy Fawn. Being married by a priest only means that he says some words, reads from a book, and writes in another book."

"But maybe it would be a good thing to do. Would he do it for us, that priest?"

"I don't know. Probably not, unless we were baptized first."

"What is that?"

"We can talk about it another time if you want to. Those are heavy logs and I'm tired."

She put wood on the fire and seemed to search for something more to do.

"If you would not want to go with a white woman, how is it that you have hardly touched me?" He could hardly hear the faint, frightened words.

"I didn't know if it was—all right to touch you now," he said gently. "I've never had a wife, before you, nor a son."

"I came here, to your valley, didn't I?"

He reached out to her, but she caught his hand and held it.

"I want to please you. You are my husband and yet sometimes you are very strange to me. Your strangeness makes me feel afraid because I don't know what to do."

He drew her close and put the robes around her. "Am I strange now?"

"My mother says I tease you too much, that you spoil me. Marie says—"

"I sometimes like your teasing. It is for us to decide, how we will be with each other. I don't want you to go to the post, ever again. I want things to go on being just as they are."

She drew back a little to look down at him, the small smile beginning to play around her eyes. She touched him and he drew a breath of pleasure that was very nearly pain.

"Like this, Blake?"

VIII

BLAKE DID NOT STAY long at the post that next spring, only long enough to do some bookwork, order some things, and pick up his trade goods. Connall was angry with him.

"They're going to close out this post soon," he said worriedly. "Rumors of that get stronger every time I hear them. I had in mind that you'd go to Vancouver for me this spring, pick up a great train of goods. I want to be well supplied before the old H. B. withdraws. It looks like a certain thing that we're going to be a part of the Oregon Territory here, of the States."

"What will you do then?"

"I'll do as I've done through the years: trade and farm. Most of the time, it doesn't make so much difference, to the little man, what government he's living under. I only wish they'd get the matter settled and have done with it."

"Well, we couldn't get to Vancouver now anyway, till some of the snow's gone."

"That I know," he said impatiently. "I'd thought you'd stay here until then, doing your job."

"I'm sorry, Connall, but—"

"The hell you're sorry! What hold has that country got on you, aside from the girl, I mean?"

"I have a son now."

"A son, is it! Well, that's news to me. When did this happen?"

"In the fall, the beginning of November."

"Is he a strong boy?"

"Yes."

"You needn't act so bashful about it. These things will happen and I can see from your eyes you think you've done something special. God knows, it took *me* long enough to get a son. But, lad, having the girl and the baby doesn't mean you're tied to that place. Don't you want to see other things at times? What's so special about that one valley?"

"It's—home."

"Blake," he said reprovingly, sadly, "more home than where whites live?"

"Yes."

"Still, lad, you can never change what you are." Connall looked unhappy, worried, He changed the subject. "You've heard we're to have a priest this year?"

"I've heard."

Blake did not look up from the stacks of blankets he was counting, thinking what a strange thing commerce was. Skins had been the only blankets known in this country until a few years back. Now those skins, from mountains and prairie, were traded away happily for these bright-colored blankets, woven on far-away English looms, priced too high and with half the durability of the blankets of the old days, while the skins went to England to make garments for ladies and gentlemen who would find these Indian trade-blankets something to laugh at.

"I don't know where he'll be wanting to put his mission," Connall was saying, "but I think it won't be too far from the post here. He's sent word he wants an interpreter."

"There are twenty less blankets here than the invoices say."

"Oh. Aye, I remember. Some Coeur d'Alenes passed last week. I forgot to write down that they bought some blankets. Would you interpret for the Father?"

"No. What else has been bought that you didn't write down?"

"Never mind that now. Lad, he'll need someone who's good with the languages and that he can trust. Why can't you help him?—for a little time at least."

"Why can't he use an Indian that he saves? Won't he be able to trust his own flock?"

171

"What is it that's made you so bitter about Christianity?"

"I seem to remember some pretty harsh words you had to say about Mr. Prewitt and—"

"This is another matter entirely. A good Father coming here will make the country a better place, for all of us."

"How?"

"Goddam it! you don't need that question answered. You're worse than an Indian. At least there's sometimes a chance of reasoning with an Indian."

"*You* can interpret for him."

"*I* have a good deal to do," Connall said coldly. "Perhaps the best thing for both of us is that you *do* go on back to the Medicine Rock. You're being here only seems to serve to make me angry these days."

Snow still lay deep in the valley. Everyone was restless, talking about beginning the journey, but it could not be done yet. Blake hurried with putting away his trade goods, eager to get back up to the cabin.

"Small Coyote and I are ready," said Shy Fawn. "We can live in the brush shelter with these mats to keep out the cold, while you work."

"Maybe you ought to stay here," he said reluctantly. "It won't be very comfortable living like that."

She went on placidly, getting their things together.

Blake thought he had solved the problem of getting the walls up alone. He could prop and brace some logs to roll other logs up, using a horse or two and rope tackle. He lashed together a rough, heavy sled for hauling stones from the stream bed for fireplace and chimney. Shy Fawn, with the baby on her back, insisted on getting the stones. She had better luck controlling the sled horse than he did.

The walls were as high as Blake's shoulders when Hawk's Shadow and Smiling Fox appeared one bright day. They came up silently behind Blake as he wrestled with a log and Smiling Fox leapt on him with a cry.

"If the Blackfeet came here," said Hawk's Shadow soberly, "or some Crows or Snakes, you would be dead if it were not that your woman is a good guard. Then what good would this cabin thing be to you? And that is not a thing to do to a good horse, harnessing it like that. The poor animal has no pride left. We have come here to save the horse and because you are our brother, no matter what we may think of you. What is it we must do to have this thing finished?"

The roof had to be of the heavy meadow sod, laid on poles. Blake had neither the tools nor the experience to make shingles. Hawk's Shadow and Smiling Fox went away to hunt as soon as the walls and the roof poles were up.

"I won't bring you game," Hawk's Shadow warned testily. "If you were doing something worthwhile, perhaps I would feed you, for the sake of Shy Fawn and the boy—"

"We have the elk," Blake pointed out mildly. He had shot it two days before.

"The People will be leaving soon. You'd better come down and look to your trade goods."

With Shy Fawn's help, he got the roof on. He had been working, when he could, on the chimney, but it was only waist high. There was no chinking in the logs—so much still to do.

"Blake, the village is ready to go," Shy Fawn pointed out nervously. "Tomorrow I think they will be moving down to the Medicine Rock for the ceremony of leaving."

"You go down," he said absently. "Look after our things and go down with them. I'll come before you're out of the Valley."

He longed not to go at all, to stay here and finish the cabin, to see the summer in his little park, but he knew such a suggestion would dismay and bewilder her. It was not the way things were done. She had already come so far in trying to meet and satisfy his strange whims.

On the last day, Blake stood in his doorway and admitted that it was really not much of a cabin. There was so much still unfinished, so much that might never be finished. He had cut a hole for a small window but did not yet know what he would use to cover it with. The floor was dirt and it would have to be left dirt for a while. He shrugged slightly, trying to dismiss such things from his mind. None of that really mattered. He had found the valley and built the cabin. In the fall, he and Shy Fawn and the Small Coyote would live here. On that wall by the fireplace, above where the pots would hang, he would

173

build a shelf for his books. He would put up a lean-to for storing meat and wood and tools. Shy Fawn would weave good mats to cover the floor. He would make furniture as best he could. The village was near enough for easy visiting in most weather. Perhaps she would not be too lonely. And sometimes, on winter nights, they would be here alone, the three of them, quiet and secure, with Never Summer standing silent and majestic outside, with the sky—vast, ever-changing and changeless—bending close above them.

Slowly, he walked as far as the lake edge and looked back. It was not much of a mark he had made on the land, not really. He had never wanted to change it much, only to know that something of his making, something of himself would be here while he was away and when he came back, to set it apart, only a little, as his own.

It was a good year for food. The root and berry crops were lush and buffalo were plentiful. It seemed to Blake that more Indians from west of the mountains made the journey than he had seen before. His trading goods were quickly exhausted.

Hawk's Shadow, with his new rifle, brought in a great deal of game. He was pleased, but said that it was not so satisfying this way, somehow, as with arrows.

"Don't use it," Blake said. "I only brought it to use on hard things, like a buffalo bull. Most of the time, you don't need it, so long as your arrows last."

"I have it now," Hawk's Shadow said. "I should get the good from it."

Beaver Tooth was jealous about the rifle and told Blake sullenly that he might be willing to trade his best horse to Hudson's Bay—not to Blake—for such a gun.

"Though it seems," he said petulantly, "that you could get one for me without need of the horse. A man such as I am should not have to use a musket when one such as Hawk's Shadow has a better gun."

The Blue Mountain band had never been able to persuade any of their missionaries to accompany them on their journey east of the Divide. In fact, several members of the band had stayed behind this year, regretfully, to help with the unaccustomed farmwork. Nez Perce and

Flatheads from the area around Camas Post were sure that next year their priest would be coming with them. Several members from these bands had stayed behind at the post to welcome the priest when he should arrive.

There was little more than brief skirmishing with the enemies that year. The Snakes seemed subdued and large war parties of Crow and Blackfeet had gone south again to harass whites on the Oregon Trail and around the new forts.

"What is this—army?" Red Sky asked Blake.

"White warriors, I suppose you could call them."

"Why would they come here? This is no business of theirs."

"Their people are crossing the country on the trail to the south. They think they must be protected."

"They must not come to our country, neither the settlers nor this army. Our country is nothing to do with them. You will tell me now about this priest. Beaver Tooth and many others say he has strong medicine. What will he do with it?"

"Mostly, I think he will want the people to follow his religion."

"And what is that?"

"Red Sky," he said uneasily, "I don't understand it very well myself. I think I can't explain."

"Were you not taught this white religion as a child?"

"I was taught one kind, but not that of this priest."

"You have no confidence, then, in his medicine?"

"No."

The chief looked at him intently. "What is your religion?"

"I—I don't know. In men, maybe, that they try to live as best they can. In the mountains and the sky . . . ."

"This is what you were taught as a child?"

"No."

They were silent for a time and Red Sky said, troubled, "These are good things you have said, but I think it is not a good thing for a man, alone, to try to make his own religion. Do many whites do this?"

"Not many, I suppose."

"It is better to learn from the old ones who go before us, to take their teachings and use them for our own lives.

Then we are not alone . . . . Perhaps, some day, I will hear what this priest has to say. Things do not feel the same for me without Crooked Wolf. Many Bears has good medicine. He is my cousin and my friend, but he is not Crooked Wolf. I am told of a band of Crows that had a priest. Once after he made medicine for them, they fought the Cheyennes in a great battle, taking many scalps and horses, and no Crow was killed."

"I think, mostly, priests don't approve of battles."

"Of what use is their medicine then?"

Blake met Father Robidou when he and Beaver Tooth and some others went down to the post on their return from the buffalo country. The priest was a round, white-haired little man with a warm smile and kind, intent brown eyes behind glasses. He had brought another, younger priest and some lay brothers in his party. With help from willing Indians, they had laid the foundation of a church at the junction of Camas River with Clark's Fork, and he had plans for a school, a communal farm, and other innovations.

"I've been eager to meet you," he said warmly to Blake, finding him working alone in the office. "Connall and others have told me what strong feelings you have for the Indians, how well you seem to understand their ways. From what I've seen, I believe this country needs more men like you."

"I'm not Catholic," Blake said coldly. The Father had seated himself, and Blake sat down again at the desk, his eyes turning back to his work.

"That's not at all what I meant," Father Robidou said gently. "My chief reason for being here is, of course, salvation, but I would also like to bring to these poor people some of the benefits of civilization."

"What benefits?"

"A better sort of life, one where they can know the joy and satisfaction of work well done, of seeing their crops grow, of living in decent, permanent homes with a church and a school nearby, of sharing Christian fellowship."

"Why?"

The priest stared at him, disconcerted. "I don't understand."

"Neither do I," Blake said angrily. "They've been happy enough for a lot of years, with their lives as they are. Why do so many whites feel compelled to come here and try to make things different?"

"Because it's our duty," said the Father with quiet simplicity. "We have been privileged to know God, to have the blessings of civilization. As Christians, we have a responsibility, a duty to share those things."

"Civilization is all blessings," Blake said derisively.

"Of course it isn't. There are many things wrong with it, but those of us who come here are doubly blessed because we have new ground to work with, both figuratively and literally. We can have the joy of sharing only the things that are good."

"And you decide what those things are to be."

"I try, with guidance. When these people find Christ, this country could be a kind of paradise."

"You really believe that," Blake said, staring at him. "This is the place where rust doth not corrupt nor—whatever the rest of it is."

"I see you know your Bible."

"I did once. I've tried very hard to forget most of it."

"What has made you so bitter?"

"People. Good Christian white people."

"Would you care to talk about it?"

"I would not."

There was a silence. Blake was writing columns in the ledger.

"I truly want to do good here," the priest said quietly, earnestly. "Perhaps I am vain in that my ideas, my hopes are too large . . . . Your French is very good."

Blake said nothing. Actually, he was having difficulty with the French. These days, when he was upset in any way, both French and English were coming hard for him.

"I'm told that you understand the languages of all the tribes in this part of the country. I'm beginning to get a little knowledge of the Flathead tongue. I hope to make a written language of it some day. I've heard about the people you live among, that they've had very little in the way of white influence. Do you think they would let me visit in their valley?"

"I don't know." He did not look up.

"It would be of great interest to me to be able to come to know them."

"So you could save their souls."

"That is always my first concern, but I am something of a student, too, when I have the time. I would like, God willing, some day to make a history of some group in the area and it would be a great help to have one to study that has not already been too much influenced and changed by the whites."

"I think the word is corrupted."

"Yes, I'm afraid you're right, generally speaking," he said sadly.

"You could study them and then do all you could to bring changes—the *right* changes, of course."

"Changes must come," the priest said gently. "They began long before you or I came here. Yes, I would like to see them have access to the good things and I hope that I can ease the—revolution for them, a little."

"With prayers."

"It can't hurt, can it, my boy, to help them come to know a higher power? One who has strength and love and patience to help through the bad times, the adjustments?"

"Why must there be an adjustment?" he cried. "Why in hell can't they be left alone?"

"Because things are never like that. The outside *will* come in. And, as you say, of course, because of Hell . . . . Many of these Indians have already been exposed to the very worst in whites, and only to that. Wherever it's possible, they must have opportunity to know and share the better aspects."

"What is better," Blake cried, "about submission and docility?"

"It's what God asks of all of us."

"Oh, for Christ's sake!" he said in helpless frustration.

The priest nodded, with a gentle smile. "Exactly . . . . It's quite clear you have no liking for me or for anything I stand for but I must tell you that I find you a very interesting young man. I think we could find a great many things to discuss."

"I can't think what they would be," he said coldly.

"You're refreshing to me. I suspect you have an excellent education and that you have done a great deal of thinking for yourself. I am held in reverence here and that is not always a comfortable position to be in . . . . What do *you* reverence?"

"Freedom," he said immediately, curtly. "I'm very busy, Father—"

"Yes, I see that you are . . . And yet you are the one who has begun taking trade goods to your Medicine Rock People. I'm told you brought your wife here last spring and that some of the People have come here with you now. Are you not trying to bring changes to them?"

"Only those that might help to—"

"And that is what I hope to do, to help."

"It's not the same at all."

"Ah. It never is, is it?"

"I'm not trying to convert anyone. Every person has a right to—find his own way."

"Just so. Each person must give what he is able to give and those to whom he gives must take what they get as they see it. We are, each of us, very much alone at times, but we go on reaching out to others. Some of us are led to try to help others as they seek their way. If we truly feel that we have been given this privilege of trying to help, would we not be wrong, sinners, to shirk our duty?"

Blake had no answer. He felt battered, beaten down, a little ill. He knew what he believed to be right, but it would never change anyone, certainly not a priest.

"You think I'm a pompous, bigoted fool," Father Robidou said softly, with no malice. "I can understand that very well. I hope that you will come to understand that I am doing what I feel I must. I have a great love and respect for these people."

"Then you *do* think they're people," he said wearily. Why could he not be left alone? Why did he keep making these comments of his own?

The priest was staring at him. "People? Of course I—"

Connall came in then, jolly, a little blustering, to take the Father away to dinner.

"I expect you were being ungracious to the Father," he said severely to Blake later in the day.

"The Father is a—"

"Now, lad, we'll have none of that. There are some things I need to talk to you about. Are you ready now to make that trip to Vancouver?"

"I can't, Connall."

"And why not this time? The fall work here is nearly done. You've had your summer's trading and your trip to the buffalo country."

"I have other things to do. I want to go home."

"What is it you're hiding from, up there in the Medicine Rock?"

"Nothing. It's where I like to be, where I'm myself, more than anywhere in the world has ever been."

"Well, then, I think you're not very secure about being yourself. Being yourself comes mostly from inside, you know. When a man's secure of himself, he can be sure about it wherever he is. He has no need to be buttressed by things from outside, such as running off to some certain place."

Blake was very tired. He longed for his little valley, for Shy Fawn and the boy, for the peace of simply being still and looking up at the mountain, with a yearning that was very nearly physical pain.

"All right," Connall said, sighing, "never mind about Vancouver. I'd like to send a clerk down there, but I suppose Emmett and the others can manage it. Has he told you how well we've done, trading down on the Trail this year? We're not going to Hall next year, but farther east; Laramie, I think. That is, if the Indian troubles can be settled down. I can't spare men enough to guard a herd through that country if the Blackfeet's hearts are bad. I wish to God they'd settle back to fighting the people who've always been their enemies. The Oregon Trail isn't even through Blackfoot country.

"And that's another thing, Blake," he said uneasily. "Your friend Beaver Tooth has a good Hawken rifle. He says you sold it to him. You know I can't stand for that."

"He paid a good price, what the white trappers have to pay, some prime otter and—"

"Goddam it! You know that's not what I'm talking about."

"You trade guns to the Indians, have done for years," he said doggedly.

180

"Of course I trade guns to the Indians, muskets, as you very well know. We can't have them getting those good rifles."

"I saw some Snakes with Hawkens this season."

"Well, that's the stupidity of some American trader, besides yourself. We've given them muskets, made hunting that much easier—"

"You've *given* them nothing and neither has any other white, ever. And don't forget that with all this generosity, you've also made it a little easier for them to kill one another off, so why not go all the way, with rifles, and have it over?"

"You know as well as anyone that having rifles won't do for them." Connall was trying to be patient. There was something of sadness, mixed with the anger and impatience in his blue eyes. "I had thought, with H. B. pulling out, that you and I might think of going into business together. I think we might have had a damn good arrangement except that you've no sense. You'll trade no more rifles out of this post to Indians."

He left and Blake began immediately to get his things together, though he had intended to stay two or three more days. He had had Connall's blacksmith make a crane for his fireplace, and the things he had ordered in the spring had come in from the east. Included among these things were a number of books. As he packed them, he let his mind be distracted, soothed, by the thought of the cabin on winter nights.

While he was loading his horses, one of the new "Mission Indians" brought him a package from Father Robidou. Irritably, Blake opened it and found to his surprise that it contained, not religious books as he had supposed, but a beautifully bound set of Shakespeare. He was touched, not wanting to be. Surely such books had meant a great deal to the priest. He had fully intended, when he took the package, to send it straight back as soon as he had looked inside, but he found, to his great frustration, that he could not bring himself to do so. He had never seen a set like this, not even in Etienne St. Croix's library, never had the opportunity for so much exposure to the English bard. He could read them, over the winter, he told himself, while the priest would be too busy saving

181

souls to look at them. He would give them excellent care and return them in the spring.

Gradually, the tension of the anger and arguments and uneasiness from the post left Blake as he was thoroughly caught up again in work on the cabin. He showed Shy Fawn how to chink the logs with mud and moss and she did the job well. He finished the fireplace and chimney and felt reasonably pleased with the work. They banked dirt around the lower part of the walls, as was done with lodges, to keep out the winter cold. Blake made a rough frame for a bed and laced it with ropes Shy Fawn had woven. She was uneasy about the bed.

"I've never slept in a thing like this with space under me," she said dubiously, laying fresh-dried grass for a mattress. "Suppose it should fall down."

"My wife has woven the ropes," Blake said with sober conviction. "They'll never break."

She glanced up at him with her little mischievous smile. "No matter what we do with this bed?"

"No matter what."

He made some furniture, crude, but the best he could manage with the tools he had, some shelves, a heavy table of split logs, some stools that were little more than slightly shaped sections of log. Both he and Shy Fawn preferred to lie on the bed for relaxation, as they had done in the lodge, with woven willow backrests to lean against. Blake had brought some oiled paper to cover the window—there was no glass to be had in this part of the country. It let in some light, but it also let in too much of a draft when the weather grew very cold, so they had to hang a skin over it. The floor was covered with Shy Fawn's good reed mats and with skins. Shy Fawn became inordinately proud of the fireplace, of the easy work it made of cooking, with its crane, the Dutch oven, the new pots and kettles, though she did not think it provided quite so much heat as did the central fire of a lodge.

At the end of November, Blake went hunting with several other men. They shot a great many deer and elk. When he stopped at the village for his family, he suggested to Shy Fawn that they might give a feast up in their valley, a small feast.

182

Red Sky's family came, and Many Bears' and some others. The cabin seemed packed with chattering women, looking into everything. Red Sky put his head in only briefly and turned back outside again, looking puzzled and uneasy.

They had guests often, when the weather was not too cold for moving around. Smiling Fox and Cricket, in particular, liked to come and stay with them. Blake began teaching the children to read. It was a slow process, not because they were not good learners, but because there was a delay, seemingly at every other written word, while he tried to explain meanings.

They were not alone at the cabin often enough to please him, but he told himself that there was a lifetime ahead for those times, that not only Shy Fawn and Small Coyote were his family, but all the rest of the band. Shy Fawn was always delighted to have guests and, with a pride that she tried hard to keep within reasonable bounds, to show off her things to them. She was still a little bewildered by this kind of life, but she made the very most of the parts of it that pleased her.

Small Coyote was strong and lusty as his first birthday came and went. His mother's pride in him was a great fierce thing.

"Why do you never talk to him in English?" she asked Blake. "Don't you think he is smart enough to learn two languages?"

"One language is enough when he's not even talking in one yet."

"Of course he's talking. He says many words. It is only that you don't understand . . . . And you teach English to Smiling Fox and Cricket and to whoever else asks you."

"They are old enough to ask. When Small Coyote is old enough, if he wants to, he can learn."

"And you never call him Alec."

"If he wants to be called Alec when he's older . . . ."

"That's not the way to bring up a child," she said severely, "to leave him to make up his own mind about everything. Children are not always wise enough to know what are the things they should do. Even the Small Coyote is not that wise.

183

"Blake, Beaver Tooth has told us much about the priest. He thinks he has great medicine."

"Beaver Tooth talks a great deal."

"He saw him, at the post, baptizing children. Is this not a good thing?"

"Maybe, Shy Fawn, if people believe it is good."

"Do you know about the places called Heaven and Hell?"

"I know what I've been told."

"Beaver Tooth says those places are written about in the priest's book."

"Yes."

"Have you read this book?"

"Yes."

She looked at him with a little awe. He said quickly, "The book is not just for priests. Others may read it."

"But I think you don't believe the things it says."

"Some of them, no."

"Is not everything that is written down in a book a true thing?"

"No."

"How can that be?"

"Because things that are written down in books have been written there by people. People think differently. They make mistakes and they are not always truthful."

"We have been taught, always, that to lie to one's own people is the worst thing one can do."

"That may be so, but still, people lie."

"Beaver Tooth says the priest says his great medicine book was written by God, that this God is a mightier spirit than all the others put together. Is this so?"

"Some think it is."

"Blake," she said uneasily, "you will *not* answer my questions. Why must you make things so difficult? Either a thing is so or it is not so."

"No," he said slowly, "a thing may be a great truth for one person and nothing at all for another."

"How can that be? I think you don't believe a thing like that yourself. You look very troubled."

"Only because—ideas are very hard to explain."

"What is this word 'ideas'? What does it mean?"

"Shy Fawn, let's not talk about these things anymore now. Let's just be as we are and—"

"But when I hear of these new things, the kind of things Beaver Tooth is saying and that I am trying to get you to tell me about, I am no longer sure who I am. It makes me wonder about some of the old things . . . ."

"Please don't," he said earnestly. "Only be Shy Fawn, daughter of Red Sky and my wife."

She smiled a little to herself and was silent for a while, then she said in a lighter tone, "I think the best thing we might do for the Small Coyote is to make him some brothers and sisters. If we are going to live here, far from the village, he should not be a child alone."

"Well, no. Probably not."

"My mother and Little Rain ask me if something is wrong that we have no more babies coming yet."

"And what do you tell them?" he asked resignedly.

"That we try, very often." She giggled. "Don't look angry, my husband. Do you think they don't already know it is like that with a man and a woman?"

During their evenings alone, she often told stories or sang songs of the great heroes of the People, of Coyote, Fox, Eagle, and Beaver, and of a few Men who had become legends. While she talked or sang, her hands were always busy with some work.

Blake often worked on something for the cabin, and sometimes he drew pictures, usually of Shy Fawn. She was a little embarrassed by these pictures, and also tremendously pleased. He read the books he had brought. In the reading, they seemed fewer than they had in the hauling up to the valley.

Sometimes, Shy Fawn asked him to read to her and she would watch him reading with an awe that had a little of fear in it. He found the translation almost impossible and it made him uncomfortable, having her watch him like that. He was always relieved that she lost interest quickly. There was the same situation when she asked him to tell stories or sing songs. She felt no awe about spoken words but he could never finish a sentence because he had to stop to try to explain some different concept. He was glad that she soon grew restless or impatient or brought up some other topic. It seemed that the more she asked him

185

about things and he tried to explain them, the less settled grew their lives.

One night when they had been through a particularly harrowing few moments of trying to come to grips with what he was reading, which happened to be an account of the decline of Rome, she shrugged away her own puzzlement, smiled her clever little smile and said, "I think, when we are wondering and trying to understand such things, the best thing we could do is go to bed. It is very cold tonight. I want very much to lie close to you, in your arms, and perhaps to think about brothers and sisters for Coyote while the wind blows outside."

IX

ON A COLD, STILL, CLEAR DAY which Blake judged to be mid-January, Father Robidou came to the Medicine Rock. Beaver Tooth had persuaded Red Sky and the others to allow the priest and the Flatheads with him to come in and stay at the village. Hearing of the visitors, Shy Fawn wanted to go down. She saw Blake's displeasure but he could not bring himself to ask her not to go. She was away for several days and when she came back, the priest was with her.

"I wanted the Father to see our cabin," she told him in a small, frightened voice. She felt such pride in her husband and in their place, but Blake's frown frightened her. "I will get water now, for the cooking."

Blake had just brought water, she could see it there, but she had displeased him. Perhaps it would be all right if she quickly left the men alone. They stood outside the cabin, Father Robidou looking around the little valley with appreciation.

"This is a beautiful place," he said quietly, after a while. "Your wife is very proud of the cabin, of everything. May I look inside?"

Saying nothing, Blake held aside the skins that covered the door. The priest looked about the dim cabin, standing in the doorway. Finally, he drew back saying, "It's an idyllic place. You are a fortunate man . . . . Truly, Blake, I did not know it would upset you to have me come here. I have been in the village for several days and have so much enjoyed looking around at everything. Shy Fawn asked if I would care to see your home. I hoped we might be friends."

"Why?"

"Because I think I like you. There aren't many people in this country with whom I feel I can discuss Shakespeare and such things."

"I hope you'll take your books back with you now."

"The books are yours. Books are things to be shared, passed on. Will you tell me what it is, my boy? Is it me, myself? Is it that I am a priest?"

"I only want to be left alone, as I am."

"I am not trying to take that from you. I think you are not very secure in it, though, or you would not need to be so defensive . . . . Is it that you want nothing to do with any whites?"

"Something like that."

"Yet you can't change yourself, can you?" he said gently. "No matter how much you want to *be* an Indian, you are still white, with a white background and white thoughts. Are you ashamed of that? of things such as knowing Shakespeare?"

"I don't want to be troubled," he said without thinking. "I don't want decisions to make or . . . ."

"Yet you keep reading. I saw that you have several fine books."

"That means nothing."

"Of course it means something. It means that you are thinking. No one can read books like those I saw on your shelf without thinking . . . . Do you think you are being fair? Don't you feel some responsibility here? Don't get angry, please. Only listen to me for a moment. You are a thinking, well-educated young man. I think you feel you owe something to your family, your adopted people, something more than simply taking your share in providing food and shelter. These things are with you, the knowledge, the thought. You can't escape them and with them comes responsibility.

"Little Rain has told me how troubled your wife is about many things. Shy Fawn has not spoken to me about these things, but I think you must know about them. Isn't there a great deal you could help her to clarify in her mind? And couldn't you help the others, too? *I* believe you want to help. The chief himself is very troubled . . . ."

"I should help them to accept your religion. Is that what you mean?"

"You are oversimplifying and I'm sure you know you are. I *can* think of things other than my religion. You could help them to understand a great many of the things that are new in their country."

"There are many things *I* don't understand and there's a great deal I don't want them to try to understand."

"None of us comes near to understanding everything, but I think your attitude toward the People is a very selfish one. You claim you want the Indians' lot bettered, yet it must be done only in ways that serve your own purposes, not necessarily for the greater, common good."

"I'd like you to go, Father. I think we have nothing, really, to say to each other."

The priest was silent for a little, looking out over the Medicine Rock Valley and up at the mountain. Then he said, with a gentleness and concern that were far more threatening to Blake than an angry harangue would have been, "I have heard a great deal about you, from Connall MacPheirson and other whites, from the People here. I've told you before that you interest me. I have thought of you often. It seems to me that you are a young man fighting battles within himself. All of us must do this at times. I think you are truly trying to know who you are, how you fit into things, where you will belong in the scheme of these changes that are coming to this country you love. Sometimes, when one is going through such a period of inner upheaval, it helps to put things into words, to talk of them with one whose concepts about life may not be altogether different from yours. You have no such person to talk with thus, here, I think. You would not care to talk with me? I promise you, religion would not enter into the conversation."

Blake said nothing. He was afraid of this man who seemed to know too much.

"Then," said Father Robidou quietly, sadly, "I have one more question to ask you, a commission, really. We have set up a chapel in one of the lodges in the village. Tomorrow, I will hold a mass there and baptize some of

189

the young children. Several of the People will come. Your wife would like to be there, but she won't come without you."

"No."

"Do you not believe in God at all, Blake?"

"I've told you, we have nothing to talk about." Why couldn't he just tell the man to go to hell, to get out of his valley?

"If you *were* to come," he persisted with that frightening, inexorable gentleness, "it would give strength to the people who are beginning to believe. I have seen that they laugh at you, ridicule your ways, but what you do, how you seem to see things, is very important to these people."

"I won't come."

"I think you know that, whatever your own convictions, however you have come to them, you do wrong to stand in the way of the beliefs of others. Shy Fawn would like your son to be baptized."

"My son is of the Medicine Rock People," Blake said fiercely. "When he is old enough, he will have his medicine dreams. That can be his religion if he thinks he needs one."

"Your wife feels, though, that it is wise to have the best of all she can find for the boy. You don't agree with that?"

Blake looked away from him, confusion making his face burn. It was a little like trying to stand up and argue with his grandfather. He hadn't a chance, yet he could not stop himself from trying to answer.

"If a thing *is* best, then I . . . "

"Are you wise enough, always, to know what the best things are?"

This time he made no answer.

"Are you not at all concerned about the safety of the boy's soul?"

He said savagely, "I'm not interested in putting thoughts of guilt and vengeance and eternal damnation into anyone's mind. *That* is the unforgivable sin. It is the thing people do to their children that binds and strangles their thinking, their being . . . . I'll ask you again, Father, to go. Don't come here again."

"Yes, I'm going," said the priest thoughtfully. "I apologize for adding to your disturbance. Perhaps I'll see you some time during the spring and summer. I'll be going with my band of Flatheads for the buffalo hunting. Meantime, Blake, I'll pray for you."

Blake hardly spoke to Shy Fawn through the rest of the day. He went out to cut wood they did not need, from trees that were frozen and dangerous to be chopping at. She trembled at her work and was cross with Small Coyote when there was no need to be. When her husband came in, perhaps he was going to tell her to go away, back to the village. How could she live if she did not live with him?

He ate little that night and she was too frightened to urge him or to ask if something seemed wrong with the food. He sat and stared into the fire, not speaking. She wanted to creep into bed and hide under the robes, but perhaps he would tell her to go away if she went to the bed. Small Coyote slept. She sat in the shadows, her hands trembling as she tried to mend some leggings. She could not really see the work.

"You can have the boy baptized," Blake said. He spoke quietly, levelly, but his voice had startled her.

"Blake, I have made you very angry. I have displeased you. I—I see now how unimportant these other things are, beside your anger. I am a stupid woman. It is a thing the village is talking about, how the spirits of their children must not go to this place called Hell if they can prevent it, and I thought it would be a good thing for the Small Coyote. But you are so much wiser—"

"Don't do that," he said vehemently. "I don't want you to be humble. You're as capable of thinking as I am."

"I did not know your heart was so bad toward the priest and the things he talks about. I will never talk of these things again."

"But you'll always wonder," he said gently. "I want you to take Coyote down tomorrow and put your mind at ease about this."

"No, not if my husband—"

"Stop it, Shy Fawn. There are two of us here, not just one. You have as much right as I to make decisions about the boy. In fact, I think you are better at it than I."

"Blake, it gives me pain to hear you talk like this."

She was near tears. They sounded in her voice.

"I *want* to understand," she insisted. "Something troubles you very much. It is here in the cabin with us. I can feel it."

"When I was a boy," he said slowly, not looking at her, "I was told every day that I was bad and evil. A part of the reason for this was that my grandparents, who raised me, believed very strongly in one kind of white religion and they twisted its teachings to fit their own purposes. I believed in that religion, too, then, because it was what I had been taught. I believed there was a great deal of evil in me, that I could never be pleasing to anyone. I was afraid of hell. Sometimes I had nightmares about it . . . ."

"You could not have been bad," she said in wonder.

"Probably, I was no better or no worse than most other boys, but *they* believed I was and *I* believed it. Now—I don't believe it—so much. I feel that I was tricked, cheated, made unhappy by things that were not altogether true . . . . but religion doesn't have to be like that. It *can* be a very good thing, for some people, if they do not twist it and let it become too all important. I couldn't see Small Coyote tied up by it, or by anything else, and made afraid the way it was for me. I want him to be free of things such as that. He can believe in God or in whatever he chooses, but I want him to have choices, to believe, too, in himself, in the earth and the sky . . . ."

"In the mountain?" she asked softly. "In Never Summer? Sometimes I see you looking at Never Summer as if he were speaking to you . . . . Does he speak to you, Blake?"

"I don't . . . . in a way, he has seemed to speak sometimes . . . ."

She looked at him with awe. "My medicine spirit is only the deer . . . . you have the mountain."

"Shy Fawn, it's not—"

"Will you teach this to Coyote?"

"I can't teach it to him. You know that whatever he finds of this kind, he must find for himself."

"Yes," she said slowly, "but . . . ."

"So take him down tomorrow and let him have Father Robidou's blessing. You are right, it will be a good thing to have. I'm sorry for being unreasonable."

"You were very angry," she said in soft admiration. "You have a great and most fierce anger. I have not seen you like that before. And now that I understand, a little, I don't feel the need to take Coyote to the priest. He has you for his father and you are most wonderful. Don't frown again, my husband. This is a true thing and I—I love you."

He smiled, his eyes blurring. "That is what a mother says to her child," he said, teasing her, his voice unsteady.

She began to smile. "No, it's not the same at all. If you come with me now into this bed, I'll show you that it is not the same. Also, I'm very cold."

"And so," said Hawk's Shadow happily, smugly, "while most of our enemies were passing the pipe in council with most of our friends, we went down to that big camp some of the Blackfeet have to the south and stole a large number of horses."

"I really wish you hadn't done that," Blake said dryly, wearily.

There had been trouble all through the buffalo hunting. Hawk's Shadow's small party had caught up with the main camps only now, when they were already moving out on the journey back over the mountains.

"Why not?" asked Hawk's Shadow, surprised, exasperated. "We did nothing wrong. Some of them are pretty good horses. Come and look at them. You should have been with us. We didn't even kill anybody, though we could have, or we could have taken a lot of prisoners. Many of the Blackfoot men were at the council. It might be good to have one of those Blackfoot women for a wife. It would be an interesting thing to tame one of those women, to try to make her become one of us . . . . I don't understand, anyway, why you sat in that council. My father was there only to see what would happen. I know *he* promised no peace with Blackfeet or Snakes or Crows. Did you go to hear Beaver Tooth talk? I am told he talked a great deal."

"You know that council was the idea of the whites, the army, the traders, the missionaries."

"I know this," Hawk's Shadow said. "We all know this. They think that if they can get our enemies to come north here to fight or council or whatever, the white trail to the south will be safe. It would be better for them if we all destroyed each other but it sounds better to say we are having a peace council. But you are not one of those whites. Why did you go? Did you speak?"

"I only translated. Red Sky asked me to do that."

"The priest asked you also, and the Red-haired One and the army. Did you tell everybody what everybody was saying? I am told that most of them said there would be peace, the Flatheads and others, even some Nez Perce. They are like dogs, panting to do as the whites tell them, so that, maybe, they will be thrown a bone. I know that Beaver Tooth wanted to agree with them. He says we will all do better with such a peace."

"Well, I think the whole thing, for whatever it was worth in the first place, has been shot to hell now, with your horse stealing."

"Little Rain tells me that, in the priest's book, it says that stealing is very wicked. We did not steal those horses, you know. We took only what belongs to us. The Blackfeet have often stolen horses from our people. It was time we went and took back the colts of those horses that were ours. You should have been with us. Come on, now. We're going to have some races."

They crossed over the Divide, still several bands traveling together, with the young men who shared Hawk's Shadow's views still celebrating their victory. One night as they were playing the hand game—Blake had become sought after for the game because, as Red Sky kept telling him, he always looked so guilty that the other team felt sure it was a pretense—a group of exhausted Cayuses came into camp with word that a party of Blackfeet was behind them.

The people made ready for battle. The men went back a little, to shield the camp, and waited. They had time, then, to paint themselves and their horses, to sing their songs, to get properly ready for war. In the morning, when the Blackfeet had not come, they rode back to find them.

It was a large party, with women and children, not wildly eager for a fight, but ready. They fought with taunts and songs and wild riding. Several people were

194

killed on both sides. The people from west of the mountains took some scalps and some prisoners and withdrew.

Only two men from the Medicine Rock band had been killed and they would have considered themselves very fortunate except that Red Sky had a musket ball through his shoulder. He lost a great deal of blood before they could get the bleeding stopped and his arm hung stiff and useless.

The women and children and the few men who had been left with them had moved the main camp to a place of good defense and relative safety and they decided to stay there for a while, to hold a war and scalp dance. It had been a long while since they had had scalps and prisoners and the immediate need for battle readiness, all at once.

Blake was appalled by the dance. The prisoners were forced to stand in the midst of four lines of people, holding the fresh scalps of their friends and relations aloft on poles. The two inner lines of dancers were made up entirely of women, who took immense satisfaction in jeering at the prisoners, hitting them, jabbing them with sticks as they moved back and forth past them. The outer lines, made up of the men, simply danced and looked on, finding vast pleasure vicariously.

Blake went away into the darkness. Shy Fawn, bringing Small Coyote with her, found him eventually.

"Come back to camp," she said urgently. "It's not safe to be so far from the others here. The Blackfeet may come."

"I don't want to see what they're doing."

"No one will be killed. I know you do not like it so I did not dance and I have brought Coyote so he will not see, but we can't stay out here so far. Besides, the priest has come in with some Flatheads and he is asking for you."

What Blake wanted, desperately, was to take his family and go on west, but it would have been a stupid, foolhardy thing to do.

"Can't you stop this?" asked Father Robidou. He looked ill.

"It's not my place to try. This is the way things have always been done."

195

"You *want* to see those people tortured?"

"I've tried not to look."

"Don't you have any feeling? any humanity?"

"Father, I don't like what's happening here, but I'm not a world reformer. Chief Growing Tree is here, of the Flatheads. I'm told he's a convert of yours. Maybe he has some influence."

"Will you translate for me if I talk to them?"

"No."

"Why not?" It was a cry of anguish.

"I want to be one of the People. I don't agree with all they do, but this is very important to them. I won't show that kind of disapproval. You know the language. You don't need anyone to translate."

"Can't you see how upset I am? I can't think in their language this way, with all this noise . . . . You won't do *any*thing?"

"No."

Haltingly, the priest tried to stop the dance. Some of the people became very hostile. This dance, they said curtly, would go on several hours a day for five of six days, if they were left alone that long by the Blackfeet. It was good medicine. They had vengeance to take and they needed the strength that the ceremony gave them. Others, trying to reassure the priest, told him that the prisoners were not being hurt much, that they would be cared for and well treated between the sessions of dancing. They tried to spur his interest by pointing out that the prisoners were behaving quite admirably—for Blackfeet.

By the second night, Father Robidou had talked with enough of his converts and prospective converts, made them uneasy enough so that there was sufficient dissension and criticism to spoil the pleasure of the dance. They moved on, many of them feeling angry and cheated.

There was no more trouble. The bands began to drop off, one at a time, going home.

"It will be good to be back at the cabin," Shy Fawn murmured one night. They had reached the Camas and were now only two days' journey from the valley of the Medicine Rock. "You are right, my husband. Sometimes it is good to have a place that is only ours. Before the winter is over, there will be another baby."

On the last morning before they reached the Valley, they were attacked. The party of Blackfeet was not a large one. They fired some bullets and some arrows among the Medicine Rock People and withdrew, taunting them unmercifully.

"Take a good party," Red Sky said to Hawk's Shadow and the others. "We need only a few men here to guard the women into the valley. Chase them back over the mountains if you can't kill them all. It is time an end was put to this."

The chief looked thin and tired. His arm, though it had been treated in several different ways, was still useless.

"I think I won't ride with you," he said heavily. "It might only slow your going."

"I can look after all our things," Shy Fawn said to Blake under the noise. "I will sing my song to the deer spirit for you."

He wanted desperately not to go with the war party.

"I don't like the feel of this," Hawk's Shadow said worriedly as they rode off to the west, following the raiders. "They should be running to the east or the north and there should be more of them. Perhaps they will try to lead us into an ambush by a larger party of their people. I don't like it that so many of us ride away from the People this way."

'They will be safe in the valley," said Beaver Tooth. "No one can harm them when they are in there with the canyon guarded."

"I thought you had become a man of peace," Hawk's Shadow said scornfully, a little absently because he was trying to understand what the Blackfeet had in mind.

"As Red Sky says, this thing must be finished. All the men want to go and have this last fight before it is winter and before we decide to change our ways. Is it that Hawk's Shadow is afraid?"

"Hawk's Shadow fears nothing," he said fiercely. "I only want to use good thinking and I do not understand these Blackfeet."

Riding hard, skirmishing now and then as they went, they stayed wary of ambush, but they were out in the open valley of the Camas. After a time, the party of Blackfeet turned north, then back to the east. Blake and

Hawk's Shadow, coming to the realization at the same moment, stared at each other in horror through the dust.

"Ride quickly!" Hawk's Shadow cried to the men. "Back to the Medicine Rock! Today, we have all been fools."

The larger party of Blackfeet had raided the band as soon as the Medicine Rock men had been led away. Wailing from the village came out to meet the returning warriors. Owl Woman and Little Rain came miserably to Blake and Hawk's Shadow. Red Sky was dead. Shy Fawn was dead.

The Blackfeet had swept down on them just as the People, with their long file of horses, were about to enter the canyon. Red Sky had shouted to the women to go on into the canyon while he and the few other men who had stayed behind held off the enemy. As they ran, Shy Fawn remembered that there was a musket on one of their pack horses.

"My father can't use his arm," she had cried to her mother. "There are not enough men back there. I will take this other gun to Red Sky. Blake my husband has taught me to use this musket. I can shoot Blackfeet."

"She was as brave as any warrior," said Owl Woman with fierce pride and began to wail again.

Twenty men of the Medicine Rock People had been killed and scalped, twenty men and Shy Fawn. Blackfoot corpses were scattered among them in the rocks, the trampled brush, and grass. Blake could not look at any of them. He rode dazedly up into the valley to help catch fresh horses for the warriors to ride.

"Your son lives," Owl Woman reminded him suddenly when they were ready to leave. "Will you not look at the boy, or speak to him before you go?"

Blake pulled his arm away from her and swung up onto the mare that had been given him when he became Red Sky's son.

"They are going to the pass on the trail we always use," Hawk's Shadow said stonily when they had followed the clear trail of many horses a little way down the Camas. "That small party that led us away will join them up there somewhere. There is another pass, on this side of that one, there to the south, much harder, but if we ride as hard as we can and use that trail, we can be across the range before them. If we get there first, there is a place I know where we can wait and we can kill them all. We will turn east here and go straight up into the mountains."

Blake turned his horse with the others', but Hawk's Shadow, trembling with his own loss and anger, kept glancing apprehensively at his friend's hard, taut face. Did he really know anything that was happening now, or had his true consciousness ended when he had stood, for that brief moment, looking down on Shy Fawn's battered little body?

They rode through the night. There was moonlight and they knew the Blackfeet would be riding. Somewhere on the steep, dry, torturous trail, the mare West Wind fell, groaning. Cursing, hardly knowing what he did, Blake took his gear from her, put it on a spare horse, and went on, to kill the animals who had done those things to his wife, to the good man who had become his father.

"They have always been our enemies," Shy Fawn had said to him, that night of the scalp dance. "They are cruel without need, vicious people. They hate us."

"This kind of thing is a game more than anything else," Blake had tried to soothe Father Robidou.

He was so benumbed now, so ill with pain and fury, that he did not see the others around him, did not hear their war songs. He had the good Hawken rifle. He had a knife.

They reached the narrow defile Hawk's Shadow had had in mind. They came to it in mid-morning of the second day and they were there, ready, when the Blackfeet came down. They were heavily outnumbered now, but they had the advantage of surprise, of ambush.

Blake lay behind a rock and tried to keep the sweat out of his eyes, taking careful, deliberate aim so long as he had powder. He had traded away too much of his powder on the journey, but he had meant to go down to the post as soon as the people were settled in the Valley, to get ammunition and other things. Shy Fawn had wanted some cloth and needles.

He stood up and ran down into the midst of the fighting. The Blackfeet were almost all off their horses, seeking good cover. With his knife, Blake caught a tall, naked man in the chest. The Medcine Rock men were swooping down around him, both groups singing their songs of war and death, shouting their inexorable defiance. Blake did not hear them. He pulled out his knife from the man's chest, not feeling the knife of another gash his arm.

The Blackfoot he had stabbed had fallen to the ground, but he was not dead, still conscious, with blood gushing from the wound. Staggering, dazed with rage, Blake bent and took the scalp lock, sticky with bear grease and paint, into his right hand, jerking the man's head up to meet his left hand, holding the knife. He made the circular motion, feeling the bone as the knife hit it, only he was not aware of that at the time. This was the one who had killed her; Blake did not doubt it for a moment, there in the midst of that madness, the man for whom simply killing her had not been enough. For an instant, he looked at the face, slack now. He did not know he looked at it, but later he could remember every line.

He held the scalp dazedly. Both his hands were covered with the warm blood of the Blackfoot. He had to turn, then, to face a screaming attacker with a war club. Perhaps, after all, he thought, maddened, *this* was the one who had . . .

"We lost six men," Hawk's Shadow said wearily.

They were riding back toward the west, had been riding for a long while, exhausted, silent for the most part. Hawk's Shadow had brought his horse beside Blake's. It was important, he thought, that Blake should speak to him now, should be roused somehow to full awareness again.

"I saw you take one scalp. Were there others?"

Blake looked at him, then down at his own hands, still bloody, holding the reins.

"I don't know."

"Where is that one?"

"I don't know."

"This will not be so hard, my brother, when some days have passed. We will go back to the Valley and bury them and—"

"I'm not going back." His voice was dull, toneless, his eyes filmed with exhaustion, as were Hawk's Shadow's.

"It is not good for a man to mourn alone," Hawk's Shadow said with awkward concern. "You will go to the post, maybe, for a while, and then—"

"No. Not the post."

"We will stop at the stream down there and bind up your wrist. You have lost much blood and you look very white. You would not let us touch it before. Do you remember?"

Blake looked down at his arm, seeing the knife cut, feeling nothing.

"It's not bleeding now. It doesn't hurt."

After a silence, Hawk's Shadow said hesitantly, "Death is always with us. It is another part of living . . . . If you think you must go away for a time, to learn to live with it, then know that the Small Coyote will be my son until you come back."

At the river, where their way turned upstream, Blake rode on west, saying nothing, hardly aware that he had left them.

"He should not be alone," said Storm Coming Out Of The East. "There may yet be some Blackfeet. I know that he has no powder for his rifle."

"We will have to let him go," Hawk's Shadow said heavily. "I think he is wishing now that there were more Blackfeet, that they would kill him too."

Blake crossed the valley and began the long climb up the western range. He went on, scarcely conscious, until his exhausted horse stopped, its muzzle drooping into the water of a small stream. Blake slid down painfully and lay in the water. It was cold.

He felt the coldness and thought of Shy Fawn, with him, bathing in the lake in the little valley. He felt more than the water then. The numbness, the fury, the horror drained out of him and into the vacuum left by those protective feelings rushed pain, a pain so intense that he gasped for breath, moaning, writhing in the water.

After a long time, he was able to drag himself from the stream. It was night. Clouds covered the moon. Coyotes yapped far away on the mountainside. The horse was cropping diligently at the sparse grass. Blake went to it and unsaddled it, wrapping the blanket around him. He was shivering violently in a small, vagrant breeze. His arm

201

throbbed mercilessly, but it was as nothing compared to the aching inside him.

He did not tie or hobble the horse. What did it matter if it went away? He remembered that he had no food, no powder. He tried to think about that, of what he ought to do about it, but he could not keep his mind on it long enough to decide anything.

"Death is a part of living." . . . . "Women are all alike." . . . . "She's scrawny and her tongue is sharp." . . . . "What do you reverence?" . . . . "What is your medicine spirit, Blake?" . . . . "You are my husband. I want only to—"

His closed, burning eyes seemed to have her face, with its little, vixen smile, imprinted inside their lids.

Then he was seeing it all again, riding back to the wailing village and out again, the face of the Blackfoot he had looked on with such unknowing intensity, Shy Fawn, lying still, broken and mutilated . . . . These pictures moved relentlessly through his mind, round and round, in varying sequences as the night dragged on. Sometimes he was aware that he was feverish, burning, moving restlessly, unceasingly. In another moment of near sanity, he knew that for some reason the horse had not left him.

"The sins of the fathers are visited upon the children, even unto the fourth generation." . . . . *"That* man!" . . . . "Do not let the sun go down upon your wrath." . . . . "The fathers have eaten sour grapes and the children's teeth are set on edge." . . . . "What is your religion?" . . . . "I will sing my song to the deer spirit for you . . . . The deer is not a brave animal, but he is very useful and good." . . . . "Don't you know that you are doing a great wrong to stand in the way . . . . ?" "Does the mountain speak to you?"

"I can't go back!" he cried out of his misery. "I can never go back!" The cry was in the language of the Medicine Rock People.

"And yet you can't change what you are, can you?" . . . . "It is a thing a mother says to her child." . . . . "No, it's not the same at all." . . . . "Do you not believe in God?"

"No! I believe in nothing. Men all have the same brutalities. They killed her and I killed them. How can I believe in anything?"

202

In the chill, still hour before dawn, he struggled up stiffly, numbness and weariness having again eased the pain a little. He saddled the patient, resentful horse and rode on, climbing the mountain, his face turned away from the place in the sky where the light that presaged sunrise was beginning to show.

BOOK TWO

BOOK TWO

X

He sat on a bench in Boston Common, in weak, striving March sunlight and read the papers. The *Florie* had come into harbor yesterday, his first time back in the States in more than three years.

The papers were filled with indications of political unrest, shifting and maneuvering for the balance of power between North and South, or to overthrow that balance—the "border" troubles in Kansas and Missouri, angry speeches and threats in Congress. Impatiently, he tried to find something beyond that. Kansas was not the border, not the frontier of which he sought news.

Last year, 1849, there had been an agreement with England as to the establishment of a border between Canada and the United States in the west. Oregon was a territory now, all that vast northwest country. What had the change meant to Connall MacPheirson, to Paul and Jesse and all the others, to the Medicine Rock People?

In that same year, California and the southwest had become United States territory, after war. "Manifest destiny!" The words leapt out at him from an editorial.

"It's a fantastic country, the United States," Captain Walker had said once, thoughtfully. "My grandfather fought you people in the Revolution. Just thirteen colonies then, seventy years ago, who couldn't agree on anything. Look at the size of her now, and imperialistic as hell."

"And still not agreeing on anything," Blake had said dryly, but he was glad to be back.

One of the newspapers carried some outraged commentary about the Mormons, how the army should be, must be, sent to deal with them. Reading between the lines, Blake gathered that Brigham Young's people must be doing amazingly well in the deserts of Zion.

He found a great deal about California, gold, immigration, politics, but no word of the Oregon country.

"What will you do now?" Captain Walker had asked him as they lay outside the harbor, waiting out a fog. "You've not done badly for yourself these past months. Will you come out with me again? We'll be picking up the cargo here for France, then I plan to go to Liverpool for more goods to take out to India."

"I think I won't go out again," Blake said.

He knew he was going west, going home, but Captain Walker had never tried to delve into his past or his future and he saw no reason now for going into any details. They had been friends in a rather aloof way, talking sometimes about books, about philosophy, about the troubles of the world, but neither of them had ever talked about himself.

Blake had known for several months what he would do when the ship reached Boston, since a night with a heavy moon and equatorial stars when he had stood alone in the bow of the *Florie* with heavy, warm spray on his face and Never Summer had called out to him, reaching halfway across the world with that great, awesome quietness, saying: It's all right now. The pain that is left will be bearable. You can come back and live with yourself where you belong. Isn't this the only place you've ever really belonged?

Yes, he thought, swept by a fresh wave of the old desolation. I belonged. I wanted to be one of the People, Shy Fawn's people, Red Sky's people. Sometimes, I almost was. It's the only place I've wanted to belong, where I felt I did belong, but maybe belonging isn't meant for me. You know what happened.

When one belongs, said the gentle, comforting, inexorably indifferent Quietness, there can no longer be such questions. Once you have belonged, to a person, to a group, to a place, to a feeling, it has become a part of you and you of it. There have been effects, interrelationships that make you a slightly different person from what you were before. Don't you want to come home now?

Yes.

It had taken him days, weeks, in that summer that now seemed so long ago, so nightmarishly unreal, to reach Fort Hall. He had come on a band of Nez Perce along a small tributary of the Salmon. He had no idea then of how long it had been since the battle with the Blackfeet or of where he was going or why. He scarcely knew who he was, dazed with grief, exhaustion, fever, and hunger. He was unknown to any of the Indians in this small group, but they gave him food, clothing, a little powder for his rifle. They said to each other that he was crazy, touched by a strange madness that whites sometimes got in the mountains. Blake never let them know he understood their language. Speaking it, during those days, would have been more than he could bear, though his mind still insisted remorselessly upon thinking in that language. He rode with that small band as far as the fishing grounds where they had been bound when he came upon them, then he went on to Fort Hall, not stopping at the Indians' camping place for fear of meeting others who might know him and ask him things.

John McCandless, factor at Fort Hall, was called from his supper table by word that some wild-looking half-breed with funny eyes wanted to see him. McCandless recognized Blake, who asked for work, for something that would take him out of the country. He asked to borrow scissors and a razor, but looked no better, McCandless thought, for a very poorly done shave and haircut. McCandless was sure the young man was very ill, that something dreadful had happened, an Indian attack probably. He was concerned about his friends at Camas Post and tried to learn some details. Blake told him that, so far as he knew, things were all right at Camas and he would say no more.

There was a small party of Mormons at Hall. They had been "called" to go out into the Spanish country to work for the expansion of their embryo nation and they wanted a guide. Blake had not crossed the desert to the west, but with what information he could gather, he thought he could guide them. He had to get away. Then Jesse Harris arrived, up from some trapping and a summer spent in the southern mountains. He agreed to go along so the trip was easy for Blake, who did not notice.

They went all the way to San Francisco and by then it was winter. Blake could not bear the town, the people, most of all himself. He went to the waterfront and signed on the *Florie* as an ordinary sailor. She weighed anchor almost immediately, bound first for the Sandwich Islands. There were storms all the way. Blake was glad of the storms. They made him newly, highly aware of the present moment, of trying to be alive.

The ship was a kind of salvation for him, a way back from the half-world in which he had been living since he had looked down briefly at Shy Fawn, dead, since he had ridden in long hours of stupor and pain, since he had killed men in sheer animal fury and a kind of maddened, horrible ecstacy. He had never been particularly fond of the sea and perhaps that was what made it bearable. There was little here to remind him of the mountain country or the life peculiar to it—or the death.

They went round the Horn to New York, then to England, and on to India and the East. Eventually, Blake became what Captain Walker called his "third mate," handling cargo manifests and other paperwork in port, working harder than he had to when the ship was at sea, seeking the balm of exhaustion and nonthinking, waiting dully for what would come. Could there be some sort of reconciliation, healing? A time came when he began to be able, slowly, to believe there might be.

And, on that hot, windy, equatorial night, his mind clearly saw Never Summer, with snow on his head and shoulders, and heard the mountain silence saying: Come home again. It's past time you thought of your son, and it's past time you began to practice some tolerance, of others and of yourself. The world goes on. This time, don't ask for so much. You believed the People were beautifully simple, that you understood and could be one of them. Then you killed as they killed, with, perhaps, the same feelings they have at such a time. Why could you not bear that? It's human, in the horrible way that some of man's shortcomings are human and shared by all at one time or other. There are very few uncomplicated human beings. Why did you think that the People, or you, had become so simple? Make the most of what there is. Don't go on with questioning, with anger, with bitterness. You will only hurt yourself. Come back and try to be content with coming to know yourself. You haven't nearly accomplished that yet. You thought you had made a beginning, but perhaps your identity had become too dependent on Shy Fawn and the others. With the mountains, the streams, the forests, the sky, you will find a measure of security and certainty. Keep a little aloof from others and you will not be hurt like this again. Only be reconciled to living with yourself, with acceptance. Aren't you ready now for peace? for submission, to yourself, to other things as they are?

Blake stiffened in the spray-wet wind. No, not submission.

And the Quietness said gently: Ah, you're not ready for that? Then think of this. Father Robidou was right in what he said about your duty. You knew it then. Knowledge, awareness, do have their responsibilities. Come back and see what is to be done about the boy.

I wouldn't know what to do. We'd be strangers.

Still, he's your son.

He's Shy Fawn's son. He belongs to the Medicine Rock as she did.

You never knew a father. Will you let that happen to another boy? He's half white and you can't avoid awareness of that, no matter how far away you go. What's happening now to the People? Shouldn't you know that, for the boy's sake, at least?

In the depths of a Boston newspaper, Blake found that at a Cambridge museum there was a new display of artifacts from Indians of the western plains and mountains. He went out to look and left the museum feeling frustrated and irritable. The signs identifying items had been dramatic and, in great part, incorrect. He went, rather doggedly, to the office of the professor whom he had been told was responsible for the display.

"No, I haven't been west myself," the old man said uneasily, "but I have made a long and careful study of the materials and—"

"The Nez Perce don't weave blankets," Blake said. "They never have. Those horn bows your signs say came from the Sioux are not Sioux at all. The saddle you identify as being Blackfoot was made by the Crows . . . ."

"What makes you so sure about these things? You've been there, haven't you?"

"Yes. I'm going back."

The old man's eyes lit eagerly. "Perhaps we could work together. You could collect materials and send—"

"I don't know," he said, feeling suddenly empty. "So long as there are things to look at, the truth about them doesn't really matter, does it? to anyone here?"

"But," said the professor earnestly, "time passes. Things change. Before we know it, there'll be none of that kind of aboriginal art and culture left."

Agreeing vaguely that perhaps he would send some things some day, Blake left as quickly as he could. They're not *things,* objects to be studied. They're Shy Fawn's people, the boy's, mine, more than any others will ever be. Will I always keep thinking that because I know that I can make other people see it? The whites are people too, after all, and both sides have a kind of block against recognizing the humanity of the others. Perhaps that wall can never be torn down. What difference does it really make to anyone if they put the wrong sign on a blanket or a bow?

Back in the city, he stopped at a large bookstore and placed an order to be delivered to the train station. He went to the *Florie* and picked up his few belongings. Captain Walker, he was told, was having lunch with some friends. Just as well. There would be no uneasiness about saying good-bye. He went to the station and bought a ticket for as far west as the railroads ran.

"Blake! Laddie! I couldn't believe it was you when Marie told me. My God, I'm glad to see you! Where have you come from? You're back to stay, aren't you?"

Connal's voice was not quite steady as he kept pounding Blake's back with one hand and gripping his hand in the other.

"Marie, get us some rum. Where the devil have you been, lad? McCandless told us about your coming to Hall that time. We were afraid you were dead somewhere when no one heard anything more. Finally, Jesse Harris showed up in these parts again and said he'd left you in San Francisco, but we couldn't trace things any farther. You look fine."

"So do you, Connall."

"Ah, but I'm older," he said, sobering. "Four years older. I don't much like the sound of that these days."

"And you think I'm not older?"

"Well, I suppose, but at your age it doesn't matter nearly so much. Now, tell me where it is you've been all this while."

Blake told him a little of it.

"India, is it? Another colony of Mother England's. You must know that we're all Americans together here now?"

"Yes. How is it?"

Connall snorted. "Perhaps the best thing about it is that we're still so far from the seat of what government there is that they forget about us and we can go on living, mostly, in peace. There are a lot of whites farther west, close to the coast, for the most part, and they do the damned politicking. Here, in the interior wilderness, things are not so much changed. We're far enough off any beaten trail and there's nothing here they've decided they want yet, so things go on for us. We've got the post still, as you see, and I do what trading I can. It's expensive when I have to supply everything myself, with no company to help with the financing. There's not a great deal in the way of furs now, and not so much demand for what there is, but I'm doing well enough with horses. The army needs them, and the settlers, and those idiot miners breaking their necks to get to California. It's far, to drive stock down from here to the Overland, but I'm glad of that, always have been, glad to be able to just sit up here, quiet at times. Aye, it's the stock-raising and trading that's going well. I've got in a good deal of grain and hay and such. You must come and look over the place after dinner. I'd close the post entirely, I think, if it wasn't that the Indians count on its being here."

"Is Emmett helping you with the farm?"

"Oh, no. Emmett's converted, or whatever they call it, and married a Mormon girl. Her family was living down around Hall somewhere, but I've heard that he and his

213

wife went with some others to found a mission to the Nez Perce, on the Salmon, to convert them and teach them farming and such. So, you see, Emmett's a missionary after all. I saw him last year, just before he married. He promised me he'd take only the one wife, but I don't know if he's kept his word.

"Those Mormons all seem to get to be so ambitious and so prosperous, it's very nearly frightening to a decent man. They took away a lot of my stock trade, down on the Trail, not only stock but they've got hay and grain and fresh garden truck to sell to the immigrants. I'm doing business more with the army these days. The army won't buy from the Mormons. It's against regulations. Part of the reason they're out here is to see about putting the damned heathens in their place. If some sort of stop isn't put to them, they'll have an entirely separate country. That's what they're aiming at."

"And Paul?" Blake asked tentatively, afraid of the answer.

"Ah, poor Paul died, here at Camas. It's been nearly two years now. Wait! I was forgetting."

He went into the warehouse and returned, laying the worn case on the trading counter.

"The fiddle was all he had at the end. He said you were to have it if ever you came back."

Blake touched the old case gently . . . . *If you go on living with the Medicine Rock People, Blake, you'll take a scalp* . . . . Had it been anything like the same thing for Paul, when he'd taken his first scalp? Had he known . . . . ?

He said levelly. "Paul had a family. Shouldn't the fiddle be sent to them?"

"He said not," Connall replied sadly, "said he had nothing at all for them. He did ask me to write after it was all over, and I did that. From the address he gave me, his wife's from one of the wealthiest, most powerful families in Quebec, so there's no need to worry about their being provided for. There's a long, sad story there, lad, if we but knew the whole of it . . . . Paul was here, sick, for several months. It was a pitiful thing to see him just wasting away. Still, the way he's always been about the drink and all . . . . He worried about you. We'd found out what happened, though it took some time and doing. He said

214

he hated to think you might have gone completely bitter from trying to be more than any man could possibly be. Paul was a deep one, and fond of you."

A boy of about six ran into the trading room, stopping short at sight of a stranger. He was a big, husky boy with bright red hair and quick blue eyes in an Indian face, striking to look at. Blake smiled at him.

"This is the one," Connall said, trying to conceal his pride a little. "The eighth was a boy, you'll remember. There have been two more girls since but, by God, Marie had the one boy. Con, say 'Hello' to Blake, and I'll thank you to speak English."

As quickly as he could, young Con sidled out of the room to stand outside by the door, peering around it from time to time.

"Nine girls we've had now, and just the one boy," Connall sighed, "but he's all right, that lad, though I think he won't take much to farming. Liz and Mary, the two oldest, are about finished at the convent school. They'll be coming home and I'll be having to think what to do with them. The others go to St. Denis as they get old enough."

"What's St. Denis?"

"Why, the mission school, Father Robidou's mission down the river. It's become quite a place."

"So he stayed."

"Oh, aye, he stayed. He's got the church and the school, several Indians farming, two young priests, and some sisters to teach. He may even take on my two girls to help with the teaching when they come home.

"A fine man, the Father. His health's not as good as it might be. He's past sixty now, you know, but he spends all the time he can traveling around from village to village. He says that's his real calling, to live among the Indians, not just to sit at the mission and wait for them to come to him.

"And speaking of old men, I'm told Mote Stanley's more of a banty rooster than ever these days. He's scouting for the army, out of Laramie. Come on, there's Marie calling us to dinner."

The two men ate. The boy sat with them, looking awkward and proud while his mother and sisters waited, serving them. Blake thought that one of the little girls, about three or four years old, was the prettiest child he had ever seen. She had thick auburn hair, great, liquid, dark eyes, a clear, vividly colored little face. Connall said her name was Katy.

"It's a funny thing," mused the father. "After seven Indians came the two with red hair. Now we've started on Indians again; you see the baby there. Aye, but they're a fine lot, though I don't know what I'll do with them all."

They went out to look at the farm. Connall had a lot of land under cultivation now, grain, hay, a large vegetable garden, all doing well. He had herds of cattle and horses, some oxen resting up from the Overland Trail, a few sheep and hogs. He showed Blake where and how he planned to build a new house, one day. Just now, all his building efforts were going into barns and fences.

"It's a good start toward an empire," Blake said with some admiration.

Connall laughed. "Aye, well—manifest destiny, you know. Would you want to ride down and see what they've done at the mission? We could stay out a few days, do some hunting."

"Thanks, Connall, but I want to be going on up the river soon."

"You're going back then."

"Yes. If I can."

There was a silence and Blake said softly, "Tell me about the Medicine Rock."

"I'll tell you what I know, lad. It's not a great deal. They stayed in the valley, of course, after that thing with the Blackfeet. They'd lost nearly half their men, I was told. They didn't even go to the buffalo the next year, feeling, I suppose, that they couldn't properly protect themselves. Father Robidou went up there, when he heard about the massacre, and stayed several weeks with them. They've had their own kind of political upheaval, you might say, with Red Sky killed and Many Bears dying a year or so afterward. Beaver Tooth's chief now."

"Beaver Tooth?"

Connall drew on his pipe, looking out across his land to the river.

"Aye, and he's a better one than you might think. He and his wife and children have been baptized, along with several more of the People. He comes here to trade at least twice a year, brings some good fur."

"A white man Indian," Blake said. He couldn't quite hide the disdain, the hurt about the People.

"I suppose you could say that, but, lad, nothing else really makes much sense these days, does it?"

"What about Hawk's Shadow?" he asked more quietly.

"Red Sky's son? I don't know. I seem to remember Father Robidou saying something about his wife being a convert, but I've not seen nor heard anything of Hawk's Shadow himself . . . . Some of those horses there I traded from Beaver Tooth. Last fall when he was here, he went down to look at the mission school. I think he's to have a young one or two in school there this year. He brings several bucks and their families down with him when he comes, but some of the rest of them keep just as much to themselves as they always have.

"They've had trouble, I guess, choosing a chief and deciding about Christianity and such things. There's been a great deal of trouble all around lately. I hear the Protestant missionaries over west are having a great lot of unrest among the Cayuses and some others, and of course there's always been trouble among the tribes. The Blackfeet seem to have turned most of their wrath on the Snakes and Crows these past few years. Father Robidou's been down among them, too. The Mormons have come in and started intermarrying like mad. They claim the Indians are some lost tribe of Israel, or some such nonsense, that they've been sent to save. Also, they're trying to get as many of them as they can on their side before the army gets to them. And the army! I never saw such a bunch of fools. They're worse than the tribes for making alliances with first one and then another.

"The Protestants blame the Catholics for unrest among the tribes. The Mormons blame the army. The army blames trappers and traders. God! It's a mess."

"And the Indians are in the middle."

"Aye, I guess they always will be."

"Have they got a chance, Connall?"

"Of what?"

"Of staying—anything like the way they want to be, of—of any kind of freedom?"

217

"Who's to say what they want? Some want to be whites, which they can never be. Some want to go entirely back to being savages and wipe out everybody; that we can't allow. I suppose maybe they vary, the way whites do, in what they think they want, and not one in ten, white or red, really knows what it's best for him to want. We're going to have more trouble, though, and I don't mean just down on the Overland. With all this maneuvering and pulling one way and another, the savages have no idea what or who to believe. More immigrants come each year, more are killed and now there are those miners and soldiers. To tell God's truth, there's not a hell of a lot the Indians *can* believe. The tribes are beginning to see, I think, that they ought to stop fighting each other and go after the whites. And if that ever happens, there aren't many Indians who are going to be much concerned about making distinctions, just like whites claim, some of them, that they can't tell one Indian from another."

"What then?"

"What? Why, nothing then. It won't happen, not fully, because they can't get along with each other and, for the simple reason of wanting to go on living, if for no other, we can't let it happen. But it'll be sad if we have to see them destroyed. If it comes, I'd rather see it in one great, glorious battle than seeing the ground cut from under them a little at a time as things are going now. They'd know, at least, how to handle a big fight, and they could take some pride in dying that way."

Blake watched a hawk, circling high up, wondering how, in past years, he could have felt the contempt and exasperation he recalled feeling for Connall's opinions. He still did not agree with Connall. The man had his prejudices, his superiorities, but he also saw things, from his own particular angle, with a good deal of clarity. And anyway, Blake chided himself, who am I to try to define clarity?

Connall said, smiling tentatively, "Have you stopped struggling then?"

"What?"

"A few years back, if I'd said the things to you I've just been saying, you'd have been ready, in your idealistic way, to fight."

"Maybe I've grown up—some. I still don't want you to be right."

"Aye, well, life's seldom an easy thing. There are often bits and pieces we'd rather have different . . . . You've not told me, lad, just how you came to be here today."

"I came with some miners to Laramie. They were in a hell of a hurry and needed someone to show them how to make camp on the trail. And then I brought a party of army surveyors up to Yellowstone Lake."

"What were they surveying?"

"They weren't, much, not while I was with them. Mostly, they were just looking around."

"And did you just leave them there, alone?"

"No. Some of Bridger's men came along, with a party of Snakes. It was Bridger's fort where the surveyors had wanted to get to, so they went along with them."

"Going out to survey Mormons," Connall said dryly.

"I went up to the Three Forks and north from there, thinking I might find the Medicine Rock People hunting, but they'd already come back west. I was far enough north when it came to crossing over that it wasn't out of my way to come here."

"Were you traveling alone all this while?"

"Just part of the time."

Connall said, with a musing smile, "I don't know what it is, luck, lack of sense, or what, but you're one of the few whites I've ever known who seems casual about traveling alone in this country. I knew, the first time I saw you with old Henry Melton, that you were meant for this country."

Blake looked at him, surprised. "You did? It seems to me you managed to conceal thoughts like that very well."

Connall laughed. "That's not to say you weren't green as a gourd. You're still a greenhorn, I suspect, in the way you look at many things. I don't see how people like you go on holding to ideals the way you seem to do. In some ways, you'll always be a babe in the woods and that's a kind of amazing thing. But still, it's always a little surprising to me to find you've been going about the country alone and such things. I can well recall a time when you couldn't find your butt with both hands."

Blake grinned and said warmly, "I've missed the mountains, Connall. It's good to be back."

"Aye, they get in a man's blood."

"Do you know anything about—Coyote, my boy?"

"Not really, lad. I've asked Beaver Tooth about him. He said the boy was well and I've heard as much from Father Robidou, but I've not seen the boy."

Blake stood up from the log where they had been sitting, feeling restless now, eager to be moving.

"Are you still charging Montreal prices for your goods?"

"A man has to live. But you're not going now, surely."

"Yes. I wanted to pick up a few things here first."

"But you'll stay the night at least. It's only two or three hours now till sundown. I'd had it in the back of my mind that you might find time to brush my ledgers up a bit. They've not been properly done for some while. Paul kept them while he could. You could take it out in trade."

Blake smiled. "Another time, Connall. I really have to go now."

"Aye, well . . . . I'm hoping some of these girls may be good with figuring and that sort of thing. Surely a man with so many daughters ought to be able to find one clerk among the lot."

It was August. The valley lay still, immobilized under the sun. High up on the mountains, fall colors were showing in the leaves and new snow glistened here and there. Never Summer was a presence, bulking reassuringly, cutting off the horizon to the south. The creek ran low and the grass had browned. Harvest flies dinned frenetically in the willows.

Blake found that his breath came a little hard as he rode slowly up through the canyon. He caught sight of a guard, high up in the rocks, and gave him the old sign, with a tight feeling of anxiety and anticipation in his chest and throat. The guard came down, uncertain of whether or not he ought to be allowed to pass.

"It's you!" he cried, coming closer. "Don't you know me? I'm Smiling Fox."

Blake thought that he would have recognized him anywhere, under any circumstances, as one of Red Sky's children. He had grown tall, taller than Hawk's Shadow, and very handsome, but his face was not much changed, still with the sly little smile that brought a stab of memory and pain.

The village was smaller, with fewer lodges, but some things were as he remembered, beginning with the noise as all the dogs rushed out at him. He didn't recognize the first People he saw, but then a familiar voice behind him said, "Get off the horse, white man, and don't touch the rifle."

"Hawk's Shadow!" He slid down and they held each other's hands in the Indian way, both of them smiling, not quite able yet to look directly at each other.

"Ah, Green Eyes, I thought you couldn't stay away for always."

"I am of the Medicine Rock," Blake said softly. Neither of their voices was quite steady.

Little Rain, holding an infant in the crook of her arm, gave them food.

"You have another son," Blake said.

"He is the third we have had since you went away, but two did not stay with us."

"And Owl Woman . . . ." Blake asked hesitantly, afraid she might be gone.

"She is out gathering herbs. She has said you would not come back."

He found he could not ask the question he most wanted answered. Hawk's Shadow said to his wife, "Where is Coyote?"

"They went to hide and watch some beaver, he and Little Chief and some other boys. I think they will be back soon."

Beaver Tooth had come in, and Storm Coming Out Of The East and others Blake knew. They all ate, talking and asking questions.

"Let's go somewhere," Hawk's Shadow said to Blake quietly. "This is a noisy lodge."

As they were leaving, the boys came back. Catching sight of the white man, they stopped scuffling with each other and stared at him soberly. Blake caught the eyes of one, briefly—green eyes. This boy was smaller than the others, younger. He was slender and quick with a serious, fine-looking face.

"Coyote, come here," said Hawk's Shadow.

He came, slowly, looking at the ground.

"Do you know who this man is?"

"No."

"Look at him."

He did, solemnly. Blake tried to smile. He wanted to reach out and touch him, but knew the boy would not like that. He himself was feeling painfully shy now.

"He is your father," Hawk's Shadow said impatiently. "How can you not know that? Speak to him."

The boy had dropped his gaze. It seemed to Blake there might be fear in his face. He said gently, "Another time, Hawk's Shadow. Coyote will be hungry now, after watching the beaver."

The boy looked sideways at his uncle until Hawk's Shadow, with a little sound of disgust and disappointment, made a gesture, permitting him to go.

"He is not usually shy like that," Hawk's Shadow said apologetically as they rode slowly up the Medicine Rock. "What do you think of him?"

"He's grown."

"Did you think he would still be two years old? Yes, he's grown, but he's not so big as Little Chief was at that age . . . . Why have you stayed away so long?"

"I wanted to come before but I've been far away. It took a long time, getting back."

Blake was having trouble with the language, speaking awkwardly.

"We might go hunting," Hawk's Shadow said, "but I came back only yesterday, with meat. Have you heard news of us?"

"I was at Camas Post."

"Then you know that Beaver Tooth is chief."

"Yes."

"Ours was a sad village when you went away, with all we had lost. Many Bears died, too, soon after that . . . . Is this the way white men deal with sorrow, to run away for four years?"

"I don't know what others do, Hawk's Shadow. You know I've never been very brave."

"Was it that Shy Fawn died or that you took scalps?"

"It was—all of it."

"You were as one mad then."

"Yes."

"And are you well now?"

"I am well."

"I will show you her grave when we go back, and the grave of Red Sky my father."

"Yes."

They were silent for a time and then Hawk's Shadow said, "Have you heard also that Little Rain, Beaver Tooth, and some others are fine Christian people now?"

"Are you?"

"No. I am still—as I have always been. The priest came here, that winter after you went away, and persuaded several of the People. I thought of being converted . . . . Do you remember that time, long ago, when we hunted the eagle?"

"I remember."

"And the thing I told you then?"

"Yes."

"It's still the same with me. I see nothing and I hear nothing, except what is—there. When my father and the others were buried, I went into the mountains and I tried again, for many days. I fasted and waited, and nothing came to me. I decided then that I would not try again. Whatever it is that's wrong with me, I have no power to know or change it. When the priest came, I listened to him for a time, but then I thought that if our own spirits want nothing to do with me, what could I expect from the white man's God or medicine? So I only wait to see what will happen. What else is there to do? I am Hawk's Shadow, son of Red Sky. I hunt well. The people listen to me, often.

"When I came back from the mountains that time, Beaver Tooth had got himself elected chief. He was afraid of my coming back, I think, and the People were, but I was glad he was chief. My father would have been disappointed in me. He often was while he lived. I never wanted to be a chief, and surely not now, with all the things to be decided and all the differentness.

"When the priest came, I thought that my father would have sent him away. Red Sky wanted to know about his book and his medicine, but that was not a time for him to be in the village. The people were mourning and confused and the priest's words had great power with some of them. Then I remembered that I was not chief and did not have to decide anything like that. This was a relief to me, a good feeling.

"I went away again, alone, for a time. This time I did not fast. I only went about the country and after a while I felt something as a boy feels, wandering about like that. Some of the sorrow left me. My mind grew quiet. Do you think that was wrong? to leave the People in that way?"

"How can *I* say it was wrong?"

Hawk's Shadow looked at him, startled. "We have done the same kind of thing, you and I, and I did not see it until now, only I was hunting, looking at the land, doing right, worthwhile things. From what you told us back at the lodge, it was not so with you. But that is only to be expected, from one such as you, I suppose."

He was smiling, a little, and Blake smiled back, both of them feeling a kind of resignation, an ease with one another.

"And when I came back again, we had all those Christians. Not so many, it only seems like many. My mother is not one. She is the same as ever, but Little Rain . . . . I am the cross she bears. For one thing, I won't marry her in the white man's church. We have been together a long time now and I see no need for that. Do you think I ought to do it?"

"It's not my place to say—"

"You have always run away from questions, Blake. It was a thing that worried Shy Fawn, the way you never wanted to say a thing was simply one way or the other. She sometimes felt, I think, that you were not very sure of what truth is. Now that you are back, you must not do this anymore. I ask you only what you *think*. I make you no bargain to *do* as you think."

"I think," he said slowly, "that if it's important to Little Rain and not very important to you, then you might do it to please her."

Hawk's Shadow sighed. "The priest says this same thing, but she nags more now that she is a good Christian. I often have little wish to do anything just to please her . . . . She has had the children baptized, your boy, too. She and Brown Leaf have learned many things from the priest's book and they tell them, always, to any who will listen. Now Little Rain wants to send our children to the mission school. Beaver Tooth's boy is there already. I have said that she can send the girl and, perhaps, this baby when he is old enough, but not the Little Chief. This one will be as the People have always been, a right kind of person.

"Do you remember my little sister Cricket? She grew up to look good and have a sharp tongue. Last year, at the fishing grounds she went to visit the band from the old days. While she was there, some whites came to the village and she married one of them, called a Mormon, and they went to live over on the Salmon. Whites seem to have an attraction for my sisters. Sometimes I think there may be something wrong with all my family. What is Mormon anyway?"

"Only another white religion."

"I know the priest has not much liking for it . . . . Why do there have to be so many things? If they were one at a time, perhaps we might get some understanding of the ones that interest us . . . .

"There are the horses, yours with them."

"Mine?"

"You have not changed," he said with disgust that was only half-feigned. "When I talk to you, I am not sure you listen. When I say a thing such as 'There are your horses,' you seem as if you are coming back from somewhere else and are not sure what I mean. I have kept them well for you, and for Coyote. My mother and others said you would never come again, but I thought you would be back. I had seen you, you know, looking at the mountains . . . . Did you see the boy's hands? He is going to be good with horses. Can you tell which are yours? There are a lot of them now."

When they had spent some time looking over the herd, Hawk's Shadow said, "Do you want to go up to the little valley? I've looked at your cabin sometimes. Last winter a bear used it, but it's there."

It seemed to Blake he had been yearning for the valley, steadily, for four years, but now he hesitated.

Hawk's Shadow said, "You want to go up there alone. I understand that. I will ride with you only to where it grows steep . . . . Where did you get this horse you are riding now? He is a white man horse, too big and heavy for this country, like that black we once rescued for you from the Blackfeet."

As they rode slowly on, he talked of trouble among the tribes.

"After what happened to us with the Blackfeet, we did not go to the buffalo country that next year. There was a council of the Nez Perce, Yakima, Cayuses, Palouses, some Flatheads and Walla Wallas, Coeur d'Alenes, and others and we sent what warriors we could. In the next fall, many warriors from those peoples fought a great party of Blackfeet. Few of them have come to the Camas since, though they make big talk, as they always have. We have not had much trouble, either, from Snakes or Crows. I am glad, though I would not say it to anyone else, and if you said I said it, I would say you lie. War is all right when it's other people's fathers and sisters who are killed . . . .

"I have talked with no whites since you left, but from what I hear of them, from Beaver Tooth and others, it seems to me they are happy to see us fighting each other. With these Christians among us, though, war is not supposed to be a good thing anymore. They have Christian names even. I forgot to tell you that Beaver Tooth is Thomas and Little Rain has become Mary. They say these names are in the priest's book. Is that true?"

"Yes."

"And whites keep coming. Now there are all those rushing along their trail to the west to dig in the ground, I am told. What is gold, anyway?"

"It's a metal, sometimes yellow and shiny. They usually find it first in streams."

"And what do they do with it?"

"It's used as money."

Hawk's Shadow frowned, grunting contemptuously. "I think I have seen some of this gold here in the valley," he said casually. "I will never understand about the things whites put high values on. Why would anyone go many miles for this?"

Blake was looking at him sharply. "Have you said this to anyone else, that you have seen gold here?"

"No. How could I? not knowing it was gold? I only thought it was a kind of sand, good for nothing. I still think that. I've seen it in that little stream that comes down by your cabin. I can show you."

"But don't mention it to anyone else, not ever."

"They would come, wouldn't they?" he said wonderingly, incredulous, still, at white follies.

"They would come," Blake said heavily. "Nothing could stop them."

It was not changed. Climbing up along the stream, his breath had come hard, with anticipation and with apprehension, with the fear of being, somehow, disappointed, but as he stood on the lip of the valley above the last brawling little waterfall, he knew it was all right. The valley lay there before him in the late afternoon sun, a faint, woods-scented breeze touching the long grass and the water in the lake, empty, still, beautiful.

He turned his horse loose and looked back, over the Medicine Rock and across at the mountain. There were two eagles above the peak, soaring, majestic. He was home, safe.

The cabin was in bad shape. Shy Fawn's floor mats, tattered and dirty, had been dragged into a corner, no doubt by the bear Hawk's Shadow had mentioned. Small things had been living there, rats, mice, chipmunks. She wouldn't have minded their using her things as beds and nests. The pain rose up in him, but it was not the tearing, lacerating, destructive thing it once had been.

Looking at the fireplace, he found it blurring in the dim light. He could see her there, it seemed, bending to adjust the crane, looking back at him over her shoulder, with that smile. You are my medicine spirit, his mind said tenderly to the apparition, and her small, gentle, teasing

227

voice said, "I am only here to please my husband, to keep his fire and his lodge and . . . ."

He turned to the doorway, trembling, stumbling because he could not see. He went to the stream and dipped up the cold water to wash his face. Covering his wet face with still unsteady hands, he sat there on a damp mossy rock. After a time, peace came back to him, gentle, nostalgic, healing.

He went back up to the cabin. Her presence was still there, but it did not hurt him now. Perhaps she would be there always.

Some chinking had fallen out from between the logs. The grass that had been a mattress for their bed was an old, moldering, scattered heap on the floor. Something had been gnawing at the ropes she had woven for springing the bed, the bed about which she had had uncertainties in the beginning.

There were no coverings for the window or the door, and the skins from the floor were gone, too, dragged away, no doubt, by various animals, chewed up long ago. The sod of the roof needed replacing. It would take a good deal of work to get the cabin ready for winter. He would be glad of the work. Perhaps, some day, he would split logs and put in a puncheon floor.

Before they had left for the journey in that early spring four years ago, Blake had nailed his books and a few other things into a wooden box. It stood at one side of the hearth, its corners showing the marks of tiny teeth. He opened it. There were some of his drawings there, several pictures of Shy Fawn. The books were in as good condition as he could have expected. At one side, in the bottom of the box, crushed and crumpled by the other things, was a deerskin shirt, the first thing she had made for him after she became his woman.

He had worn the shirt for a while and she had cleaned it for him, with white clay, as the People did. The skins, worked to a wonderful softness, had grown even softer from the use and the cleaning. When they had been gathering their things and setting the cabin in order, preparing to leave for the buffalo country in that last spring, he had put the shirt away with the books, without her knowledge. The People did not often save things, keep souvenirs. She would have said it was wasteful not to use the shirt, that she would make him another when it was worn out.

He carried the shirt and the drawings into the light now, sitting down on the log of the doorsill. The pictures were not nearly so good as his vision of her had been. He held the shirt over his arm, tenderly touching the decorations she had embroidered with porcupine quills. He remembered her working on this shirt in the lodge that had been their first home together.

The sun was low. Never Summer stood, sharp with light and shadow, awesome, utterly calm. Three deer had come out to browse, indifferent of his presence, on the other side of the lake. The wind had shifted, as it usually did in the heat of a summer afternoon, and it blew down from the mountain, cool, smelling faintly of snow. The big pines around him, warmed by hours of sun, gave off their warm, sweet smell. A bluebird in the willows along the stream above the lake sang its tender, unbearably sweet song to the evening. The water made a faint, pleasant undertone for the silence. The Quietness did not speak to him. Simply, it took him in, folding around him, warm and quiet.

Reluctantly, he roused himself after a while and put the things away, closing the box again with care. He wanted to stay here, to begin the work that needed doing when he was ready, when he had absorbed enough of the peace and beauty so that he would want to go on with other things, but they would be hurt, at the village, if he were to keep away after only that brief visit.

He wished he need not think of anything for a long while, need not hear people talking, need not be made aware of the things that troubled them and himself. Now that he had seen the cabin, it might even be necessary for him to go back to Camas Post for some more things he would need before the weather grew bad with autumn. There would always be things from outside his valley—duties, necessities—but the valley and the mountain had been here always. The cabin, the awareness of the presence of Shy Fawn, the peace of it all, would always be here.

XI

ON AN AFTERNOON in November Blake sat resting in the
sun against the cabin wall. He had finished the work that
had to be done. Two days before, he had come back from
a good hunt with Hawk's Shadow and others. His meat
hung in the lean-to. He had traded in the village for cakes
of dried roots and berries, skins and other things. The
books he had bought in Boston and the older books, the
new drawing things he had got together, waited now for
winter.

A few inches of snow lay over the valley now. Morn-
ings saw a skin of ice on the lake, thickening around the
edges. The peak of Never Summer was white. The winter
was coming and, today, Blake was feeling a heavy, sad
loneliness, a kind of desperation, mixed with disgust for
the fickleness of his feelings. He had yearned so long for
this place and its solitude and now he was restless and
sad. The valley had lost none of its meaning, the quiet joy
it had always held for him was not diminished. What
seemed to be troubling him was the fear of not having
enough to keep his mind and body sufficiently occupied
through the long days of winter. There was always the
village, he told himself sternly. He could go there whenever he liked and the People would visit him. It was only
that, through those other winters he had spent here in the
valley, Shy Fawn had been with him . . . .

He got up impatiently, resolutely, and went into the
cabin. It was time he found something more to do. Paul's
fiddle lay on the mantel and he took it from its case. The

instrument needed new strings. The hair of the bow was worn, but he thought, rubbing rosin on it, that he could repair the bow.

He carried the fiddle outside, tuned it with difficulty and began to play, tentatively, with a slightly desperate obstinacy, very badly. The horses he had brought up from the lower valley lifted their heads and twitched their ears, looking, he thought, pained and offended. Blake frowned, concentrating, biting his lower lip, trying to find one of Alec Douglas' reels in the recalcitrant strings.

From a corner of his eye, he saw the horses fling their heads to look in another direction. Someone was coming up to the valley. He was glad.

The boy rode a small paint pony and a big, awkwardly gamboling brown-and-white pup was with him. They had talked, a little, in the village from time to time, being almost painfully shy of one another. Blake had said, "I'm going to be living up in the valley. Have you seen it?"

"Hawk's Shadow my uncle has shown me the valley and the cabin."

"Would you want to come there to live?"

"If you tell me to."

That had disturbed Blake. He had said, almost curtly, "You know the way. You can come when you like."

The boy rode up slowly now, looking small, diffident, a little defiant.

"Hello, Coyote," Blake said softly.

"I have heard strange sounds," the boy reported soberly.

"It was this instrument," Blake said apologetically.

"Smiling Fox my uncle plays the flute sometimes, for the girls. *It* makes pleasant sounds."

"Will you stay and let your pony graze? Maybe he is hungry."

He slid easily to the ground and the dog jumped on him excitedly.

"This dog is called Bravest Of The Brave," he said, putting the dog off, looking shyly as if his dignity might have been shaken. "He will be the biggest dog in the village when he is grown. Owl Woman my grandmother gave him to me when he was first born."

"He is a fine young dog."

231

"When I am older, he will not be my dog anymore."

"Why is that?"

"Don't you know that only women and children have dogs? They are not for men."

"I think that will make Bravest Of The Brave very sad, not to be your dog anymore."

"I've told him how it will be. Sometimes we wrestle, this dog and I, but when I am winning, he bites."

He had taken the gear from his pony and now turned him loose, saying judiciously, "You have brought some of your good horses up here."

"They're your horses too. Which do you like best?"

"The stallion. He's a very good paint, though my uncle and others think him too big. Which do you like?"

"The black mare, the young one."

"A black is not so good."

"Why not?"

"Because, paints are best."

"Does color make so much difference?"

"Yes."

"But it's only on the skin. Other things, many other things, count too."

He didn't bother to answer that, but said, "This is a good little valley. The grass is good."

"Do you know," Blake said eagerly, "that, probably, this valley was once filled with ice?"

He looked around dubiously. "Snow . . . . ?"

"No. Ice. It was a long time ago and many things about the earth were different from what they are now."

"When Winter Thunder came?"

"Long before that. Long before there were people here, of any kind. People are only just beginning to think these days of what might have happened to the earth in those times, to begin to understand such things. The snows fell and did not melt. They packed together and grew heavier, forming ice. The ice began to move down the mountainside and to cut this valley. That took many years."

The boy was listening, watching his face intently, dubious still, but with interest.

"Very slowly, the weather grew warmer and the ice began to melt. You see the lip of the valley there. That's where the ice dropped some of the rock and dirt it had dug from the side of the ridge. When it first melted, maybe the whole valley was a lake for a time. The extra water began to make the cut where the stream is, by running over the lip. People call those places where the ice dropped what it was carrying a moraine. Now it is just a little ridge, you see, well packed together, with trees and grass and brush growing on it."

Coyote was staring at him. "How can ice dig?"

"It was very thick, very heavy, and it tried to move, always down the mountainside, almost like a river of ice. Many of the things under it and in its path were moved along as it went. All this happened very, very slowly. People are only beginning to understand about these things. I have seen places, in other parts of the mountains, where there is still ice like this."

"Hawk's Shadow and the others have told me that you know many strange things, but how do you know about this ice, here, if it was so very long ago?"

"I've read about such things in books."

"Is it written in a book about this valley?"

"Not about this one, but about others like it."

"How do you know they are like it?"

"The books tell me they are alike, in some ways. When you read things and think about them, you find there are many things in the world that are like many others."

"Do you write in a book about this valley?"

"No."

"Could you?"

"I could write, yes, but . . . ."

"Maybe you should make a book about this valley and the ice."

Blake smiled, feeling totally inadequate to answer that.

They were silent for a time, the boy looking thoughtfully around the little park.

"Will it come again, the ice?"

"If it did, it would take many years for the weather to grow cold enough for it to begin, much longer than a man lives."

"Could I go with you one day to see those other ices?"

"Yes. Such ices are called glaciers."

"This is an English word."

Blake nodded.

"I have an English name. I'm told you gave it to me when I was very small."

"Do you want to be called Alec?"

"I think it may be good to have two kinds of names."

"Your mother thought that too."

"She was very brave, my mother, they have told me, and they have said that you were brave too, sometimes. They have told me many stories, Hawk's Shadow and my grandmother and others."

"I have some drawings of your mother. Would you like to see them?"

They went into the cabin. The boy moved around shyly, trying to look uninterested, tentatively touching things. He had little interest in the drawings or in the deerskin shirt, after looking at them briefly. The pictures were of a woman of the Medicine Rock, doing ordinary kinds of things; the shirt was like many others he had seen.

"Which books tell about the ice?"

"This one, but it has hardly any pictures, only words."

"I could learn to read those words and understand them."

"I'm sure you could, if you want to. Are you hungry? I think I'll cook something now. Maybe you'd like to try some biscuits and other things you haven't had before."

"White man's food." There was scorn in his tone.

'Yes," Blake admitted, trying not to mind.

"You will cook it?"

He nodded.

"Cooking is woman's work," the boy pointed out severely, disapprovingly.

"There is no woman here. Should we starve?"

He frowned. "How can you be a man if you cook and keep this cabin and such things? I am not even sure that men should read from books."

"Coyote—Alec—it's not only the things a man does that make him a man. There are things inside us that—"

"In the village, they said you think strange things because you are white. All whites are strange."

"When you're older," Blake said slowly, "maybe some of these things won't seem so strange, especially if you

234

decide you want to learn more about some of them. You're half white. Maybe you will come to understand both kinds of people."

"I'm not white," the boy said calmly, looking at him directly. "I am of the Medicine Rock, grandson of Red Sky. I will go outside now, if you are going to cook. Will you teach me to shoot with that rifle?"

They ate, mostly in silence. Alec tested the new food cautiously, judiciously, and then ate well.

Drinking his coffee, Blake thought of how Shy Fawn had made it, how the other women still did, putting half coffee and half sugar into a pot of water and boiling it for a long time. He had never liked coffee with sugar, nor boiled like that, but had never had the heart to tell her so. She had always taken such pleasure in making coffee for him. Coffee at the cabin had never lasted long in those days because their guests had liked it very much the way she made it. He looked, now, at the large, full coffee can on the shelf, thinking he would give that and everything else he had if she were here with him to help him know how to bring up the boy. Alec must be happy and secure. He must know the things from two worlds, if he wanted to know them, and still be able to be at ease with himself. It would never be an easy thing.

"They said," reported Alec thoughtfully, "that you should not stay up here all alone through the winter."

"Have you come to stay with me then?" There was a feeling of tightness in his chest.

"I would like to go and be with the boys sometimes."

"You can go down whenever you like."

The boy looked uneasy. "You are my father. Does a father not tell a boy when he may or may not do things?"

"All right," Blake said gently. "When you want to go down, you will ask me and I will tell you if you may or not."

Alec's face cleared for a moment, but then he frowned again. "Only I hope you won't tell me I have to do woman's work."

It was a long, cold winter and Blake was not lonely. He and Alec grew, for the most part, very comfortable with

235

each other and the time passed quickly, pleasantly. The boy's eager mind was a delight, a marvel to his father, who remembered all too vividly the frightened, circumscribed, bleak life he had led at the age of six.

"You are strange," Alec said to him one evening in the midst of a writing lesson when Blake had been trying to explain the meanings of some words, "but sometimes I like your strangeness. It makes me think about things."

Blake cut a little fir tree and set it up for Christmas, drawing small pictures of animals and other things as decoration. Alec was dubious at first, but then he began to help. The innate talent he showed for drawing seemed so beautiful to Blake that he found it almost frightening. Alec was, for the most part, well pleased with his own work and he enjoyed doing it, but he was still doubtful about whether he should enjoy such things quite so much. They made a large star for the top of the tree, coloring it with the brightest paints they had. It was not a star, Blake thought, smiling, that truly religious people would have wanted to have.

"Father Robidou has told us that Christmas was the day Christ was born," said Alec. "Last year, he was in our village at Christmas. I like the holy pictures he brings. It's odd to see a man weeping as Jesus does in those pictures."

"Men *do* cry sometimes," Blake said a little absently.

He was trying to draw a bighorn ram, standing on a boulder, thinking a little of the ewe he had shot long ago, the first large animal he had ever killed with an arrow.

"But it seems to me this is not a thing to make pictures of," Alec said. "It seems to me a great weakness for a true man to cry and that it should not be put into a picture. A picture of such a thing makes a man a captive of that thing . . . . The Father and Little Rain my aunt say that Christ weeps because people are so wicked. If the Father comes this year, will you come and hear the things he says?"

"I'll go down to the village with you, but I think I won't go to the chapel."

"Why not?"

"Because I know the things the Father says and I—I don't believe as he does."

"Then I won't believe either."

"Alec, as you grow up, you must decide for yourself what to believe."

"I don't understand," he said, perplexed. "You are white and the Father is white, and yet you say you don't believe the same."

"Believing is not a matter of what color the skin is. Too many people think that way. That kind of thinking binds the mind so that it has no freedom. Do you understand at all?"

"No, but it doesn't matter, probably. I think I don't want to be a Catholic. When I am old enough, I want to go away and seek a medicine dream. They say that good Catholics don't do this."

"If it's what you want, then it's what you should do, when you're older."

"But how will I be two things, white and Indian?" he said, deeply thoughtful. "It seems that things should not be so hard."

"Try not to worry about it. It is a thing you should not really have to think about very much. Only be what you are. Take things one at a time, as they come, to decide what you feel and what you ought to do about them. I'll help you if I can."

"You are my father. You should *tell* me what to feel and decide."

"Alec, I'll tell you how I feel if you ask, but you have to make up your own mind about yourself."

"I don't want to have to be spending all my time in thinking. I want to be a good hunter and know about horses. I want to play games and some day I will be a warrior. Already, I'm a little bit brave."

Blake bit back the first words that came to him. He was trying to make the boy grow up too fast, understand too much. He said lightly, "Besides being Christ's birthday, do you know that Christmas is a time when people give gifts to each other?"

"Why?"

"It's a happy time, when they're glad of their families and friends."

"Will we give gifts to my grandmother and the others?"

"Yes, if you like. I have some trading things I brought

from the post. You can decide which gifts to give to them."

"We'd better tell them about this custom so that they can give gifts to us."

"I don't think we'll do that. The real idea is to *give,* not to see how much you can get."

"Still, I think they should know about it."

After the boy was in bed at night, Blake sat up carving things for him, animals of the country, a top, two boats to float in the lake, a railroad locomotive. He wrapped the things in old, carefully saved newspaper and put them under the tree on the night before Christmas Eve.

"I will look at them," Alec said eagerly when he knew they were his gifts.

"Not until Christmas morning," Blake cautioned happily.

"But I see them there now."

"Still, you can't look inside."

"Why?"

"Because this is how it is done."

"I have no gift for you."

"I don't mind that."

"I think it's not right. You should have things wrapped up too."

"It gives me enough pleasure, giving things to you."

"Is it like that, being a father?"

"Yes, it is."

"Then perhaps I will never be a father when I am old."

Father Perry, one of the young priests from St. Denis Mission, was at the Medicine Rock village just after Christmas, but a great storm struck just after his arrival and Blake and Alec did not go down. Later, when the sun shone and a light crust was forming on the snow, Beaver Tooth and Hawk's Shadow came up to the cabin.

"Why do you have that tree in here?" demanded Hawk's Shadow, astounded.

"It is a tree of Christmas," Alec explained shyly, proudly. "We made the things hanging on it and there were some gifts. It's dead and dry now and we will have to burn it soon, but we like to look at it there."

Blake gave them coffee, boiled with sugar, as they liked it.

Beaver Tooth said, "You ought to have a woman up here. There are young girls in the village, needing husbands. It seems to me you should take one."

When Blake made no answer, he went on, "Since that battle with the Blackfeet, we do not have enough men for our women. *I* would take another wife, simply to give one of those young girls a place, but the Father tells me that good Christians have only one wife. You have no wife at all and you are not a Christian."

Hawk's Shadow said restlessly, "It's time we hunted. There is a crust coming to the snow now. We could catch the deer and break their necks because it's not yet a crust thick enough to hold their hoofs. We would save arrows and powder this way and it is fun to hunt like that sometimes. Will you come with us?"

Blake said he would come.

"When Father Perry was with us," Beaver Tooth said soberly, "he told us of a great council that will be held next summer near Fort Laramie. It is mostly for the tribes of the plains country, but we of the mountains have been asked to come, too."

"It is called by the army of the whites," Hawk's Shadow said with distaste, "and by traders and missionaries and such. I think they are going to try to tell the tribes what to do. What do you think?"

"I think you're right," Blake said reluctantly. He dreaded being drawn into this.

"Hawk's Shadow and some of the others," said Beaver Tooth, "think we should not go, but I have told them we should. It is better to know for ourselves whatever may be said there than only to hear of it from others."

They waited, looking at him expectantly, each for his own reasons. Finally, he said, "That may be true."

"A few of the People," Beaver Tooth said unctuously, "are still very old-fashioned. They hold on, very hard, to the old ways. I am their chief. I have told them I will go and bring them back a report of this council. But they have asked Hawk's Shadow to go as well and he has said he will go only if you will."

"I know nothing of whites," Hawk's Shadow said unhappily. "I do not know their language and I don't want to know it. There was a time when I thought I wanted to

239

know such things but I was very young then. Now I think it is better not to know them. Still, if I am to go and sit in this council, I must believe I will have a true translation of what is said."

Beaver Tooth frowned, looking very important. "*I* understand their language. I have been at Camas Post many times. I talk with the Fathers. My son is at the mission school. It is a shame to the People, some of them, that my cousin Hawk's Shadow has no faith in the words of his chief . . . . Will you come, to set his mind at rest?"

Blake did not want to go and he knew he would. The words about duty nagged at him.

"I've told Connall MacPheirson I'd go with him and some of his men to meet a supply train at Fort Laramie in the spring. I suppose I could go to the council."

"It will be at about the time when the buffalo come," said Beaver Tooth. "The Father says that we will all be friends together, counciling and hunting."

Hawk's Shadow made an ungracious sound.

"I have said to the village that there are things we can learn from the whites. They have much in the way of goods and their lives are easier than ours. Why should we not learn what is good for us of their ways? Then we will have the best of both ways of living, here in the Valley, and be better for it. Don't you agree? The Fathers say I am right."

"If that was all there was to it, I'd agree," Blake said.

"Is it not what you are doing? Living like a white and like an Indian?"

"I do not like this word 'Indian,'" said Hawk's Shadow irritably. "It throws us all together like snakes in a hole. We are different tribes and bands and peoples and not the same at all."

"He has little understanding of the whites," Beaver Tooth explained tolerantly. "He only stays here, holding to the old ways—"

Hawk's Shadow said hotly, "And you become a white man Indian. That kind *is* all alike, like snakes in a hole. Crooked Wolf your grandfather, Red Sky and the others would not—"

"They were great men," Beaver Tooth said with self-control, "but they are gone now. Things are not the same.

There was a time like this before, for our people, when they first began to have horses. We all know those stories, how some held to the old ways and others did not. Those others began to raise fine horses, the best in the country. They traded them for things our people had not had before. They went to the buffalo country. They were mighty in war. Are those bad things? Yet they were new things once and different, feared and ridiculed by some."

"As long as I live," Hawk's Shadow said in a kind of fierce helplessness, "there will be at least one of the Medicine Rock People left who does not sell himself to the whites."

He went outside, his face like a storm.

"He is a good man," Beaver Tooth said, magnanimously and with real concern and something of sorrow, "but he truly does not understand."

He picked up a book from the table. "I have learned to read some words of English from the Bible and I am practicing to sign my name."

Blake left him looking at the book and went out to stand silently near Hawk's Shadow at the edge of the frozen lake.

"It makes him very angry," Hawk's Shadow said after a long time, "that some of the People, mostly the older ones, say that you and I must go to this council the whites have called. I can see in his face and hear in his voice that he is angry, but he does not say so. Is this something a man learns from the whites, not to say what he truly thinks and feels? Is this supposed to be some clever way for a chief to behave to his own people?"

There was silence again and then he said, "I do not want to be chief. I am glad not to be, and yet I go on worrying as only a chief should have to . . . . What will come of this white council?"

"Probably not much that will touch the Medicine Rock. I think they want, mostly now, to make their trails and forts more secure, so they will be talking mostly to the plains peoples."

"But it is our hunting ground, too, that they disturb, and what of later? They seem to be without number, those whites, Every year, more keep coming out of the east. When will they want our country?"

"Hawk's Shadow," he said painfully, "can't we think of the council and those things when they come? The Medicine Rock is as it has been. Let's just think of our hunting tomorrow and—"

"You run away from thinking again," he said heavily, sadly. "Sometimes, you are like a man covering his eyes, Blake. You must take away your hands some time and what you have been trying not to see will still be there. I wish you would tell me just what it is you are trying not to see because I can't seem to know. I feel only a badness. I see nothing of this clearly yet. I think you *do* know, my brother. Is it that you feel as I do, not wanting to be a chief, yet with a great feeling for the People?"

"Yes."

"Then warn me of these things you are trying not to see, yet seeing. You know that I have no medicine spirit. I have always believed you do have one, though you have said you don't. What will happen? What should we do? Together you and I may be able to—"

"Hawk's Shadow, I don't want, ever, to tell anyone else what to do, about anything. Even if I knew what to tell you now, I think we could do very little. Two men, alone, cannot stop the world."

"It would not be two men only," he said quickly, vehemently. "There are still many who have respect for my father, even for me. If I knew what to warn them of, I would go to the other bands and tribes, the Palouses, the Yakimas, the Cayuses—"

"No. We can't."

"Is it that we should make ready for war? All the tribes? I know what you think of war. I don't understand it, but I know. We could fight the whites together and kill them. Then things would be as they used to be, as they should be."

"Hawk's Shadow—"

"You are afraid of war," he accused angrily.

"Yes, I'm afraid. If the tribes fought the whites, all together, they might hold them back for a time, but not for long, and then, for those people who were left, things would be much worse. There are many of them, as you've said. They would keep coming."

"They can't," Hawk's Shadow cried fiercely. "Who has told them they should come and take our country?"

"They feel it's their country," Blake said reluctantly, "even more now than they used to. It's a part of the United States now—"

"What is this?"

"The nation of the whites, their country."

"But this land is ours! A country does not belong to a people simply because they *say* it does."

"I know that, but they believe that it is theirs."

"They have not lived and died in this land, nor hunted . . . ."

"But they want to. They're beginning to."

"And many more will die," he said fiercely. "They will *not* have it."

"Hawk's Shadow . . . . if the Medicine Rock People could keep this valley, as it is, and go on living in the old ways, it might be enough—"

"Now your whiteness is showing. Would you have us be farmers? We could not just stay in the valley, you know that. We must have the camas grounds, the fishing, the buffalo. It might be right to share those things with a few whites, as some of the tribes have always shared them, but whites have no mind for sharing. They say, 'This is mine. Keep away from it. Do not touch it. You have no right to a share.' I know this from things I have heard about lands they have taken in other places. Is it not true?"

"It is true," Blake said unwillingly.

"Then we cannot let them begin to think of coming here. You say you are of the People. Will you fight for us?"

There was a silence, and Blake said painfully, "I'll try to fight, Hawk's Shadow, but not with rifles and arrows. That might work, but only for a little while. I'll go to the council and listen to the whites and see if I can find what they are thinking of doing. Then we'll see what can be done if—"

"What other way is there to fight but with rifles and arrows?"

"White men have laws, rules written down, by which all the people are supposed to live, and courts—"

243

"The whiteness in you now hurts my eyes," Hawk's Shadow said with great, fierce, disappointed intensity. "Battles cannot be won with words and talking papers."

"I've seen Red Sky and other great ones do mighty things with words in councils."

Hawk's Shadow made an angry, helpless gesture, saying bitterly, "I do not like all this talking. You talk, Beaver Tooth talks, and I cannot always find ways to argue with you because words do not fall out of my mouth so easily, yet I know you are wrong. Can you believe these whites will be held back by words?"

"Probably they can't be, but neither can they be held back by guns and arrows. I want to do what I can to help the People, but each man must do what he is able to do."

"I have said to you once that I don't like war and yet I would do everything I could to bring the peoples together to fight. I would be willing, even, to be allied with the Blackfeet for that, and what will you do? It is your whiteness that makes you like this. You want to be of the People but there is always that differentness inside you. Before you went away, I was beginning to have hope that you might be a right kind of person one day. At that time, I think you would have stood with us, while Shy Fawn and my father lived. Would you have fought then?"

"I don't know."

"You know, Blake," he said accusingly. "You always try to escape by saying you don't know if you can think of nothing else to say. Do you not believe they would want you to fight this thing still, as a man ought to fight?"

"I think Shy Fawn would not have wanted such a war, and maybe your father—"

"Women are sometimes different in thinking about war. They know very little. Yet Shy Fawn died as bravely as any warrior, fighting, as did my father."

"I'm trying to tell you, there are different ways of fighting."

"You have tried to tell me there are many different ways of almost everything. I have believed little of that. There are rightness and wrongness, goodness and badness. It seems to me another way you try to escape, saying that everything may be all right, perhaps not bad nor good. Also, I think that while you were away, you

244

changed. You have lost what you had gained toward becoming a right kind of person."

"I am only trying to accept some things because there are those things in the world that I can't make different, that none of us can, so that we have to adjust to be able to go on living . . . . Would you go down to the Medicine Rock and bang your head against it until you were dead, trying to move it to another place?"

Hawk's Shadow stared at him stonily. "Why would I want to move the Medicine Rock? If you are going to go on thinking and acting like a white man, I don't know why you stay here."

"It's my home," Blake said around the hurt that had risen in his throat. "Red Sky called me his son. You have called me your brother. My son is Shy Fawn's son. I love the Valley and the People. I have always felt I belonged here . . . . but you're right, I'm white. I can't help the way I was born or the things I know and think. If you say I should not be here, I will go. It's the land of the Medicine Rock People, not really mine."

Another silence and Hawk's Shadow said angrily, but more softly, "You wound with your words."

"And you with yours." Blake's voice was scarcely audible.

"And you have almost made me say that you are right about being able to fight with those words."

"It should not be so between us."

"No." The anger was going out of Hawk's Shadow; he looked tired. "Beaver Tooth is coming. Tomorrow we will go after the deer. Let's take our boys. They should see such things."

"Hawk's Shadow, listen," Blake said quickly. "It may be that there is nothing that can do any good, words or anything else. I am not wise. You know that well. I only want to do something if I can. That does not mean—"

"We'll hunt tomorrow. Each day we'll do what must be done and we'll see what comes. We will find ways. We are of the Medicine Rock, sons of Red Sky."

That spring, the spring of 1851, Blake began working again for Connall MacPheirson as a trader. He still had some of the money he had earned on the *Florie* and could have lived for some time on that, with his small financial needs, but as the weather began to moderate, he admitted unwillingly to himself how restless he was growing. His little valley was the place he wanted to be. It held all the beauty, peace, and joy he could want, and yet thoughts of the summer's council, of all that could or might be coming to the country would not allow him simply to be quiet. The advice he had heard so clearly in his mind, standing in the bow of the *Florie* half a world away, words about keeping himself a little aloof, was good advice, counsel he wanted to take, not ever to be hurt so much again. All right. He would hold himself a little apart from people, from what happened to them, but the need to *know* what was going on, to try to think of what might be done, drove him down to Camas Post and about the country. Eagerly, Alec went with him.

Connall was investing that year in wagons, oxen, mules, and horses, in addition to new farming equipment and cattle, going into the lucrative business of freighting.

"So much is wanted in the way of goods, in California and the rest of the west," he told Blake. "I can't afford *not* to go into the carrying trade. The trouble I'm having is in finding men to run this thing. *I* don't want to have to be forever driving a wagon over some God-forsaken trail. I've other things to do, but it gets harder every year to find men a man can truly trust . . . . I don't suppose you'd want to take charge of some of it?"

"You're supposing right," Blake said. "I couldn't live on those trails either. They're too civilized, too white."

"Aye," Connall said glumly, "with all those poor souls scrambling to get to the gold or grab off the best farm lands or whatever their reasons are. Still, Blake, every man's got the right to do what he can to better himself."

"The God-given right," Blake said bitterly, "whatever it does to anybody else. Have you been reading that stuff in the papers about white supremacy?"

"That's the Southerners talking, justifying this mess they've got into."

"Yes, but don't ever believe most whites don't feel that way about Indians, or about anybody else if the idea suits their convenience. It can make damn good justification for almost anything."

Connall's face had grown stubborn, his blue eyes a little defiant. "Well, there's some shred of truth in it, lad."

"Connall—"

"Now wait! We won't talk of it much. When you were here last year, back from your travels, I thought you'd changed, mellowed a bit, become more reasonable. I'm afraid now that that was just an idea I had at the time. I want us to stay friends so we'll not talk of this supremacy much, but I need to say just one or two things.

"Your claim has always been that Indians are human beings, and that's true, but they're not the same as whites, lad. They don't know, just as an example, what to do with the land, to make it work for them. Some whites do. They've had to learn it over a long period of time, but now some do know. Doesn't that show a kind of supremacy? Granted, they've had advantages the Indians have never had, but still, most whites, one time or another, have worked for those advantages, for the learning or know-how or whatever it is they've got. I believe they've earned, or their grandfathers or somebody have earned for them, the right to use those things in their best interests."

"What do you mean by 'advantages' and 'best interests'?"

"Ah, Blake, don't start to complicate things with exact meanings of words. I've never enjoyed such things. You know as well as I what those words mean. Now, what I'm saying about this land business is that this land's here, waiting, and there are some who know what properly ought to be done with it. Doesn't that prove there's a purpose to it all?"

"Connall, the oceans are there, too. Does that mean we've a manifest destiny to take them away from the fish?"

Connall brought his big fist down jarringly on the table. "Don't go clever on me, Blake. You're making no sense at all, just playing around with words. I've never been any good at that kind of thing. I'm only trying to explain this one point to you. I don't want this land taken up, but it's going to be. I'm only finding out myself how good it can be. They've done some irrigating at the mission farm and the Mormons are building dams and irrigating like mad—

men. I'm trying it myself, and it's a wonderful difference it makes in the land. A great deal of this could be good farming country and, so, I suppose it ought to be."

"*Why?* Land's not needed. There's plenty of it, still, in the east that doesn't belong to Indians, that's close to markets—"

"I don't know what it is about whites, lad. They seem to have to keep spreading, reaching out for something more. I see it in myself, and in you. Both of us might have made pretty good lives, just living as the Indians do, but we can't feel that that's enough. Also, the government encourages all this pioneering. It's a good thing for business, and for politics. Right now, the big maneuvering is between the free and slave states, who'll end up controlling the most country. I think that'll come to war, one day."

"I hope so. Maybe it'll stop immigration."

"You've not much charity, lad. A civil war would be a sad thing."

"It's not a sad thing, what's happening out here?"

"Ah, it is, but let's talk of other things. You're stubborn and I'm stubborn and we'll never get this thing settled between us. Have you seen in the papers, too, those things about what the ladies are doing back east saying they're equal with the men—Lord love 'em—asking for the vote? Sometimes a man must just sit and wonder what can come next."

Blake traveled a good deal that spring, renewing his acquaintance with the country and the tribes west of the mountains. He saw restlessness and uneasiness everywhere, dissatisfaction on the part of the Indians with the missionaries and other whites among them, contention and jockeying for advantage among the whites themselves. Father Robidou's group was kindly spoken of by *his* Indians, and not so much resented as some among most of the others. The southern Nez Perce and the Snakes seemed to think reasonably well of the Mormons who were coming among them, but the Protestant missionaries over along the Blue Mountains, Mr. Prewitt's group and others, got hardly a word of defense, even from the Indians they considered to be their own.

When the spring trading season was done, Blake and

Connall, with their sons and several other men, took the things for which they had traded down to Fort Laramie to make use of Connall's new wagons for sending the goods east. Father Robidou traveled with them, on his way to the great plains council.

Working among the tribes, Blake couldn't help remembering the words of the old professor at Cambridge, "That aboriginal culture will be gone . . . ." Almost against his will, he began collecting a few very fine things, representative of the art and the everyday lives of various tribes and bands. He told himself that perhaps he would send some things east one day, only to try to set the scholars straight. He went on, looking for examples for the collection as their party moved east of the mountains. Sometimes, by the evening's camp fire, he drew a scene or an activity he had seen that day.

"You have a great deal of talent."

Blake looked up at Father Robidou, studying, over his shoulder, the almost finished picture of a Snake woman, dressing a deerskin.

"If I could draw like that," said the priest, "I could give our order a much better idea of the things we're doing here. Would you consider coming to St. Denis to make some sketches of things there? The church, the farm work, the school?"

"I might," Blake said evasively. "Some time."

The priest had aged a great deal since the last time Blake had seen him, at his cabin in the Medicine Rock. Father Robidou's beard and hair were entirely white now, his shoulders bent, his face thin. His blue eyes, perhaps more earnest than ever, seemed dimmer behind his glasses.

"You really should come and see what we're doing, whether you would sketch or not. You'll be wanting to send your boy to the school soon. May I sit down? How old is Alec now? Six?"

"He was six in the fall. You're welcome to sit down, Father, but Alec won't be one of your students."

"Why not? It seems to me he shows great promise. Don't you think he should have the preparation—"

"Promise of what?"

"Why, of intelligence."

249

"That's true. His intelligence is not going to be channeled, though, into the best ways for his becoming a good, humble, docile half-breed."

"I don't think I follow you. We don't at all—"

"I've seen some of your students, Father. You're doing some good things at St. Denis, I don't doubt, but you're also adding to the confusion of those youngsters. They're becoming a little bit of this and a little bit of that, and they don't belong anywhere. I don't want that for Alec."

"You're going to let him grow up simply as an Indian then? You don't feel he needs to be prepared for living anywhere but in the Medicine Rock?"

"I'm not sure what you mean by 'simply as an Indian.' I'm believing more and more that there are very few simple people, whoever they may be. I want the boy to grow up as Alec Westfall, whose mother was a Medicine Rock woman, and whose father still isn't sure about a lot of things. He's learning to read and to think. I hope he's also learning to be. The humility you encourage at the mission wouldn't help him much with those things. The students I've seen this spring have too much knowledge to be the old kind of Indians and too much docility to be whites. I know you believe in what you're doing, and some of it is good, but you're helping to make a whole group of people who can't ever be anything, who won't really belong anywhere."

Father Robidou looked into the fire, his face thoughtful, troubled. "You add to my burdens," he said gently, smiling. "It's much easier on the conscience to know that one is right. You insist on trying to make me question. I'd been told by Connall and others that you were somewhat changed after your time away from the mountains."

"And now you think I'm not."

"You're as interesting, as disturbing to me as you've ever been. Perhaps you've grown more tolerant, less angry."

"I want to apologize, Father, for that time I asked you to leave my cabin. You made me very uneasy then, very unsure, but I think I can live with that now, better than I could. In those days, you see, I was trying to be truly of the People, as though I'd been born in the Valley. Only I couldn't love Shy Fawn as an Indian loves his wife, and I

250

couldn't kill Blackfeet as an Indian would have done. It was hard to have to know those things."

"These must be very hard things for you to say. I feel you are doing me an honor."

"No, they're not so hard. Not anymore."

"And what do you feel yourself to be now?"

"Just—a person . . . . As I grew away from the way my grandparents raised me and from the kinds of life I led before I came west, I'm afraid I got to feeling rather superior. The attitudes of some of the whites I knew added to those feelings. There was a short time when I thought I had most of the answers. The Indian ways seemed very simple and, for the most part, good. I thought I could just shuck off being white and still have the best of both worlds. Only I couldn't stop feeling and thinking like a white. When we fought the Blackfeet, I hated as a white man because I loved Shy Fawn and Red Sky as a white man loves. I didn't want those feelings. I had to go halfway across the world to begin coming to grips with them, to begin to accept them, to accept that I can't change such things in myself or change the basics of what others are. Now, I think I don't want to try anymore. I want to be of the Medicine Rock, as much as I can be, because it's home to me and to Alec. I'd like simply to live and let live. It's a trite expression, but it would be a beautiful kind of life, if it were possible."

"But you don't think it's possible?"

"I don't see how, with people like you in the world and with things going as they are. Do you?"

"No. You see, we agree again."

"To some extent."

The priest smiled sadly. "I'm sure you realize that I couldn't possibly give up beliefs in what I know to be right. Granted, I'm not practicing live and let live as I believe you mean it. I have been given a trust to help others, to try to direct their lives toward God. You have a block where religion is concerned. I'm afraid that may never change, but I'll go on praying for you."

"I'll be glad of that," Blake said quietly.

"And do you still look, for your answers, to the mountains and the sky?"

"Not so much for answers. It seems to me that answers

have a way of changing from day to day until I don't believe there are any standard ones. They vary, with the situation and the people involved in the questions. But there's peace in the mountains and the sky, tolerance, things I can count on staying pretty much the same."

"I think you have a great deal more of faith than you care to admit."

"Not in your kind of God; not in my grandparents' kind. I can never again believe that a supposedly omnipotent Being would care about loading men, who already have almost more problems than they can bear, with a burden of congenital guilt. Why should He bother with a mean, petty thing like that if He's already omnipotent? If you're going to interpret God to people, why not give them some hope, hope for tonight and tomorrow, not just for after they die? Isn't the way you do it just a way of keeping people in line, for the convenience of the Church or whatever?"

"Ah, now you're interpreting."

"Yes, I am, and I'm sure that seems like some kind of heresy to you. To me, it seems like my prerogative as a living, thinking human being. If there *is* a God, it seems to me He's a little different for every individual. It's no one person's business to try to tamper with another's concepts."

There was a silence and the priest said softly, "You have changed since I first knew you. I could almost wish you hadn't become able to put your thoughts into words . . . I'm holding a mass in the morning. Will you come?"

"I think not, Father."

"Will you allow your boy to come?"

"If he wants to."

"But you won't send him to us at the mission?"

"Only if it becomes very important to him."

"There is still the question of his soul."

Blake made an impatient gesture. "I had thought that that was a part of what we've been talking about."

"The things you've been saying make me think, perhaps even question some things a bit, but I have no doubts about the immortal soul and the need, the responsibility, for its salvation."

"Salvation, it seems to me, if there is salvation, is another private, personal matter, like God."

"But some of us are given the privilege of seeing the way more clearly. It's our duty to point it out to others."

"I can't believe that, Father. It's like going out to wait for a medicine dream—"

"You compare such heathen things with Christianity?"

"Aren't they the same kind of thing, really?"

"Oh, Blake, you are confused."

He smiled. "The more we talk, the less confused I feel."

"You're a great worry to me."

"I'm sorry about that, Father. I'm only trying to be myself, which seems to me the most worthwhile thing any of us can do, to be ourselves, bound by our own rules. Perhaps you can think of me as the devil's advocate."

Father Robidou stood up stiffly, a shadow of anger passing over his face, and changed the subject. "That is really a fine drawing. The woman looks almost as if she might speak to us. Why the sadness in her face?"

"Because that's how she looked."

"I think you have a great feeling for people. I think you try to hold yourself a little apart from them, but your sensitivity shows, in your pictures and in other things."

He had taken the finished drawing and studied it in the firelight. Now he held it out.

"Keep it, if you like."

XII

"My grandmother says you are making a woman of me," Alec reported.

"I know she does," Blake answered calmly.

They were weeding their garden on a hot day at the beginning of August. They had spent most of this summer in the valley, not going, this time, with the Medicine Rock People to the buffalo country. The growing season was short but intense, and their vegetables were doing well. Blake had planted a few fruit trees, though he had no great hope of their being able to survive and produce. He had bought a few cattle, and Beaver Tooth, too, had become a cattleman in a small way. Blake's excuse for spending the summer in the Medicine Rock had been to keep an eye on the cattle while the rest of the People were away. He and Alec had been working on the construction of a small barn and on putting a floor in the cabin. Alec went on now, about his grandmother.

"She says we're both growing stranger all the time and that you should bring a woman up here to do this kind of work in the garden and such, before it's too late and we're both lost to manhood."

"I know what she says. What do you say to her?"

"That we're happy enough as we are. Then she says again that you're making a white of the grandson of Red Sky and so I tell her it can't be helped, how I was born . . . . They should be back soon. We could give her some of these beans and things."

"Yes, we will. As soon as someone else is here to

watch the stock, I'll be going down to the post again. Do you want to come or stay at the village?"

"I think I'll come with you. Con MacPheirson is my friend. I want to see him again. Do you think Hawk's Shadow would let Little Chief come with us?"

"I don't know. We'll ask him."

"Will the new books and things be there, I wonder."

"Probably."

"When we were at the post in the spring, I heard you and Mr. MacPheirson talking about a trip to St. Louis. If you go, could I go with you? I've never seen a city or any of those things."

"You can go, I suppose, but I doubt there'll be a trip now, not with the trouble there's been to the west."

"Would it be dangerous for us to go?"

"I don't know about its being dangerous, Alec. It's mostly that I just don't want to be away now."

"You never want to be away," the boy said comfortably. "Look. The deer have been in here again."

That afternoon, they saw the Medicine Rock People coming back into the valley. Alec went down and when he came back the next morning, Hawk's Shadow and Little Chief were with him.

"You did not come down," Hawk's Shadow said to Blake, after greeting. "What kind of guard are you for the valley if you missed seeing so many people coming in?"

"I saw you, but I didn't want to come down until the village is set up."

Hawk's Shadow grunted. "You're wise to keep away, I suppose It's a noisy place now, full of women's arguments."

"Are the People well? And was the hunting good?"

"A few old ones and babies died on the journey, as they always do," he said and named them. "The hunting was not so good, but we are good hunters and we have meat. You should come down and get some and, while you are there, you should take a woman. It's been a long while, Blake, since Shy Fawn died. Some of us worry that you are not even as normal as you once were. We have had homosexuals among the People before but not for a long time. When they were among us, they had their own lodge and lived, in those ways, as they saw fit. They were

255

men still; some were even good warriors, I am told, but that seems to me a sad kind of life. Women can be very trying; still, they have their place and their uses. I don't want to see you become one of those kind of people nor make such a person of the boy. It is a worry to Owl Woman my mother."

"It isn't happening," Blake said quietly. "None of you need to worry that it will."

"There are several nice young girls you could choose from. One of them is Falling Leaf, Beaver Tooth's little sister. You could be of the chief's family again, though she would make you marry her in the church."

"Red Sky's family is the family of my chief."

"Beaver Tooth would be pleased, I think, if you married his sister. His heart has changed toward you, now that he is a white man Indian and you are both raising cattle. And that reminds me." He laughed. "Beaver Tooth's heart is not so good, just now, toward me or toward Little Chief. Little Chief and some of the other boys were being scouts as we came back to the Medicine Rock. They were still excited about the buffalo and other kinds of hunting. As they rode into the Valley, one of those cows was shot. Don't look angry. It was a cow of Beaver Tooth's, not yours.

"Little Chief is very good with a bow. When Beaver Tooth asked why it was done, he said that the People needed fresh meat to celebrate being back in the Valley again. Beaver Tooth has other thoughts, but, to me, this seems very reasonable. The cows are raised for meat, aren't they?"

"But, Hawk's Shadow, they aren't the boys' cows to kill."

"They're in the valley, eating the grass. The Valley and the grass belong to the People, all the People. You have killed a cow or two of yours, to share the meat with the People."

"I wouldn't like it if they had been killed without my permission."

"What do you mean by 'permission'? Listen, I have heard talk of this all season, from those Cayuses who live near the white missionaries to the west. The missionaries have told those Cayuses they want them to have the benefits of the white man's ways, of farming and things like that, but those Cayuses have begun to come to their senses, finally. They are not so blinded anymore by white medicine from the Bible-book, or any of the rest of it. None of those things have helped them in making war, and white man's diseases have come among them that the whites can't cure. Also, they now see that farming and such is not fit work for men. Still, the whites keep telling them they want to share, and the Cayuses try to believe they don't lie, about everything.

"Last year, I'm told, almost nobody stayed there to help with the farming. There are a lot of whites living over in that country now. They can do such work themselves. When the Cayuses came back from hunting, the crops were ready and they did as the whites have been telling them all this time and shared in the harvest. This made those whites very angry. Can you tell me why that is?"

"Why do you pretend to be so innocent?" Blake said, smiling. "You know the answer to that as well as I do. Those Cayuses did no work for the crops. They had no right to share."

"But the Cayuses say, wisely, that they did no work to raise the buffalo or the camas or any of these things."

"The Cayuses, and you, know there's a difference."

"We have brought buffalo meat and other things which you can share, yet you did no work at all for those things."

"I'll trade for them."

"Kettles and things," he said scornfully. "I think it becomes more a world of women every year. The trade goods are mostly things for women. The men are made to do women's work, except you, who have always done it willingly. Nothing has felt quite right for some time, and it's been worse since that disgraceful council two years ago."

Blake said nothing, thinking back to the gathering of whites that had taken place at the fort prior to the council of the tribes; how he, Connall, Father Robidou, and a few others who tried to take the Indians' part had been scorned and ridiculed, called squaw men and white Indians and worse things, not only by the new army officers

257

and government emissaries sent from the east, but by a few old mountain men from whom they had hoped for more understanding and support.

Ellis Williams, who had fallen asleep years ago while hiding from the Blackfeet, and who claimed with perverse pride to have fathered at least a dozen half-breed children whom he had left behind without a qualm, had been made an agent to the Snakes. But there had been a few others whom the advocates of the tribes' interests had hoped they might depend on and who had disappointed them.

"Just get the savage bastards onto a reservation," they had clamored. "At least, that way they can be watched better. We can't have any more whites killed."

"What about their hunting?" the few had tried desperately. "What about—"

But the decisions had already been made. The council had been called only for putting those decisions into effect and those few whites who refused to do what they could to be helpful were blacklisted by their fellows, looked on as having become not only something less than white men, but less than human as well.

Hawk's Shadow was saying now, "Beaver Tooth says it's a lot of money those plains tribes got, a lot of trade goods, for signing those papers that say they will live only where they are told, but you have told me it's not so much and that the whites are not keeping their word about it. Well, then, the tribes needn't keep their word either. Both sides were fools to talk of such things in the first place. How can the whites believe they can make any group live only on a certain piece of land, hunting only what game happens to wander there, not being men anymore, in exchange for a few beads and blankets?"

"Still, they did sign."

Hawk's Shadow made a sound of disgust and derision. "It made me ashamed to be of the same color as they are, sitting there, hearing those chiefs of the Crow and Snake and Blackfeet and Sioux say how good their hearts were toward the whites, what friends they were, and all that buffalo shit about the father in Washington. Anyone who knows anything, knows that was just talk. They like to move their jaws, those people, and try to see who can look the most important. You felt the same about most of what was said there. Didn't you walk out of the council and make the whites very angry because you wouldn't play the game? Yet now you take the whites' side, saying only that those chiefs signed."

"I'm not taking anybody's side. You are right, saying that it was like playing a game. I think it was like that for both the Indians and the whites, only each side was playing a different game, with little understanding of what the other was doing. That is going to prove to be very confusing. And they did sign."

"But they were fools to do that and now they know they were fools. People do sometimes make mistakes. Must they suffer for those mistakes forever? Must their children, who had no part, go on paying for those mistakes?

"And why do you not come with us on our journeys anymore? You only sit here like a farmer. Does the buffalo hunt not give you pleasure anymore? Don't you see that one day there may be no more buffalo? . . . Or is this why you don't go?"

"Hawk's Shadow, I've been thinking. Suppose that next year we caught some young buffalo and brought them here to the Valley, alive."

"Why?"

"For meat. Then the People wouldn't have to go out to the plains. They—"

"Many years ago when we saved you from the Blackfeet, your head was broken and it made you crazy. I have always thought you never got over it and now I see I have been right again."

"It's not crazy. We could—"

He interrupted with feigned patience, "It has always been our way to go to the buffalo country, to move about in the land, gathering the things that were put here for us. What kind of men would we be, raising buffalo like tame cattle and staying shut up in the valley? What kind of life would that be? It would be like living on one of those reservations."

"But it would be your land, the place you chose, not they."

"This is a thing you should talk about with Beaver

Tooth. You and he think more alike, with your nonsense, every day. Perhaps he would like this plan. No doubt you and he could herd your buffalo down to sell to the whites on their trails. I would never have thought that you could imagine us living, only and always, on one small bit of land. *All* this land"—he made a great sweeping gesture—"belongs to the People."

"Hawk's Shadow, you don't want to hear this and I don't particularly want to say it, but the whites are people too. In their different ways, some are just as—"

"No!" he cried. "They are not the people of this land. This land belongs to those who were here first. If it was not meant to be ours, then why are we here? This land has given us our needs since the beginning of the world. We have loved it and fought to protect it. The blood of our people has soaked into it with the rains. *It is ours!*"

They were silent for a long time, both of them looking across at Never Summer, where fall brightness was beginning to show in the leaves of the highest trees. Alec and Little Chief were swimming in the lake, shouting and splashing.

"Will you be going to the post soon?" Hawk's Shadow asked finally, wearily.

Blake nodded.

"There is a thing I was forgetting to tell you. There is smallpox west of the mountains this year. They say it comes up from the western ocean. There will be trouble from this, Blake. The tribes have enough problems without having to suffer from white men's diseases. So people are saying those diseases have been brought deliberately, to help in killing us. Some Cayuses and Walla Wallas, even some Nez Perce, have very bad hearts. You should be careful not to meet any of them when you travel."

Hawk's Shadow looked again at the mountain and said quietly, "I think we should not talk again of the signing of papers and the herding of buffalo and such things. Such talk does no good, but only makes us angry. I think it may be that every man in this country will need his friends, so we will leave such things alone. Anger has no real place between us. So we will leave it, and decide now which woman you should choose from the village."

"Blake, I'm glad you've come," said Connall, a momentary relief in his troubled face, "though there'll be little trading to do. Con, you and Alec run away somewhere, only remember what I've told you about staying within sight and call of the post.

"Here, lad, fill your pipe and sit down. I've things to tell you if you've not already heard. Did you meet anyone, coming down along the Camas?"

"No. What's happened?"

"There's been a massacre over at the Blue Mountains settlements, twenty-five or thirty whites killed as near as I can seem to get the straight story. They've had the smallpox over there—you must know that—and trouble over the farming and the church and such for some time now. I've only had word of the killing from Indians so far, and they're apt to change things around to suit their own purposes, but it seems that a boy died of the pox just after they got back from hunting, the young son of a chief, and that was the last straw. You know it's all right, among them, to kill the medicine man if the patient dies. The chief was wild with mourning for his boy and he hit the white doctor with something. There were several others around and that's what it took to set them all off. That band's been peaceful for years, but the blood came out in them, killing and scalping. They took some prisoners and burned up most of the settlement."

Blake was silent. Connall kept glancing uneasily at him, waiting, but he said nothing.

"They say the whites who are left have sent for the army, to Bridger, Laramie, the coast, wherever they might get help. They've barricaded themselves in the church to wait. Father Robidou's sent word he's getting together a party to go over there. I thought you might want to go along."

"Why would I, Connall? I'm sorry it's happened, but I don't know what can be done now."

"You might lift a hand to keep more white people from being killed. You're friends with a lot of the bands. You could talk to them."

"I doubt that any more will happen if they're just left alone for a while. They'll turn over the prisoners in good condition, if they haven't done already, and their hearts

261

will be good, so good they'll probably do anything they're told."

"I don't believe you're at all sorry about the mission people."

"Of course I'm sorry. For one thing, their never-ending ignorance and stupidity will mean trouble for this whole part of the country."

"That's no way to talk of the dead. And I did hope you'd try to help and make yourself useful. Father Robidou sent special word that I was to try to find you. You'd be welcome to leave Alec here with us. . . ."

"You're not going?"

"I'd not be much help. I don't know the languages over there much. Besides, I have the family and this place to see to. I'm only waiting to learn what will happen next. We may have to leave on a minute's notice."

"Leave? Would you do that?"

"Aye, I'd do that. I think I've said to you before that if their hearts get bad enough we're all going to look alike to them, and whatever there's been of good feeling in the past will be forgotten."

"Where would you go?"

"Across the mountains. To Laramie or Union, I suppose, for the winter at least. I'm trying to convince Father Robidou to bring his people along, if we do go. It may not be safe here for any whites."

"Connall, you've been at Camas a long time. Do you really think the people around here would—"

"Ah, Blake, don't be completely foolish. They'd kill me, right enough, and I'm not even saying they'd be entirely wrong to do it, not if you can think a little as an Indian thinks, that is. Some are mighty upset, and not without their reasons. If they begin to kill, which they've already done, then they're apt to become rather like a good dog that bites for the first time. If it bites in fear or pain or anger, the starting to bite only adds to its disturbance, and it's apt to do real damage. When things get that bad, the dog doesn't care anymore who's been its friend."

"I don't think that's true."

"But you only *think,* lad. You don't *know,* do you?"

"I guess I'll get together the things I came for, so we can start back in the morning."

"Blake, I want you and the boy to stay here. It's liable not to be safe—"

"Surely you don't believe I would be afraid of the People."

"I doubt you've sense enough to be afraid of anything, but you know it's not just the Medicine Rocks I'm talking about. It's a long, empty way, up the valley."

"Beaver Tooth and some others came down with us. If they want to start back when I do, it'll be a fair-sized party."

"And if they don't?"

"Then Alec and I will be all right."

"Lad, stay," he said earnestly. "Why must you always be so bull-headed?"

"For one thing, I'd like to be the one who tells Hawk's Shadow and the People first about the trouble to the west. I want to be home in the Valley if there's to be any more trouble."

But no particular trouble came to the Medicine Rock. Beaver Tooth and some of his particular partisans traveled around the country that year, as long as the weather permitted, talking with other bands, gathering news, trying to promote calm, doing as Robidou asked them. It was an unusually mild winter. The village, left to Hawk's Shadow's guardianship, did well. After the first flurry of excitement, the trouble to the west was not much discussed. Hawk's Shadow said to Blake, "This time, I think Beaver Tooth is right. Those of us who have no interest in licking the boots of the Father and other whites will just stay here in the Valley and be as we have been . . . . We need eagle feathers now, Green Eyes. Suppose you and I, with our sons, climb up on Never Summer and see what can be done."

In the spring, Blake found that Connall and the others at the post had wintered safely. Some Coeur d'Alenes, far to the north, had killed a trader in from the coast, a stranger to them. Far to the south, a great deal of unrest was reported among the Snakes; mostly it was directed at the Mormons coming among them.

"And now we've got the army here," Connall finished his report, "because of the Blue Mountain business. There are a few troops camped down near the mission. One of the young priests was a prisoner of some northern Flatheads for most of the winter. They didn't do him any damage, just wouldn't let him come back to the mission while they argued and tried to decide if they ought to do anything. The army has said the mission school must be closed for a while. Some mission stock was killed or stolen over the winter. It's my opinion the Church will close the whole mission, at least for a time. I've heard that a great deal of bitterness has come out in the Indian converts because of this mess, though most have stayed pretty well in line. They've sent several delegations to Father Roubidou, telling him how much they resent the ways he's been trying to change them—telling them it's wrong to be polygamous and to kill and torture their enemies, trying to make farmers of them and the rest of it. It's come as a shock to him. He believed they were truly converted and changed. I'm afraid he's a sorely disillusioned old man, and twice as bewildered with the Church telling him to pull out, just when he feels he's most needed.

"I was down there last week, at the mission. He asked if you'd come in yet and he sent you a message. The army plans to turn the mission into a fort if the priests and others leave. With the weather fit for traveling, they'll be looking around now for another site or two for forts. Father Robidou wants you to come and see him and talk with the army people. He thinks, if they'll listen, that you might give them some good advice and I think he may be right."

"The army doesn't want advice, Connall. You know that."

"But you do have a way with Indians. The languages come easy to you—"

"I don't want to sit in any more councils gotten up by the army. If I did, I mightn't be able to overcome the temptation to stop translating and only tell the chiefs what *I* think of what's being said."

"Aye, that's something of what the Father said. He said, 'Blake's got a real feeling for the Indians. He'll tell them the straight of things and maybe they'll listen. He won't want to come,' the Father said, 'but I think his conscience will compel him. Any of us who can do anything at all that might ease things, must do it. It's not a place anymore,' he said, 'where a man can hide and ignore the world. If Blake loves the people as I think he does,' he said, 'then he'll at least try to help them now.' "

It was the beginning of autumn, 1855. They rode up the Camas Valley, Blake and Alec, together with several of the Medicine Rock People, coming home from a council. This one had been held at the confluence of the Clearwater with the Snake, and it had been only for the tribes and the whites west of the mountains.

The army had been in the country for over a year now. There had been some sporadic trouble, raiding, some deaths. The white settlers along the Blue Mountains had a fort and garrison and detachments of troops were scattered about over the rest of the land. St. Denis Mission was now an army post called Fort Pierce. The tribes were growing quieter, some even seemed penitent. The army and the agents had things their way at the council. Ellis Williams had been appointed agent to the Shahaptian peoples—the Nez Perce, Cayuse, Palouse, and others. His new agency was headquartered at Fort Pierce. Beaver Tooth thought him a fine man, for a white.

The tribes had had reservations outlined for them at the council, mostly the lands where they already spent much of their time. They had their fishing places, their camas, and kouse and bitterroot grounds, the sites of their winter villages and, according to the papers they had signed, they would have those lands forever. They were to be encouraged, by the issue of beef and other goods, not to go to the buffalo country, to become sedentary, agricultural people. More schools were to be provided, along with other "civilizing" influences.

For Blake, it had, in more ways than one, been a frustrating, angry, defeated time.

"It's not all that bad," Connall had tried to console him. "Tell me what's really so different now. The Medicine Rock People are hardly affected by these things at all."

"The People are hardly the only ones involved," Blake said irritably. "And they're granted their lands 'henceforth and forever.' Just how long do you think 'forever' will be, Connall? When somebody decides they ought to

265

have the country to put a road through, or for farming, or for anything else? They've got chiefs' names on those treaties. That doesn't mean a hell of a lot to any Indian and it doesn't mean anything to the government, but the government can use the damned treaties to its advantage and the Indians never can. If anybody decides whites ought to have some of this land, or if anybody gets a grudge against some band, all they have to say is that the treaty's been broken somehow. Then they can feel justified in wiping out any number of Indians or in doing anything else their goddam manifest destiny may seem to dictate."

Beaver Tooth had signed the treaties, making a long and eloquent speech first, about the greatness of the Medicine Rock People and their good hearts toward the whites. He said, to his own people, "We have our Valley and all the same things we have always had. Besides these things, we now have a share in the goods the whites will be dividing among the tribes each year. The goods will cost us nothing. All we have to do is go to the agency and collect them."

"Cost us nothing!" Hawk's Shadow had cried, almost weeping. "You have put your name on their papers as our chief. It's as if you have signed away a part of the spirit of the people. Surely, my father is weeping now, and Crooked Wolf, and Winter Thunder."

Blake had said as little as possible. What good were opinions, his or anyone else's? There was no way out now. The people were caught, trapped, pawns, as they had been for a long time, between fur companies or religions, between settlers of various aims and persuasions, between countries and territories vying for the best and strongest political positions. But what could be done about it? So except for translating, he tried to keep silent. In a way, he tried to convince himself Beaver Tooth was right. Perhaps it was better docilely to sign the treaties, to share the meager advantages that might never materialize, and then to go back home to the Valley and go on with living. Had the papers not been signed, the people would, without doubt, have been more liable to immediate interference and harassment from the army. Blake had convinced himself, a little, that there was simply nothing else to be done. All he wanted then was to get away from the army and the agents, to get back to the village and the cabin, with the winter ahead in which to try to reconcile himself to the new ways. He had to think, to rest his battered emotions and prepare for the next things that would come.

Then there had been trouble of a more personal and painful nature, which had left him utterly bruised and uncertain, filled with a new desperation of self-doubt.

"What does it mean," Alec said softly now, "to be a bastard?"

He and Blake were riding a little apart from the others. The boy kept his bruised, swollen face averted, looking at the river and up at the brown hills on its other side.

It had been several days since the thing had happened, and they hadn't yet talked about it, not really. Blake tried to tell himself he had been waiting for Alec to be ready to broach the subject, but, in part at least, he felt it was his own cowardice and reluctance to face it that had postponed their discussion so long.

"A bastard is someone whose parents were not married," he answered quietly.

"Is that so bad?"

"There's nothing bad about it, except in the way each person sees it. Alec, people do all they can to build themselves up, to try to feel good about themselves, to seem important. For some people, being able to do that seems to mean they have to tear others apart. Such people are sad. They are small and petty and cruel. The least bit of differentness in another person frightens them. It could be a threat to their security. They strike out. They point to the differentness and say it is wrong or bad. Does this make any sense to you at all?"

Alec glanced at him briefly. His face was troubled, the green eyes bleak and restless.

I'm trying to make him grow up too fast, Blake reproved himself miserably, because it might be easier for me that way. He's a child, a hurt, confused child. What the hell good is philosophy to him at a time like this? Just how wrong have I been? about how many things?

He said softly, "Will you tell me what happened?"

"Con told you, and Little Chief and others."

"I'd like to hear it from you."

There was a long silence. The wind came fitfully, with a touch of coldness. Dark clouds were hurrying across an uneasy sky. Finally, Alec began, keeping his voice level and disinterested.

"You were sitting with the other men in the council that last day. We watched for a while. They signed the last of the papers and they kept sitting there smoking and talking. We saw the presents being given. Beaver Tooth got his fine bright chief's coat and Little Chief said he was a traitor to the People and that we shouldn't stay there anymore. We were tired, anyway, of watching and listening and being quiet, so we went away, down by the river, Little Chief and Con and I.

"There was a soldier down there, washing his shirt. This seemed funny to us, that a warrior would do this with all the women that were around. We said nothing to him, but I think we smiled. He asked us who we thought we were and what we were laughing at. He knew me and he knew Con. Little Chief told him he was the son of Hawk's Shadow of the Medicine Rock People and I translated what he said because the soldier seemed to want to know. He asked what was so special about that, and he laughed and began shouting at us. He said we were all bastards but that Con and I were worse than Little Chief and others because our fathers were—were dirty squaw men. He said any white who came and lived in this country of his own free will was sick—mad, I think he meant—and that any who lived among the Indians ought to be tarred and feathered. I don't know the meaning of that either. He said that we were breed bastards and that decent people would not want us to live.

"Some boys had been swimming in the river, a lot of them, all kinds. We had come down there to swim with them, but they came up to see why the soldier was shouting. Some of them were Nez Perce boys from the village there, some were Flatheads, a few were from other tribes. Some were half white sons of Frenchmen and others. A few understood the soldier. The Indians started looking at the ones of us who were half white and making fun, saying our skins were ugly, pale, and sick. Con knew many of those boys. He said to them to pay no attention to the soldier, that he was new to the country and knew nothing about how things are, that we were all friends together and that we should go away and play some game.

"But they got very angry. I don't know why. Some of those who were all Indian said they would have nothing to do with us, though we had played together all through the time of the council and been friends. One of the Flatheads who had lived at St. Denis Mission said our fathers were wicked men who slept with all the Indian women they could find because they had devils in them, and that the children born to those women had devils. He said it showed in things like Con's hair and my eyes. He said that no Indian with respect for himself and his people would have anything to do, anymore, with half-breed bastards.

"Little Chief had been asking me what the soldier said and I couldn't tell him, but he understood the Indians all right. He yelled at the Flathead that I was his cousin and Con our friend, that he couldn't say those things. He said many of the Indians there, men as well as boys, were cowardly women because they listened too much to whites. He said all who sat in the council and signed the papers and got gifts were stupid, being led around by their noses by the whites and selling their own people. The Flathead hit Little Chief then, and we all started to fight.

"I saw that the soldier had sat down on a rock. He was laughing. Some other soldiers came and watched, and some Indians. There were maybe eight of us—breeds—and probably thirty Indian boys. The grownup Indians were shouting, some of them, that their boys should kill us because we were white. Little Chief fought for us and a few others did, but we were losing badly. An officer came down and he made the soldiers who were watching stop the fighting. I think they were afraid, but he shouted at them and they used their rifles as clubs. Some of the older Indians helped them a little.

"That officer—you know the one, his name is Hamilton, I think—called Con and me to come with him. We can't hide, Con and I. People keep recognizing us. He sent for you and Mr. MacPheirson, and Little Chief brought Hawk's Shadow.

"We were bloody and very angry. Con was cursing in a way I had not heard before. We thought the officer was going to shout at us and say we made the fight, but he didn't. He told us to wait in his tent, and he told a soldier to bring water so we could wash off the blood. The soldier cursed us and said that because of what we had done, the council would probably fail. He said that breeds like us were bad for everybody because we belonged nowhere. The officer shouted at him from outside and he went away. Then you came, and the others."

"Alec . . . . I'm sorry. I truly don't know anything else I can say. . . ."

"Are you sorry I was born?"

The boy looked at him directly now, for the first time, his eyes bright with sparks of anger and a background of tears.

"Of course I'm not sorry you were born, son."

"I think more whites will keep coming," he said rapidly. "I think some day the People may have to go and live somewhere else. Con says they will. Maybe it will be a place I don't want to live, or maybe I will want to work some place like Camas Post. I don't really mind being half one thing and half another, but I don't like it when people call me names and hit me. Maybe the Flathead was right and I don't have a place and a people where I really belong."

"You belong with me, Alec, and with the People. No one in the Valley has ever made you feel you didn't, have they?"

"But the Valley is not the whole world, and the things you tell me are different from the things Hawk's Shadow and my grandmother tell me. Now, I don't think I know what is true anymore, or who I am."

"You're Alec Westfall."

Alec shook his head, biting his lip. That was no answer.

He said, "One of the boys there who is part French was yelling at us, along with the Indians. He said that, though he is a breed too, his parents were married in the Church and he is no bastard. He said that he has a right to his father's name and that I do not. This is not true for Con. His parents were married in the Church."

"It's not true for Little Chief and most of the other Medicine Rock boys. Don't you think they have a right to their fathers' names if those names were passed on in that way? I loved your mother, Alec, and I love you. It doesn't matter about being in a church. Your mother and I were married. There was a ceremony, the Medicine Rock ceremony, when she became my wife. That's a marriage, as surely as any other kind. It's how two people *feel,* what they want that counts, not the kind of ceremony. For some people, being married in a church is very important, but no one has a right to try to force his beliefs on others."

"Why did you not start fighting those people at the council, as Hawk's Shadow wanted to?"

"It wouldn't have done any good. It could have wrecked the council and brought trouble for a great many people."

"Then my battles are not yours?"

"You know that's not true," Blake said painfully. "Striking out like that, without thinking, usually only makes things worse. You can't force anyone else to accept or try to understand by hitting them."

"The army has done that. They rode around the country with their guns, telling the people of how many more soldiers and guns there are in the east, and the people allowed them to build forts. The people went to the council and did as they were told there."

"But force is not—"

"Some day, maybe I won't be living in the Valley. What will I do then, about being a breed bastard?"

"I can't answer that, Alec. All I can say for sure is that if and when the time and the circumstances come, we'll decide—"

"*I* must decide. You are white."

The next day, they reached the Medicine Rock. The village was troubled and uneasy. Hawk's Shadow, looking worried and ill, wanted Blake to stay for a while, though he would not put the request into words, but Blake thought it would be best for Alec if they went on to the cabin. The boy looked pale and tired, his eyes full of struggling and uncertainty.

That night, when they had put away some of their

things, eaten and sat by the fire, the boy said, "What do you think should be done now?"

"I think we should—just go on as we have been," Blake said slowly. "I'm not sure I understand exactly what you mean."

"I want to know some answers. I thought you might help me."

"Alec, an unhappy, cruel thing has happened. It hurts me that I disappoint you, that I can't give you what you're looking for, but, to a thing like that, there are no quick, ready answers, not that I know, at any rate. All I can tell you is that we're the same people we were before we went to the council. A man's strength comes from what he is inside, not from what anyone else says or thinks. We'll have the winter here, being as we've always been. We can only take things as they come and deal with them as we have to. You and I are not changed."

Alec looked into the fire and said heavily, "*I'll* never be the same as I was."

It was a long time before Blake slept that night and he knew that Alec, still though he lay, was not sleeping either. When he woke in the morning, it was later than usual. Alec was moving softly around the cabin and he seemed a little startled when he found Blake awake.

"I have decided," he said stiffly, "to go up on Never Summer for a few days."

"Would you have gone without telling me?"

Blake got up and went to the door to look up at the mountain.

"I supposed you would know."

"There may be a bad storm. It's been threatening for two days."

"I think it will clear."

They were silent for what seemed to both of them a long while.

"Alec, I—I wish you well. I'm very proud of you and I wish there was something more I could . . . . There are a lot of things I've not done right. Some day, I hope we'll . . . ."

Alec said tensely, "You are to come for me after a time. You know that, don't you?"

272

"Yes."

"It should not be before five days."

He went down across the little valley and disappeared.

There was a great deal of work that needed doing—they had been away most of the summer—but Blake could not concentrate on or force himself to stay with any task for more than a few minutes at a time. His thoughts were a turmoil and finally he gave up trying to work.

He stood by the lake and looked at the mountain. For the first time, he felt something from it besides peace and anonymity. There seemed to be a hostility, a threat, a brooding portent about it, though, as Alec had predicted, the sky above it was clearing.

The boy would not have had time yet to cross the valley of the Medicine Rock and begin climbing the mountain, but Blake found his eyes straining for some sign of movement, high up at the tree line. His mind saw Alec clearly, slender, looking taller than he was, looking from the back much like Little Chief and others of Red Sky's descendants. Alec did not smile often, but when he did, it was his mother's smile. But his eyes . . . . What have I done?

Blake turned from the lake and walked up into the woods, following the little stream. He climbed beyond the big spring, moving steadily into the afternoon, glimpsing Never Summer now and then through the trees, not wanting to see the mountain. From the top of the ridge, he knew, there was a great wide vista of country to be seen, the Camas Valley, and the eastern range on its other side. He did not go to the top. This was not a time for looking at panoramas, but at things much closer, much harder to look at.

He turned back, finally, and, near sunset, he came again to the spring. He drank a little water and sat down wearily, leaning against one of the boulders that was of the same color and material as the Medicine Rock . . . . Alec would have no water, no food. He was alone on the mountain with night coming on, waiting for a medicine dream.

He's so young, Blake thought miserably, not quite eleven yet. It was the way of the Medicine Rock boys to go out at about this age, seeking to know their guardian spirit, but Alec was not ready to be a man because his father had made life too complicated for him. I've given him nothing, Blake thought, no bases. I've told him only, be yourself, think for yourself, and that's not what a boy needs. The way I was raised, wrong though it may have been, at least let me know, in no uncertain terms, where I was supposed to stand. I've been trying to make Alec understand things that I couldn't comprehend until long after I was grown. He's smarter than I ever was, but I've asked too much. He's had no real childhood, what with trying to decide between what I say and what the People say. How has the time gone so quickly? How could I have been so unfair to him, using him as something to experiment on?

Maybe when I came back five years ago I should have taken him to some large city in the east or in Europe, where they are more used to people who are half one thing and half another, and where people are not so ostracized for thinking differently, for thinking at all. Yet I wanted him to be proud of what he is, to know and respect his mother's people—my people. I didn't take him away, though, mostly because of what this place means to me, what *I* find here.

Blake looked out over the country and his mind said, Shy Fawn, it's good you haven't had to see this, the changes coming to the People, the boy hurt as he has been while I'm so helpless to help him. I don't understand all of it and I couldn't begin to make you an explanation. He's up there now, looking for a medicine dream and I hope to God he finds something. It will give the Indian part of him strength and confidence. And the white part? Perhaps the kindest thing I could have done for him would have been to keep away from the Valley, once I'd left. But I came back and I've made him think, partly as a white. *I* want to be myself, not categorized and classified as white, Indian, or anything else, only to be Blake Westfall; but that's not a fair way to try to make the boy think. While I've thought I was setting him free, I've allowed him no roots at all.

An evening wind, down from Never Summer, sighed bleakly in the evergreens. The autumn twilight would not be long and there would be no moon tonight. He ought to go on down, out of the woods, before it grew dark. He did not move.

But now that I realize where I've been wrong, what will I do? I can't change what's gone before, but surely there are things I can do to make the future a little easier. Alec is more a half-breed than most of the children like him, and I've done that to him. A green-eyed Indian . . . .

I ought to be able to do something to give the white part of him more stability. I've done little enough but criticize other whites. There'll be more of them in the country every year now. Maybe I can begin by trying to think more kindly, more tolerantly of them, try to help us both to see that most of them are not really hard and selfish and without feeling. Together, maybe we can look for things in some of those others that we can identify with. It will be another experiment to subject Alec to, but I can't think where else to begin. We can't stay here in the valley always, where it's safe. Alec isn't going to be that kind of person. It's long past time I stopped trying to explain abstractions and did something he can see.

He stood up, unable to bear thinking and sitting still any longer. His hand touched the rough boulder and he looked at it in the dim light. Suddenly, into his mind, came the picture from Alec Douglas' old, tattered book, and Alec Douglas' words: "It doesn't have to be a castle like this one in the picture. A castle is a thing of the mind. A man must do what he *can* do. Do you understand at all? Never mind. It will come one day, when you're older."

Blake slept little that night, his heart aching for the boy, alone on the mountain, his distracted mind seeing the dark boulder, laying out lines on it.

In the morning, he took some tools and spent the day by the spring, marking and planning. Why? He could not say, but some day a miniature castle would come from the boulder. Somehow, it was a concrete symbol of what he wanted to do for Alec, and for the future. He would never try to explain it like that, he knew, because he was far from understanding it himself.

He worked on the boulder every day until it was time to go and find Alec, leaving the work around the cabin for later. It would be a long slow process, this castle, something he could work on through the years as other things allowed, something he could hold in his mind when other things intervened. Perhaps it was, in a way, he thought, looking up at the mountain, his own small, insignificant, individual answer to Never Summer, his own special mark to leave on the land, his defiance, his acceptance.

When the time had passed for Alec's waiting, Blake put his tools away. There was going to be a storm, a major one, by the looks of the sky and the feel of the air. He would do no more work on the rock this season. That did not bother him. The castle was a thing he would finish, must finish, one day, but he felt no compulsion to hurry. It must be a good job, the best he could possibly do, not to be rushed. The rock, like Never Summer and the valley, would be here, waiting.

XIII

IN THE SPRING, the Medicine Rock People held a guardian spirit dance. It was their first such ceremony in several years. Hawk's Shadow gave the feast. His elder son Little Chief, who after the dance was to be called Eagle Feather, had, to the father's vast relief, gone out and found a medicine dream. The children who would participate in the dance kept their dreams, their new names, their guardian spirits more or less to themselves until the time for the ceremony, when they performed symbolic acts and sang their songs—if they had been given songs—to tell their visions to the People. Some of the young people no longer sought medicine dreams. They had been told by the priests that it was a pagan practice, instituted by the Evil One. But some still held to the old ways, and watching his son prepare for the dance, Hawk's Shadow was quietly, deeply grateful to the Old Ones, happier than he had been for a long while. Little Rain, the mother, was cross and uneasy. What would the Father say?

"The Father has gone away," Hawk's Shadow pointed out shortly. "It was wrong for him ever to be here in the first place. He brought teachings that have no place here and now he is gone. The land and the people were too much for him. Whoever heard of saying it's wrong for a man to have more than one wife if he can hunt and fight for more than one? Why is it bad to kill in war, or to take prisoners and torture them if there is the chance? Is this not the way we have always lived? Is this not what our enemies do to us whenever they can? Why must we, all at once, begin living as some white man tells us? We are the People. How can it be wrong for our young people to seek medicine dreams? You say that Christ is supposed to be the only medicine spirit, but how can that be? We see life all around us. How can anyone believe there is only one spirit? I would rather have a deer or a bear or wolf for my guardian spirit when I am hunting than the spirit of a man who never saw this land and knew nothing of us and our ways."

Little Rain sighed heavily, her face creased with worry. She crossed herself and, while she ground some dried bitterroot to add to the stew, she prayed earnestly for the souls of her husband and her son who would not be shown the right ways.

Beaver Tooth's eldest son also danced that year. His new name was White Wolf. The wolf spirit was one of those most highly desired as a guardian. The good Christians among the People looked askance at the boy's dancing, but Beaver Tooth explained smoothly that it was a good thing to try to please all the spirits. "We can never know who may be watching."

Alec took no part in the dance. He sat a little away from anyone else and watched quietly. Trying to read his half-averted face in the flickering shadows. Blake thought he looked wistful and sad.

"It is the white in him," said Storm Coming Out Of The East quietly, sympathetically, sitting beside Blake. "Perhaps it was not really to be expected that he would have a vision, being half white, but it is hard for the boy."

Storm's own son and daughter, twins, were also dancers.

Blake thought back to the day he had gone to find Alec on the mountain. The weather had changed abruptly from autumn to early winter. The previous day had been unsettled with a seeking wind, veering restlessly from one direction to another, and, in late afternoon, several violently intense thunderstorms had spawned themselves against the mountains, the wind settled into the north and the clouds began to thicken. The next morning dawned raw and bleak. There would be snow.

He found Alec around on the far side of Never Summer, at timberline. The boy lay without movement beside a small pile of stones. His eyes opened sluggishly as Blake came up to him.

"Has it been five days?" he asked dully, automatically.

"Today is the sixth," Blake said gently. From the look of the boy's eyes, he feared there had been no dream.

Alec struggled to his feet, shrugging away Blake's proffered hand irritably. He had had no food, he had walked a long way, and there had been all those days of tension and emotional strain, but he stood alone, swaying.

Blake had led a horse for him. Alec dragged himself into the saddle, not speaking. They had gone only a short distance when he lost consciousness completely. Blake tied the horse's reins to his saddle and held the boy before him, his own heart as bleak and troubled as the sky.

When they reached the cabin, he had only to heat the broth he had left ready in a pot. Alec ate a little and slept deeply. Blake worked through what was left of the day, in the beginning of a heavy storm, trying to make the cabin ready for winter. In the evening, Alec woke and ate a little more, then got back into bed, shivering. Blake sat a long time by the fire, trying to read, not seeing the written words before his eyes. Finally, they lay in bed in darkness. Wind buffeted the cabin and sometimes they could hear the driven snow sifting against the logs or spattering down into the low fire.

"I had no dream," Alec said quietly, dully.

Blake moved to put an arm around him. It was a kind of reflex, the only answer that came to him, but the boy's slender body stiffened at his touch, drawing away.

"Dreams don't come to everyone," Blake said painfully. "It's not a thing to feel so very badly about, Alec."

"I think I did all the right things, but maybe I slept too much. There were sleep dreams, but I could have had those here, in the night, or anywhere, any time."

"Are you sure those, or one of them, wasn't the dream you were searching for?"

"Yes. You know the medicine dream comes from another kind of sleep."

"Maybe it did come and you don't remember. You were very tired. Maybe later you'll—"

"No."

After a long silence, Alec said thoughtfully, "You saw the storms on the mountain?"

"I saw them."

"I was up there, above where the trees stop, and the lightning came down. Once it touched some rocks very near me and I felt a great, strange tingling through the ground and all through me. The thunder was so loud that I could hear nothing and I could not move."

"But wasn't that a special thing?" Blake said, shivering at the thought, "that you were there like that, in the middle of the storm and you were not hurt?"

"I thought it would be," Alec said heavily. "I thought that something *must* speak to me then, either in the midst of the storm or as it passed on. I wanted to run down into the trees, but I thought it must be meant that I should stay there. Besides, I couldn't move. I thought surely it must be the time."

"The spirit of the storm," Blake said softly. "Are you sure that this was not what you went out to find? I don't think you realize what good fortune was with you that you were not hurt or killed. Maybe you should just wait and think about it for a while, then, when it's time for the guardian spirit dance, perhaps—"

"No one, nothing spoke to me," Alec insisted dully. "There was only the storm around me, first rain, then sleet that cut my skin, and the great lightning and thunder. I was inside the cloud. It seemed to last a long time . . . . Are you saying I should make up a story that something came to me?"

"Alec, I think that, rather often, people add a little to their visions, something they should have seen, but perhaps didn't, quite, and it all blends together to become what really happened. It's not a wrong thing to do. Think of the dreams of others you've heard about, of the medicine bundles some of the people are given. Couldn't it be that they go after their dreams and collect those things, rather than having them given by the medicine spirit during their dream? And if they do, but *say* those things were given at the time of the dream, that's not wrong. It's only—"

"That would be a lie."

280

"Not really. Don't you see that there are shades of lying? That if—"

"I suppose you can never understand," the boy said wearily.

"I'm truly sorry. I'm trying to understand, but you need to understand, too, that very little that any person does or that happens to him is really perfect in his own eyes. Each man is more critical of himself than any other man can possibly be, and the more he thinks and tries to know who and what he is, the more critical he becomes. Perfection is a relative thing and it's not always wrong to try to add what we can to it in the eyes of others. A part of the way we see ourselves comes from a kind of reflection we get back from the way others see us. Each person has so many difficulties in trying to come to terms with himself that it's not necessarily wrong to—to polish the reflection a little when he can. A long time ago, Red Sky your grandfather told me that it's good for a man to talk in council about the good things he has done. Red Sky said that talking about such things would make that man want to do more of them. Do you see at all? . . . . Perfection and reality and truth are all such relative things, relative to a particular person and a particular situation. If someone adds a bit to a medicine dream, for instance, because he thinks it is expected of him—"

"No, I don't understand," Alec said angrily, "Unless what you are saying is that there is no right and no wrong."

Of course he doesn't understand, Blake thought, angry with himself. It's taken me more than thirty years to begin thinking this way. How can he possibly understand now? He said carefully, "Such a storm came to Winter Thunder your great-grandfather years ago, by the Medicine Rock. He was told to be a leader, to bring the People here. How do we know that he didn't already have those things in mind before the dream? He was very young. He must have known the People might not listen to him unless he had a very powerful dream. Yet what he was doing was the best thing for the People. If he wanted that dream and it came to him, perhaps with help, who can say he was wrong?"

281

"You're saying you think Winter Thunder lied?" Alec's voice was awed, horrified.

"Not lied, Alec," Blake said earnestly, "only helped to make reality for himself into what would be a more acceptable reality for others."

Alec moved restlessly. Blake lay still, feeling utterly helpless and useless. A heavy gust slammed against the cabin and there was a long silence.

Alec, rejecting such impossible ideas, went wearily, doggedly on with his story. "When the storm had passed, I went down into the trees. I had left my blanket there in the early morning, under the shelter of a rock, and I was very cold. Now I think I should have stayed up there, where I had been in the storm. If I had not been so weak, thinking only of the coldness, maybe . . . . but I went down and took off my wet clothes and wrapped myself in the blanket. It had stayed nearly dry and the place in the rock shelter was not very wet. I lay down there and slept . . . . I think if it were not for white blood I would not have come down like that. One truly of the People would not have been so concerned for his body's comfort at a time when other things were so much more important."

There was another silence. Even the storm seemed to quiet briefly.

"I slept," Alec said softly, "and I dreamed of my mother. I don't remember what the dream was, only that I saw her there. She did not talk. I only felt very warm then, and quiet. What kind of dream is that, even a sleep dream, for one to have who is a boy trying to become a man—a dream of his mother? . . . . I don't remember that I ever dreamed of her before. She was very beautiful and young in the dream. I'm not even sure how I knew who she was, except she was like your drawings. Her face was sad. I felt, in the dream, that she knew I would have no medicine spirit."

"The storm," Blake said a little desperately. "Are you so very certain that the storm itself was not—"

"Nothing spoke to me," Alec said patiently. "It was only, in the storm, that I could not move and I was—frightened."

"Then perhaps it was your mother, coming to you like that—"

"I have told you, I was asleep then, and how can a woman be a medicine spirit, especially one who says nothing? Don't you know the people would laugh if I tried to show them something so foolish in a guardian spirit dance? No," he said with a dull and final resignation, "I had no medicine dream. I am half white and it is not given to me to have such things."

Blake was sorely tempted then to tell him Hawk's Shadow's secret, but he could not quite bring himself to do it. It would have been a betrayal of Hawk's Shadow's confidence, a revelation of what Hawk's Shadow considered his shame and disgrace, but the chief thing that stopped his words was the certainty that Alec would not believe them. Perhaps later, when the boy was older—

"Why did you wait until the sixth day?" Alec asked, sounding drowsy now.

"I thought," Blake said slowly, "that you might like having another day. Older boys sometimes want more time. You are not of that age, but—"

"It's good you waited. I wish you had waited longer."

"It was turning colder, Alec. The storm was coming. I couldn't wait any longer."

He wanted to add "because I love you," but Alec already felt that he had let him down. There was a weakness, a betrayal in the fact that white blood ran in his veins. He would have considered love or the expression of almost any emotion at this time a further manifestation of the white shortcomings he was struggling so desperately to deny.

"I know how you feel," Blake began gently, tentatively. "I wish—"

"Nobody," Alec said quietly and yawned, "*knows* how anybody else feels." He slept.

Blake got up miserably and put wood on the fire. He filled his pipe and lit it without thinking of what he did. The storm roared, pushing against the cabin.

So he knows that, he thought bitterly, that nobody *knows;* that, when it comes down to most of the things that truly matter to a human being, he is, must be, more or less alone. Someone else's love, or any other feelings a person may have, don't really figure much in the problem. It keeps coming back to the same thing, that each of us has, in the end, only himself to rely on. I want to know how he feels; I think I do know, but he's right, I probably don't, I can't. How much of my wanting to know, to share those feelings is just a search for something to ease, a little, the way *I* feel about what's been happening to him lately? How reasonable or compassionate is that? to want *him* to help *me* at a time like this? It's my doing that he realizes no one knows how anyone else truly feels, how alone we all are, and what good is that to him when he needs . . . . I don't know what he needs. The dream did not come, not in a form he'll accept, though I don't know what more he could possibly have expected. What can substitute for a medicine dream?

He felt Shy Fawn's presence in the cabin then, more strongly than he had felt it in years. In his mind, her large dark eyes were questioning, pleading, frightened.

I don't know! he cried, his lips moving soundlessly. I can't find answers for anyone, no matter how I want to. Please! I just don't know what to do.

It seemed that she moved restlessly around the room and stood for a long moment by the bed where Alec lay sleeping. In the dimness, the boy looked so small, so vulnerably young.

Why does all this have to begin so early? he cried within himself. Why can't he be just a little boy, only for a while longer?

It seemed that Shy Fawn left the cabin then, restlessly, worriedly. He even felt the icy draft from her closing of the door, and shivered.

He lay down again after a time, his thoughts running in tight, tense circles. The ultimate answer was, perhaps, that there was really nothing he could do. Alec must find his own easement, make his own adjustments, discover his own answers. Perhaps the realization that no one truly understood anyone else was a kind of beginning, but such a bleak, deserted beginning for one so young! As a boy he, Blake, had known of a certainty that his family had no understanding of him, no slightest wish to understand, yet he had been always hedged about by their religious precepts. They had been painful things when he could never measure up to them, but they had been there, things he could count on, references for living and thinking. He had given Alec nothing like that. Even now, at a time when Alec was so terribly lost and uncertain, he seemed only able to offer theories, things that, for the boy, were only more uncertainties.

He had thought often, at times had wanted desperately, to bring another woman to live with them at the cabin. One of the reasons he had not done so was to give the white aspects of Alec more of a chance, to keep the boy as free as he could be to make his own decisions, to see things from at least two angles. But if there had been a woman, a second wife and mother, wouldn't the boy have been better? If he had become entirely a Medicine Rock boy, would that have been an undesirable thing? He might conceivably have missed some intellectual exercises, but, almost without doubt, he would have been a happier, better-adjusted boy.

Perhaps if he had tried to talk to Alec about his own feelings for Never Summer and for all the country, how medicine dreams might come in a variety of shapes and forms. Blake was afraid he could not really talk about the mountain. Even with Shy Fawn, who would have understood more than anyone in the world, he had been able to touch only the edges of those feelings. He was afraid the boy would not understand. He despised himself for that self-protection. He began to wonder then if he was or ever had been capable of truly loving anyone. Perhaps, somehow, his feeling for the mountain stood between him and the full giving that had to make up such a great part of love. "Keep yourself a little aloof," the words had come to him so far away, "so that you won't ever be hurt like that again." They said he hid here and they were right. He wanted no part of the striving and struggling of the world. It was not going to be like that for Alec. Alec was no drifter with tides. He would fight and struggle, Blake feared, for his place, his niche, and that niche was not likely to be a hidden, almost inaccessible valley. His peace of mind and contentment were not likely to come from looking at a mountain. What could he, Blake, do to help? Perhaps nothing, but, still, as his father . . . .

It was near morning when drowsiness finally began to ease the tension of his body. Into his exhausted, tormented mind came thoughts of the rock, the castle up by the spring. He felt guiltily that such thoughts were a kind of escape to which he was not entitled, but his mind, obdurately insisting on respite, began systematically laying out lines, thinking of depths, seeing his castle come to life from the boulder in bright warm sunshine. Perhaps in the spring he would show it to Alec. Perhaps they might work on it together, or at least talk about it. He could tell him more about Alec Douglas, not just facts about that other Alec, but about how he, Blake, had felt about the man. Alec Douglas had helped him in those other years to get away from theories of religion and evil; perhaps he could help him now with these other things. There would be a tower at each corner, rising dark and delicate and beautiful in the sun . . . .

In the days following his return from the mountain, Alec seemed almost his old self again, quiet, eager to learn, thoughtful, taking a greater interest in books and other things from the outside world than he had ever done before. He was too sober and intense for an eleven year old, but he had always been a serious child. He seemed to have come to some adjustment with things and himself as they were; Blake was grateful for a relief he feared would be only temporary, but both of them enjoyed the winter, and it had passed quietly and companionably.

Glancing covertly at his son through the progress of the guardian spirit dance, Blake hoped that the boy was no longer so upset by the withholding of the medicine dream he had sought. His mind seemed more fixed on other things now. What were those things? Was it respect for Alec's privacy or Blake's own wish for self-protection that kept him from asking?

As he watched White Wolf telling in the dance how the wolf spirit had come to him, there was a touch on Blake's shoulder and he looked up at Hawk's Shadow, who gestured him away into the darkness. Hawk's Shadow's face, which had been so smiling, so filled with pride and relief as his own son danced, was sober now and angry.

"The guard has come," he said hotly as they moved away from the gathering. "White soldiers are down there, wanting to come into the valley."

"What do they want?"

"They have said to the guards that they want talk. I want you to come and talk to them, tell them to leave."

Beaver Tooth joined them hurriedly, looking irritated, uneasy and important.

"You will not want to leave," Hawk's Shadow said to him absently, "while your boy is—"

"I am chief here," Beaver Tooth said shortly, but with dignity. "It was wrong of the guard to come to you with this and not to me. We will go now and see what those whites want."

There was light from a full moon. The air was warm for late April. Medicine Rock Creek ran full and noisy as they rode beside it. Blake found that he was thinking of that first spring he had known in the valley, of Red Sky, of how certain of everything most of the People had been then.

The group of soldiers waited near the end of the canyon. They had built a small fire and were preparing their supper. The lieutenant in charge came a little away from the fire to meet the three riders. He was on foot, a tall, good-looking blond man with brown eyes that tended to merriment. He kept his eyes sober now. He had been told how important that was in dealing with Indians.

Blake slipped to the ground as the soldier approached. Hawk's Shadow and Beaver Tooth remained mounted, solemn and impressive in the ceremonial dress and paint they had donned for the guardian spirit dance and the feasting.

The lieutenant had a Flathead youth with him as interpreter but he was relieved to see Blake. He held out his hand.

"Mr. Westfall, I'm Wyeth Hamilton. Maybe you don't remember me but—"

"I remember you," Blake said curtly. His first impulse was to ignore the hand. It had been Hamilton who, after the boys' fight at the council on the Clearwater, had brought Alec and Con MacPheirson into his tent. Then he remembered his resolve of the autumn before, to try to be more friendly with some whites. He shook Hamilton's hand briefly.

Beaver Tooth had dismounted. "I am Beaver Tooth,

287

chief of the Medicine Rock People," he said, gravely offering his own hand.

The officer shook it warmly, but he looked uneasy.

"I've not been here quite a year yet," he explained almost apologetically to Blake in a very marked southern drawl. "I can't seem to get hold of the languages. Roaring Bull," indicating the Flathead boy, "is a real good interpreter in the country up north of here but he doesn't know this language too well either. I was hoping we'd find you here."

Blake explained this to the others and Beaver Tooth began a speech about the People and himself, pausing for translation. Hawk's Shadow sat his horse, soberly scowling.

"What do they want?" he demanded finally, breaking into Beaver Tooth's dissertation.

Beaver Tooth, offended, gestured to Blake to try to answer the rude question.

"Lieutenant Hamilton," he said, "you've come at a bad time. There's a very special ceremony going on in the village and we don't want to miss any part of it. What is it you want here?"

"We've come mostly to talk," explained the officer. "We're out to visit all the villages in this part of the country. Captain Shadran thinks that's the best way to handle it and he's had orders to that effect from Washington."

"To handle what?"

"Well . . . . any ideas that might come into anybody's head about—making trouble. We're supposed to talk with the chiefs and ride through each village at arms—"

"Has there been some trouble?"

"Not that I know of. This is, I guess, what you might call preventive medicine."

"What's he saying?" demanded Beaver Tooth impatiently. "I have learned English words but they don't sound like the ones he speaks."

Blake managed not to smile. The lieutenant's drawl was a mild disruption even to his own understanding. It had been a long while since he had talked with anyone from the Deep South. He gave Beaver Tooth the translation and added, "I think they only want the People to see them, with their arms, and to talk with you about what the army is ready to do if there is trouble, to impress us with their strength."

"Do they have much strength?" Beaver Tooth mused and Hawk's Shadow said, "White men are not welcome in the valley of the Medicine Rock. We have made no troubles for them—yet. Tell them to leave now."

"You can't come to the village," Blake said to Wyeth Hamilton. "I've told you this is a very special time for the People."

"Would they mind," the lieutenant said slowly, a little shyly, "if—if I watched their ceremony? The other men needn't come in now, but I'd like—"

"Whites have never been allowed in the Valley."

"You're here. I understand you've lived here a long time, and the priests used to come."

"Lieutenant, no one here is making any trouble, or plans any that I know of. You're the one asking for problems if you try to insist on coming in where you're not welcome."

"Those are my orders," said Hamilton and his full mouth, which was more inclined to smiling than to any other expression, set.

Beaver Tooth said solemnly, "I will hold a council with this officer, tomorrow. My son, who will now be called White Wolf, is, at this moment, telling the People of his medicine dream. I cannot go on staying here, waiting to find out nothing. He is saying, isn't he, that they have not come for a battle? Then tell him his soldiers will be allowed to make camp where they are, for the night, and tomorrow I will come here, with you and others, and we will talk."

The lieutenant shook his head uneasily when Blake had told him this. "We're to ride through the village. I don't see any reason why it can't wait till tomorrow, but we have to come into the valley."

"I suppose it's very important to your captain and those people in Washington that the women and children be duly impressed," Blake said dryly.

"Have you got any idea," asked Hamilton earnestly and with admiration, "what fighters some of these Indian women are?"

"Yes, I have."

Hawk's Shadow said fiercely, "There are not many of these soldiers. A few of us with muskets—"

Blake said quickly, "Why not let them wait here until morning, as Beaver Tooth says? They can be watched. Maybe they will be ready to leave after some talking."

"Why talk? *I* have nothing to say to white-eyes soldiers."

"You have hunted and made meat for this feast," said Beaver Tooth a little patronizingly to his cousin. "Don't you want to have a part in it, when your son has just finished telling the People of his medicine dream?"

"They say they want us to see them with their guns," Hawk's Shadow said coldly. "We have looked. Is it part of the paper you signed, Chief Beaver Tooth, that we must now let them come here to the Valley whenever they like?"

The lieutenant said awkwardly to Blake, "Why don't we just wait here for the night and then see about it in the morning?"

Blake smiled. "I didn't think the army asked permission for anything."

Wyeth Hamilton looked at the ground, feeling a flush creep up from his neck, glad of the sunburn that covered it. He was twenty-eight years old, but this country and the people in it had a way of making him feel ridiculously young and foolish most of the time.

"I'm new at this, Mr. Westfall," he said quietly. "I'd like to do things right, not to rile anybody more than I have to. That can get a little tricky sometimes. Sergeant Wilcox over there has been in this country a long time, down south, mostly, in what used to be Mexican territory. He bases his thinking on that old thing about the only good Indian is a dead Indian. He said we ought to ride right on in in the beginning, shooting if we had to. I can't believe things have to be that way and I know the Indians have got rights, or rights to rights, same as anybody else, but what I've got is orders. I'd like to carry out those orders without having or making any extra trouble. I can understand about the ceremony. Maybe *I* can understand about their not wanting whites in the Valley, ever, but I don't really count for much with the army."

"All right, Lieutenant, I apologize," Blake said, looking away from the earnest, intent face.

Beaver Tooth had remounted his horse. "I will send extra guards so that they are well watched," he said and galloped back toward the village.

"You will be a guard, Blake," Hawk's Shadow said firmly, angrily. "If they are to be allowed to stay here, then you will stay with them and listen to everything they say. All of us are not friends to the whites as our chief is. How do we know they will not raid the village in the night?"

The lieutenant said diffidently, "Mr. Westfall, I was wondering—when the ceremony is over, would you mind coming back here for a while? I'd like to talk to you."

"What about?"

"Well, about the country, the people. I'd like to learn what I can."

They sat by a small fire; it was well past midnight. Coyotes barked down toward the Camas and the roar of Medicine Rock Creek was pleasantly muted by a little distance. The soldiers, except for sentries, slept.

"It's quite a country," Wyeth Hamilton said a little stiffly into a long silence. "How long have you been out here?"

Blake counted back and it hardly seemed possible. "I first came fifteen years ago."

"They said, some people I talked to, that you wouldn't talk to me. They said you don't like whites mostly."

"I'm here, Lieutenant, because I was asked to watch you and your men. I'm talking because you said something about being interested in the *people,* not the Indians or the redskins or the savages. I thought, from that one word, that you might be worth talking to."

"The captain, the sergeant, most everybody figures I'm a fool . . . . Would you mind calling me Wyeth? It seems more friendly and I guess I get a little lonesome sometimes for something that seems a little like home." He smiled. "Actually, it's pretty much like home, being called a fool. I was raised, my sister Corie and I, by our half-brother Byron, and Byron's always been certain I wouldn't amount to anything, couldn't run the plantation or anything worthwhile like that. He said that maybe military life would make something of me, but he'd be disappointed if he could hear me talking like this to a stranger. He'd feel smug and justified in thinking I'm a fool and a waster of time if he knew how much these people and this country interest me . . . .

"There're some things, though, that I like about the army. I don't usually mind taking orders. Most of the time, I don't mind carrying them out, and sometimes I like giving them. The best part about it, though, has been being sent out here. There must not be anything in the world like this country. I'd like to live here when I'm out of the army, though that's liable to be a long time . . . . I mean to ask you about your boy. He's doing all right, is he?"

"Alec's fine . . . . You were kind to him last fall. I never thanked you."

"Kids can be sonsofbitches, can't they? The way they gang up and look for somebody to pick on. But that business at the council was started, you know, by one of the soldiers, making fun of the kids, egging them on to fight. It would be nice to believe that grown people would know better, but sometimes it seems like they're a hell of a lot worse than kids to pick at people and find fault . . . . Is there much trouble like that?"

"Like what?"

"Well . . . . about people being half white and half Indian."

"There wasn't much, so long as there weren't many whites."

Wyeth drew on his pipe and exhaled a long slow breath. "What is it about whites, I wonder, that causes so much trouble. Our part of the country, Mississippi, was Indian country once. The whites got to wanting the land, damn good land of course, so they took it, just took it, moved those Choctaws to a country they'd never even seen before. That's not right. It just ain't right. A good friend of mine, when I was a kid, was one of those Choctaw boys. We used to hunt together a lot. I wonder sometimes how he and his folks are doing now. It bothered my

292

brother Byron a lot, that that boy and I were friends. Byron's a great one for wanting people to stay in their places. Corie and I have always been a trial to Byron and his wife. Our mother, Papa's second wife, was very nearly what they considered white trash. Really, she was the finest, kindest, most sensible woman that ever breathed, but in their books, she just wasn't a lady. She just never did take much to living in a big fine house and being waited on and staying ignorant about the world, or pretending to be ignorant and genteel.

"Anyway, I've seen whites mistreat Indians before this, and there's been the trouble with the blacks where I come from for a long time. Now I guess things are getting hotter and hotter among the whites themselves. I guess we'll all be called back east one day, to fight each other."

"You think there'll be a civil war then?"

"Oh, I'm nearly certain of it. The North claims it's over the wickedness of slavery, but it's because they want to get hold of the cotton fields that supply their factories and a lot of things like that. They want all this western territory to be theirs in a political way, and the South wants the same kind of things."

"And will you fight for the South?"

"Sure, I will," he said, surprised. "Not for slavery, but because I can't just stand by and see one part of what's supposed to be the same country run over another part the way the North means to do . . . . That will be an awful kind of war, if it comes, the worst kind there can be. It'll take a hell of a long time to be over with, after any kind of political peace comes. After it happens though, if it happens and if I live through it, I'd like to come back here and live, do some stock raising or something.

"But I know my wife wouldn't like it out here. I've got two boys, you know, just little fellows, two and three years old now, and I've got to think about them. A papa's not much good to kids if he's always far away somewhere. I'm supposed to stay out here another year or so and then be stationed some place where I can have the family with me. I guess Mary Lou, my wife, wouldn't mind if I just stayed on out here . . . . Mary Lou's Byron's idea of a lady. That's not to say she's not a fine girl, but, well—she and I have never got on real well. We married mostly because our folks thought it was a good idea. I needed the civilizing influence Mary Lou's people have, they're Courtneys, an old family from the Virginia tidewater country that kind of fell on hard times, and the Hamiltons, my people, have got a lot of land in the past couple of generations. It works out fine for me and Mary Lou, so long as we don't see each other for long at a time, and I wouldn't trade having the boys for anything.

"But, you know, what's going to ruin the South is all that goddam civilization. I never saw how it really is till I got away from it a little. People like Byron and his wife Matilda build their whole lives, everything they are, on nothing but a bunch of snobbish crap. They think a person's important because of how he holds a teacup or gives orders to a servant or what he says, or doesn't say, to a lady at a dance. It's all so silly when you stand off a little and look at it. When you look at something like these mountains, how can you care anymore how somebody combs his hair or whether he says ain't or not? And that's exactly what Mary Lou and people like her would hate. This country sort of shakes a person all around and makes him feel small . . . . You're lucky since you want to stay here, to have a wife that belongs to the country and probably understands how it is. That must make a lot of things easier."

"It did," Blake said, "but my wife died a long time back."

"I'm sorry," Wyeth said softly and with feeling. "Nobody told me that."

"Do you think the South will lose then? If there's a war?"

He nodded emphatically. "I wouldn't say that to another Southerner. Fact is, I don't know why I'm saying it to you, or most of the other things I've been saying, except that a man does get lonesome sometimes. I've been North, seen their factories and things. Mostly, people in the South just talk. So far as I know, they're doing almost nothing about making cannon and ships and such things; too damn sophisticated, I guess, and the ones the aristocracy considers fit for such work don't begin to have the know-how."

294

"And yet you'll fight for the South."

Wyeth peered at him in the dimness. "Sure I will," he said almost angrily. "It's my country, my people. They're wrong, some ways, but so are the Northerners. I don't know enough to even begin trying to decide who's most wrong, and, even if I did, it wouldn't matter much. Wouldn't you fight if it was your people? Nobody's ever all the way right, are they?"

Blake liked him immensely. His artless honesty was a kind of marvel. He had never thought of meeting a white man like Wyeth, certainly not a Southerner nor a soldier.

"Anyway," said Wyeth, knocking out his pipe, "while I'm here, I mean to learn all I can. The army's not the best place for learning. Things are set pretty firm, and it's a kind of unwritten rule that you don't pay much attention to the natives, wherever you are, except for trying to make them do as ordered, but I've been wondering a lot about the Indians around here. They're not much of anything like the Choctaws I knew when I was a kid and it's made me realize that one Indian, tribe or person, can be as different from another as whites are. I've heard stories about these people here in the Valley, that they're different, some ways, from the rest of their tribe. I wanted to see their ceremony tonight, not to make fun or anything like that, but because I'd like to know, a little what their life is like . . . . A person like you ought to write a book or something for whites. Maybe some would come to see, that way, that the Indian ways have got some merit, even though it's not by white standards . . . . How do these people come to be living here, so far from the rest of the tribe?"

Blake told him, briefly, about Winter Thunder and his vision and how the People had come to the Medicine Rock. Wyeth was silent for a time when he had finished speaking. Finally he said, "It can't be easy for any people to have foreigners, strangers, come in the way we have and start lording it over them, with no consideration whatever for them and the ways they live. I see that and still I've got to do as I've been told. Do you think they'll let us come into the village all right tomorrow?"

"I think it will probably be all right with Beaver Tooth."

"And what will they do?"

"It wouldn't be very fair, Wyeth, for me to forewarn the enemy."

Wyeth smiled, then looked unhappy and earnest again. "I really am trying to do halfway right, you know. It's pretty hard to think things out and decide what might be best when I never know what to expect. The army people I know seem to be of two kinds. Either they're like Captain Shadran, green and scared and stuffed full of their own importance, or like Sergeant Wilcox that I mentioned to you before, bored and critical of everything that doesn't have to do with killing somebody. As far as my rank will let me, I'd like to think that maybe I'm a little more humane than either of those kinds.

"So far, since we left the fort, we've been mostly up in the Flathead country. They weren't entirely new to me. There have been some Flatheads around Fort Pierce all winter, but this is a new band, a new tribe for me. I'd like to think a little about how I could best deal with them, do what I've been told to do, with as little uneasiness as possible, for all of us."

"There'll be talk if there's to be a council," Blake said, relenting a little. "Lots of talk. That's about all I can tell you."

Wyeth smiled grimly. "Yes, I've heard lots of talk from the Flatheads, and I'm supposed to give them back as much as I get. I'm supposed to talk a hell of a lot about the Great White Father in Washington and the mighty Captain Shadran and his cannon, how everybody's only looking out for the Indians' best interests, particularly that beneficent agent, Ellis Williams. There's a lot of bullshit."

"You know, don't you, that some of what they say to you falls into the same category?"

"I thought so, but do they know that what I'm saying is sometimes just a bunch of manure?"

"Of course they know. At first, they believed most things whites told them, but they're learning, some of them are."

"Then I wonder why any of us bothers."

"I wonder why you're working on this assignment."

"It's part of the job."

"But how were you chosen to lead this expedition? It seems to me somebody is slipping. It's been my limited experience that soldiers out here aren't supposed to think the way you've been talking."

"I asked for this job. I wanted to see the country on some mission where nobody was supposed to be killed. The other officers—there aren't many—are as green and ignorant as I am, but I thought that just maybe I could keep things in hand. Actually, I'm a fair officer, as lieutenants go. And I also like to believe I'm human."

Blake smiled. "You give me hope for the white race."

Still, he let the Medicine Rock demonstration, which he felt sure would take place, remain a surprise.

The soldiers made their parade through the village next day, and the people watched with great solemnity. Then the council insisted that most of the contingent be sent back down the valley to wait, under observation, while the talking took place. Sergeant Wilcox made dire predictions about what would happen to the lieutenant but Wyeth sent them away. A little doggedly, the officer told the People the many things he had been instructed to tell them. His boyish face showed due solemnity but he sometimes stumbled and hesitated in his speech though he spoke in English. Once, when he began to translate a sentence, Blake said first in English, "Never mind, I'm making it sound impressive as hell," and Wyeth coughed, hiding a disgruntled grin.

Beaver Tooth spoke for a long time, recounting the history and great deeds of the People, saying that they were friends of the whites, with good hearts, but nonetheless a proud, independent people who hoped there was room in the land for all peoples to go their particular ways. Other men spoke then, but not Hawk's Shadow. He sat in the council only on demand of the People and the deep scowl never left his face.

Just at the proper moment, when everyone who wished to do so had spoken, there came yells and shots from the distance, and the thunder of galloping hoofs. As a courtesy to each side, no one in the council was armed.

"Jesus Christ!" Blake heard Wyeth whisper as his face went pale.

For the first time that day, Hawk's Shadow was not

297

scowling. He threw Blake a glance of pure smugness and complacence.

"It's only a parade at arms," Blake said mildly to the lieutenant in the midst of bedlam as young warriors circled the council lodge. "A gesture of peace and friendship."

"You knew they'd do this," Wyeth accused. "You'd better hope those boys down the valley don't hear it and—"

"I think your interpreter Roaring Bull was told about it. He's with them. He should know enough to tell them it wouldn't be diplomatic to interfere."

They had all come outside now, to watch the demonstration. The young men were showing all their prowess at horsemanship, standing up in their saddles, hanging from one side of a horse by fingers and toes, flinging themselves back and forth under the horses' necks at a full gallop. The riders shouted, every dog in the village barked, the women and children cheered. Those who had sat in the council watched stony-faced because the white man was there, but there was a proud, defiant sparkle in their eyes.

"God, what riders!" breathed Wyeth, awed. "Isn't that your boy on the gray? Look at that little devil ride! I didn't know he was old enough to join a war party."

Neither did I, Blake thought dully. He's not.

When the whites finally left, there was hearty laughter among the People and the day's happenings were carefully recounted. Hawk's Shadow said aside to Blake, "All whites are like you in that they show everything in their faces. Did you see the officer's fear when the riding began? What children they are!"

"The officer is a good man," Blake said quietly. "He would like to do the right things."

"Then why was he here where he is not wanted?"

"Because he was told to come, by his chief."

"Once," Hawk's Shadow said ominously, "we did as we were told by a chief, but if a chief is a fool, a man who may be wiser does not always listen. The young men even frightened Beaver Tooth to begin with. Did you see that? I suppose he was mostly afraid of losing some of the presents the white chief sent him."

When Blake made no answer, he looked at him sharply and said uneasily, "Are you changing, my brother? Growing whiter?"

"I'm just as I've always been," Blake answered a little stiffly.

"Will you stay in the Valley through the summer?"

"No. I'm going to guide some surveyors, Hawk's Shadow. They're planning to build a military road."

The scowl came back, dark and unhappy. "You have not mentioned this before."

"I heard in the fall that they were planning it. The officer talked about it again last night. They need someone who knows the country."

"Why will you be the one?" cried Hawk's Shadow fiercely. "Will you betray the people who—"

"I will help them," Blake said wearily, "because they are thinking of putting their road across the valley of the Camas, along the trail the People use for going to the buffalo country. I will go with them and show them a better way, a way that will keep their road farther from the Medicine Rock. I don't like being called a traitor."

Hawk's Shadow followed sullenly as Blake went to look for his horse.

"You talked with that soldier all through the night."

"You asked me to go and stay at their camp."

"But I did not say you should—"

Blake turned on him, his eyes flashing. "Do I measure your words when you talk with a man?"

He walked on and after a few moments, Hawk's Shadow walked beside him again.

He said softly, "In my heart I know you would not betray us. Hardly anything is certain now and that makes me, almost, distrust my brother."

"Do you think things are so certain for me then?" Blake had not meant to say the words or that his tone should reveal so much turmoil.

After a moment, Hawk's Shadow said kindly, "Will you leave the boy with us while you are with those people?"

"No. He'll go with me."

"He should stay, Blake. He is not so old as Eagle Feather, but there is much he should be learning."

299

"He has to learn from whites too."

"You have decided to make him white? Is this because he had no medicine dream?"

"It's because he *is* partly white."

"A man need not have a medicine dream. You know that."

"But Alec doesn't know it."

Blake roped his horse and stood holding the rope, looking at Hawk's Shadow. "If—if you told him that, he might believe it's true."

Hawk's Shadow looked away and said heavily, "I can't tell him. It's my shame that I ever told anyone, though it was a comfort at the time to share my wrongness. I could not say such things to a boy, or to anyone . . . . But . . . . if you think it would help him, you are free to tell him."

"No. It wouldn't be the same, coming from me."

"He will not make a good white, Blake. He is too good a person. Did you see him riding today? It may be that he will be a better horseman even than Eagle Feather."

"I saw him," Blake said.

"Does he want to go with you?"

"Yes."

"Has the grandson of Red Sky decided to try to turn white?"

"Hawk's Shadow, the boy has enough trouble in his own mind. Leave him alone. Please don't ever say a thing like that to him."

"That is what you always think, leave things alone," he said hotly. "Others will say those things to him, or whites will ask him why a white man's son tries to be of the Medicine Rock."

"I know that, but those things don't have to be said here, not by you. Surely you see that, if he can, he wants to be—"

"It is not possible to be both things," Hawk's Shadow said adamantly, with finality, "for him or for you . . . . You will come back here in the autumn?"

"I don't know. Will we be welcome?"

"The land is not mine to give."

300

XIV

CONNALL GREETED him weakly from the bed. It was mid-summer of 1857 and Connall was recovering from a fever of which Marie had died.

"It's good to see you, lad. It's been a while."

"I'm sorry, Connall, about Marie."

"She was a good woman," Connall said softly.

He lay propped against pillows, looking very thin and pale, his blue eyes tired and sad. There were streaks of gray in his red hair and beard. With a little shock, Blake realized that he was nearly fifty. They were none of them getting any younger.

"It's not a fatal illness," Connall said, "not for me, but it's going to take some time getting over. The weakness of it is slow to go. Thank God for my girls. That was Elizabeth, you know, that showed you in. She was here for a visit from her teaching job and now she says she'll stay on to see to the house and the young ones."

Of Connall's nine daughters, three had died in infancy or early childhood. Mary, the eldest, had married in Montreal where she had gone to school, Elizabeth had been a teacher in a Canadian mission school, Anne was married to a settler living over near Walla Walla, Brigid had married a Coeur d'Alene boy, and the two youngest were still in school. These two, Katy and Nancy, had been spending the summer holiday with their sister in Montreal and Connall said now, "It's a mercy those two young ones weren't at home this year. I'm afraid they'd have caught the sickness. Con is here, of course, but he's strong. It didn't touch him."

"He looks as healthy as a bull," Blake said.

Connall smiled a little, pleased. "Tell me about yourself, lad. It's been a long time. I know you were with the surveyors last year and how you kept the road away from the Camas, though I could have used the business its passing would have brought to the post."

"You have plenty of business as it is, selling stock and things to the forts and along the road," Blake said, smiling.

"Aye, well, now that you mention it, and not to brag, you understand, but the demand does sometimes outrun the supply these days. Just when I was thinking the Mormons had done me in, taking all my business in the south, the Lord sent the army."

Blake grimaced. "So that's who we have to blame for them. I think you'd make money, Connall, if you were alone in the middle of a desert—you and the Lord."

"I told you long ago that a farming and stock-raising operation would be a good thing to have here and, admit it, Blake, having the army in the country hasn't been such a bad thing for us so far. No settlers have tried to come to the Camas, but we still get some of the military business. The Indians are quiet, except for the bits of reservation trouble . . . . Where have you been since winter?"

"I've been working for the army again."

"You? Two summers in a row? There must have been a miracle somehow. What have you been doing? Scouting?"

"In a way I have been. They sent out what they call a reconnaisance group, but not for fighting. They've been trying to map the country west of the Divide, from the Canadian border south to a line running west from Laramie. It's damn well time somebody got decent maps of the area."

"How was it they got you to go along?"

"Wyeth Hamilton led the troops."

"He seems a fine boy."

"Yes. He's being sent back east."

"Why?"

302

"Because he's got too much sense, too much feeling, I think. Shadran, who's just been promoted to major, is more than a little afraid of him. Wyeth's been too much on the Indians' side too often. That reservation trouble you mentioned, do you know what it was about?"

"That some Indians wouldn't stay where they'd agreed to stay. I know it's a hard thing for them to understand, after having the run of the country all this time, but they did sign—"

"Some of them didn't sign, Connall. Chief White Water, for one, of one of the Palouse bands, signed nothing. His mark is on the papers, but Ellis Williams put it there."

"That's quite a charge to make, Blake. Have you got any proof of it?"

"White Water's word and the word of quite a few others."

Connall shrugged weakly. "You can't go by that. You know—"

"It's true, Connall, and it's why Wyeth is being sent east. When he heard about it and couldn't get Shadran to do anything, he started trying to find out what he could and he asked me to help. Williams gets an allotment at the agency for White Water's band. Those goods are sold and Williams and Shadran divide the money. Three of White Water's people have been killed this year because they refuse to be penned up where they never agreed to stay in the first place. Wyeth wrote a letter to the Indian Bureau and they contacted Shadran. He told them the lieutenant is a troublemaker and asked to have him reassigned. That's supposed to be the end of it."

Connall sighed, shaking his head. "Such a mess. They can't be making more than a few dollars apiece out of that junk that's supposed to be issued to the Indians. I knew from the first minute I saw him that Ellis Williams wasn't worth the powder it would take to blow him to hell, but I would have thought a little better of Shadran. Still, I suppose a thing like that shouldn't come as too much of a surprise. It seems to be a fact of life that where man goes, he takes such things as politicking and graft with him. I suppose it has to be expected that people in

303

authority as well as those who aren't will have a certain percentage as crooked as a dog's hind leg. I don't see that there's anything to be done."

"You could write some letters, Connall. You're a well-known, respected man all over this part of the country, if they cared to check up on you. *I've* written, but if anyone bothered checking on me, they'd just decide I'm a crazy mountain man past his time, with too many pro-Indian prejudices to be listened to. But you're a man of property and standing. Your word ought to count for something."

"Aye," he said thoughtfully. "I could do that. I could dictate the letters to Liz. She writes a fine hand, much more refined than yours, since she holds her pen in the proper hand, and she's good at keeping the books too. I might suggest they put somebody else in Williams' place. Would you want that job?"

"No."

"Why not? There couldn't be anybody better."

"I wouldn't work for the government."

"You've been working for the army."

"Only temporarily. I'm through with that now."

"The Indians need you, lad."

"Not like that. Not as anybody's employee. Don't bother writing if that's—"

"All right. Just rest easy. I'll only say they should get Ellis out and I'll name no other names if you want it so."

"They ought to get rid of Shadran too."

"Yes, both of them. I'll get Liz to write it after dinner. . . . . If you're through with the army, what do you plan to do now? You seem to be coming back to the white world these days, in spite of yourself."

"I don't plan to do anything except go home. Alec and I have been away from the Medicine Rock since March and we were away all through the good weather last year."

"He's a fine-looking boy, Alec, a lot better looking than that redheaded scoundrel of mine, though he seems a bit light built for his age. What are you going to do about his education?"

"Nothing. He's been having his education since the day he was born."

"But formal schooling, I mean. He's going to be thir-

304

teen soon—isn't he?—and he's never darkened a school-house door."

"He reads better than anybody I've ever seen."

"I don't doubt that, wild as *you* are over books, but there's more to schooling than just what comes out of books. We owe these boys something extra, Blake. Life is going to be hard for them, at times, in some ways that most other youngsters never even have to think about. They're breeds."

"That's one of the reasons I wouldn't send Alec east. Another is that he doesn't need it. He knows more now, in many ways, than most boys going to college. Formal schooling tends to try to take a lot of that kind of knowledge out of kids. Those so-called educators want them all stamped out of one mold. They can't take into account too much thinking on the part of their students; different-ness, innovation scares hell out of them. Those things would make the teachers' jobs too hard and complicated. *They* might have to think a little if kids didn't go by the book."

"Well, I can't argue with you there. For one thing, I'm not even sure what innovation means, but what I do know is that one day there are going to be a lot more people out here. Some day, this may even be a state and I mean for Con to have a place in it. I think that, to have that place, he's going to have to learn some things in the ways most other people know them, so as to be accepted. He had the one year at St. Denis before they closed it down, but it's past time he had more. The girls went to school in Canada; the two are still going there. That was the place to send them when we first opened the post and I've gone on with it because it seemed better to send the little ones where they already had sisters. We're a part of the States now though, and I've entered Con in a school in St. Louis. He's to begin in September. I'd planned to leave to take him there next week. I've also got some business matters that need taking care of there before there's a war. There's going to be a civil war, you know, as surely as the sun will set. Do you think you'll be fighting in it?"

"No. Why should I?"

"Well, it's your country. I only wondered."

"*This* is my country. It's not my war."

"You don't think it will spread here somehow?"

"I suppose there will be individuals, small groups, maybe, who will hate each other and fight, but I don't see how any southern army could come here, or why they'd want to. They might want to try to take California because of the gold that's still there, but there's nothing here but country."

"What does your southern military friend Hamilton think?"

"About the same. That the South will have its hands more than full trying to hold the territory it already claims."

"Well, I'm glad to hear that. God knows I'd hate to think we'd have to change governments again. Do you know that, except for Jesse Harris, I've never seen anybody who was even part Negro? Have you ever seen a slave?"

"Yes."

"What do they look like?"

"Why, like—Negroes. I don't know what you mean."

"I mean, do they wear chains and such like that?"

"Not that I know of."

"Have you heard about this book, *Uncle Tom's Cabin?* These old newspapers we get are full of it. It seems to have the country, North *and* South, up in arms. Elizabeth says she's got a copy, but she didn't bring it, not knowing she'd be staying. I want you to find it for me when you're in St. Louis."

Blake had been looking from the window, watching Alec and Con where they sat on a corral fence, seeming easier together now that the awkwardness of reacquaintance was passing. He turned sharply to Connall, his eyebrows raised.

"St. Louis? I think I must have missed something."

"I thought it was settled that you'd be taking Con there for me." Connall spoke casually, smiling, but his brow was slightly furrowed and there were tension and worry under the lightness of his tone. "The arrangements are all made with the school and I can't go. I'm weak as a kitten. I was counting on making this trip. I've been fairly often to Montreal, but I know almost nothing about any part of the States outside the Oregon Territory. And there're the

306

business matters that have to be seen to. You can go and be back here before winter closes up the passes, travel being what it is these days. You've not been out of here for a long while."

"I don't want out."

Connall said gently, "Blake, it seems to me that for the past year or so you've maybe been trying to show Alec a little something about whites. Wyeth Hamilton's a good man, but a lot of soldiers are scum. Some are all right, but even so, the army often makes a difference in people. Oughtn't you to show him people in more normal conditions? Give him a look at people with homes and families and that kind of life? At least let him see one city. I'd planned to ask the two of you to go with Con and me, but now I just can't make it. There's nobody else I'd rather trust my boy with, or my business in St. Louis."

"You've just been talking about war," Blake pointed out. "You don't want Con in school in the States with a war going on, surely."

"He can get in at least this one year before that happens. You know how slow politicians are to get anything started or stopped, and they have to consider the people with money invested, both North and South. They'll be given time to pull out with as little loss as they can manage. I think there'll likely be two years yet . . . . Will you do this for me? For Con—and for Alec?"

"I don't think Alec would want to—"

"Ask him. Look at the two of them out there. I'll bet they're talking about it right now. Will you do it if the boy wants to have a look?"

"I—don't know, Connall. I'll have to think about it."

"When can you tell me?"

"We just stopped by. We'll have to be going soon. I'll decide before we leave."

"Well . . . . there's something more."

Blake was watching the boys again, Con talking mightily with grand gestures, Alec listening intently, his face solemn.

"I shouldn't mention it now, I suppose. You being as you are, it's liable to make you turn down the St. Louis thing, but I'd like you to think about this too. I'm going to be all right from this sickness but I'm not a young man

307

anymore. I doubt that Con will ever want to run this business. He's not certain what he wants to do with himself, except that he says he's sure he won't be running a farm and trading post. I'd like it if you'd come here . . . . Liz is a fine strong woman. Who's to say the two of you mightn't work something out one day? There'd be no obligation in that way, you understand, but it's not right or natural for a young man like you to just go on living alone. One day, before you know it, Alec will be grown and gone off on his own."

Blake's immediate reaction had been irritation, but the look of concern and apprehension on Connall's pale, thin face made him try to put the feeling aside. He said mildly, "I'm not that young, Connall. I was thirty-eight in the spring. Don't worry——"

"When you're my age, you'll wish to God to be thirty-eight again."

"You're getting to sound like a really old man," Blake said teasingly, "trying to put the world in order before you——"

"Being sick this way and losing Marie, I've been feeling an old man, and I've worried about you since the day I first picked you up at Laramie. But it's not just you; it's me, too. I'd like to feel easy about this place. All along, I've supposed that if Con didn't want it, one of the girls would marry somebody who'd want to take over, but they haven't. There's only the two in school left, and Liz. Liz is twenty-five now, but there's naught wrong with her. The reason she hasn't married is that there was a time she thought she'd be a nun. That didn't work out, and she went to teaching. Since then, she tells me, there's been no one she's wanted to marry. I think the two of you might get on if you both weren't too stubborn. She's a great one for the books and a good worker."

"Connall, I——"

"As I say, there's no obligation about that if you decide to come here and run the post. It's a thing I'd like you to think about is all. You could have a home, perhaps other young ones."

"I have a home. I'm going for a walk now. I'll talk to Alec and tell you about St. Louis when I come back."

"Have a look at my pigs. Have you any idea what the army's willing to pay for a hog carcass?"

"And pork-eater used to be a dirty word," Blake said dryly, "when I was called one."

"There'll be ham for dinner," Connall said with satisfaction. "How long since you've tasted pig ham? And you'll have a fair chance to see what a fine cook Elizabeth is."

"How long since you've heard the word subtle?" Blake asked wearily.

"Never heard it that I know of."

"I don't suppose you'd consider looking it up?"

"How do you spell it? I'll ask Liz."

Blake sat by his fire while a wet, heavy spring snow fell on the valley. It was early evening and very dark. He had eaten some supper, for which there had been little appetite, and now he sat turning the pages of a book restlessly. He had brought back a large number of books from St. Louis, more than he had ever purchased at one time, but it had taken an amazingly short time to read them all through once. He had built new bookshelves in the late fall, and spent time in repairs and small additions to the cabin, making it more comfortable and ready for winter, but when winter closed in, he found he could not stay there. It was too lonely. The peace his little valley had always brought him was not enough. Finally, resignedly, he had made a pack, strapped on showshoes, and left.

He worked for Connall and others, small jobs that took him about the snowbound country. There had been more Indian trouble and rumors of trouble in the fall and few men were willing to travel the country alone. In early March, he had come home again, exhausted, ready for the respite of the cabin. But that had been several weeks ago and now, to his disgust, he was restless again.

He got up from his place by the fire and looked at a calendar. Connall would have left by now to pick up the boys. They could not be expected home before the end of June.

Blake had been surprised and a little disappointed by Alec's eagerness to make the trip to St. Louis. Perhaps he had had a premonition when they first talked about it that the talking, the visit itself, would not be the end of the matter. They had gone with a small military detachment as far as Fort Laramie, and from there east they traveled with one of Connall's freight caravans. At a little Kansas town that was the end of a stage line, they left their horses and took a coach. Blake had chafed at the necessary slowness of the freight wagons, but the plains would not have made safe traveling for a man and two boys alone. He chafed, too, at stage travel, but the boys wanted very much to try it. They were trying to see how many "firsts" they could achieve. Alec was even keeping a written list of their firsts. Water in the Missouri was low with the season, but as soon as they reached a point where boats were still able to come up, they left the stagecoach for a steamboat.

In the city, they had two rooms at a good hotel. Blake would not have had money for such accommodations, but when he had protested about them, Connall had said angrily, "You're making the trip as a favor to me. I'd have had to spend the money anyway and now I'll hear no more of it."

The boys took in everything with wide eyes. Con was always vociferous with comments, admiration, criticism, sometimes ridicule of all the new and unaccustomed things he saw. Alec, except for an occasional question, was quiet and thoughtful. Blake took them to museums, to plays and concerts, to anything he could think of or they could find might be of interest, but their favorite thing to do was walk the streets, watching people, looking into the windows of business establishments, prowling through stores and examining merchandise.

They arrived in town a few days before Con could move into his school and filled all the time with sightseeing. Finally, there was one more day left. Blake, though he had enjoyed some of the things they had done and, even more, had enjoyed the pleasure the boys had found in them, was relieved that he and Alec would be leaving soon. He had had an uneasy feeling about the trip from its beginning and wanted fervently to be home again.

He did not go out with the boys on that last evening. They were out walking again, and he had work to do on the report and accounts of the business he had been transacting for Connall. He had left the buying of Con's school clothes until the last day, needing to do some observing on his own of what was considered appropriate these days in the way of school clothes, and was wondering if perhaps he had left too much for the last minute, when he heard the boys come back into their room next door. After a time, Alec came quietly through the door that connected their rooms, closing it behind him.

"Con's gone to bed," he said and sat on Blake's bed.

Blake, looking up from his paperwork, thought the boy looked a little flushed. His eyes were restless.

"Guess who we saw."

"Who?"

"Mr. Williams."

"Ellis Williams?"

"Yes. He was coming out of a bar on Front Street with some others."

"You shouldn't have been on Front Street at this hour of the night."

"He said, 'Well I'll be goddamned! some breed boys from my part of the country!' and then he told those men how we make trouble for Indians and whites both and aren't fit to be either. They were all pretty drunk. We wanted to fight him, but the other men made him come away with them."

Blake could feel anger burning in his face. "Alec—"

"Oh, you don't have to say anything," Alec said almost nonchalantly. "I don't much care. It's kind of strange how I don't care. I was mad while we were there but it didn't last long. Con's making all kinds of threats about how he's going to find him and do things, but I told him it wouldn't make us any different . . . . Did you know that at his school they don't even know he's a quarter Indian?"

"Yes. Connall told me."

"Well, he doesn't *look* Indian, but I can't see why they want to keep it a secret. I asked him if he's ashamed and then I thought *I'd* have to fight him."

"I think it's because, if people object to something, it does no good to hit them over the head with it. There are more tactful ways."

311

"Like what?"

"Well, when Con's made friends and come to know his teachers, then he could let it get around that he's part Indian, if he wants to. Some of them, if they'd known before they knew *him,* would have had their minds made up about a lot of things and they'd be much harder to change. It would take a lot longer to get them to see and accept that he's just another boy."

"But why bother?"

"Because Con and his father think it's worthwhile doing it this way and I think they're right."

"Con says his father says you've changed a lot the past few years. Would you want me to say I'm not Indian?"

"That would be up to you, but you wouldn't really have to say that you're *not.* Probably, it would be a matter of just not saying that you *are.* I can't see that there's ever much point in asking for trouble."

"I know you can't," Alec said and Blake looked at him. The bitterness was there. The boy said, "Are you ashamed of it, when we're in a place like this?"

"Alec, I have never been ashamed of you about anything, any time, anywhere."

There was a silence and Alec, trying hard to keep his voice casual, said, "Well, I didn't come in here to talk about Mr. Williams. I just thought I'd better tell you about that and have done with it because Con will still be ranting in the morning."

Blake waited and finally said tensely, "There's something more then?"

"Yes . . . . I want to stay here and go to school."

Blake could not look at him. This was the thing that had been in the depths of his mind all along, the reason for his uneasiness and fear of the trip.

"I've been thinking about it a long time," Alec said levelly. "Con wanted me to take those tests he had to take, just for fun, and I did it because I kept thinking I might be staying. Did they talk to you about the tests?"

"Yes. Your marks were all excellent."

"I knew they would be because it all seemed so easy."

"But, Alec, I don't think there's really a lot you can learn here—"

The idea of leaving the boy here alone frightened him

to the point of despair, but he struggled, making himself admit that a good part of the desperation was for himself, for the long winter and being alone. There was no shred of fairness to Alec in that kind of thinking.

"Could you pay for it?" the boy asked relentlessly.

"Yes, only—"

"How?"

"I could—sell some horses, I suppose."

"You wouldn't have to sell Ceres or Persephone or Jason."

"No."

"I could learn a lot of things. You've told me for as long as I can remember that a lot of the most important things people have to learn don't come from books. Con says his father says that most of the jobs you've taken lately have been so I'd see more whites. Don't you think I need to see schoolteachers and people in stores and homes and those things? Maybe I could find some kind of work to help pay for the school."

"How much influence do you think Con's had on you in thinking about these things?" Blake asked and wished he hadn't. Why shouldn't the boy be influenced by someone his own age, with some of his own particular problems?—someone who was, in many ways, closer to him than his father could ever be.

"Some I guess," Alec said thoughtfully, "but I had thought about going away before I knew he was going. I asked Lieutenant Hamilton about schools and things in the States. He said I could probably learn more by studying at home, but he doesn't understand how it is, being half something I don't know anything about. I thought, two years ago, that I wanted to be just Indian, but then I had no medicine dream, so I have to look into the rest of it."

"Why do you have to be one or the other? Can't you be happy being both? Because both is what you are."

"I don't know. Aren't I doing just what you've always told me, trying to look at all sides of a thing and then think about it for myself?"

There was some derision in his tone. Looking up at his father's scowling face, he changed it and said innocently, "What's the matter?"

"It seems to me," Blake said slowly, "that you've begun to feel a bit sorry for yourself about being a half-breed, to use it as a crutch, or rather as a battering ram. It's a thing I don't like to see happening . . . . About school: it begins the day after tomorrow. I doubt you could get in this year."

"There were some boys from some of the southern states who were registered and now they won't be coming."

"All right, Alec." He felt ineffably weary. "I'll think about it and we'll decide in the morning. You do realize, don't you, that there would be no way of getting home until spring?"

"I know," he said carelessly and went back to the room he shared with Con.

The headmaster was pleased to have one of his late southern withdrawals replaced. Blake sat at a desk and filled out the necessary papers with Alec watching closely over his shoulder. The master smiled nervously, watching him write.

"Are you left-handed too, young man?" he asked with false joviality.

"No, sir, I'm not."

The master was relieved. "No offense, Mr. Westfall, I'm sure you understand that, but some of our teachers are not very—ah—enlightened about that sort of thing. I *cannot* persuade them to realize it's not—unnatural."

Looking down at the papers, continuing to write, memories rushed into Blake's mind of beatings and harangues from his grandfather. "It's the devil in you—pure, stubborn wickedness! You won't try to use the right hand! There's nothing I know to help you about them evil green eyes, but with the Lord's help and patience, I'll see you quit using that left hand." He couldn't. It was such an automatic, natural thing and his right hand was always so awkward. There had been a period of several years when he had stammered badly. They had said that was the devil too, that he wasn't right in the head. He remembered crying once, thinking that he might cut off his left hand with the ax. That must have been when he was very young because he had stopped crying early. Finally, he had known

314

that, wickedness or not, left-handedness was a part of him, something he couldn't change. Perhaps that had been the beginning of the end of his bondage. Alec's difficulties were, in a small sense, something of the same thing.

The master had excused himself and left the room. Alec said softly, "Could I have the pen?"

Blake gave it to him automatically, then looked at another sheet of paper where the boy was writing. The sheet was headed "Information About Student's Family," and on the line that requested "Mother's Full Name," Alec was writing "Shy Fawn, daughter of Red Sky of the Medicine Rock Band."

"Alec—"

"If they don't like it, they can keep their school. Let's see what he does." The boy was smiling a little.

The master became flushed and embarrassed as he looked at the papers.

"We've never had an—an—"

"The word is Indian," Blake said coolly.

"Yes, I—I thought so, from the information here about the—ah—mother. We've never had an Indian student apply here, Mr. Westfall. I'm sure you'll understand that schools must have their—policies. Perhaps—ah—Alec would wait outside."

"I'd like him to stay."

The harried man cleared his throat, shuffling papers. "There is a school, perhaps you haven't heard of it, for Indian children and children who are—are—"

"Half-breeds?"

"Exactly. It's a very fine school, on the other side of town. Perhaps they could . . . ."

"This school is supposedly open to people who are willing to pay."

"Well, yes, but I'm sure you'll understand that some room must be left for—ah—selectivity. With the volume of applications we have—"

"You told me, not a half hour ago, that you still had openings."

The old man's face was flushed. He shuffled the papers with distraught hands. Blake felt a little sorry for him and he did not like the hardness that had come into Alec's

315

face. Still, this was supposed to be an educated, enlightened man and the thing had gone this far. He said reasonably, "Mr. Curtis, suppose I had filled in Alec's mother's name as Mary Smith. You would never have known the difference. Alec is only another boy who wants to go to school. You've seen the tests he took. You told me yourself that he's ready for your highest form."

"But that was before I—I mean—it wouldn't be a good thing for him to be a student here—for Alec's sake, I mean. He would be the only one of his—kind. You must know how cruel children can be . . . ."

"I also know that, mostly, they pick up that sort of cruelty from adults. I know about the Indian school, Mr. Curtis. I know that, unfortunately, its scholastic standards aren't nearly as high as yours. Alec would be wasting time and money there. Will you take him?"

"It would call for a full meeting of our staff and administration. This—ah—sort of thing has simply not come up before. Perhaps we could begin discussing it as soon as possible and let you know our final decision later in the day."

"I can stay for the meeting," Blake said calmly, relentlessly.

"Oh, I assure you that won't be necessary. Parents don't usually—"

"I'm rather concerned in this, Mr. Curtis, and Alec is. I think I might find the meeting interesting."

He sent Alec and Con away to begin choosing school clothes, wishing he had not let Alec stay in the office at all. He felt trapped and angry, not wanting to stay himself, but the thing was begun. He could not simply let it drop as he would surely have done had it concerned only himself. Alec's burning, defiant eyes, if nothing else, left him no escape.

With a few well-chosen, derisive phrases, Blake browbeat and badgered the uncomfortable staff, and Con and Alec moved into the school dormitory. When he had left them there that night, Blake stopped at a saloon on his way back to the hotel. Later, he met a girl. She was young and thin and sad and he was sorry for her, hating himself, but he felt a little better in the morning.

He called on the district head of the Indian Bureau that

316

morning, talking forcefully with him about Ellis Williams and the treaties, wondering if he was going to have to go on with his life now, in this active, demanding way forever. The official assured him some immediate action would be taken, and Blake left with no feeling of hope or satisfaction about the matter.

Back at his hotel, he wrote a letter to the professor at Cambridge, reminding him of their meeting seven years ago and asking if he was still interested in authentic items and facts about the western tribes. Perhaps the old man was dead. What had come over him, fostering all this activity?

He visited the boys briefly that evening. They seemed a little lost, but reasonably happy.

"They watch Alec real close," Con whispered, giggling. "There's a lot they want to know, but they ask me instead of him. I think most of them are afraid of getting scalped in their beds."

Alec said little, only looked defiant, adamant, a little frightened, and very young.

Where will this end for him? Blake wondered miserably, walking back to this hotel. He tried to convince himself that the year at school might be the best thing that could happen, but he could feel only guilt about leaving the boy, worry and concern for Alec, and some sympathy for Mr. Curtis and the others.

On Blake's return to the Medicine Rock village, it was Owl Woman who demanded first to know where Alec was. She was bent and old and terribly wrinkled now, but her sharp dark eyes were hard on his face as she listened to his answer. Little Rain and the wife of Smiling Fox went on with their work, listening carefully. There was a little relief for Blake in the fact that both Hawk's Shadow and Smiling Fox were out hunting with other men.

Owl Woman said harshly, "You have deserted the boy in a place of whites. The grandson of Red Sky, the child of his daughter, has such a father!"

Blake put down the food bowl they had just given him and left the lodge sadly. There would not be much for him in the way of winter's companionship in the village. Hawk's Shadow had been cool and distant since the time the soldiers had come.

He turned at a touch on his arm and found that Eagle Feather had followed him from the lodge.

"I hurt my hand," the boy explained. "I can't shoot yet so I did not go hunting today."

"I'm sorry. Does it grow better?"

"Yes . . . . My grandmother's tongue is sometimes very sharp. She is old now and does not always think what she is saying."

"Yes, I know."

"I will miss Alec."

"So will I."

"Does he like it there, do you think?"

"It was his wish to stay, not mine."

"Sometimes he has talked of a thing like this, of going away to a place where only whites live. Will he come back?"

"In the spring."

"To stay?"

"I don't know."

"I could come to the cabin sometimes," the boy said shyly. "You have begun teaching me to read and to know English. I should know more."

"What does your father think of that?"

"He complains of it very much. He says I am in danger of growing up to be like Beaver Tooth. I have tried to tell him this will not happen, but he does not listen so now I no longer try to tell him. But it will be all right. Alec and I have talked about that, too, sometimes. Alec is younger than I but, in some things, I think he is wise. He says that some day there may not even be a People. This I do not believe, but I think that, to help the People if I can, I should learn to read and write and know English and about white men. I don't want to know only enough of these things so that they will give me presents and then laugh at me."

"Yes, I understand that."

"My father is not happy about it, but so long as he can hunt and have the country, his unhappiness is not too heavy . . . . I will come, then, to see you?"

He came often, sometimes staying for a night or two. Hawk's Shadow and Storm Coming Out Of The East and a few others came occasionally. Blake hunted with them

318

for the winter's meat. They urged him to get a woman and would talk of little else. He was tired of the subject and could make no satisfactory explanation, to them or to himself, of why he did not want one. There had been women, occasionally, like the girl in St. Louis, but only for the briefest time, only to satisfy the tormenting physical needs. He had not known their names or anything about them, had not wanted to. He was afraid to risk any close relationship. Such things always seemed to end only in pain. Finally, he told the men curtly that he would be leaving the Valley again soon.

He stayed on at the cabin as long as he could, nervous, restless, yet reluctant to go. When the weather was good, he spent a great deal of time in careful working of the boulder by the spring. The outline of the castle was taking shape under his hands. He could look up from his work, through the trees to Never Summer, watching it change as winter came on, and feel quiet and still for a time. He thought that perhaps it was never quite enough for a man simply to love a country. To be truly a part of it, he had to mark it somehow, as animals marked their territories. First he had built the cabin; now there was the castle about which no one else knew. Perhaps, he thought, that was why farming and such things were so important to others . . . . But what will I do about Alec?

It grew too cold for working on the boulder. He left the valley for a time, and now it was beginning to be spring, in the reluctant way spring always began in the high country, and he was back, sitting by his fire, trying to reread one of the new books, unable to remain still or to keep his thoughts from intruding. And his horses in the meadow whickered uneasily. He went to the door and found Eagle Feather coming up through the heavy snow.

"My father asks that you come down to the village. Cricket my aunt has come with three whites and their children."

Blake built up his fire and sat down by it with Emmett Price. The cabin was crowded. Emmett's wife Amanda and her brother Eli, who was Cricket's husband, were there. Amanda lay in the bed with three small children, sleeping, and two other children slept wrapped in skins on

319

the floor. Cricket was down in the village, in the birth lodge. Little Rain had been hurt and offended when Cricket's children had shown fear of being left in her care. Blake had been uneasy about bringing all of them here; it was a long hard way up into the little valley in this weather, but Amanda had insisted, very near hysteria. She had never spent a night in an Indian village.

"That was a good mission we had," Emmett was saying in his slow, careful way, warming his hands gratefully before the fire. "We had real good farmin' land, an' things was goin' good, with us an' with the Indians around. The Mormon Church is some different than the one my folks belonged to. They want to convert the Indians, a course, but they don't, most of 'em, look down on 'em the way some do. Things was workin' out good till the army started messin' with ever'body. They've had a big bunch of soldiers at Fort Bridger all winter, waitin' till spring to come down on Salt Lake City.

"We begun to have some trouble some time back, nothin' to speak of at first, just—things wasn't easy the way they had been at first. Then—you may have heard of it, the army started workin' to turn the Indians against us— against us Mormons, I mean, sayin' we'd multiply like rabbits an' take up all the land, things like that. After a while, we began to have real raids. Some of the Indians that had settled around left us. Finally, we had to send to Salt Lake for help, for more people.

"This spring, they sent word they couldn' spare nobody, for us to close things up an' come down there. That was a hard thing. We'd worked mighty hard on that land an' we was just gittin' it in what you could call good shape. We talked about it an' thought maybe we'd just try to stay. Mostly, when you're called to do somethin' by the Church, you just do it an' it turns out just right, but we thought they didn' really know, down there, how it would be for us to have to leave all that work we'd done.

"An' then—there was a real fight. Three whites an' about a dozen of our Indians was killed an' we *had* to go. Cricket, she's been sickly now for several months, an' she'd been askin' to come home. Eli wanted to bring her. We've all been right worried about her. This was a lot closer than goin' to Salt Lake, though hard country to git

320

through, an' I don't know what the Church is goin' to say about it."

Eli said uneasily, "I didn' like just leavin' her down there like that. That old woman purely looks and seems like a witch."

"She's Cricket's mother," Blake said, trying to make it a little easier. Eli's gaunt face was creased with worry and exhaustion.

"An' Cricket was so glad to git here," Emmett added. "Maybe ever'thing'll be all right now . . . . They let us right in, Blake, down at the canyon. Cricket gave the guard some signal an' hollered to him who she was . . . . This seems like a good place you've got here, though I couldn' see much and it's mighty hard to git to. You doin' some farmin' here, are you?"

"No, just grazing some horses. I've got a few cattle down in the main valley."

"When I was here, years back, I remember thinkin' what good farmin' land some of the country around here would make. It's been a long time, ain't it?"

Blake nodded, thinking, with the surface of his mind, how much older Emmett looked. There was a lot of gray in his hair and his shoulders stooped. And he, Blake, was a few years older than Emmett. As if reading the thought, Emmett said, "You look like you've stood the years good. I can't see any gray hairs. Course this light ain't very good . . . . I thought you had a boy . . . ."

"He's in school in St. Louis."

"Oh. Well, that's good . . . ."

Blake had to ask the question that had been occupying most of his mind. "Emmett, were they Nez Perce that raided you?"

Emmett's face was sad and uneasy. "They was, Blake. I hate to say it, but they was. We worried about that, but Cricket felt like there wouldn't be any trouble, this band bein' separate from the others for so long an' all. What do you think?"

"I don't think there'll be trouble for you here. There's not much to do but wait and see what happens other places."

Emmett said desperately, "Blake, ain't there no place a man can go an' *have* what he works for? I remember how my folks got put off their farm in Missouri. A man pays for land, one way or another. What gives somebody else the right to tax him like they done my folks? They was just barely makin' enough for the family to eat out of that old hill land, but it was supposed to belong to them. They wasn' botherin' nobody, not askin' nobody for nothin', makin' their own way . . . . We sweated an' cried an' prayed over that mission land an' the gover'ment sent the army to turn the Indians against us. We meant good to them people an' we wasn' doin' wrong to anybody . . . . I don't know, anymore, if there even *is* such a thing as rights an', if there is, who's got a right to have 'em."

XV

As you will see from the enclosed documents (ran Headmaster Curtis' letter), *your son has excellent marks. I must tell you, in fact, that some of them are the best of record for our school. His scholastic achievements have been, indeed, outstanding. However. . . .*

Blake looked up from the letter at Alec, who sat by the old, rough log table, engrossed in some drawing, his face intent, but calm and untroubled.

"You've read this, I suppose."

"Well, yes, I have. It never was really sealed. I think Mr. Curtis intended for me to read it."

" 'Sullen, uncooperative, and recalcitrant,' " Blake quoted, looking at the letter.

"I did the schoolwork. You can see the records they sent."

"I've looked at the records, but what's been the problem with 'recalcitrant' and the rest of it?"

"The whole place is full of a lot of stupid rules, like that you can't talk during meals. Why? Nobody could give any explanation for most of their rules, except that they just *had* them, they'd always had them, and it was against the rules to ask about them. And those final marks I got: In some things, I had to take three or four different examinations because Mr. Curtis and the others couldn't believe that 'an—ah—Indian' could do so well. It almost killed them to give me what I had coming. They were going to give me just average marks until I found out what was going on, and when I tried to talk to them, they just said it would be better for me not to have a swelled head. What could *I* do with school records anyway, they wanted to know, but I wouldn't stop talking. I'd had those drawings and paintings and things shown, and things in the newspapers about the exhibit, and they said that that was more than enough to make me impossible to live with, but I wouldn't shut up about the grades. I couldn't. I told Mr. Curtis that if I didn't get what I'd earned, I'd go to the newspaper and tell them his school was discriminating against Indians. Discriminating is a really good word to use with someone like Mr. Curtis. It upset him. So then they made up some new examinations that none of the others had had to take, and I did them."

"Farther on in the letter," Blake said thoughtfully, "it says 'dissension and radical thought among the other students, leading to disciplinary difficulties.'"

"Well, I told the other boys what was going on about the exams and things. They might as well have heard my side of it. It may have been the first and only time some of them will do any thinking about injustice and the complacency of people in authority.

"To begin with, Mr. Curtis was upset and embarrassed about the art exhibition. He said that my working for Mr. Kirchner at the museum was one thing, good discipline for a boy to work to earn his keep, but it was a little uncomfortable for him to have one of his students with artistic talent. He didn't ever say talent; that would have broken his mouth, but, anyway, the school doesn't teach art. It doesn't consider such things necessary or quite proper for young gentlemen. It doesn't teach music either, or anything else of any cultural value. People who have only what they're taught there don't really know much of anything, even about their own country, except for a lot of propaganda to make them want to fight somebody. Latin and Greek, math and ancient history and things like that are all right, so far as they go, but what good do they do you when you don't have anything to eat? Or when you have to get from one place to another and there are no roads or stage lines? And that's another thing: Most of those boys think the United States ends just west of St. Louis. The school didn't even have one map that went farther west than the settled parts of Kansas. I drew them some."

"Yes," Blake said dryly, "I'm sure you did. But you say that in the beginning Mr. Curtis was upset about the art exhibit. Do you remember that I had a letter very much like this one last year?"

"Well, yes, but there won't be any more because I'm finished."

"I realize that and it looks as if the teachers are relieved about it."

"That was another thing. It didn't seem right to them for me to be through so quickly. They had an awfully hard time coming to accept that."

"If you're determined to have a wide education," Blake said, "then that's part of it. Most people feel most comfortable doing things the way they've always been done. They get very uneasy about something a little out of the ordinary. If you want to go on living closely with a lot of people, I think you'll just have to accept that and go along with it, to some degree."

"Why will I?"

"Because it will make your own life a hell of a lot easier, if nothing else."

Alec smiled, unconvinced. "Well, at least I shook up Mr. Curtis' school a little. I think I was good for it. They kept saying things like: 'If we *allow* you to graduate after only three years here, what do you intend to do with yourself?' One of the teachers, Mr. Schaeffer, kept trying to persuade me to go on to the university. He's a nice man, in his way, and he would have helped me get a scholarship. I think he was hurt when I said I didn't want it. He said it would be a shame and a waste for me not to go on with something. I told him all I was really interested in going on with, that somebody else could teach me about, would be something to do with art. That was a shock for him. I told him I could come home and draw and paint all I liked, at the same time working to raise good horses and roaming around the mountains and such things. He wanted to know what good a formal education would be in a situation like that and I told him I'd been wondering the same thing, but that I could do things like conjugating Latin verbs while I skinned an otter, just for my own satisfaction. He looked like he might cry, and he said that my biggest problem seemed to him to lie in the lack of a decent, basic upbringing.

"They all wondered, one time or another, why I couldn't be like my friend Con, who showed some proper respect for what he was getting. Con's been in a hundred fights these past three years. He always had all the demerits he could carry, for fighting, missing classes, things like that. Sometimes his marks were only just barely passing, but all that was fine. They said Con was a quite typical young gentleman and you had to expect some extra rough edges on someone brought up so far from civilization. Con has decided he wants to be a lawyer and they think that's awfully commendable. Con never asked them any questions . . . . Do you see in the letter where Mr. Curtis says I'm an iconoclast?"

"I've read all the letter. I wish you weren't quite so pleased about it."

He drew for a time and then said, "Things got really interesting at school when the southern states started talking secession. Most of the teachers were Northerners, but quite a few of the boys were from the South. That was the only fight, physical fight, I had this year, when I said I wouldn't fight on anybody's side because none of it had anything to do with me or with anything I cared about and why should I risk being killed for nothing . . . . Con says he's going to join if there's a war, but don't tell his father. He'll be going back to school in the fall if things don't get too hot, and he'll join the Union army from there . . . .

"Look at the light on those big rocks on the mountain. There's no light anything like that in the east. I'm glad to be home . . . . We heard a lot of talk, coming out, about the gold they're finding down south and there are lots of people on the road. Have you heard about it?"

"On the South Platte? Yes."

"We could take some stock down there to sell, couldn't we? You ought to see those people. Most of them don't have anything. If they ever did have anything, they just left it and are rushing out to get rich. Some say there's gold all over the mountains. Mr. MacPheirson says some people have been digging up here. Maybe we'll have a rush here one day. I've seen sparkly stuff in a lot of streams."

"I hope to God you haven't been going around saying that to people."

"No, but they'll come looking, won't they? We've got farmers in the Medicine Rock now. I suppose we could stand a few miners."

It had taken Cricket a long while to get well after her baby was stillborn. During those weeks, spring came to the valley. Emmett and Eli had brought some seed and a little equipment from the abandoned Mormon mission. Their hands itched and their muscles tensed to begin working the good land along the streams.

A few braves from one of the bands along the Salmon had ridden over to tell their version of what had happened at the mission. Hawk's Shadow and some of the others were uneasy and angry that the whites were among them. Beaver Tooth called a council, to which he asked Blake to come, to present the whites' proposition to the People.

"They cannot stay here," Hawk's Shadow said adamantly. "Whites have no place in the Medicine Rock. No!"

"Yet Cricket is your sister," Storm Coming Out Of The East pointed out mildly. "She wants to stay. She says and the men say they will make no trouble. They do not want to make a mission here. They only want some land; that land up the north fork of the creek. It would be well away from the village. We need never see them. They have been driven from other land. For my part, I can see how it would be with them. We do not use that land."

"We hunt on it," Hawk's Shadow said shortly. Then, staring bitterly at Blake, he added, "My sisters are fools for marrying all these whites. It has been nothing but trouble for my family and the People."

"Still," said Beaver Tooth calmly, "it has happened and these people say they will pay us money for the land they use, and that they will do nothing to interfere with us. Also, to have them here will make it better for us with many other whites. They will see that the Medicine Rock

327

People truly have good hearts and they will not need to send the army to bother us and such things."

"The army helped to drive out these whites from where they were," cried Hawk's Shadow angrily.

"If they do not do as they have said, we will make them go," said Beaver Tooth.

Hawk's Shadow made a rude sound. "You should know how whites are. When they get hold of a piece of land, they will never let it go. There is a great deal of land. They need none here."

"They are going to raise some cattle, besides growing food for themselves. They will sell those cattle and pay us for the land. This pay will be divided among the People; it will be a help to us all. Isn't this true, Blake?"

Blake was startled by being addressed and did not want to try to answer. There was no answer.

Hawk's Shadow said accusingly, "Blake wants all those people out of his cabin. That's all he's thinking about. He would say it's all right for them to do anything."

Emmett and Amanda, Eli, and all the children had been living in Blake's valley for weeks now and it was true—he was very tired, more than ready to have the place to himself.

"They have told me," he said slowly, with all their eyes on him, "that they only want to farm and raise some cattle. They say they are through with being missionaries and only want to make their own lives. I've known Emmett Price for a long time and I believe he means what he says. I think that some day other whites will want to come into the Valley. Perhaps, if that has to be, these are better than most."

It had always been a tacit rule that a council should go on until there was agreement. This was a very long one, lasting until Hawk's Shadow walked out.

Emmett and Eli and their families went into the branch valley drained by the north fork of Medicine Rock Creek and began their clearing and planting. They felled trees for a two-room cabin which the two families would share and talked excitedly about irrigation and other undertakings for the future. There was not so much good land along the north fork as in the main valley, but there was as much as the two families could use for some time to come, and there was access to good high meadows for grazing. Emmett went down to Camas Post and got a few pigs and cattle to start their breeding operations.

Blake helped them for a few days when they were felling trees and building. Despite his own uneasiness and lack of resignation at having other people come into the Valley, he had always liked Emmett and liked seeing him so happy and eager.

"Nobody could have worked harder than most of us did on that mission land," Emmett told him, "but it wasn't the same as this. I'm thirty-five years old an' this is the first place I've had that's been really mine. It does wonderful things for a man, havin' his own place, don't it? I don't think I've ever felt so good in my life."

Blake was away most of the summer and did not go up the North Fork again until fall. He found only Amanda at the cabin, with the small children. The others, she said, were up in the meadows, getting in wild hay.

"Come in. Dinner's nearly ready. They'll be back before long, to eat."

"You've done so much," Blake said, looking around at what they had accomplished in those few months.

She sighed, bending over the fireplace. She never felt easy with this man; he was odd, some ways, and now she was doubly uncomfortable and uneasy because she was heavily pregnant and trying to pretend that neither of them noticed it.

"We've all worked real hard. I guess we'll be all right now, for the winter. Our garden stuff done good and the Indians are maybe goin' to leave us alone, though I still can't hardly feel easy about them. My papa was killed in that trouble at the mission, an' Emmett's folks was both killed some years back, over west. I know these here are different people, but I still can't git myself to trust any of 'em . . . . I'm glad you come by. Emmett's been wonderin' about you, wantin' to show you things, an' I wanted to ask you about somethin'."

She twisted her apron, looking at the dirt floor. "Cricket says that when they was kids, you taught her an' her brother to read some. We got, between us, three younguns that's ready for some learnin' an' I aim, one way or another, for mine to have some. None of us has got learnin' enough ourselves to teach them anything about books. It's been all right, before this, for just common folks not to know much about them things, but some day, I hope to the Lord, this country'll be more settled up, an' I won't have my kids looked down on. We was wonderin'—would you teach 'em?"

"I'm not a teacher, Amanda."

"Emmett says you taught your boy an' whatever Indian children wanted teachin'. Down at Camas Post, they told him that that school in St. Louis says your boy's one of the brightest pupils they ever had, so it must have been good teachin' you give him. I don't want to have to send my young'uns off somewheres to school. You can't never tell, at them places, what they'll learn that they oughtn' to, an', the older they git, the more we'll need 'em to help with the place. At least if we'd gone like the Church told us, there'd be some kind of school for 'em to go to. The Church always manages to have a school. I don't much like bein' here if you want to know the honest truth, an' not havin' any school is just one of the reasons. I know there's just about nothin' would make Emmett leave now. Once he's turned over some ground it's nearly all he can think about, but I look ahead to what things might be like for the kids. If they don't have some education, they won't be any better off than them Indian kids. I got nothin' against these Indian kids here, you know. Me an' Cricket has always got along good, nearly like sisters, but I don't aim for other white people to say my kids is no better than Indians.

"Couldn' you come here sometimes an' git 'em started learnin' things? We could pay you in milk an' butter an' such. If you want it that way, we could have the Indian children to come up here that wanted to learn somethin'. It would be nearly like a reg'lar school."

"I appreciate that you think I could do it, but I don't think I'll be able to. I'll have to be away a part of the winter and—"

"Well," she said shortly, "if you won't, we'll just have to see about gittin' somebody in from outside. Emmett said I wasn' to say that to you, but I think you ought to know just how strong I feel about this. That's why I was glad you come while the others was gone."

Blake excused himself and went out and chopped some wood, thinking wearily that it had really begun now. Wherever people came, most of them couldn't wait for neighbors, a church, a school.

When Emmett came, he asked if Blake thought some of the Medicine Rock People would want to join them in a wolf hunt. "Can't have the country full of varmints," he said complacently, "with us tryin' to raise stock."

Blake went up to his little valley, feeling desolate and empty. He sat a long time on his doorstep, watching the clouds around Never Summer. Some people never have the chance, not even one day, he told himself, to know a country like this. I've had it for more than seventeen years. But he could find little in the way of consolation for the future in that.

Looking up again from his drawing now, Alec said, "Eagle Feather says Hawk's Shadow still talks about burning them out on the North Fork. I guess he won't ever really do anything though . . . . Eagle Feather says Beaver Tooth's talking about building himself a house . . . . It's different around the village with Owl Woman dead, isn't it? She was almost the only really old person left . . . . Don't you think we could drive some stock down to the Platte and see what's going on?"

"Not with what I've been hearing about the Blackfeet."

"We could make up a good big party and be all right. Con would go. I guess his father would want to send some cattle and horses. Eagle Feather is different since he married. A lot of things seem different now, or maybe it's mostly me. Anyway, I don't think I'll ever marry. Women make more changes than anything else does.

"I was looking at what horses I could find of ours on the way up. They look good. I especially like the looks of Persephone's colt, don't you?"

"We need to sell some more," Blake said. "I think the army will be pulling out soon, going back east."

"Will they close down Fort Pierce and the others?"

"Probably, if there really is a war."

"What will the tribes do then?"

"Nothing, I hope. Maybe things will be more normal for them for a while. There's a new district agent in charge at Walla Walla. He may be a better man than some have been."

"What's happened to Ellis Williams?"

"Connall says he went over to the coast for a while .... You remember Mote Stanley?"

"That little old man who talked so much? Yes."

"He died last winter. He'd been living by himself, way up on the Kootenai, and no one found him until he'd been dead for months."

Alec looked at him soberly. "That could happen to you."

Blake was startled and he tried not to smile. "I think I've got a while yet. Mote must have been nearly eighty."

"But, still, maybe you ought to get married. Sometimes I've wondered why you didn't .... Oh, I nearly forgot to tell you. Mr. MacPheirson's got a new wife, a Flathead girl about my age, and Elizabeth's going back to school-teaching. I guess there'll be some more breed kids on the Camas."

Alec chose the horses they would sell. He had always had a marvelous eye and an innate intuition about horses. Chiefly through his selections, theirs had become the best breeding stock in the area. In mid-summer, they took herds of horses and cattle down to the new-sprung towns of Denver and Auraria.

Connall was with them and he couldn't hide his excitement over the wildly bustling, thrown-together villages, whose noisy exuberance only appalled Blake. Since he was there, Connall invested in some land.

"Just for the good of the country," he said blithely. "If I don't make a profit from it, somebody else will."

Autumn was well advanced by the time they returned to the Medicine Rock. After a few days, Alec went, with Eagle Feather, White Wolf, and others down to the post for supplies and Blake was deeply grateful to be alone in his valley. He was tired with a weariness that was more than physical and that he could not be rid of.

He went up, almost doggedly, to work on his castle, but could find no pleasure or respite. Looking up at the mountain, he felt little more than coldness and hostility in its grand indifferentness. It would be good, he thought, to go hunting with Hawk's Shadow—eagle hunting, maybe—if things were as they used to be, but he and Hawk's Shadow had been more like acquaintances than brothers the past few years. Everything was different . . . .

Maybe Alec's concept of his age was more nearly correct than Blake's own. He had had his forty-first birthday in the spring. Forty-one was not old, and yet age, like everything else, was relative. So many things had happened to him and around him in those years. Today, he wished that nothing more would come, ever—that he could only rest and be quiet.

It was a warm, poignant day, utterly still, soft, heavy with a nostalgia for the summer that was gone, but warmly remembered. The work he was trying to do somehow irritated more than it pleased him and finally, disappointed, he gathered his tools and went back to the cabin.

It was dim inside and almost cold. He got into bed and pulled the skins and blankets close around him, beginning to feel drowsy almost at once. Sleep would be good.

He had almost stopped searching for answers, for Alec and for himself. The boy was, basically, what he had made him. There were things about the boy that Blake did not approve of, a few things he did not even like, but they were done. Alec was his own person now, brilliant, restless, dissatisfied, not often happy, but he was, for all practical purposes, an adult. He would not be asking now for many answers.

Blake slept heavily. His sleep lasted well into the following day.

"I thank you for coming, Mr. Westfall," said Tom Allen warmly.

He was a small, balding man with a weathered face and quick gray eyes.

"I've been wanting to meet you since I came out here and, as I told Connall MacPheirson, I simply didn't have the time to go way up the Camas to look for you. Of course, the trip's as long one way as another and I want you to know how much I appreciate your time and trouble."

It was almost the first white man's house Blake had

been in since his days in New Orleans. This was nothing like those houses, but, compared to the cabins of the country, it seemed to him filled with luxuries. The house had four or five rooms, built of fine sawn boards, with smooth pine floors. Tom Allen had a small, neat, gray-haired wife who had brought them coffee and brandy with a warm, quiet smile.

Before coming to the agency, Blake had walked around the community in the moist, sunlit air of late spring. There had been a fort here for a long time, but most of the town itself was new, smelling of fresh-cut lumber from the sawmill. It was a busy place, but it had a feeling of stability, unlike the mining camp towns they had visited last summer, shack villages which were filled almost entirely with the frenetic activity of people in a hurry to get somewhere else. The agency buildings were roomy and sturdy. Walla Walla had been made district headquarters for all the tribes of the interior northwest.

"I wanted to tell you myself what seems to be going on," said Tom Allen candidly, "because I hope you can help me. Probably, you've heard most of it."

"I've heard about the miners," Blake said grimly.

Allen nodded. "And you know that they began to pull most of the military troops out of this area as soon as word came about the firing on Fort Sumter.

"We used to live in Santa Fe. I was a government representative there while all that country still belonged to Mexico. Then we were sent to the Indian Territory. I didn't know a thing about Indians to begin with, but I'm truly interested, which I think you know many agents are not, and I've tried to learn. I've never felt in such a precarious position as I seem to be in here this year.

"You're right, it has to do with the miners. Last year, some men came to see me, led by a Mr. Robinson. He said that about ten years ago, he was with a small party, trapping over on the Clearwater, and that they found quite a lot of color—gold—in a little creek there. No one thought much about it at the time somehow. Anyone interested in prospecting couldn't stop in those days till he got to California. This Robinson himself went on to California and did rather well, but he kept that spot on the Clearwater in mind. He seems a restless man, wanting to be always on the move, the kind this western country seems to attract. He went back up there last year, with a small party, just to see if it really was gold he'd found."

He paused, waiting, and Blake said wearily, "And it was."

Allen nodded. "Quite a lot for placer mining, they said. They told me the details, but I don't know much about that kind of thing. At any rate, the details don't matter. What happened was, as you probably know, some Nez Perce braves came along and told them they'd have to leave. That's part of their reservation. So Robinson came here. He asked me to open up the reservation for mining and I told him I couldn't do that. I learned later that some of his party went right back up there. Mr. Robinson didn't. He told me he'd try to work it out through channels, and I suppose you could say he's done that. He certainly contacted our territorial government. I think every single member has been in touch with me, one way or another, over the winter. Robinson and several others have written letters to all the federal agencies that could possibly be even remotely concerned and of course our territorial representatives have been in Washington, talking up gold in Oregon . . . . Have a cigar?"

"No, thank you."

The man's silence bothered Allen a little, made him self-conscious. Westfall did not even look at him steadily, but kept glancing out the window as if, perhaps, he were not really giving him much attention.

"Do you know a man named Ellis Williams?"

"I know him."

"Well, he seems to be another channel that this group is working through. He's spent months now, talking with various bands and tribes, telling them they'd be rich if they sell the mineral rights. I've heard that while he's been doing all this traveling and talking, he's also found time for some prospecting of his own."

"That sounds likely," Blake said.

"He, and others, have convinced some of the chiefs, and the Indians themselves have come to me about it."

"You can't do it," Blake said with a sudden violence that surprised the other man. "It would be the end of the country as it is, of—of everything. Have you seen country

335

that's been mined? the way the people are? They come in and destroy the country and each other and leave it. It's . . . ."

"I know," Allen said sadly. "That's the way I felt when Robinson came here. It's how I feel now and how, I suppose, I'll always feel. Unfortunately, the country and the people who feel as you and I do are not nearly all that's involved in this. The big strikes are over in California. There's friction down around Denver about which government is going to get that country in the end. The Union government would dearly love to have some big discoveries made in this area. They have suddenly become very much aware of the existence of the interior northwest. Their land ties to this area are likely to be much more stable than to California. They can send miners out here with very little risk of having them attacked by Confederates, and there's far less danger that gold shipments from here would be hijacked."

"But the people—the Indians . . . ."

"Exactly. I hope you'll believe I'm deeply concerned for them, but I've had my instructions now and there's not much I can do. I've sent out word that there will be a council in the fall. At that time, I'm to offer new treaties, wherein a good portion of most of the reservations will be ceded back to the government. In return, there's to be a small per acre payment, received mostly in the form of goods and services over a period of time, food and clothing, farming equipment, workers to teach farming, some new schools and so on."

"My God!" Blake groaned, putting his hands to his face in an automatic, defensive, helpless gesture. "Six years ago, Mr. Allen, I was at the Clearwater Council. I saw treaties and heard solemn oaths that this land would be henceforth and forever . . . . That was six years ago, *Six years!* It's a thing that's not to be borne."

The older man's eyes were sad, commiserating. "I know. And yet what can we do?"

"If that's why you sent for me, I'm afraid I can't—"

"No, no. I couldn't ask anybody for an answer like that and expect to get one. It was a rhetorical question, just a—a cry, I suppose." He relit his cigar and went on with reluctance.

"There's certainly nothing more *I* can think of to do. I am, after all, an employee. There have even been times when I have liked my job, enjoyed it. We have planned, my wife and I, that I would stay on in it until retirement—it won't be long now—but in these past months I've thought very often of resigning. If I did that, though, they'd only assign someone here who would be willing to rush things through.

"I hope you understand that I truly have no choice. When I said I felt the situation was precarious, though, I didn't mean just for myself. The army is going now and I think you must know that those prospectors are *going* in. Several parties are already roaming the country and more go every day. The military couldn't, wouldn't stop them, even if there were enough troops here to try to do so. Yet, if they go without an agreement or understanding with the Indians, there's going to be very bad trouble. We've already had a taste of that. Bannocks killed two prospectors down south last month."

"And if there's an agreement," Blake said angrily, "do you think that means an end of trouble? You must know that not all the people, not nearly all of them, are going to agree to what you've been telling me."

"But several of the chiefs have come here, asking that something like this be done. The Indians listen to their chiefs and see that their word is made good."

"White men are teaching them that that doesn't have to be so. It's one of the contributions manifest destiny has made to the people here."

"I'm sorry, Mr. Westfall. I can see now that this is very difficult for you. But if the Indians don't agree, then soldiers are to be sent back here, many of them. The government is busy with a war. If they sent an expedition here, its mission would be very harsh, very severe. The Indians would have to allow the miners in, ultimately, and I'm afraid if there was any retaliation, they would simply be wiped out. So you see, I'm in something of a bind. I've sent out word about the council and I've sent word back to Washington that this is being done. I see no other way.

"I asked you to come here because I know you know the country, that you've been out here a long time and are sympathetic with the Indians' problems. I must send out a

337

party to survey what will be offered as new reservation boundaries and I'm asking you to act as head surveyor and mapmaker. You are the only man I know of for the job of whom I can feel really certain. I want the tribes given the best lands, what they want and have been using most. I want them to have their hunting and fishing, roots and berries, as much of what's home to them as can be managed. I feel sure you are a man who wouldn't put a boundary through such areas simply because you thought there might be gold there."

Blake said nothing for a long while. When he spoke, his voice sounded hoarse.

"What about the Medicine Rock?"

"I have no instructions about any specific band."

Mr. Allen got up and went to a large map that hung on the wall.

"They're very isolated from the rest of their tribe, aren't they? So far as I know, no one is wanting to make any claims in that country yet."

Blake cleared his throat and said heavily, "I can't do what you've asked."

"Will you tell me why?" Allen looked disappointed, distraught.

"I've told you, I've seen how long these treaties last. They're none of them worth the paper they're written on. I won't take any part in the drawing up of another one. I do know one band, Mr. Allen, my—the Medicine Rock People. I know how much the country and the freedom to use it means to them. I can't . . ."

"I understand," the older man said quietly after a little silence. "I truly appreciate your coming here and listening to me and I hope you will believe that the only reason I asked you to come here was that I thought it was the best thing I could do for the Indians."

Blake would not go to the council. Beaver Tooth wanted him as an interpreter and he refused.

"Your son White Wolf is good with English. You don't need me, Beaver Tooth. You don't need anybody. Your mind is already made up."

Hawk's Shadow would not go. The People were divided in their feelings and there were tension and anger in the village. Alec rode along with Beaver Tooth's contingent as an observer.

"I won't do or say anything," he assured Blake blandly. "I just want to see what goes on."

And he came back with a full and thorough report.

"Beaver Tooth and a lot of the chiefs feel that it really means nothing now, signing the papers, except that the government has to give the goods they've promised. They say, among themselves, that the People can just go on, doing as they please, and that the whites are fools to set such value on marks on pieces of paper. Beaver Tooth says that since the Medicine Rock People were not even asked to give up any land rights, why shouldn't he sign and have a share in such goods?"

Blake went on with the drawing he was making of two otters he had watched, playing, that morning. It was all such an old story now.

Gradually, the anger and dissension in the village subsided. Beaver Tooth and a few others had built themselves log cabins and were building up small herds of cattle, along with their horses, to sell to hopeful prospectors farther west and north who were willing to pay almost any price if they had the money.

Hawk's Shadow spent more and more time alone in the mountains. He was away, off and on, almost all of the following summer. As he came back down the valley, returning from a solitary venture that had occupied most of August, he came upon Blake, with Alec and Eagle Feather, breaking horses.

"Ho, Green Eyes!" he cried, coming up behind Blake and seizing his shoulders. "If I were a Blackfoot, I would have had your scalp."

Blake was incredibly relieved to find him smiling. "You're almost as much a stranger as if you were a Blackfoot."

"Well, I have been resting my thoughts in the mountains. Probably I will go back again soon. Maybe you will come with me, down to that stinking country again. I have a wish to go there."

"That would be a good thing," Blake said softly, his eyes burning.

"Look at those two boys of ours," said Hawk's Shadow proudly.

They were riding, Alec on a bay, Eagle Feather on a pinto, both horses newly broken. From behind, they could have been twins, slender, wiry, with heavy, straight black hair.

"Eagle Feather is more than three years older," Hawk's Shadow said thoughtfully, "but Alec has caught up with him. The difference is no longer a thing that shows. Is my grandson born yet?"

"Several days ago. Only it's a girl."

"Well, a girl is all right too, this once." He sighed. "We grow old, Blake. I have been thinking of that, up in the mountains. I have thought that when a man begins to know that he is old, it is no longer a time for bitterness. The young should be angry sometimes. It is good for them. They should spend some of their energies on fighting battles, but the older ones should take a little time for resting."

"Hawk's Shadow, we're not *that* old. I mean—"

"I am," he said firmly, complacently. "I've decided it in these past days. I could not be a chief. If the People had chosen me, I would not have been good for them because I think too much of myself. Beaver Tooth also does this, but he makes many believe he is thinking of them. One thing I have decided is that there is no need for me to fight Beaver Tooth quite so much anymore. Being in the mountains is what makes me happy. Some day, Beaver Tooth may sign one paper too many and make it so the People are no longer supposed to live here. Why should I not just—be here while I am here? Also, some day I may die."

"Would you leave?"

"No. I would not live anywhere else. Eagle Feather would not, and a few of the others. That may be the time when I, and others, will die. So . . . . for now, I will just live and see what happens. Is this not what you have told me you try to do with all your life?

"Still, when I am here, I will not make things *easy* for Beaver Tooth. That might frighten him. Since I am an old man with a granddaughter now, perhaps I may forget myself and call our chief He Who Pisses Into The Wind

340

in council, or some such things. You know how the mind of an old man can wander back to his youth."

They went to the Yellowstone, the Stinking Country, and it was an idyllic trip, as if both of them had, briefly, gone back to their youth. They went alone, Blake and Hawk's Shadow, having agreed not even to invite their sons, who would have spoiled the dreamlike quality of the journey merely by their presence.

On the day they returned, the village was astir with something new. Cricket had been there for a visit and had tried to explain some new white law Emmett and Eli had heard about.

"It says," reported Smiling Fox, "that whites can take up land with just papers that say they own it. Cricket says her husband says many settlers will come here now."

"What does it mean to us?" Beaver Tooth asked Blake. "Whites are always talking with papers. Can we get these papers?"

Snowbird, Eagle Feather's pretty young wife, came shyly with a crumpled newspaper sheet in one hand and her tiny daughter on her other arm.

"Cricket brought this," she said, offering the paper to Blake. "They thought you would want to see it."

Blake said, "You have a pretty little girl there. Where are her father and Alec?"

She looked down, smiling, pleased at the compliment. "They have gone to fish in Camas River."

The men waited restlessly, uneasily, while he read. Looking up finally, he said, "The Congress of the United States has passed what they call the Homestead Act. This law says that settlers can come onto government land and choose one hundred and sixty acres of it for themselves, for each family. They then file a claim, they—sign papers that show just which land they want and agree that they will do certain things, cut trees, build a cabin, plant crops, within a certain amount of time, and then the land becomes theirs."

Hawk's Shadow said unexpectedly, "This does not seem unreasonable, for whites. How much land is that, for each man?"

Blake showed them, in the meadow, about what the boundaries of a quarter section would be.

"Very little," said Hawk's Shadow derisively. "Not even one deer would stay to live on so little land."

"It's enough for farming," Blake said heavily. "If it's good land, it's all a man and his sons can care for."

"But what is so special about *this* law?" asked Storm Coming Out Of The East.

"Before this, most whites, in the east, have had to pay for the land they got, with money. This law gives them free government land and most of it is in the west. I suppose they've passed the law at just this time because the federal government wants to get as many northern sympathizers into this country as they can, in case the war goes badly for them. Then——"

"Don't begin talking about those whites' war," Hawk's Shadow said shortly. "What does this thing mean for *us*? What is government land?"

"Almost any land," Blake said wearily, "that isn't already owned by individual whites."

"Ours?" asked Smiling Fox, his eyes widening.

"We have this valley by treaty," Beaver Tooth said scornfully. "I have seen its boundaries on maps and written on papers. What does it say, Blake? Something like 'the watershed of Medicine Rock Creek forever'?"

"But you have said"—Hawk's Shadow looked at Blake accusingly—"that this is not a part of the main reservation, though I know that the main reservation itself is not safe if they want it. If this is not part of the reservation, then does that mean——"

"Who can sign such papers?" asked Storm Coming Out Of The East.

"Male citizens, over twenty-one."

"Does this mean that one must be white?"

"Yes."

"Who would want to sign them?" demanded Hawk's Shadow. "Signing means nothing, and who would want to bother with just that little bit of land?"

"It would be better than none," Blake said slowly.

"Mr. Allen, the chief agent," Beaver Tooth said worriedly, "is a good man. He will not let the valley be taken. Even Blake says he is a good man."

Hawk's Shadow made a sound of derision. *"We* are all good men, far better than any white, and yet——"

342

"Wait, Hawk's Shadow," Blake said absently, trying to think. "Listen . . . . Miners are going to be here sooner than settlers. Very few settlers can come this far before next year. The miners will come first. They'll be following every stream as the trappers did, only it'll be worse because there'll be more of them. I don't know what rights homesteaders are supposed to have about minerals." He looked back at the paper. "It doesn't say anything about that here, but it might be that—"

"I think I will go and sleep for a while," said Hawk's Shadow, yawning. "This paper-signing has never been my concern."

"No, wait. The paper says claims for this area can be filed in Crownsville. That's where the army post was, and St. Denis, on Clark's Fork. They opened a land office there last month. There are a lot of new people passing through there and none of us would be known to any of them. If we were to go there and file, every man here—"

"You said it has to be whites," said Smiling Fox.

"Yes, but . . . . if you cut your hair and wore cloth shirts and trousers and no ornaments—"

"You are crazy!" cried Hawk's Shadow incredulously. "I have always known you were a crazy man. Do you think I would do that? I am of the Medicine Rock. Why would I hide it? Do you think I would try to pretend to be *white,* just to sign a paper?"

Alec and Eagle Feather came riding up the valley then, shouting about the many fish they had caught. They sobered and fell silent at sight of the men's faces. Blake showed them the newspaper. Eagle Feather frowned deeply. He could read well enough and English came easily to him, but he did not see the ramifications.

"They'd have to have new names," Blake finished his explanation. "White names."

"Do you really think we could get away with it?" asked Alec, delighted, smiling the smile of Red Sky's children. "What a fantastic thing to do to the government!"

"I don't know," Blake said soberly, "but it might be worth trying. When settlers start coming, this valley is going to look very good to them."

"Even if we could pull if off," Alec said thoughtfully, "they'd find out about it some time."

343

"Yes, but going through the courts takes a long time. If we had those legal documents, somebody would have to go to court to have them nullified."

"Would they? For Indians?"

"We could damn well try to make them. I know Emmett would help us, probably Eli, and Connall."

"We met Emmett down the valley. He and Eli are going to file tomorrow. He said Connall has filed—that's where Emmett got the word from—and that Connall has rounded up every breed he can find with a proper last name to file for him, on more land."

Hawk's Shadow said, "You are wasting talk, both of you."

Beaver Tooth said, "That's true. This does not concern the People. Our affairs are not dealt with in an office in Crownsville or in the newspapers."

Eagle Feather said slowly, "I think we should call a council."

Several others had gathered around them now, and they wanted a council, simply to find out what was going on and all that had been said.

Blake went into the lodge and smoked with them in the ritual way. Beaver Tooth made the usual sort of speech, about the People and himself, a long speech, and then he asked Blake to tell them about the newspaper and what he had suggested.

When he had done that, Blake left the lodge as unobtrusively as he could. By now, they were well accustomed to having him do that and he felt his presence might make things more difficult. Eagle Feather and Alec were there and could answer their questions. He took a long walk, looking at the Valley, lying quiet as the autumn day ended.

It was twilight when he came back and they still sat in the council lodge. He entered quietly and sat down by the door.

"And," Alec was finishing, "it would be a good trick to play on the government. This country has belonged to the tribes since before there was time. The government thinks it has a right to take it with papers. Why can't we give it back some of its own papers and laws? It would be a funny thing."

344

Blake, his eyes adjusting to the dimness, found that Beaver Tooth and most of the older men were no longer there. Hawk's Shadow was, and Storm Coming Out Of The East and Smiling Fox, but the rest, about a dozen of them, were all young men.

"But it is such a little bit of land," Hawk's Shadow said softly, almost automatically.

His son had just spoken, his first real speech in council, impassioned and impressive. It had seemed to Hawk's Shadow that he saw Red Sky, perhaps even Winter Thunder there before him. He could not go against Eagle Feather.

"Having this paper for one hundred and sixty acres," explained Alec, "doesn't mean that anyone can make you stay on just that bit of land. You can still go where you like, do mostly as you have done. It means only that if you or anyone else wants to put a fence around his hundred and sixty acres, to say that others must stay off, he can do that. It is one man's land to do with as he likes."

"And you say," mused Storm Coming Out Of The East, "that we must take white names."

"Just for this signing," answered Eagle Feather. "They would not be our names afterward, unless we wanted them."

One of the young men laughed, "I think it would be a good thing to do this. Then Beaver Tooth could not always be saying in council that he is the only man of the Medicine Rock who has put a name on white men's papers."

"What names would we have?" asked another.

"Just—maybe names from books," said Eagle Feather, "like George Washington and—"

Alec shook his head. "Well-known white names like that would make them suspicious at the land office. I can make up ordinary names for you."

"If I am to have a white name, even for a day," Hawk's Shadow said firmly, "it should not be an ordinary one. Is Westfall ordinary? Blake once tried to tell me about it, but he really seemed to know nothing and it made no sense, having two names that mean nothing.

Still, I think I could have Westfall as one of my names, for one day."

And then they all wanted to be called Westfall and Storm Coming Out Of The East said, "Call a woman to bring us some food, and tell her to bring fire too. We need light for you must teach us to write these white names. If I am going to do this, I don't want just to make a mark."

One of the boys went out and they became aware of Blake's presence.

"You can't all be named Westfall," Alec was telling them patiently. "It's a family name that relatives would have, brothers, cousins, men of one family. The people at the land office would think it strange to have so many men of that name wanting to file and they would look at us closely. We don't need that."

"My name and my father's will be Westfall," said Eagle Feather proudly, "because we are of your family. Mine will be—Patrick Westfall." And he said to the others, "Patrick is a good white name. In a book of Blake my uncle's I read of a man named Patrick Henry. Once, when things were very bad for him and for his country, this Patrick Henry said, 'Give me liberty'—that is freedom—'or give me death.' Is this not a worthy thing to say?"

"Perhaps he was not all white," Hawk's Shadow said softly. "Perhaps his heart was of the People."

BOOK THREE

XVI

"CONNALL!" BLAKE CRIED, coming down out of the woods. "I'll be damned!"

"Where were you?" Connall demanded irritably. "A man comes all the way up here, he ought to be able to expect a decent welcome."

"I was just—up in the woods. There's a spring up there and .... There's not anything wrong is there?"

"Damn right there's something wrong. Alec said you wouldn't come down to the Fourth of July celebration and I've come to fetch you. This is a nice little place up here but it's hard enough to get to. Come on. Get ready." He was changing his saddle from the horse he had been riding to the fresh one he had led. "I've got to get back to tending my store tent. I've left Sally and the girls with it, but that's a rough place, your Harmony City, and they can't count on any help from Con. He and Alec and all the other boys are out racing and such. A man came in just as I was leaving and said Alec's cleaning up. That boy's a riding fool, Blake. I never saw anything like him. Come on, lad! I don't want to miss anything. This is a little like the old fur company rendezvous. Tomorrow, there'll be speeches and a great community picnic and all that."

"Connall, I don't like speeches and all that, and I can't stand Harmony City. God, what a name they chose—"

"Aye, well, don't be so picky. What does the name matter? How long since you've been to any white doings? This is the day before Independence Day, plus we have to celebrate the establishment of Idaho Territory, separate from Oregon."

"But none of it really matters—"

"Blake, Alec tells me you haven't been any farther out of here than Medicine Rock Canyon since late last summer. That's not good. You can't just go on hiding up here."

He sighed and turned resignedly to the cabin for a clean shirt.

"And don't suffer about it all the while," Connall called peremptorily. "You wouldn't have any rum in there, I suppose."

"No. Sorry."

Impulsively, Blake pulled a wooden box from under the bed and took out the first shirt Shy Fawn had made for him after she became his wife. It was badly creased and wrinkled, but it would smooth out all right with wearing.

Their horses went carefully down the steep trail into the main valley with Connall talking all the while.

"Most of the People from the Valley are down there, I guess. I saw Beaver Tooth and some others. Do you think Hawk's Shadow went?"

"He's gone off in the hills somewhere."

"Emmett and Eli and their families are down there. About how far is it, would you say?"

"Maybe fifteen miles from the mouth of the canyon. How did you get in?"

"Oh, I know one of the guards. Can't think of his name. His father is Storm Coming Out Of Somewhere. I wanted you to tell me about this homesteading business. Is it working out?"

"It's been nearly two years now since we filed the claims. Nobody's said anything so far. Of course we're trying to keep the word from getting around. Nobody knows about it, I hope, but you and the people here in the Valley."

"And you've had no trouble from miners with things going on so close?"

"Some have wanted to come in, but the guards have been able to manage them. So far, they're all going on up the Camas."

"Yes, and they've brought a good little bit of dust down from the gulches up there. I don't know, Blake. It seems a dangerous business, going on with trying to keep people out of here. Those Indians are liable to start shooting and any of those gold-hungry fools would surely shoot back. They're crazy, the lot of them. Some of them must be decent, ordinary people, but when they go after gold they're like buffalo stampeding. If they were to get the notion they're being kept out of here because the Indians have got gold . . . . It's like sitting on a powder keg, isn't it?"

They passed through the cool, shadowed canyon and out into the dry, dusty heat of the Camas Valley. Harmony City had sprung up, literally overnight, at the place where the old Indian trail crossed the river, going toward the eastern range and the pass leading toward the buffalo country, and west over the range to the watershed of the Salmon. There had been a minor rush of prospectors to the Salmon last fall and this had been the shortest way for them to go from the valley of the Beaverhead and other places east of the Divide where they could not find suitable claims. Some had stopped off to prospect the Camas. Others, seeing tracks leading up the river, had decided someone must know something and followed them, then others. A few suppliers and speculators pitched tents in a huddled hodge-podge in a cottonwood grove by the river. They laid out a town in lots that were changing hands furiously . . . . Harmony City! The very thought of it made Blake feel sick.

"I don't suppose," Connall said, trying to sound casual, "that you've heard about the news at our house? that Sally and I have a boy, born in April?"

"Yes, Alec told me, Connall, but . . . ." He made a physical effort to drag himself out of depression and be pleasant. "I'm sorry I hadn't mentioned it. Congratulations."

"He's a good strong boy named Philip. Sally fancied that. She likes Bible names, from going to school at St. Denis. I used to think that if I ever had another boy, I'd name him Hudson's Bay MacPheirson, for the old days, but when it came down to it, I couldn't quite do that to the boy . . . . Did you know Con's home again?"

351

"Alec told me."

"He's been reading law with a man in Montreal but he says he's back to stay now, thinks he can go on with studying on his own. Thank God I was able to keep him from running off and enlisting. He sees now how foolish it would have been, but if I hadn't gone to St. Louis to get him in the spring of '61 he'd have done it for sure. It didn't even matter much to the idiot boy which side he fought on. He just thought it would be fun to go to war .... Anyway, he's thinking of going into politics. It seems to me he's young to start that, but I suppose not, with this being a brand new territory. Nearly everybody that's not scratching for gold seems to be in politics, one way or another. It might be helpful, one day, to have a United States senator or some such in the family.

"Did you know, then, that my girl Brigid and her husband have come back to Camas Post to live? She's the one married to the Coeur d'Alene, you know, the boy that's Sally's cousin. They're going to run the farm and all for me. They've got three fine boys."

"What are you going to do? Retire?"

"Ah, no, not yet. I'm moving my business to Harmony City, except for a little trading that Brigid and High Cloud can carry on at the old place. That's where the money's to be made now, that scabby little town. Those that have money let it run like water. No need for a thinking man to go panning and digging in the ground. We've brought up several wagonloads of goods and have more coming from the east. We've got a big tent for a store, though not big enough, and a covered wagon to sleep in. I'll build soon, if it looks like the place has any staying power. I rode up and bought some lots as soon as they had them laid out, just in case, and before they went up.

"My girls Nancy and Katy are home. Nancy has two more years of schooling but Katy's finished now. They're pretty girls, Blake, the prettiest I've got. It scares me a little with all these wild men around. And now I've got to start all over again, with Philip and maybe a whole new bunch, though I wouldn't be complaining. Which reminds me, have you got any horses to sell?"

352

"I don't quite see the connection, but no, we're down to breeding stock. Everybody in the Valley is."

Connall sighed. "So am I, and I could sell a hundred this very week. Con tells me Alec's getting rich. Where's he been getting all those horses?"

"He and Eagle Feather have been west and north, buying them from the tribes."

"The way you did when you were his age, but prices have gone up some, haven't they?"

"So he says."

"Oh, come, Blake, try to make the best of it. There's none of it we can change."

After a time Connall said, "You've heard about the new trail—they're calling it the Bozeman Trail—that comes north from the Overland, through the Yellowstone country to just about straight across the Divide from us? Did you know they're building two or three forts along it? I guess the Crows and Blackfeet are giving them a hell of a time. And there's a good-sized garrison at Fort Boise now, a lot of mining around there. I've heard two or three more whites were killed by Bannocks down south. And did you hear about the camels?"

"Camels?"

Connall laughed. "Aye, somebody decided they were exactly what's needed for packing in this country so they tried them on that military road you helped lay out. Con and the girls were in Crownsville on their way home when the camels came through there. The people with the train intended stopping there for the night but the people held a town council or whatever it is they have there and asked them to go on their way. They claim the smell of the beasts was something fierce, drove strong men away from the bar at the Crown Saloon, they said, so they had to move the train on west. They were supposed to go all the way to Walla Walla but I've not heard what became of them. That would be something to see, wouldn't it? I'd like to see your friend Major Shadran riding a camel."

"He's probably a general now," Blake said, smiling at the thought of the nervous, fussy little man on camelback. Then he said soberly, "Have you thought that it's a little strange how they can suddenly afford to supply all those soldiers at Fort Boise and along the Bozeman Trail? When they pulled them out three years ago, they said this country wasn't worth protecting with a war to fight in the South."

"I don't understand you. Are you complaining that the army was gone from us for a while? It's to protect the gold and all that they've come back."

"*That's* what I'm complaining about, but never mind it now."

Connall was thoughtfully silent for a time and then he said, "Three white families have settled and started ranching between here and Clark's Fork."

He wanted earnestly to cheer Blake up, to have him share his own enthusiasm, but all he knew to talk of was news of the country and that seemed to serve only to make his friend angry and more morose. He tried again.

"I keep hearing and reading that the Confederacy has fallen on hard times. Perhaps the war won't last much longer."

"It's a shame it won't last long enough for them all to kill each other off."

"Ah, now, lad, don't be like that. I know you don't mean a thing like that."

"Connall, don't you know that when it's over people are going to come pouring out here—"

"You've been saying almost this very thing since the first time I set eyes on you."

"And it's been happening. It's going to be worse."

"But, lad, accept it, *live* with it. What else can you do?"

"Oh, hell, I don't know . . . . Nothing . . . . I'm sorry."

Connall was excited about the new developments, irritated by Blake's portentous gloom. He *would* go on talking.

"All the politicians that the government's sent out here to run the territory are Republicans, you know, but a lot of the people coming in are Democrats. There are going to be some hot times in politics. Most people get God-almighty loyal to a party or the Union or Confederacy or whatever when they get this far from home. Did you know there are a few people in Harmony City that have Negroes? They claim they're not slaves, but I expect they

354

were till a short while back. There was a fight last night, started between a Union man and a Confederate. Damn near the whole town was into it before it fizzled out. It all reminds me of stories my dad used to tell about before the war of 1812. Trappers and such that hadn't given a hoot about what country they came from, all of a sudden when they heard there might be a war, got to be very good Americans or Britishers. It's a funny thing, when you think about it, what this country'll bring out in a man."

"Like the way most mountain men felt about the Mormons," Blake agreed dryly. "It was all right, they said, for a trapper to have an Indian woman and several kids in every other village, but Mormon polygamy was a sin in the sight of God."

"Goddam it!" Connall cried, completely exasperated. "I'll not stand any more of your gloom. Look at the sky. You've clouded it up with all your sulking."

"I think I'll go back, Connall," he said miserably. "I truly am sorry, but I can't seem to—"

"You won't go back," Connall said with angry finality. "I made the trip to fetch you and I'll not have it go for naught. Listen to me now, and if you get angry I'll hit you. They've got a lot of things in Harmony City. It's a dirty collection of hovels, but it's something different for people like you and me and you ought to take an interest. It would take your mind off what's tearing at you. Knowing you, you may never come back again, so why can't you make the most of it? There's lots of whiskey down there to drink, different kinds of people to see, and a whorehouse. They've already built a shack for that. It's not even in a tent like everything else. Best business in town, always busy. I want you to go there. It would do wonders for you. It's expensive. Everything is, but it would be well worth your while for improving your disposition. You're going to lose what sanity you've got, always up there brooding in the woods over things you can't do anything about . . . . Will you do it?"

"I wasn't—"

"Oh, don't answer. Just think about it. That reminds me. I haven't got to the bottom of the matter, so to speak, but I understand Ellis Williams has at least a part interest

355

in this place we're speaking of. That man does get around. I also hear he's thinking of going into politics."

They came in sight of the small, disorderly scatter of shacks, tents, and wagons, swarming with people. The noise came out to them, mingling with the sound of thunder rumbling up the valley to the south.

God told Noah to take his wife and his sons and their wives and go into the ark. The thought moved tensely through Blake's mind. God, what *is* wrong with me? he wondered with a twisted, half-hysterical smile.

A brief rain fell on Harmony City. People sought shelter but the noise did not die down. Connall's store tent was jammed and each group carried on its own independent conversation in stentorian tones. Blake took a glass of rum from Connall, who became busy with customers. The rain stopped and the place was temporarily empty.

"Our wagon's right out in back there," Connall said. "We'll have supper soon. I told Con and Alec to be back here about this time. Tomorrow there's to be a community cooking down by the river."

The boys came in then, flushed and laughing, their shoulders and hair wet from the rain. Con had invited two more guests, young men he had met in the course of the day, and Eagle Feather was with Alec.

Connall's wife Sally, her young son strapped on her back, brought in supper, assisted by the two girls, Katy and Nancy. They put the food on the store's rough board counter and did not eat with the men.

"Alec's won a half dozen horses and some gold dust," Con said happily. "The rest of us did all right betting on him, for a while, till everybody found out his horses couldn't lose."

"This is sure *some* place," breathed one of the young strangers.

His name was Jed Vogel and it irritated Blake, the way he and his companion kept staring at everything, their mouths all but dropping open. They ogled the women and were markedly uneasy about having Eagle Feather eating with them.

"Wide open night an' day," agreed the other, who was

called Sam. "Have any of you heard much about these places called Alder Gulch and Last Chance Gulch, over east a ways? I've been hearing they're makin' some real good strikes over there. The trouble with this country—one trouble—is that it's so goddam hard to get anywhere. Any place you want to go, it's over some god-awful bunch of mountains. Anyway, when this celebration gets over with, I think I'll just go look around over that way."

"I thought you two had some pretty good prospects around here," said Con.

"Well, maybe not bad," said Sam restlessly, "but I've about decided to sell out my part of this claim. A fellow can almost always do better."

Jed said, glancing around uneasily and speaking conspiratorially to Con, "I was wondering if, after supper, we could maybe go down to that Indian camp down the river and look around some. I'd like to see what it's like. I've heard some all-fired things about Indian girls—men, too, for that matter—that they'll let you use their wives for a night for a drink of whiskey, things like that."

Sam laughed. "That'd be one hell of a lot cheaper than the prices bein' charged in town."

Jed glanced from Eagle Feather to Con. "Would he—uh—show us around, do you think?"

"It's not my camp," Eagle Feather said quietly, coldly.

The strangers looked startled and more uneasy. They had not supposed he understood any English.

Some customers came in and Connall went jovially to wait on them.

"I thought," Sam said a little defiantly, "that all Indians were supposed to live on reservations." He turned directly to Eagle Feather, raising his voice and enunciating carefully. "Now I don't mean no offense or nothin'." And to the others, "I just never thought that there'd be so many of them, roamin' around all over the place like they are. A couple of bucks even come around our claim the other day and—"

"This is Indian country," Con said lightly. "They've been around a long time."

"Well, yeah, I heard that an' I guess it's all right, only it can make a feller uneasy, times like at the races today, with 'em all around . . . ."

357

"Have you done something that gives you a guilty conscience?" Alec asked blandly.

"No, I ain't. It just—makes me uneasy, an' that's no offense to you." He had raised his voice again with this last phrase, for Eagle Feather's benefit.

"You'll get used to it," Con said and was going to change the subject, but Alec pointed out, "You're still surrounded. We're mostly Indians here."

They looked from face to face, their eyes pausing on the deerskin shirt Blake wore, its decoration more ornate than that of Eagle Feather's.

"Con and I are breeds," Alec went on smoothly. "Those girls you've been staring at, bringing you food, are breeds. You could be tackled and scalped before you could make a sound."

Con threw him an irritated glance and said a little stiffly, "If everybody's finished, let's go take a walk through the saloon."

Jed and Sam moved eagerly, but Jed said, "Well—oh —I don't think we can do that right now. We got some things to see to and . . . ."

They went out hurriedly.

"Bastards!" Con muttered. "But, Alec, why do you always have to stir people up?"

"Because people like that make me madder than hell," Alec said casually. "Eagle Feather and I are going down to the camp to play the hand game. Do you want to come with us? We're going to clean out those Flatheads and then I'm going home. I couldn't stay here tomorrow and listen to their speeches about how goddam great this country is."

"You're boy's a troublemaker," Connall said to Blake with some consternation, when they had gone. "Anybody knows you could guess he's yours."

Blake went out into the asymmetrical area that was being called Main Street, to a tent with a crudely lettered sign that said "Nugget Saloon." He edged his way to the makeshift bar and bought a whiskey. The price staggered him and it was not good whiskey. As he was about to leave, his whole body tense from the noise and crowding, a hand fell heavily on his shoulder. He looked round, a

358

little dazedly, at a fat, round-faced, balding man in dapper city clothes.

"I don't believe you know me, Blake. I'd know *you* anywhere. You haven't changed much. It's been a long time."

"It has, Ellis," he said slowly, with no smile to answer Williams'.

They had not seen each other for almost nine years, since the Clearwater Council. Ellis had put on weight and aged incredibly since then. Blake could hardly think what it was that made him recognize him.

"Let me buy you a drink. I been hoping I'd run into you one day."

"No, thanks. I just had one."

"Well, have another."

"No."

Ellis held on to his bright smile. "You still live up there in the Medicine Rock?"

"Yes."

"Still nurse-maidin' those Indians. What I wanted to see you about was that business in St. Louis when you went to my boss and tried to get me fired as Indian agent. I wanted to thank you. That was about the best turn anybody ever did me. I got in with some mining interests after that and I'm doing just fine. I thought I'd let you know, in case you'd been worrying about hard feelings or—"

"I wasn't worrying, Ellis."

"Well, it's good to see you. A lot of things have happened in this country, haven't they, since you first come to Camas as a greenhorn. I hope things are going good for you. Anybody found any gold in the Medicine Rock yet?"

"No."

"How's your kid? I heard he went to school in St. Louis."

"I heard you ran into him there."

"Listen, Blake, I hope you won't take this wrong. I mean it to be friendly. You ought to have a talk with that boy or do something about him. He's got notions and talk 'way beyond what's good for him. I've heard stories about

359

him all around the country this summer. It don't do for a breed kid to have a smart mouth. It riles people."

"Does it?"

"I've always said, the best thing a white man can do when he finds out he's planted something in a squaw, is get away and leave it alone, let it be an Indian. The kid's a hell of a lot better off that way. It don't do nothing but make trouble for everybody if you try to educate 'em, get 'em thinking they're white. Somebody's going to take that kid of yours down a few notches."

Blake turned and made his way out of the tent, not looking back. He heard Williams' loud, falsely hearty voice, hailing someone else.

"Say there, Harvey! Got something to talk to you about . . . ."

Twilight was deep along the river now. The mountains stood back somberly, more felt than seen, the last of the light just touching the peaks and the sky above them. Blake remembered achingly, in the midst of the noise, that it had been at just about this point along the river where Shy Fawn had said to him, "I wouldn't want to go back to the post with you in the autumn because your son should be born in the village."

A group of men waited, a little awkwardly, outside the shack whose sign said "Harmony Palace." As Blake walked distractedly past, one was saying, "They got one Chinese girl, but the other two are white."

Another said, "Well, it looks to me like they better get some more in here. How'd you like to have money invested in *this* business?"

Blake had walked through all there was of Harmony City and he turned back toward Connall's store tent, hurrying. His horse was tied there. He was going home.

"Blake! Blake Westfall!"

A rider was picking his way through the crowd, waving.

"Wyeth!" Blake's heart lifted with something very near to pain.

"Sonofagun! Connall said you were here somewhere, but I didn't expect I'd find you in all this mob and racket. Are you doing anything special? Get your horse and come on out where we're camped, so we don't have to holler."

Wyeth Hamilton was no longer in an army uniform. He wore tattered, stained butternuts. His left hand had been amputated; the wrist was heavily bandaged.

"A cannon blew up," he explained as they rode out of town. "I was too close to it. That's been a year ago now, but I still keep hurting my arm. I just—forget the hand's not there and keep trying to use it."

"How long have you been back?" Blake asked, now that they could lower their voices.

"Just got in here last night. We've been over at Alder Gulch—what they're calling Virginia City now—since last spring. These towns are a mess, aren't they? Corie said she wasn't camping any closer to this one than a mile. I don't know, it just seems like people are not meant to live on top of one another the way they have to in these camps, shows up the worst in them, seems like. Some that I've met are just nice, ordinary folks when they can forget about gold for a minute and have a chance for a little privacy.

"How have you been, Blake? How's Alec? God, I'm glad to be back. It's kind of odd how much like home this country feels to me."

They had a tent with a small fire burning in front of it, in a little, scattered grove by the river. Wyeth proudly introduced his sister Corie and his boys, George and Courtney. The boys were about ten and twelve years old and they looked at Blake with shy, wide eyes.

"Daddy's told us and told us about you," said George, the younger one, in a drawl so heavy that it made Blake smile a little incredulously, "but we were gettin' to think we'd never get here."

"You two better get on to sleep now," Wyeth said. "You've had a long day, with the races and all. Blake'll be here in the morning. You will stay the night, won't you, Blake? We don't have very much, but half of it's yours."

They sat down near the fire and Corie gave them coffee.

"We've got some fried dried-apple pies left from supper if you'd care for one," she offered.

"It's been hell, getting here," Wyeth said contentedly

361

when his pipe was filled and drawing well. "There's a lot to tell you."

He stretched out, leaning on an elbow.

"When I was being reassigned, I went home for a while. Mary Lou had died of a fever just before that, so I resigned from the army. I'd have had to do that anyway, with the secession and all. Corie and her husband Ben Sullivan were taking care of the boys, but I wanted to be with them, especially with all the trouble that was coming on. Then, of course, I had to join the Confederate army and, after a while, I lost my hand. Real early in the war, Corie's husband was killed. I was sent home for a while, for my arm to heal. I could have gone back, done paper-work or something, but Corie and I got to talking. I'd told her some about this country and we decided we ought to try to do what was the best thing for the boys. The middle of a civil war ain't a place for young-uns. I still don't feel just right though, sometimes, thinking about it. In some ways, we were like rats leaving a sinking ship."

"It wasn't like that when we left," Corie pointed out in her calm, soft, definite voice. "We left just after Gettysburg and some other battles that had gone real well for the South, when it looked like there might be a good chance."

She had just come out of the tent and sat down close to the fire, to sew a patch on a pair of trousers.

"I guess I'm still influenced too much by our brother Byron and the way people like him felt about what we were doing," Wyeth said. "They thought we were some kind of criminals. But, anyhow, we left. We started out with a good lot of stuff. Corie, being smart and stingy like she is, had hung onto some of what Ben left instead of turning it over to the Confederacy, so we had all kinds of household goods, a little money, and a nice little herd of breeding stock. Lord! that stock has been a lot of trouble. You got any idea how hard it is to hold onto cattle in this country these days? Some people'll sell their souls for a piece of beef, or steal it any way they can."

"But we've still got 'em," said Corie with a small, grim smile.

She was a rather tall, slender, strong-looking woman of about thirty, with dark blond hair and warm, direct brown eyes. The skin of her face was sun- and wind-burned, sprinkled with freckles. It was not a beautiful face, perhaps not even pretty, but there was a candor about it, a kind of wholesome, perceptive strength that made it very pleasant, reassuring somehow. Her casual participation in the conversation was a new and vaguely disconcerting thing for Blake. He had been accustomed, most of his life, to women who kept quiet when men were talking. He rather liked Corie's being there, though it made him feel a little shy.

She went on dryly, "We've had to leave most everything else, one place and another, but we've still got the cows."

Wyeth said mildly, "Don't get ahead of the story. We had a hell of a time crossing Arkansas and Kansas. There was skirmishing back and forth and, a lot of the time, we didn't even know which side of the lines we were on. We had some niggers with us, a few people that wanted to get away from the plantation and come west. We've still got Jonas. He's out now, watching the cows and horses. I don't know what we'd have done without him. His girl Delcie and her husband came, too, but they stayed over in Virginia City. They're cooking in a restaurant there, doing real well most of the time, when people don't make them trouble. They just got worn out and said they wouldn't cross any more mountains.

"Anyway, we had some trouble over them when we'd get into Union territory—were they slaves? and was I a deserter?—that from both sides, till they'd see about my hand. That's a funny thing, what a difference it makes to people. I can still shoot and do most of the other things I always have done, but seeing the hand gone changes people right quick. I guess there may have been a few times I took advantage of that, but it helped get us through.

"We wintered close to Fort Laramie with the family of a sergeant I'd had. He was killed in Tennessee. He'd told me about this place he had, that his family was trying to hold onto while he was gone. They were having a struggle, his wife and his old daddy, and I hope we helped them some, over the winter. As soon as the weather would let us, we came on."

"*Before* the weather would let us," said Corie. "Wyeth

just couldn't stand himself till he got into the mountains. I was beginning to think he was purely touched in the head about mountains."

"But she caught the fever too," Wyeth said placidly, "once we got here."

"Maybe, a little," she admitted. "But I'd have been willing to stop a good way back somewhere. It's a nice country, but not to travel through. Seems to me one place is about like another."

"Well, we had to come on to some place where I could make a little money," Wyeth said. "I did some pretty profitable panning out of a little creek over there near Virginia City and then sold my claim. I never figured to be a miner, but I had to get some cash for land somehow, and since we were that close, I wanted to come on back to the Camas country. Connall tells me I can take up a homestead and buy more land. I'll need a good bit for grazing in this dry country.

"I was sure glad to find Connall. When we heard they were making a town here, I expected he'd be around somewhere, cashing in. He tells me you've got homesteaders in the Medicine Rock."

"Just two families," Blake said. He wanted to tell Wyeth about the claims the People had filed, but did not quite trust Corie not to spread the word. He told him how Emmett and Eli had come to take up their land.

"You don't suppose they'd let me come in up there, do you, the Indians? I've been itching for that valley since the first time I saw it."

"I don't think they would, Wyeth. They'll remember you as a soldier and they've been pushed pretty far lately."

He sighed. "Well, I guess I'll just have to make do with second best. I thought maybe the upper Camas, though I've heard now that there are a lot of prospectors up there. Anyhow, we've got to find a place and get settled in before winter. Maybe you'd do some riding with me tomorrow? help look around? Or are you here for the political speeches and all?" He grinned.

"I was on my way home when you found me."

Wyeth nodded. "Connall thought you might have already left." He sighed. "It bothers me to think of farmers in the Medicine Rock. I knew, all the time I was looking over this country, years ago, that God never meant it for anything but grazing land."

"Why," Blake said with sudden heat, "does everybody who comes out here know just what God meant for the country, and it's always a different thing?"

Corie smiled. "Wyeth's just talkin'. He wouldn't recognize God if He was to walk right up here to this fire."

Wyeth grinned. "He wouldn't be here, not this close to Harmony City."

"Well, that would show good sense," she said shortly.

"Corie's a little tired of mining camps," Wyeth explained.

"Corie's a little tired," she amended. "We're all about worn out with living in tents and wagons. I'm going to bed now. That pot's nearly full of coffee and you can tell Jonas his supper's in the Dutch oven."

Wyeth knocked out his pipe and began refilling it as she went into the tent.

"I've got to go and relieve Jonas pretty soon. We have to keep a guard on the stock all the time. The boys can watch them all right, day times, but they're a little young for the responsibility at night . . . . I was at some of the races today and saw Alec there, but I didn't get a chance to speak to him. I guess there were, maybe, a couple of hundred people there, but it seemed like ten thousand. I'm getting so I get real fidgety in a crowd like that. Anyway, Alec was busy. He had some fine horses and what a handler that boy is. He's sure grown up to be a handsome kid and Connall's boy's a big bruiser, isn't he? Seeing them makes me feel like I've been away fifteen years instead of seven . . . . I sure am glad to be back. It's like a dream coming true, a real long dream that's been, some of it, nightmare.

"When I left Fort Pierce to go back east, I thought that was the end of it. When I got home and found Mary Lou had died, well, I still feel bad that my first thought was: Now I can take the boys and go back to the mountains. They wanted to come, of course, and back home won't be a place for younguns to grow up when this business is finally over, all the bitterness and misery. We've had some of it out here. No matter how busy people are, trying to live and scrabble for money, it seems like they'll remember, once in a while, that they used to be Union or Confederate or Democrat or something. But that'll pass off, I think, a lot quicker here than it will back home. This mining business'll die down too. The ones that stay after that will be, mostly, ones that want to stay, and they'll be so busy trying to just make their lives, they'll come to see that most of that other stuff doesn't really matter much.

"Anyhow, we could never have got here, the boys and I, if it hadn't been for Corie. You talk about somebody with spunk! Corie and I have always been close, but I never knew till this trip just how much grit she's got. It's a woman that a thing like we've done is hardest on, having to make do and keep traveling and still make a home.

"Corie's not had it easy. Ben died three years back and not long before that she lost the only baby they had. She's been a better mother to my boys than their own was, though I probably shouldn't say that, and they've needed her. They've needed a lot of homelike things that I couldn't have done for them, and there have been a lot of things going on that have puzzled them, things where they've needed a woman's point of view.

"And she's done man's work, too, driving wagons and helping with the stock." He laughed. "I guess she like to have scared the livers out of a couple of men over at Virginia City that thought they'd steal them a calf. She shot all around them while they were gettin' away. They told about it in town, thanking God she couldn't hit anything, and the funny part is she could have killed them with one shot apiece. She's a better shot than I am now."

He drew on his pipe and said dryly, "Course Corie's never been one to suffer in silence. If she's got a complaint—and she's had several—she lets us hear about it, none of this delicate martyr stuff, but she's the one that's kept this outfit going . . . .

"Now, I want you to tell me about things around here, something besides prospecting and hell-raising. You've not said a dozen words."

Blake told him then about the new treaties and about the use to which he and the People had put the Homestead Act.

Wyeth smiled broadly, then sobered. "Somebody is going to be mighty surprised one day, and awfully displeased. Do you think there's a chance of making the claims stick?"

"I don't know. It seemed worth trying."

"Damn right. It ought to get interesting when the authorities realize what's been done, real interesting . . . . I saw Ellis Williams at the races today. He told me you went to St. Louis to tattle on him when our letters didn't do any good."

"I'm glad he thinks that, but I was there with Alec and Con when they were starting school."

"He seems to have his fingers into just about everything, Ellis does. He's been in every mining camp in the territory, I guess. Never seems to do any real work, but always has plenty of money. I don't feel easy about people like that. But tell me something about Alec. What kind of boy has he grown up to be?"

"That's hard to say," Blake said slowly. "He's often cynical, and distant . . . ."

"Like you."

"No," he said, a little surprised, then thoughtfully, "Well, maybe I am, a little, but I do keep hoping . . . ."

"And you think Alec doesn't?"

"I just don't know." It was the first time he had spoken of his worries about the boy and the words came hard. "It's as if he's resigned to whatever's going to be, but determined to make as much trouble as he can about it anyway, more just for the hell of it than anything else. I don't think he has any idea of what he wants."

"Well, when I see him, I'll tell him if it's ever a job he wants, he can have one from me, any time. God, I'd give anything to have him in charge of my place, when I get one, and if I could afford him."

Blake felt unreasonably irritated and tried to keep it from sounding in his voice. "He ought to do something more than that kind of thing. It would be a waste for him. He's—he could do anything, if he wanted to."

Wyeth said quietly, "I've always thought that very thing about you. We talked some, back yonder in the past, about how people ought to be let alone. I remember once you said something like 'God save us from having

367

other people look out for our best interests.' Maybe you oughtn't to worry about him so much. I can see you have been worrying. I expect that, being your kid, he's going to go his own way, no matter what. Maybe he does know what he wants. I heard people talking today about his horse business. Maybe he's got what he wants right now and you're just too close to the whole thing to see it clear.

"Well"—Wyeth stood up a little stiffly and stretched—"You can put your bedroll just about anywhere. It's a damned big, wonderful country. I'll go out and relieve Jonas. Will you do some riding with me tomorrow?"

"All right. I'll go with you now, for a while. I'm not sleepy."

XVII

BLAKE SPENT ALMOST TWO WEEKS helping Wyeth.
When he came back to the cabin, Alec was there, lying in
the shade of one of the pines, reading.

"You were away so long chipmunks moved into the
cabin," the boy greeted him lazily.

"When did you come back?"

"Three days ago. I shot a couple of deer the day before
yesterday. There's some meat inside. Snowbird is smoking
the rest of it for me. . . . Ophelia's had her colt. They're
just over there—no, they've gone into the woods, but it's
an ugly, brown scroungy little bastard. I can't think what
bred her unless it was that mangy stallion of Beaver
Tooth's. We need some fences up here."

Blake went into the cabin for food. A gun belt with a
pistol lay on the table, and beside it was a beautifully
done picture of Katy MacPheirson. He carried his food
out and sat on the doorstep.

"Did Mr. Hamilton find some land?" Alec asked,
glancing at him after a moment.

"Yes. That flat where the Darkwater comes into the
river. We got his cabin up."

"I'm glad he came back. He's the best white man I've
ever known. I thought you must have had something
ready because their camp was gone when I came back
through Harmony."

"The family moved up there as soon as Wyeth had
picked out the land. Where have you been?"

"I helped the MacPheirsons bring some more stuff up

369

from the post, and then I was looking for horses. I could only find a few that anybody was willing to sell. We've been thinking, Eagle Feather and I, of going down into the Crow country after some wild ones. People are crying for horses. I've heard that last winter around Virginia City they were paying people to pack things on their backs, as much as forty cents a pound."

He stretched, yawning. "Connall's started building his store. It'll be a nice place. They're starting a lot of building. I wonder if the boom will last as long as it takes to get things finished. I didn't get a chance to ask you what you think of Harmony City."

"I think you don't need to ask."

Alec smiled, nodding. "Still, it's kind of interesting."

"How?"

"Oh, just to watch people. They always seem to make such fools of themselves in that sort of situation, where everyone's living so sort of frantically. It almost seems as if you can see right into their souls sometimes, and even their souls are foolish . . . . It's so odd, the things that get so very important to people.

"For instance, when I came back through the other day, there had been a fight. A man was shot. These two men were drunk and the one who was shot had said that a Walker hound was a better hunting dog than a blue-tick, whatever that means." He laughed. "What a thing to *fight* about! I could understand a good hot argument but . . . ."

"What happened to the one who did the shooting?"

"Nothing. He had a couple more drinks and went back to his claim. They're going to get some law and order down there as soon as they have time for it. Ellis Williams may be persuaded to run for sheriff. Wouldn't he be just perfect?"

He looked back at his book, then remembered something more.

"Oh, some news came in from the east, garbled up as usual, but there's been a battle at a place east of Denver. Not a Civil War battle. Some Arapahoes, or maybe it was some Cheyennes—what the hell, those redskins are all alike—had a village there. They'd been told to stay there until somebody was ready for them to move to a reservation somewhere. They've been having a good deal of harassment down there, I guess, but these people's hearts seem to have been good, they were doing as they'd been told. A troop of militia came on them in the dark and pretty well wiped out the village."

Alec had sat up angrily, restlessly. "So now there's a new batch of white heroes. They were talking, in the saloon, about how if everybody around Harmony wasn't so busy, they ought to go out and kill off a few savages so they wouldn't start getting any big ideas around here. I told them where they could start, only I was wearing my pistol . . . . They're not people, those whites."

"Alec . . . . they *are* people. People like to talk . . . . Do you remember telling me, after that first year you'd been at school, how some of the boys were always talking about girls, and that you'd decided most of it wasn't true, but only talk, to make themselves look and feel more important? It's bad, but most of the things that are said in saloons are just that kind of talk . . . ."

"I won't listen to it."

"Neither would I, but I wish . . . ."

"What?"

"That you could just walk out of a thing like that. What good does it do, really, to say anything?"

"It does *me* good. I don't have any idea of getting anything through to *them*. I gave up on that when I was about ten years old."

"It won't do you much good to get yourself killed."

"I won't be killed," he said, lying back, relaxing. "I'll die of old age in seventy or eighty years. I only wish I could believe there was a chance that I could outlive all the idiots."

"Those seventy or eighty years might be more pleasant for you if you could just leave things alone sometimes."

"I can't just let things go, when I know what's happening."

He dismissed the matter, shading his eyes from the light as the branches above him shifted in a warm, indolent breeze.

"That eagle's got a hell of a nice life, flying around up there like that. I wonder what he thinks of things he sees

371

down here . . . . Did you know Eagle Feather and Snow-bird are having another baby? They can't seem to feel worthwhile until they've had a son."

Blake watched the bird for a time, then said hesitantly, "Alec, I saw the picture on the table, of Katy MacPheirson."

"It turned out well, didn't it?" Alec said absently, still following the eagle's flight. "She's interesting—to paint, I mean. There are a lot of contrasts."

"She's pretty and it's a very good picture."

"I never have been able to do portraits as well as you do. Somehow, when I try to do people, they come out looking unnatural, cold. But I got to thinking yesterday that it would be interesting to try it, with those new paints. Maybe I'll give it to Connall."

"He'd like that."

Alec looked at him then, levelly. "It's only a picture."

"Yes. What else would it be?"

"I've heard that parents do quite a lot of thinking of who their kids will marry."

"But it won't be Katy?"

"No, nor anybody, maybe. Someone like Katy certainly wouldn't be right."

"Why not?"

"Well, she's out of her element here. I guess she'd be out of it anywhere because maybe she doesn't even have an element. I don't think it was a good idea for Connall to send those girls away for all that schooling."

"And why is that?"

"Women don't need all that much formal education. They've learned things like piano playing and fancy embroidery and how to pour tea. What good's that ever going to be to them?"

"Maybe none, but there's nothing wrong with the learning. And that's not all they've learned."

"Women have no business with books or with trying to think."

"Alec, for God's sake!" he said in disgust. "Did you ever hear of a double standard?"

"Yes. I believe in it."

"What are women supposed to do with their minds?"

"Thinking too much only confuses them," he answered blandly.

"That's the biggest bunch of crap I ever . . . . women are people, after all."

"Still," Alec said with a small imperturbable smile, "this is what I think. They *are* people, but not all people are the same as all others . . . . If I ever marry, I think it will probably have to be someone like a Medicine Rock woman, only, I hope, not as talkative as most of them are getting to be." He looked back at the sky. "But I don't know if it will be a Medicine Rock woman. When I think of having kids, I can't decide if they'd be better off being white breeds or Indian breeds. What do you think?"

"I think you ought to try just letting fate take its course."

"I don't intend to live that way," the boy said calmly. "I don't know what fate is, any more than I know what God is. People make their own lives . . . . Anyway, when I think about it, I usually decide that I don't ever want any kids. There's too much responsibility, too much involvement . . . . But there's no need to bother about it. I'm not quite twenty yet. There's plenty of time and women are easy enough to come by, who don't have to be married."

They were silent for a time. Alec went back to his book. Finally, he said thoughtfully, "When I went deer hunting, I was up by the spring . . . . It's a beautiful castle. How long have you been working on it?"

Blake's eyes went to the mountain. "Nine years."

"God, Blake!" he breathed, awed. "How could I not have known? I must have been up that way a hundred times."

"I suppose the rock was covered with snow or something."

"It couldn't have been, every time. It bothers me that I could have overlooked a thing like that. It's a fantastic piece of work. When I saw it, I got the strangest feeling, as if I'd come on something that—spirits had done. When did you finish it?"

"I don't think it will ever be finished. I still work on it sometimes."

"But why a castle? I mean . . . . here . . . ?"

Blake told him about Alec Douglas and the picture they had looked at together, years ago.

Alec looked at him, frowning perplexedly. "I don't understand you. I guess I never thought much about understanding before I saw what you've done up there, but when I found it and started thinking, I— All the time it must have taken! If it were some place where people could see it, then . . . ."

"I guess that's part of it, Alec. It's mine, mine and—the rock's."

"The rock's?"

"Yes."

"Maybe you'd rather I hadn't seen it."

"No, I don't mind."

"But you never showed it to me, or talked about it."

"I suppose I would have, some time, if you hadn't found it. I always meant to, but then things would . . . ."

"It must have given you a lot of—satisfaction."

Blake was relieved. He said slowly, looking away, "It's been a kind of medicine dream."

Alec shook his head, frowning intently. "Sometimes I think . . . ."

"What?"

"That you find a wonderful lot of peace in—in things a lot of people don't know anything about. Some ways, you're more of a mystic than any of the Indians. I wish I could know how you do it. You're strange."

"I've been told that," Blake said, feeling suddenly very tired, "all my life."

"I didn't mean it negatively," Alec said quickly. "I guess I envy you for being able to—to find what you need."

"I don't often," he said wearily. "Sometimes, I think I know where I ought to look, but it doesn't always work out." He stood up. "Is there anything left of our garden or has it all dried up?"

It had been so terribly important to have Alec understand about the castle, without his having to try to explain. What he had wanted was to have the boy think, in effect, like another part of his own mind about it. He had never been able to tell him about it or show it to him, basically, because of fear that such understanding would not come automatically. That was completely unreasonable, he knew, but he was being swept now by a bitter loneliness and disappointment. We are all alone with the things that count most. "No one *knows* how anyone else feels." Perhaps, after all, Alec understood more than he thought, more than he truly wanted him to. If he truly wanted the understanding, why couldn't he talk about the things he wanted understood? Was it that he could never make or allow anyone to understand, except, perhaps, the mountain? And the mountain did not care.

Alec got to his feet, his face still quizzical. "The garden looks fine. There must have been a good bit of rain while we were away . . . . I guess I'd better cut some wood."

Blake sat by his fire, trying to write. He had written several times over the years, to the people at Cambridge. The old professor he had met there had died, but his successors were interested in what Blake could do for them —too interested, he sometimes thought. He had sent them a few things from time to time and almost every time he picked up his mail, there were letters asking for more, hungry for information and artifacts. Sometimes that made him feel hopeful. There were people who cared. At other times, he saw it as only a clinical, mechanical interest, and it irritated him. The letter he was trying to write was not going well. He couldn't keep his mind on it. Impatiently, he moved the candle, wondering if his eyes were getting weak. They had asked for information about the guardian spirit dance. What were the machinations of the Indian mind? What relation did their religion have to their daily lives? What kind of question was that? Everything, for the People, was bound up in everything else. There was, for them, a beautiful interrelation, a balance of everything in their world, so that everything made sense, had its place and reason—or things *had* been so until whites came into the country and began trying to destroy the meaningfulness of the world that the People had worked out for themselves. What business was it of New England professors coldly to analyze and speculate?

Angrily, he threw the just-begun letter into the fire. He thought he would write no more. Sending them artifacts was one thing. It couldn't hurt to have others see, perhaps some would even appreciate, such things, but he would write no more explanations. Let them make their anthropological deductions from some others, some people who were not his. He walked restlessly around the cabin, distracted, nervous. Finally, he took up some carving and sat down again.

He had planned to make some animals of the country for George Hamilton, Wyeth's boy, an elk, deer, bear, a bighorn sheep, whatever he had time for. It would be George's birthday soon.

Blake had been at Wyeth's several times over the winter. Once he had stayed several days, helping to build a barn. It was a good place to be, the most comfortable place he had ever been, among whites. Thinking of it now only increased his restlessness. It was so good there, talking with Wyeth and Corie, the friendly, easy comradeship they shared . . . .

And finally—there was no escape—he let himself think about his visitors of the afternoon.

He had been working outside through the April day. Gradually, the sky had grown heavily overcast and there had come an almost incredible warming to the air. He was afraid of heavy rains that would melt the winter's heavy accumulation of snow too quickly and send the streams rampaging. There could be a good side to that, though. Maybe the river would rise enough to take away Harmony City.

The horses, twitching their ears and nickering, had warned him that someone was coming up from the lower valley. It was two men with a pack mule. They were heavily bearded, their clothes caked with drying mud. Blake could see them consulting together uneasily at sight of him and of the buildings. There were picks and shovels, gold pans and snowshoes strapped on their mule.

"Howdy!" one called out tentatively as they approached where he stood watching by the corner of the cabin.

One was young, the other middle-aged. They might be father and son. They looked haggard, their eyes tired and feverish.

"Didn't know there was no whites up here," the older one said.

He laughed, still uneasy. They were quite near. "Never saw no green-eyed Indian."

"How do you come to be up here?"

"Why, we was lookin' at this stream down below. She started showin' a little color so we followed 'er on up. This is a nice place you got. Looks like you been here a while. What kind of luck you havin'?" He peered shrewdly, supposing he would not be told the truth.

"I'm not mining or panning," Blake said. "This is a homestead claim. When I asked how you got here, I meant how did you get into the main valley down there?"

"We come from the other side of that mountain yonder. We followed a little bitty stream that looked to show some promise. Got to the head of it an' come acrost a big high ridge an' down into the big valley, away up toward the head of 'er. It seems to me like it took months to cross over."

"Nice horses," the young one said. "How would you feel about grub-stakin' us to a couple of 'em? We ain't got no money—yet, an' I've climbed around these Godforsaken mountains about all I can stand."

"You've picked a bad time to travel," Blake said without warmth. "You're lucky you weren't caught in a slide, coming across that high shoulder of Never Summer this time of year."

" 'Bout time we got lucky," said the older one. "We been pokin' around this country for a year now, starvin' an' freezin'. They've found some pretty good claims on three or four streams comin' into the Camas an' we aim to get us some place new, an' good, staked out before the weather gets too good an' ever'body starts movin' around again. We seen them flecks in this stream down below, an' that there was a trail comin' up here . . . . well, we figgered this just might be the place."

"It's not," Blake said quietly. "This land is mine and the valley down below is Indian land. I'll have to ride down with you so that you can get out to the river without any trouble."

"We ain't lookin' for any trouble," said the young man and he stepped sideways suddenly, watching Blake carefully, and took a rifle from the mule's back.

"We don't mean you no harm," said the older one,

"but this here land's as much one man's as another for minin' claims. I got me a feelin' you've come on to somethin' real good up here. I can see how you'd want to keep it to yourself. I'd be the same way, but that ain't the way she works. There's room along this here little stream for a lot of placer claims, an' for diggin' all around."

"We was told about them Injuns in the valley," said the younger one. "Feller name of Williams told us to watch out for 'em, but he also said that ain't reservation land, he said—say, Pa, I know who this feller is. He's the daddy of that green-eyed breed they talk about down at Harmony. Ain't you?"

"Yes."

"What are you? some kind of crazy hermit?"

"A goddam squaw man," said the father with loathing. "I'd feel bad, hornin' in on a decent white man's business, but your kind ain't fit to have no consideration."

"Where's your squaw at?" asked the son, leering. "I could sure use me a woman right now, white or green."

Blake did not answer. He had begun to tremble with rage.

"I think what we'll do, son," said the older one judiciously, "is just stay here a while. It's fixin' to rain an' this just might be a right nice, dry spot. One way or another, I guess we'll be able to find us out some information."

The younger man gave the rifle to the older one and went cautiously to peer into the cabin.

"Nobody there but it's full of books an' stuff. He's got somethin' cookin' for supper."

"Show us where you been gettin' the gold," said the older man.

"An' show us where you got the squaw hid," said the other. "I've heard how friendly an' glad to please these squaws are. Folks say bein' fucked by a white man is the finest thing God ever let happen to 'em."

From the corner of his eye, Blake saw the horses become alert, twitching their ears toward the entrance to the valley.

"I've heard they'll do anything in the world to get it from a white man. Is that how it is for you? Heard they think it's a gift from heaven to get knocked up with

378

somebody's white bastard. I could start workin' on that right now."

"That's enough of that kind of talk, Silas," said the older man without conviction. "A white man lives with a squaw ain't no better'n a beast."

"I ain't gonna *live* with none," said Silas, laughing. "I'd just like to have one handy to screw when I felt like it, do some other work for me. Say, Pa, that's it! We can just set back an' watch, let him an' his squaw get the gold out for us."

The older man smiled. "You haven't thought, son, that if she's the one whelped that breed boy you was talkin' about, she won't be no young thing. Them redskin women ages fast, same as a cow does."

Blake saw Eagle Feather come up over the edge of the valley and stop, as he always did, to look things over. He had a rifle.

The young man, deflated, said, "Well, she could still dig an' pan." Then he brightened. "But here's what I bet you. I bet he's got him a young one hid away up here, maybe three or four of 'em. You know all that stuff we've heard about squaw men. Hell, two or three in a bed, all eager to please an' get planted with white men's seed wouldn' be half—"

The bullet smashed into the logs of the cabin, just past the older man's head.

"Put down the rifle," Eagle Feather called, his voice light and sharp in the heavy air.

"A goddam redskin!" muttered the older man. "Another one of your bastards I guess."

But he let the gun drop to the ground as Eagle Feather moved toward them. Blake picked it up. His movements were stiff and uncertain, as if he were exhausted or very cold.

"What has happened?" Eagle Feather asked him in the language of the People.

"These men are miners," Blake said heavily. "They came down across the valley from Never Summer. They want my gold."

"I came to tell you that I have a son," Eagle Feather said with quiet pride. "Hawk's Shadow my father is very

379

pleased and so am I. He seems a strong boy and my mother says Snowbird does well."

"I'm glad," Blake said dazedly.

"I saw that two whites had come up here. I could not think who they might be or how they had come into the Valley." He changed deliberately to English and said casually, "Shall I kill them? Or we could kill one and have a scalp dance with the other. After the scalp dance, of course, we would kill him also. It has been a long while since the People have had a good time like that."

"Listen," said the older man quickly to Blake, "if you've got a speck of white feelin' left in you, you won't let this—"

"I can take them down to the village and let the women decide," said Eagle Feather solemnly. "Remember how good our women are with torture? They will be filled with pleasure to see the blood running on these sickly white skins."

Silas said shakily, "Listen, mister, them things I was sayin' to you, I was just joshin'. You know how it is. I didn' mean—"

In the language of the Medicine Rock, Blake said, "Will you take them down and see they get out through the canyon?"

"Yes, but I will see they are well frightened as they go. Have they hurt you, my uncle?"

"No."

"You look ill."

"Just get them out, Eagle Feather. Please . . . ."

"What have they done to you?"

"Nothing. Just get them out of the valley."

"Shall I come back then and—"

"Not today. I . . . ."

"What has happened?" he asked in consternation.

Blake turned and went into the cabin, stumbling a little, nausea rising in him.

As he sat thinking of it by his fire in the evening, he had to force his hands to be steady on the carving. Why had it upset him so terribly? It had only been talk . . . . Yet if Eagle Feather had not come up, he, Blake would be dead now. He had not been so angry in a long, long while. He would have gone for them and they would have killed him. He had begun, standing there under the heavy sky, to feel as he had felt when he and the others had ridden after the Blackfeet all those years ago. And he had believed himself finished with those kinds of feelings, so violent, so far beyond his control.

His knife slipped and he had cut a great gash in what was to have been the leg of the elk he was carving. A little blood from his hand stained the wood. He threw it into the fire, feeling an abject despair far beyond that merited by the small accident.

Without knowing he had moved, he found himself standing in the doorway, looking out into the sad, slowly falling rain and blackness. A light wind made heavy slow sighings in the pines. One of the horses down by the lake nickered, and Blake's already tense body stiffened further. A little jerkily, he moved to take down his rifle.

Could it be that the two miners had had time to reach Harmony City? to stir up a crowd, to . . . ? If any more of them came, he would kill them, as many as appeared over edge of his valley.

He tried to calm himself. If they had come up forcibly through Medicine Rock Canyon, he would have heard shooting. Certainly, there had not been time for anyone to come in by any other way. But maybe it was new ones who had come across the ridges . . . . He told himself angrily that he was growing more than a little insane. Probably the horse had simply felt like nickering or, very possibly, he was imagining things. But then someone called out. It was Alec's voice.

Alec was not alone. He led a pack horse and there was another rider with him.

"Katy's with me," he said as they dismounted in the darkness. "Katy MacPheirson. We got married this morning. Take her inside, will you, while I see to the horses."

Blake stood there dumbfounded, but Alec led the animals away, saying no more, so he had to do something.

"Come in, Katy," he said awkwardly, trying not to sound too dazed.

Her face was pale and drawn and she was trying hard not to cry. She had been wrapped up well against the weather, but it had been a long ride and the rain and cold had penetrated. She moved automatically to the fire and stood there shivering, looking miserably down at the hearthstones. After what seemed to them both a very long silence, Blake said stiffly, "Have you—had anything to eat?"

"I'm not hungry, Mr. Westfall. Thank you." The words were almost inaudible.

"You ought to take off your wet coat and things . . . ."

She looked up at him briefly, her great dark eyes full of misery.

"If you want to go out and talk to Alec about it," she said softly, "It's all right. Please don't feel you have to stay here and be polite. I can see how you'd wonder . . . ." She caught her trembling lip between her teeth. "I'll be just fine."

Alec had taken the packs from the horse and laid them under the overhang of the barn roof. He was throwing out a little hay for the tired animals.

"I wish we had some oats," he complained irritably as Blake came in.

"What happened, Alec?"

"I heard you had some trouble up here today."

"That's not what I'm talking about."

"Eagle Feather is guarding down at the canyon tonight. He told me about those men being up here. I suppose you've heard he's got his boy."

"Yes."

"Well, I'm going to have one—or something—in the fall."

Blake was silent and the boy said, "Goddam it to hell! Can't you say something?"

"I'm sorry that you're so unhappy about it, since it seems to have happened. You'll have to give me a little time to get used to the idea."

"You may get used to it sooner than I do."

"Do you want to sit down out here and talk about it?"

"No, but I suppose there's not much choice."

He took a bottle from his pocket, drank, and offered it to Blake.

"No."

"What did she tell you?"

"Nothing."

382

"Damn her!" he said between his teeth.

"She looks miserable, Alec. If things are this way, there's just nothing to be done. Can't you both just try—"

"Blake, for Chrissake, don't lecture me! Con's mad, Connall's mad, and there was that goddam preacher they've got now down at Harmony. I didn't do any more than she did, but I had to hear, all last night, about wronging an innocent girl."

"How long have you known?"

"I stopped at their place last night and she told me the news. It happened back in the winter. There were only a couple of times, and the first was in the fall."

"Did they know? Connall and the others? before you did?"

"No. At least she didn't do that . . . . I wanted her to get rid of it. There are women who know about doing that kind of thing, but when I said that, she started crying. Con came into the room and asked what was the matter. I told him Katy and I were talking about getting married. I didn't know anything else to say. And then Connall heard about it and he said we couldn't. He said he didn't have anything against me but that we were too young. He said he'd planned for Katy to go back to Montreal and stay with her sister for a year. We could think about it, he said, and if we still felt the same after a year . . . . That made me madder than hell because she'd told me he was trying to get her interested in Dick Vaughn—you know, that dude that's been buying up a lot of good-looking claims. Connall looks after his own interests first and he'd give anything to have a connection with that family. Also, I got the idea he thinks I'm not good enough for any daughter of his—later on, he told me that plainly—so finally I said that by the time Katy spent a year in Montreal and came back here, the baby would be almost old enough to walk. After that, all hell broke loose. There were times I thought Con would kill me and Connall yelled most of the night.

"In the morning they got that preacher and he started in about had we thought it out carefully because marriage wasn't a thing to be entered into lightly. We were all so tired we couldn't see straight. Katy had been crying most of the night. Finally, I asked him if he'd just get on with it because there wasn't much time. I told him there wasn't any more thinking to do and that if he was going to be so goddam slow and solemn about it, it would be nice if he learned proper grammar."

"I wish you hadn't done that, for Katy's sake."

"Hell, the whole thing's all over town by now anyway. Nothing's secret—or sacred—in that goddam place . . . . Blake, I'm trying to be civil to her. I just have to—tell somebody how it is."

They were silent for a time. Rain dripped dismally. Alec drank again from the small bottle and dropped it, empty.

"Is it all right if—we stay up here for a while? I haven't had a chance to think or . . . ."

"Of course it's all right."

"When he decided we'd have to get married, Connall said we had to stay down there, that he'd find some work for me to do, like it would be a goddam sacrifice on his part. Katy couldn't live up here, isolated like this, he said. She wasn't used to it. She'd been brought up like a white girl."

The hurt was clear in his voice, but then his tone changed back to anger.

"I told him she could damn well *get* used to it. What does he think? that because she's only a quarter Indian, he can pretend she's none at all? Is that what made him so mad? . . . Maybe it wasn't just that he wanted Dick Vaughn. Maybe he can't stand the thought of having any more Indian in his family . . . . But he's got a fullblood for a wife, again." Alec's bewilderment was painful.

"Probably you all said a lot of things you didn't mean or that didn't make much sense, angry as you were. When he's had time to calm down, I'll go and talk to Connall . . . . Alec, you're still angry, and hurt. A big, unexpected thing has happened but . . . . don't take it out on the girl. You must care about her if you—"

"She's a good, sweet girl," Alec said shortly. "And pretty. I like sleeping with her. I wanted to do that since the first time I saw her again last summer, after she'd been away all that time and grown up. I'm not saying this is any more of her doing than mine. I just never thought about a thing like this happening to me and that's so stupid—just plain stupid. It's such a shock, Blake. It's going to make a difference in everything . . . . I—don't know what to do."

Blake stood up, trying to sound and feel brisk and cheerful. "Well, for now, I'll get a couple of blankets and sleep out here in the hay. In the morning, I'll go away somewhere for a few days."

"I wish you wouldn't," Alec said, sounding frightened. "Would you consider staying here so *I* can go away?"

"That wouldn't solve anything, Alec. It'll be better if you're by yourselves for a while."

Alec picked up the packs, trying hard for a smile.

"She must have a ton of stuff in here. Well, now that we've got a woman up here finally, at least we won't have to do woman's work."

"He hates me!" Katy sobbed.

It was late September now. They had been married five months.

"Oh, God, Mr. Westfall! I love him so much I can't *bear* it and he—hates me!"

Blake had just come back from the Medicine Rock village. He had met Alec, coming down from the cabin, and Alec had said he was going to see if Eagle Feather was ready to go looking for wild horses. Blake had been away from the cabin a good deal all through the summer. Much of the time he had spent at Wyeth's. Alec had been away almost as much. When he was home, he was always curt and critical of the girl, when he spoke to her at all, and his temper flared often. Katy tried, with a concentration that was painful to see, to do exactly what she hoped would please him, but what Alec seemed most to want from her was to be able to forget her existence.

Blake thought she must have been crying since the boy had left and that would have been nearly an hour. It wouldn't be good for her, surely. He put a gentle, awkward hand on her shoulder.

"Please don't cry like that, Katy. Don't you think you ought to lie down and rest? I'll help you."

She sat by the table, crumpled, her head resting on it. Her beautiful, dark red, shining hair spread around her. She had glanced up when he came in, a shadow of aching hope flickering across her face, hope that Alec might have come back. Then her head had dropped again, in abject despair, and she had cried out to him. Blake had not heard her utter a word of complaint through the months, and this was not a complaint. It was a cry, wrung from a misery that Katy was being forced to believe was hopeless.

"I've tried so hard," she said brokenly. "I just don't know what to do. I was really stupid about a lot of things when I came here, things I should have known, but I've tried to learn. It can't be helped that we had a few more things to do with at home or that I spent all that time living in Montreal. I *can* do the things he wants me to, only I just have to learn about some of the things he calls woman's work. I just never knew about things like chopping wood and making camas flour. I don't mean to be a snob about it or anything like that."

"Has Alec said you're a snob?"

"No, but I think he *thinks* I am. That's the trouble, Mr. Westfall, He *says* so little. I don't really know anything he's thinking. I never have, for sure . . . . Today when he said he was going after wild horses and might be gone a month or more, I said that maybe the baby would be born by the time he gets back and he just— We haven't mentioned the baby for weeks—*I* haven't. Alec never mentions it. But when I said that, he said that I was trying to keep him hanging around for something that's entirely women's business and that he has no interest in. He said I wasn't going to hold it over him for the rest of his life, that he didn't want to be here when it's born, and I was just trying to make him stay. Oh, I do wish he *wanted* to be here, but I know he doesn't, and it's better for us all if he isn't, but I wasn't trying to *make* him stay. I only said what I did to—to *say* something. We talk so little."

She had raised her face. Her large dark eyes were swollen, her cheeks were drained of their normal, vivid coloring, pale and blotchy.

"Come and rest," Blake said gently, lifting her to her feet.

Obediently, she lay down and he covered her with a blanket. She was shivering and he felt frightened. Tears

386

kept flowing, but the rending hysteria had passed. She said wanly, "Would you—sit by me? Just for a minute?"

He drew up a chair and sat beside the bed. Her small, pretty hand, growing roughened now, was gripped tensely into a fist, lying on the buffalo robe. He covered it with his own hand. Her fingers relaxed a little under his gentle touch. She said diffidently, "I'm sorry to be such an awful baby but . . . . It's been such a long time since anyone has just—held my hand or—looked at me kindly or seemed to know I was . . . ."

"Try to sleep," Blake said softly. "If you still want to talk about it when you wake up, we will, but you have to rest now."

Blake went out, when she slept, and did some work around the barn. It was a hot day for the time of year and he was grateful for the wind which, as it did in summer, changed in mid-afternoon and came down from the peaks to the south and west, cool and fresh. There was fresh snow on the mountains, glaring in the sunlight, though there had been only a sifting of it, so far, in the valley.

Katy came from the cabin and stood watching him as he mended a bridle. Her hair stirred around her in the wind. She looked better. Her eyes, large with diffidence, were swollen and circled, but her color had come back and she tried to smile.

"Are you all right?" he asked.

"Yes. I— Mr. Westfall, could you listen to me just a little bit more?"

Her soft, lovely face set with a kind of desperate determination.

"It's wrong, I think, to talk about Alec, but he won't be talked *to* and I just don't know what to do. I'm—afraid for him."

Blake sat on an old, split-log bench against the barn wall. He indicated she should sit beside him, feeling cornered, unhappy, and helpless to resist the plea in her eyes. If there were something he could do, it would be a different matter, but . . . .

"I don't know, Katy, if there's anything I can do, more than listening, but I can do that."

She sat down, twisting her hands together nervously, looking off over the valley.

"I've thought and thought about these things. I've thought them until they've worn a path in my mind, like a dog would wear, running round and round a fence, and I don't get anywhere. It almost seems as if my mind is—sore from trying to think something different, what I ought to do about what I've been thinking.

"I know how it was for Alec, having to marry me. At least, I think I know. It wasn't like that for me . . . . I've loved Alec since I can remember. I remember him first from before I ever went away to school. I think I was just about six, the first time I can remember seeing him, and he would have been nine. As I grew up, whenever I'd think anything about any boy, I'd think of Alec, too, something he'd said or done or how he looked. When Nancy and Con and I came home a year and a half ago, Alec was at the post, helping Papa. I hadn't seen him for two years and I—just loved him.

"I know he thinks I deliberately—trapped him, so he'd have to marry me. Maybe, deep in my mind, it was there to do that, but all I *know* I was feeling was that I wanted to be with him, just close to him, always, and to have him —well, at least not mind my being there. If he just smiled at me, I'd feel happy enough to last for weeks. Most of the time, if that happened, he wasn't really even looking at me, but I'd try to believe he had been, and when we . . . . I'd have done anything. It wasn't a trap. I—I wanted to. I didn't think about anything for later. It was just that Alec—wanted me, and that was the most wonderful thing that could have happened, more than I'd ever thought would happen."

She stiffened, sitting straighter.

"You may not believe this, but I'm not completely without some pride of my own. Teachers, Papa, Mama, my sisters, lots of people, used to say, 'Katy MacPheirson, you're too strong-willed for your own good.' . . . But with Alec, I just—melt. I don't know who I am anymore. All I want, when he's there, is to be what he wants, what he'll like or notice, even a little. Sometimes, when I'm thinking about these things, it's almost as if I—hate Alec, because of my being this way, but then, as soon as I see him again, it just happens and I can't help myself.

"But I think that, besides feeling trapped, Alec hates me or whatever it is he feels, because I'm a breed."

She looked at him with a kind of defiance and Blake said slowly, "I don't see how that could be, Katy. He's—"

"It's right in the front of his mind all the time, that he's one. He'll always go out of his way to be sure people know it, daring them to make trouble about it. It's as if he feels they're going to be nasty anyway, so he'll get in the first licks. He throws it in people's faces and it's really as if *he* feels it's something bad or dirty or to be ashamed of. He hates being a breed and I think he never expected he'd have to marry one.

"I don't understand why he's like that, why it hurts him so much. For myself, I never thought much about it. It's just always been—the way things are for us. People I knew at school eventually found out we were part Indian, but it was never any big thing. Sometimes, they asked stupid questions or said silly things, but I'm sure I did the same kind of thing about them. With Alec, it's like everything he does, he has to think, *that*'s Indian, *that*'s white. Why can't he just be—Alec?

"I loved my mama. I can't ever remember thinking of her as a woman who was Indian, or half Indian. She was —Mama. When I began to know that being a breed made me seem somehow different to other people, I was proud of the Indian blood. But I'm not Indian, not the way Alec thinks I ought to be. It's not that I'm ashamed or anything like that. It has to do with the way I've been brought up, and with the fact that I'm me.

"The only time Alec has ever mentioned the baby of his own accord, he said that, when the time came, I should go to the birth lodge in the village. I can't do that, Mr. Westfall. Alec says it's because I'm ashamed of being Indian. It's not that. We've always had Indians living and working around the post, but, at home, I suppose we lived more like whites, in most ways. I've never lived with Indians. I really don't know them and their ways that well. I like Snowbird very much, and a lot of the People, but I'd be afraid, living in the birth lodge and having the baby there. I'm scared to death anyway. I'd do something to offend the women or make them angry, because I just don't *know*.

"I told Alec I'd go back to Papa's for the baby to be born, or do almost anything, but that I couldn't go and stay at the village. He said I was trying to pretend I'm not a breed. He said I couldn't go to Papa's because that would just be running away from things, trying to hide from reality."

"Do you want me to take you down to Connall's?" Blake asked.

She said, "No, I couldn't do that. It would make him awfully angry. Amanda Price said she'd come when the time comes, or that I could come and stay with them."

Her eyes filled with tears. "Mr. Westfall, I'd do anything for him. I want so much for him to be happy. I wish I could be a part of his being happy, and I can't help it if that's selfish . . . . He said, 'Be what you are, Katy. Stop being ashamed of your Indian blood.' But I *am* doing that. He's the one it's tearing apart and I just don't know what to do."

"There aren't any easy answers, Katy," Blake said slowly. "Sometimes, I think there aren't any answers at all. I hope you don't think I can just say this is how it is, this is why, and this is what you ought to do to make things all right, because I can't. Alec's been the way you've been talking about for a long time and I'm afraid it's mostly my fault. I wanted him to have the best of both ways of life, of both races, but it's turned out wrong for him somehow. I'm afraid he wants things, expects things, of himself, of life, of the world, that just aren't there. I don't believe he has any fixed ideas about what those things are. He just keeps looking for—more than there is."

"But there's so *much* for him," she said intently. "Whatever he does, he does it better than anyone else can. He's the handsomest boy in the world. He's so smart that a lot of people are afraid of him; Con is, a little I know, *I* am. He has so much talent with art and things. He works hard at everything he tries and he's making money. He could do anything he decided on. What does he *want*?"

A castle, Blake thought, a mountain, a medicine dream, things that are there, have always been there, only

390

somehow he can't recognize them. He said, "Peace of mind, I suppose, certainly about himself."

"I don't see why he can't have those things," she said almost angrily. "Why does he always have to be picking and tearing at himself? Why does he have to be so concerned about things like what's Indian and what's white? And if he does have to be, then why can't I help him at all? It just doesn't matter that much, being a breed. It's Alec that's important . . . ."

"You're right, of course. It's easy enough to see that from outside. To understand why it isn't so clear and simple for Alec, we'd have to *be* Alec."

She wiped absently at her eyes, saying distractedly, "I don't know how he's going to be about the baby, after it's born. I keep hoping it will make a difference, that when he sees his child, if he'll hold it in his arms, he'll *want* it . . . . but I can't let myself depend on that. A lot of girls would. That's how romantically they think, but I've never been able to be like that. They used to tease me, at school, about being too realistic and practical. They said I thought more like a man than a woman. It would be nice, in a way, to be a romantic, fluffy little thing, but it might end up hurting more. If I let myself be convinced that Alec will become something different just because the baby's born, and it didn't happen that way, then I . . . . only I don't really want Alec different. I just . . . .

"But if he can't love the baby, if he has to keep trying to take it apart instead of just letting it be a whole person of its own, then I think I—can't stay with him."

The tears ran down her cheeks and she was not aware of them.

"I can hardly bear thinking of not being near him sometimes, of not seeing him, and if I left, I'm afraid it might just—verify what he's known, or thinks he's known, about me and about himself all along, but I'd have to think about the baby too, wouldn't I? about what would be best for the baby?"

"Of course you would." Blake said gently.

He had put his arm around her instinctively and she leaned her head gratefully against his shoulder.

"I wouldn't stay at Papa's," she said miserably. "I

don't have the strength to be that near Alec and not beg him—to live with me. I guess I would go back to Montreal. I love it here, all this country. I think, in most ways, it must be the best place in the world to bring up kids, but I just couldn't . . . . Is that cowardly? Would I be letting the baby down?"

"There's nothing cowardly about you," Blake said softly. "I wish I'd had half your courage and your understanding of things when I was your age."

She looked up at him, trying to smile. "Then there might not be an Alec. You might never have come out here . . . . But it is cowardly of me to talk and cry like this. I ought to be able to handle it myself, to decide what ought to be done and keep quiet about it, only . . . ."

"Talking sometimes can help us work things out for ourselves." he said. "I can't tell you what to do and I don't know that I can do anything. I've always told Alec to go his own way and I'm afraid that's a part of his problem, but I don't think I can really talk to him about these things. Probably, he'd resent that very much and it would only make matters worse."

A shadow of fear crossed her face. "No, please! I don't want him ever to know we've been talking like this. It would make him—angry and, I think, it would hurt him."

"You're right," Blake said heavily, "not to depend too much on the baby's making a great difference. There aren't a great many climaxes in life, Katy, when something happens where, on one side of it, we've been one thing, and when we come out the other side, we're something else. People, after they've lived for a few years, are just not made to change that much, that quickly. There's too much involved in a personality, too many complications. Most of the changes that do come are slow things and we hardly realize they're happening. We look back, one day, and find that, years ago, we felt differently about something than we feel now. Often, we don't even know how or when we began to change.

"I know this isn't any help now, but you and Alec are both so very young. There are possibilities for the future that none of us can even think of now. You have a great deal of courage and I think you're strong enough to hold on for a while and see what happens. Alec hates this kind of thinking, but sometimes it's the only way to go on living . . . . Try to give him some more time. See how things are beginning to look after a while, to both of you."

"It doesn't take courage to stay," she said in a tone that was a mixture of irony and misery. "Sometimes I loathe myself because I'm such a fool over him. Sometimes I get so mad and I think that when he's back I'll scream and yell and say everything I can think of to hurt him and then walk out, but all he has to do is come back and I just—fall apart. He doesn't have to say anything or even look at me. I just want to start begging him to—know I'm there. It makes me ashamed and I know he doesn't like it, doesn't have any respect for somebody so weak, but—it happens. No . . . . for me, it's the leaving that would take courage."

XVIII

"IT'S BEEN INTERESTING to see, for a little while," Alec said carelessly, "all those politicians and such people, scheming for the good of the common man and getting all they could out of it for themselves—just as a secondary thing, you understand, a kind of fortunate accident. With the war over and the territory divided again, maybe things will simmer down to a boil now and those politicians can get a little rest. I don't suppose there's any reason to think that our being declared to live in Montana rather than Idaho Territory will make any real difference to anybody *but* the politicians."

It was the spring of 1866. Alec and Katy and the baby had just returned to the valley after spending most of the winter in a town that was now being called Helena.

Alec had come home last fall from his horse catching, a few days after the birth of his daughter. He had shown far more interest in the wild horses they had brought back than in the tiny girl. Katy, setting her pretty mouth a little, had made the best she could of things and, when it was apparent that Alec was totally indifferent to what she did, had named the baby Sylvia.

"He likes Greek and Latin names," she told Blake with a light brightness that made his heart ache. "He gives them to all the best foals. Sylvia means of the woodlands or something like that. It has a cool, pretty sound, doesn't it?"

She never mentioned the things they had talked about on that warm fall afternoon before the baby was born.

Alec had been home only for a few days when he left again, taking some of the unbroken horses to Helena.

"I'll work on them on the way," he said with anticipation. "Those greenhorns are so desperate for horses, they'll take anything they can get, green, wild, whatever."

Blake went down to Wyeth's for a while, one of the Medicine Rock girls staying at the cabin with Katy and the baby. When he and Alec came home again, it was almost Christmas and Katy had made the cabin beautiful for the season. She was learning, from Little Rain, Snowbird, and others, the old crafts of the People. She had made robes for the baby. She had asked Blake to make a cradle board so that she could carry Sylvia on her back when they went away from the cabin.

"It's the only sensible way, really," she said matter-of-factly. "All women ought to find out how handy it is to carry their babies this way."

Sitting by the Christmas tree she had decorated, Alec told them that he planned to go back to Helena, almost immediately.

"It's making pretensions to be quite a city. Now that they've split Montana Territory away from Idaho, the Helena people are making a bid for the territorial capital. Some eastern people are building a big hotel and they ran an ad in the paper for a local artist to paint some murals. Con showed me the article. He's speaking to me again these days, a little. They'd had only a few entries, which were really bad, and they'd about decided to send east for someone. I made a couple of sketches and they said I could have the job." He smiled contemptuously. "It's not much of a compliment. They showed me the other things that had been submitted. It's an any-port-in-a-storm kind of thing; they were desperate. And it won't be a very satisfying job because it has to be done so quickly. These are to be big paintings and they want them finished when they open the place in May or June. It'll be a little like slapping paint on a barn or something."

Katy's eyes were on him, warm with pride, but he had not looked at her. He said a little tentatively to Blake, "When we came here last spring, I said it would be just for a while. It's been a long while, but this job is something I'd sort of like to try. When I'm through, it'll be spring again and I'll see what I can do about building a cabin or adding to this one or something. So, if Katy can stay here for another winter without too much—"

She said softly, "Sylvia and I will go with you to Helena, Alec."

He looked at her where she sat in the firelight, in a rocking chair Blake had made, the sleeping baby in her arms.

"It's too hard a trip," he said flatly, frowning. "The snows came deep and early this year. The passes are hell to get through and there's no place for you to live. The town is jammed."

"It wouldn't be the first time I've lived in a tent," she said quietly, firmly. Her chin lifted a little and her hair glowed in the firelight. "I'm good and healthy now and Sylvia's strong. We'll be fine."

Still frowning, Alec went on to talk about Con's career as a kind of apprentice lawyer, about Harmony City's decline, about the few families who were trying to winter as settlers in the Camas county.

To Blake's knowledge, neither Katy nor Alec mentioned her accompanying him again, until one evening as they were finishing supper, Alec said, "I'll be leaving in the morning. I hope my clothes and things are ready."

"They are, Alec," she said placidly, and that was all.

But her things, and the baby's, were ready and at breakfast, when Alec said he wanted to get an early start, she said, "I hope you won't mind cleaning up the breakfast things, Blake. I meant to do them, but if Alec thinks we ought to . . . ."

She had got up from the table and was pulling packs from under the bed.

"What do you think you're doing?" Alec demanded angrily.

"We're ready," she said calmly, but Blake saw that her hand was shaking. "As soon as I get Sylvia—"

"I told you, you're staying here."

"You'll need someone to cook for you and—"

"I don't *need* anyone for anything. I don't want you to come. It'll be nothing but—"

"All right, Alec," she said, her voice faint but level, her eyes on the elkskin robes in which she was wrapping the baby. "If we can't go with you to Helena, then we'll go and stay with Papa and Sally until you've done the paintings and come back and built a house for us. There's more room at Papa's and he needs help in the store. We've intruded on Blake long enough. This is his cabin and it's not right or fair the way we've taken it over. I won't stay here another winter without you."

"Goddam it, I've told you—"

Blake left then. He went up in the woods to the spring and stood there, leaning against his castle. It was where he had waited while Sylvia was being born, doing some desultory detail work, thinking of Shy Fawn and those past times that had been so brief. Now the boulder was crusted with snow. He did not brush it off, but only stayed there, waiting, for a time. He could not see the cabin, nor the trail down out of the valley, so he went back, finally, with a heavy feeling of apprehension.

There was a note on the table by his coffee cup. It said only, "I hope it's the right thing. Thank you for always being kind. Love, Katy."

It was several weeks before Blake knew for sure if Katy and the baby had been left at Connall's or not. She had counted on Alec's pride not to let that happen and it had worked.

And now it was spring again and they had come back. On the surface, things seemed little changed for them. Alec still quite obviously preferred not to notice that he had a wife and child and Katy went on quietly, as best she could. She had run to Blake on their return, hugging him fiercely.

"It's wonderful, just wonderful here!" There were tears in her eyes.

She was in the cabin now, cooking while the baby slept. Alec and Blake sat in the sunshine by the barn wall. Spring this year was slow and reluctant to come. There was not much warmth yet.

"We stopped in the village," Alec said. "Eagle Feather tells me there's to be another council of the tribes this summer."

Blake nodded grimly. "I don't know why anybody bothers."

"Formalities are a kind of soothing ointment for the

397

conscience I guess. If you're some official and you've got signed papers, gone through the motions, you can rationalize away a whole multitude of sins . . . . Eagle Feather said there hasn't been any trouble about our homesteading business. I still can't believe we got away with that and that it's held this long."

"It hasn't really held," Blake said. "It hasn't been tested. What's held is the guards at the canyon and the fact that people have kept their mouths closed. When anyone has tried to come in, they've been told that the Valley is Indian land. But the only real reason I can find for our being left alone this long is that we've just been damn lucky. We were lucky that they made those big strikes east of the Divide and so many people left Harmony City and the Camas. We were lucky that the war lasted as long as it did and that this place is so isolated. We were lucky that Ellis Williams decided Harmony was too small for him before anybody got around to giving him any official duties."

"I guess I didn't know you believed so much in luck."

"It's the only explanation I can find."

"Harmony does look pretty bad. It's half a ghost town already, though there'll always be some traffic and trade, I guess, with people going back and forth across the valley on that road. Connall is crying a lot, but he's still making a profit. He'd make a profit in hell . . . . Did you know they're getting together a territorial army of militia? God, what a mess that's going to be. We have to have protection from the savages, you know. What they're going to do is sit in Helena and places and drill and collect government money. Most of them are a bunch of rabble that can't find any gold. I doubt they could hit the side of a barn with a cannon, but I hope to God they never get hold of one. . . ."

"Ellis Williams is in Helena now. People say he's going back east soon to find himself a proper lady wife. He's got land all over the place and interests in mining companies and I don't know what else. Con says he's not only going wife-hunting but that he wants to see about getting appointed territorial governor."

"Well, if he's busy with all that, maybe he'll forget

398

about the Medicine Rock. He's been after this valley since the first year I knew him. Then, he wanted the beaver."

"But you wouldn't want that sonofabitch for governor!" Alec cried.

Blake shrugged. "If it'll keep his mind off the Valley, he can be president as far as I'm concerned."

"When are you ever going to start taking a broader view?"

"I guess I'm not," he said contentedly, looking up to the mountain. "I'm old and set in my ways. You young men can fight the world's battles. I was never much of a fighter anyway. I bitch well, but that's about as far as it's ever gone."

"Now you sound like Hawk's Shadow. Every time I see him, he tells me what a kindly, sweet, resigned old man he is, and then he asks me to play the hand game, like it's his dying wish—and wins. You're not so very old. You're hardly even gray. How old are you? Forty-seven? That's not too bad . . . . But Ellis Williams! God! he's bald and looks like a mummy, a fat mummy. Can you imagine anybody marrying him?"

"Ellis is only four or five years older than I am."

"I guess you're better preserved."

"You've always had a kind heart, Alec."

They grinned at each other and Alec said grimly, "Some woman will marry him though, with all the money he's accumulated."

Blake said, "You saw the cabins they've put up on their claims down in the Valley?"

Alec nodded. "Eagle Feather's got a really nice one. He says Hawk's Shadow won't live in his with Little Rain. He's got a lodge up, near it. Beaver Tooth's place is looking like a real farm. Eagle Feather said that White Wolf was drunk again last week and beat his kids up pretty bad."

"I'm glad your grandfather can't see the Valley now," Blake said sadly. "He knew these things would happen, not exactly what they'd be, but that great changes would come for the People. But I don't know any other way we could have managed . . . . The way we've been luckiest about these homestead claims is that none of the People

399

have talked. The ones who have them know how important it is to keep quiet and the ones who don't think it's too foolish even to talk about, but there are a few, like White Wolf, who do a good bit of drinking when they can and I'm surprised it hasn't come out."

Alec shrugged and said dryly, "Who ever listens to a drunk Indian—or a sober one either, for that matter?"

"You haven't told me how the painting went."

He moved restlessly. "I wasn't very happy with most of it. It had to be done so quickly and . . . . I don't know exactly what it was I wanted but, whatever it was, it didn't quite turn out. Do you know why I took that job? Because when I went to talk to the men who were choosing an artist, they were so goddam condescending. They said, 'We ought to give the poor breed kid a chance.' Not in exactly those words, but I think they expected to have to scrape off the paint I daubed around and have their murals redone. But they thought it would be awfully humane and charitable to let me play around."

"So you showed them," Blake said quietly.

"I knocked their stupid eyes out," he said, but without much pleasure. "The pictures aren't what I wanted them to be, but I'll bet you anything you like that they're the best things of their kind west of the Mississippi, or maybe farther. A bunch of people are coming from back east in the summer, big stockholders in the mines, some railroad people, a company to sing at the new opera house, and an art critic is coming with them, just to look at the murals."

"That's quite a compliment, Alec."

He sighed discontentedly. "They've sent sketches back east and there have been some things in the papers, you know like, 'Native breed artist makes good, is able to distinguish red from blue, his right hand from his left, count up to seven,' almost that bad."

"But the publicity is good, isn't it? I mean, if you want to go on with that sort of thing? Writing people always seem to do what they can to make things a little more spectacular, one way or another, than they really are. They seem to have the idea that no one will read what they write unless it's a little bigger than life, and maybe they're right. You've always told people, before you've even been introduced to them, that you're a breed. I don't quite understand. . . ."

Alec knocked out the pipe he had just lighted. "Neither do I."

"If this is the kind of thing you want. . . ."

"It's not. Whatever I get, it's not what I wanted. Right now, I just want to stay around here and break the rest of those horses and I guess I'll see about adding a room to the cabin, if that's all right with you. I could build on my claim down in the lower meadow, but since they've passed that thing about being able to claim extra land for grazing and not having to prove it up like a homestead, I guess I won't. I've been thinking a little about going east some time. It might be interesting to see New York, maybe Paris and London. If I do anything like that, it would be better for Katy not to have to stay off by herself some place. So, do you think an addition would be all right?"

"What does Katy think?"

"She says people would gossip about the two of you. Good God! what difference does that make? If she *was* your wife, we'd all be a lot better."

"Alec—"

"Katy's . . . . she's good as gold, the salt of the earth, all those things. She's bright, sometimes she's even wise. She's patient and understanding and long-suffering and . . . . we're wrong for each other. I don't love her—not that I believe in that romantic crap from books, but there ought to be something, some feeling that's—special. Mostly, she makes me angry and it's so goddam unreasonable of me to be angry that I just get angrier . . . . I like sleeping with her; at least there's that, but that's—all, and even that's not much good because I'm so afraid of having another kid." His eyes looked lost, bewildered. "If I have to have a wife, I'm glad it's Katy, but I'm not meant to be anybody's husband or father and sometimes I get so tired of trying to know why. . . ."

Blake said hesitantly, "Maybe you'd like to go away in the mountains for a while, alone or with Eagle Feather."

Alec grimaced, trying to smile. "Eagle Feather, the future chief of the Medicine Rock People, is digging a well." He shrugged. "But thanks. I see what you're get-

401

ting at. People are supposed to go away like that and find themselves, aren't they? Only it won't work. You know I've tried before. Serenity is not in the stars for me, I guess, or wherever those things are supposed to be."

Alec tried with a visible effort to change his mood.

"I've brought sketches of the murals to show you."

"I hoped you had."

"Blake, I don't want to ruin your life here. This is your place. If you'd rather we didn't build onto the cabin. . . ."

"You *and* Katy decide about that, then we'll see what's to be done."

"Would you—go to Helena and look at the murals some time?"

They were both looking at a large puffy cloud that had got stuck on the peak of Never Summer.

"I'd like to, Alec," he said softly. "Maybe we could go when the critic is there and you could—"

"No. I don't want to be there then."

Alec had filled his pipe again. He was having trouble lighting it and Blake held up his hands to shield it from the light breeze. Alec said, "We spent last night at Wyeth Hamilton's place. They said you've been down a few times, over the winter. I was glad to hear that. Is it that you've decided not to be a total hermit after all?"

He was watching his face closely. Blake said, almost defensively, "I haven't decided anything." And Alec smiled.

Katy called to them then that dinner was ready.

"They asked us all to come down there Saturday and stay over Sunday," Alec said as they walked toward the cabin. "They're having some kind of party and some other people are coming for the day on Sunday. Corie told Katy about it and Katy said we'd probably come before she mentioned it to me. I'll be busy with the horses but maybe you'd like to go. They're really getting that place fixed up. I think what they want to do, mostly, is show it off and that's why they're having this gathering. I guess they can't be faulted for that."

Alec went down with them, after all, to Wyeth's ranch. He had sprained his arm, breaking horses, and it was too painful to do any more work for a few days. He was glum and morose, riding down, thinking privately that he would go on to Harmony City to observe Saturday night there, rather than stay at the ranch.

They arrived at about five in the afternoon to find only Corie at home.

"Why, we didn't expect you till dark," she cried happily, hurrying down the porch steps. "Wyeth and the boys had to work on a fence some today, no matter what else is goin' on. They've got a new bull that they think's the finest thing ever breathed life, but they've been havin' a time keepin' him in. Here, let me have that sweet baby. Ahhh, such a pretty little girl you are."

"I'll ride up and help them," Alec said. He had not dismounted.

"Your arm," Katy began tentatively.

"If it was good enough to come here," he said shortly, "it'll be all right for another mile or two."

"You go with him, Katy," Corie decided briskly. "Do you both good to get off by yourselves for a little while. This young-un can stay with me, can't you, sweet thing? They're up the creek there, some place on the south side."

Katy looked wistfully up at Alec and he said, "You'd better help with supper."

"Shoot, I can manage supper," Corie snapped. "You let her go along. Blake, could you cut me a little wood? I was fixin' to get some, but now I'm goin' in the house and just hold this little ole girl a while. Jonas has been sick and we've got behind with wood cuttin' and things."

Blake went around to the side of the house and began splitting logs, thinking that Corie had meant only kindness but that perhaps Katy and Alec would both have been better if Katy had not gone with him. Alec's mood was a dark one and it did not seem likely to be improved by Katy's presence. Blake had come to know Corie well in the past two years, during his visits to the ranch. Twice, she and Wyeth and the boys had ridden up to his cabin for a day, just to see what it was like in the valley. Corie's certainty about everything, her definite bent toward action, frightened him a little, though he admired it, and she was a very reassuring person to be near.

Wyeth had built himself a good house, three rooms in an L-shape with a porch in the L. He had two sturdy log barns and several corrals. It was a good place, a place that felt like home to Blake, more than anywhere besides his valley had ever felt.

He carried in some wood. Corie sat by the kitchen table, cuddling Sylvia, talking to her softly. The baby was falling asleep. When he brought in the third armload, Corie said, "Blake, there's somethin' I want to talk to you about."

"All right."

"I'll put the baby down. Get you some coffee."

When she came back, she began speaking from the doorway, her face stern and ominous.

"If you don't do somethin' about that boy of yours, I mean to. What ought to be done is he ought to be turned down across somebody's knee and spanked. It's a shame and a disgrace the way he treats that girl."

She flung cold coffee from her cup out the back door with a splat and refilled the cup.

"They were by here last week and spent the night. They'd come all the way from the James ranch that day, stoppin' off a few minutes in Harmony, and that's a long way. They were all about wore out. The baby was cross. Alec was as cranky as a sore-tailed cat, though he didn't say much, and Katy was scared to death that she or the baby would do some little thing to get him more riled. Katy was mad at him, too, but she was tryin' her best to keep things calm, so they wouldn't be any more embarrassed in front of us. Now I know this is none of my business and I expect you'll tell me so—Wyeth already has—but I've just got to say somethin'."

"You didn't say anything then?" Blake asked, half teasing.

"No, but I like to've busted."

He smiled, then sobered. "I know, Corie. It's bad, but I don't know anything to do. They're grown-ups and if things are ever to be worked out, they'll have to do it. We can't tell people how to think and feel and how to treat one another."

"It seems to me," she said slowly, "that you never have told Alec to do anything. You've told him how things *could* be done and *why* they ought to be done some certain way, but I'll bet, even when he was a little bitty boy, you never just said *do* somethin'."

"Maybe not, because I don't believe that's the way things ought to be done."

"Why not? Isn't that part of what a parent's for?"

"I wanted him to be able to grow up thinking for himself, being himself."

"Well, he's selfish is what he is. If you'd said to him when he was a little boy, 'You don't hurt people; it's not the way to do,' and if you had to give him a reason for that, you could have said, 'Because they *feel* and they can be hurt,' maybe he'd think a little more of Katy—and of himself. But that's really to one side and I don't mean to say things to hurt you. Alec *is* grown now and he ought to know better on his own. But if he can't see those things, then somebody better tell him somethin' pretty soon.

"He was drinkin' that night they were here. They'd stopped a few minutes in Harmony for her to see her folks and he'd spent the time in the saloon and had brought a bottle with him. She said he wasn't usually so mean and gloomy, but that he was a little drunk."

"Did Katy say mean?"

"Well, no," Corie admitted. "Katy said, when she got so she could talk for cryin', that he was tired and hadn't wanted them to stop in Harmony. She said he was out of sorts. Out of sorts, my foot! If he'd have acted that sulky and childish with me, I'd have put him so far out of sorts he still wouldn't be back in."

"I didn't know Alec was drinking much."

"Well, he was that night. The baby was cross and fretful. Katy was tryin' to pacify her and she felt like she had to help with supper. You could see she was so tired herself she couldn't hardly walk. Alec just sat there in the front room, frownin'. Wyeth was off up the river and didn't come back till about the time we had supper ready. Even when he got back, Alec didn't want to talk. He was poutin' is what it was. I was ashamed of him, Blake.

"After supper, the baby woke up again and started to cry. Katy was in the bedroom with her, tryin' to get her quiet and Alec went in and said somethin'. I don't know what it was, but she took the baby and ran out the back door, no wraps on either of them and it was snowin' a little.

"After a little bit, I had to go out and see about them. She was in the barn, cryin' like her heart would break. I got some wraps for them and took the baby and she went to sleep. I just stayed there with Katy and let her cry. Lord knows, she seemed to need to.

"When she began to get over it some, she started right in, makin' excuses for Alec, how tired he was and that he hadn't wanted to stop in Harmony because he don't get along with her papa. And she said he was upset about those pictures he'd been paintin'. They didn't come out the way he wanted them to. Wyeth was in Helena last month and he says they're the most beautiful scenery pictures he's ever seen—mountains and buffalo, things like that. Now I've heard how artists are supposed to be sensitive, temperamental people, but that boy's carryin' it too far. I want you to know that if he acts that way in this house again, I don't mean to put up with it.

"I think, and I told Katy so, that it's as much her fault as his, because she lets him get away with it."

Blake drew a deep breath and said tiredly, "You're right, Corie, probably, about everything, but I keep hoping that, with time, things will get better."

"How did you get to be that way?" she asked, the outrage abruptly gone from her voice, her brown eyes gentle and curious on his face.

"What way?"

"I've noticed it lots of times, in things you've said here, to us. You'll know a thing's not right and you'll go a ways toward doin' somethin' about it, and then you just do what the army calls fall back. Lord knows, there's a lot we can't do anything about, but some things we can. You quit too soon, Blake."

He looked away and said defensively, "I don't like fighting. There have been a few times in my life when I've actively tried to finish something. It's usually turned out to be a disaster of one kind or another. If things are just left alone, they usually work out the same as they would have anyway, no matter how much we've struggled."

"You struggle," she said gently. "You try to keep it all inside yourself, but it happens. I can see it."

"I can't seem to stop doing that," he said almost apologetically.

"Well," she said firmly, "part of it is that you think too much. I think that may be Alec's main trouble too. I know how much readin' both of you do, not that readin's a bad thing. I've done a good bit of it myself, one time and another, but I don't believe it's left a mark on me."

Blake smiled and she said a little defensively, "No, what I mean is, it's all right to read about philosophies and things like that, but there's so *much* of it. If you try to take it all in and make use of it, you could drive yourself crazy. You'd get so you weren't sure of anything. One of those thinkers thinks one way and you decide that sounds pretty good, and then you run onto another one that thinks just the opposite. It's enough to wear a body to a frazzle, tryin' to decide what's the right way, and I can see how a person, after a while, might come to decide there's really not any right and wrong, or much of anything."

"I guess that's about how it is," he said uneasily.

"Thinkin' is good, but there's such a thing as too much. Sometimes a thing like this with Alec just needs some action. I know a little about how things have been, from what you've said, and Wyeth, and other people. I know how Alec's mother died and you were away all those years, and I think you've thought about those things and felt guilty about them long enough. You haven't got to make up to Alec for them the rest of your life. You've done what you can and you ought to just get on to somethin' else. It seems to me you've given him just about the best bringin' up a boy in that situation could have, except that you've spoiled him rotten."

Blake said unhappily, "It's been hard for Alec, being a half-breed. I'm afraid that that's been at the heart of everything, all along."

"Shoot!" Corie said scornfully. "What's to be so bothered about that? I thought he was proud of his mother and the Medicine Rock People. I know he is of you."

"I'm not at all sure how he feels about me."

"Have you asked him?"

"No."

"Not ever? Why?"

"Because it would be an invasion of his privacy. People ought to be able to keep their thoughts and feelings to themselves if they like."

"Blake, you've built a wall around yourself and you think ever'body else has got one too, or ought to have. You could ask Alec how he feels if you want to know, then, if he didn't want to tell you, he could say so. Maybe he thinks you don't want to know. Maybe he thinks, from you always bein' that way with him, that ever'body's supposed to be that way, secret and always watchin' out so somebody can't hurt them or get too close. Do you love him?"

"Yes."

"I don't believe you told him that often enough when he was a boy, because it's plain that he believes men aren't supposed to show love. I don't see how he could keep from lovin' Katy if he'd just let himself, that is, if she'd stand up to him and show a little grit."

"Those years when I was away, Alec seemed to get a fixed idea of what women are supposed to be, what their place is . . . ."

Corie snorted. "You mean they're all supposed to be squaws. I said to Wyeth that Alec was trying to treat Katy like a squaw and he said, 'Don't you ever say that to Blake or to Alec.' Well, you just get mad about it if you have to. I don't mean it as a dirty word, the way some of the whites around here use it. I just mean to say that Katy's not a squaw. She's lettin' him try to make her one, but what good's that ever goin' to do? How can either of them have any respect for her when she's always tryin' to act and play a part she don't fit into? He ought to have married an Indian girl if that was what he wanted. And if it bothers him so much to be a half-breed, why does he always go around tellin' people about it?"

"I think he wants to be proud of it, but somehow, he isn't. That's my fault, Corie. I think he's never understood about why I had to go away for those years or why I came back."

"Tell him about it," she said simply.

"I can't," Blake said quietly, looking out across the valley. "I'm a coward. He might not understand and I—"

"Blake," she said with a sympathetic tenderness that made him flush miserably.

He went on doggedly, "When he was born, I hoped he could be just a Medicine Rock boy. After I came back, I couldn't help getting him started reading and thinking about things outside. I ruined his chances for being all Indian. The best thing, probably, would have been for me to stay away, once I'd left, but this country had become very special to me. I wanted to be with Alec, to know him and do things for him. My father died before I was born and my mother soon after. It was important for Alec, I thought, to know at least one parent."

"Of course it was important," she said gently.

"When Alec was not quite eleven, he went out to search for a medicine dream. Maybe you don't know about medicine dreams, but they're one of the most important things in the life of an Indian boy, or they used to be."

"Snowbird has told me some about things like that. She and Eagle Feather come to see us pretty often. Did he have one?"

"No. At least he's never thought so."

"I don't understand."

"Some things happened. He was in a storm above timberline; lightning struck the mountain near him; he had a dream about his mother, which had never happened before, but none of it was what he'd set out to find."

"What was he looking for?"

"I don't know, he said he didn't know, but whatever it was, he didn't find it, so then he decided to be more white."

"If he was ten or eleven, that must have been about the time Wyeth first met you."

"Yes, we'd met Wyeth just before that, because Alec had been in a fight over being called a breed in that dirty way people have."

"So when Alec decided he'd be white after all," she said thoughtfully, "he decided he couldn't ever measure up to you or to what he thought you expected of him."

Blake stared at her incredulously. "No! I never expected—"

"He simply doesn't know where he stands, Blake," she said with conviction. "Can't you see that if he doesn't want to be a breed, he doesn't have to be? *He* can't decide what he is, is the trouble and I don't believe it really has much to do with racial things. He's usin' that for his reason, his excuse. Nobody would hardly think about him bein' Indian if he didn't tell them."

"But he is, Corie. I think he wants to be very proud of it—he ought to be—only people won't let him and he—"

She had got up with an impatient gesture to get the coffeepot and refill their cups. She tried to speak reasonably.

"We've all got things about us that bother other people or that they can't or won't understand. You bein' left-handed, now. I know how silly some people are about that, sayin' it's not natural and such foolishness. There's hardly anyone that's around you long, that won't notice and mention it. Courtney, Wyeth's oldest boy, has got one brown eye and one blue one. People always have to call attention to it. For my part, I never fitted in too well with most of my family because I'm not a lady the way they thought I ought to be. They tried. I heard about it ever' day of my life. 'Cora Nell Hamilton, I declare to my soul,' they'd say"—her drawl had grown more noticeable—" 'we do ever'thing in the world, give you the very best trainin' in manners and fancywork and the rest of it, and all you want to do is go out with Wyeth and his common friends and ride a-straddle and pistol shoot. I just don't know what's to become of you, miss.' My husband Ben felt the same way. He said I was forward and just a general mess, but I never could help it. To tell you the truth, I guess I didn't try real hard to help it, because that's just me. I tried not to hurt anybody with the way I was. I tried not to shock or embarrass them too much, but I never could be Cora Nell. I'm just Corie.

"What I'm tryin' to say is that, mostly, we just have to *be* what we are. But you don't go around yellin', 'Hey, ever'body, I'm left-handed, but I'm still just as good as you.' *I* don't say to a person when I first meet them, 'My name on the church records is Cora Nell but I don't like it because that's the name I always got accused of not bein' a lady with.' They'll notice soon enough, those people, that you're left-handed and that I'm no lady. They may think we're odd or funny or that there's somethin' to be pitied or whatever, but what difference does it make? I'm still tryin' to talk about Alec, do you see?"

"I do and you're right, but—"

"And another thing," she said restlessly. "You feel guilty about comin' back here after you'd left. It seems to me like maybe you feel guilty about nearly ever'thing that's ever happened, whether you really had anything to do with it or not. You've talked some, here, about the way you was raised, your grandparents and all. I think that, in spite of all you've done to try to get away from it, you're a very religious man. I don't mean in the way of goin' to church and testifyin' and things like that. I mean you can't help believin' in the good things the Bible teaches, like love and kindness and respect for one another. I think you've tried real hard not to keep countin' on those things so people couldn't hurt and disappoint you, but you just can't help believin' and tryin' to live that way.

"Somehow, you feel like you've not got any right to expect nearly so much from other people as you expect from yourself. Maybe because of the way you were raised and other things that have happened to you, you've decided you can't be a really good person and that you're not ever likely to get any more from people than you think you deserve. You've gone up to that little valley to live because it hurts you to see people be mean and small and because you've got all these questions and guilts about yourself that you keep lettin' tear at you. You're afraid of people, Blake, and, more important, you're somehow afraid of yourself."

Blake was looking out at the sunset over the western range, feeling tense, exposed. Corie was a little embarrassed by her own candor, but she couldn't stop now.

"I wonder," she said softly, "if you don't even feel guilty sometimes that Alec was ever even born. Alec can't help feelin' those things from you, I think, whether he knows he knows them or not, and he uses them against you. That's not an unnatural thing. If you say to nearly anybody enough times, 'Hit me, I deserve it,' after so long a time, they'll probably hit. Do you see what I mean? The

411

two of you talk a lot, I guess, but I don't believe you ever really say the things that count. He uses how you are by lettin' this half-breed business always be the first thing in his mind. Ever' time somethin' don't go just the way he wants it, he can think—maybe the way you think about him—well, if I wasn't a breed it would be better, if my daddy hadn't taken my mama for a wife . . . . But you did take her and Alec was born and you've let him grow up hurtin' you when, maybe, he never really meant to be that way. And now he's doin' the same kind of thing with Katy and if somebody don't straighten him out, I may have to try it."

There was a silence. Blake looked down at the floor now, stiff with self-consciousness. No one had ever talked like this about him, and he had no reply, no defense.

With a small, tentative smile, Corie said timidly, "Are you mad?"

"What? No."

"Well, maybe you ought to be. *I* would be . . . . Isn't there something you can say?"

"I think—you've been thinking a lot, for somebody who doesn't believe much in it."

"I have, Blake," she said quietly.

"And I think," he said with difficulty, still not able to meet her eyes, "that most of what you've said is true. I've meant to do the best I could for Alec, but somehow I've never been able to make much of anything work out right."

"Now you're feelin' guilty again," she said shortly, "and that wasn't what I was after at all. I just thought that maybe you didn't *know* about all that guilt and things and that if you saw it, you could begin to get over it. I just wish you'd told Alec things like 'This is good, this is bad, this hurts me, or somebody.' A child don't have the wisdom to know about things like that for himself. A child *needs* to be told such things and then it can come to know those things are true. You've felt bad enough, long enough, about past things and you ought to try to let them go now. I'm just tryin' to say that maybe you and Alec ought to really talk some time. They say none of us is ever too old to learn."

He still looked away from her, his eyes full of pain and

confusion. He was frightened by the discoveries she had revealed. So often, he had thought he wanted another person to be able to see into his mind, but Corie seemed able to see things of which he himself did not want to be fully aware. He was deeply shaken and his impulse was to go back to the valley, to sit and look at Never Summer until its mighty stillness and indifference had washed him again with precarious quietness and peace.

Corie had come softly, shyly, to stand by his chair.

"Blake, I didn't mean to hurt you so, truly." Her hand touched his hair. "Besides talkin' about Alec, I've been tryin' to ask you, please, to stop hurtin' yourself. Stop *takin'* everything onto yourself. Let, *make* other people be responsible for what they are and what they do." Her voice was unsteady with emotion.

Blindly, Blake reached up and took her hand. It was warm and strong, with a rather large, thin strength. There were heavy callouses on the palms and fingers.

Corie said tenderly, "Has anybody, ever in your life, told you they love you?"

"Once, a long time ago." His words were almost inaudible.

"*I* love you, Blake."

He stood up then, trembling, and took her in his arms. Her body was slender and strong against him and he held her close, leaning his cheek against her hair. After a long, quiet time, she drew away from him a little and looked at him. Her eyes were full of tears but she was smiling. She was beautiful and he wished he could see her more clearly.

She said shakily, "That wasn't too ladylike either, but I was afraid you'd never know, if I just kept waitin'. I'm not much good at waitin'."

"I know," he said huskily. "I'm glad you're not."

She wiped at her eyes, standing back a little, becoming brisk and businesslike again.

"Lord-a-mercy! I've got to get them chickens to fryin'. They'll all be in here in a minute, starved to death. Wyeth's whiskey's on the shelf there. Maybe you'd want to go and sit on the porch. There's a paper there, no more'n a week old—"

"I could help you with supper."

She came to him again, holding him fiercely.

413

"Hadn't you better go on out there, or some place? I know how much you treasure bein' by yourself, and it seems to me that after all this talk, you'd want—"

He said softly, "I'd rather stay, Corie."

XIX

BLAKE AND CORIE were married in the early autumn of 1866. It had been, at times, a hard decision for him. Often, he would decide he had been alone too long, that such a change, such a beginning over, would be asking too much of both of them. But then he would want to see her again, yearn for the feelings of love and security that simply being near her gave him. That was not the way it was supposed to be, he thought; *he* was the one who was supposed to give her such feelings. He tried to talk to Corie about that.

"You feel what you feel," she said tenderly, but with a little brusqueness. "Don't you know I feel good with you, good and right, better'n I've ever felt about anything? Don't question things like that, Blake, and tear them apart, just take what there is."

"What do you think of the valley?" he asked then, relieved by her handling of his feelings, as he had felt almost sure he would be.

"That little valley up there where you live? It's the prettiest place I've ever seen . . . . but it is awful hard to get to. I don't believe I could get in and out of there winters, if I wanted or had to . . . . I was wonderin' what you'd think of buildin' down below in the main valley. Would it be awful bad for you to live away from . . . ?"

"Alec's got the land where our stream comes down to Medicine Rock Creek. Probably, it wouldn't matter to him if we built there somewhere."

"But, Blake, I don't want it that way unless you're sure

415

it will be all right for you. It's just—I was thinkin' about things like when people come to see us. I know you wouldn't want a bunch of people around all the time. Neither would I, but it's good to have friends and family and see them sometimes."

"I think it's a good idea," Blake said.

He was surprised by the relief he felt. He would miss living in the little cirque, but it would be near for him, he could go there when he liked. Most of his feelings about the little valley were for Shy Fawn, for Alec as a boy, for Blake, before there was Corie. This had been one of the things that worried him. It seemed unfair, somehow, to ask Corie to live there.

She said, smiling, "I just can't picture me bollixin' around on snowshoes. I never hardly saw snow before we came out here."

"Doing what on snowshoes?"

"What? Oh. Bollixin' around, I said."

"What's that?"

"Why, it just—a word. *I* don't know. Just try to picture me on snowshoes and you'll get the meanin' . . . . Anyway, I've thought there'd be some nice places up there to build. There's one spot, just in the edge of the woods above that meadow, where you can see up and down the main valley and over across to the mountain. It would be nice to have a cabin there, with a good big porch to sit on."

"Have you been planning this from the first?" he asked, smiling.

"No. From the second time Wyeth and the boys and I came up there. About a year ago, wasn't it?"

They laughed and he said, "Alec's been talking about adding to the cabin, but he never wants to begin it. I guess he and Katy can just have it now, if they want it that way."

"Well," Corie said a little resignedly, "I think we'd better build somethin' big enough for Katy and the baby, as well as for ourselves. I couldn't stand to see them left alone up there in that high valley in the wintertime, and Alec's gone so much . . . . And I hope we'll need the extra room for babies of our own. I want children, Blake, yours and mine, more than I've ever wanted anything besides you. I'm not real sure I can have them. Ben and I were married five years and we had just the one little girl that died before she was a year old. I had a bad time after she was born and that's always seemed so silly, big ole strong thing that I've always been. It's been a sad, scary thing to me, thinkin' I might not have other children, a lot worse, till I knew you, than thinkin' I might be a widow woman the rest of my life."

"How old are you, Corie?"

"Thirty-three."

They were sitting on the porch of Wyeth's house in the lingering twilight. She looked at him sharply, apprehension and defiance in her brown eyes.

"You're not fixin' to say some silly thing like that I'm too old to try to have babies?"

"No. More like that I might be."

"Shoot!" she said, laughing.

"It doesn't bother you at all that I'm fourteen years older than you are?"

"Bother me! I'm glad of it. Bein' an older man, maybe, just maybe you can handle me."

"I guess I could start by teaching you some English. People don't *fix* to say something, they just say it, and it's *handle,* not 'hannel.' "

"Lord!" she said happily, "if brother Byron knew I was fixin' to marry a damnyankee, he'd be here before winter sets in."

From the first, Corie had mixed feelings about leaving Wyeth and the boys and Jonas on their own. When they did tell him, Wyeth grinned happily, shaking Blake's hand and hugging his sister close with his bad arm.

"Hell," he drawled to Corie, "do you expect this to come as a surprise to me? What do you think I brought you out here for?"

Blake built a cabin of two rooms, to which more could be added later. He made it, happily, of logs. There was a new sawmill down near Harmony and he had thought Corie might want a frame house, but she didn't. The cabin did have a smooth board floor, though, and glass in its windows. Alec helped him with the building, readily, even with seeming pleasure. It was only the building of a house of his own for which he had no enthusiasm. Others

417

helped them from time to time—Eagle Feather, Emmett, and Eli. Wyeth was there the day they set the ridge pole. They enjoyed speculating what it was going to be like for Blake to be married again after all this time. For Blake, it seemed in many ways that living with Corie was a thing he'd already been doing for a long, contented happy time.

They went to Helena for a few days when they were married. Blake wanted to see Alec's murals and this was a good reason and opportunity for going. Corie did some shopping, for things for the house and for cloth to make clothing, for themselves and for Wyeth and the boys. By the time they left the town, Blake was nervous and irritable. It took him most of the way home to relax again.

It was dark when they got there, and beginning to rain, a sad, misty rain, blowing about on a little wind that would eventually settle to the northwest and turn the rain to snow. There was a fire laid in the house, a pot of stew ready to be heated, a fresh loaf of bread, and a huckleberry pie on the table.

"Bless Katy's heart!" Corie said warmly.

While they ate, she said, "It was good to see Alec's pictures and get that stuff bought and look at the town—such as it is. I'm glad we went. The Lord knows when I'll ever get you to go again, because I don't aim for you to be gettin' married just ever' year or two, but . . . . I'm awful glad we're home."

Blake still had a lot of work to do on the place. He had the porch to build and some kind of barn to get up. Corie had brought a milk cow. She said she couldn't get along, cooking, without a lot of milk and butter. She also had a rooster and a half dozen hens.

Most of the finish work inside the house had not been done when they moved in and, as they worked on it together, it came to look rather a strange, interesting, happy kind of blended place. Corie had brought a few samplers and such things, in her trunk, all the way from Mississippi.

"I don't really even know why I kept them," she said. "While I was makin' 'em, I hated 'em, and there's blood in a lot of the stitches, from where I stuck my fingers, but I guess a woman just likes to hold onto things from when she was a girl—some things."

She made curtains in the brusque, impatient way she

did most things and spread a patchwork quilt on the bed, but a bearskin rug lay at the hearth and she had discovered, packed away, Blake's collection of Indian things. He had sent the occasional boxes east to Cambridge, but had kept the things that pleased him most.

"Why couldn't we hang some of these things around on the walls?" she asked him. "They'd look real nice."

"I didn't know if you'd want them," he said gratefully.

She turned from her work to look at him. "Why wouldn't I? They're part of the country, and of you."

So there were a rabbitskin blanket, meticulously worked in beads and quills, an eagle-feather headdress, a fishing spear on whose handle someone had taken a great deal of trouble with carving, and several other things. A mortar and pestle, a basket, and a pottery bowl were on the rough mantel, along with Paul's fiddle. A long carrying bag with a beautiful design in clay paints hung beside Blake's bookshelves.

"It's gettin' to look right nice in here, don't you think?" Corie said complacently. "Now what we need for that place over the mantel is somethin' you paint."

Blake looked at the bare space a little wistfully.

"Some day, maybe, but I don't know what it would be. We could ask Alec to do something. He does so much better."

Corie shook her head. "I want it to be a picture of yours. All those critics and people say how good Alec is, and it's true, but, to me, there's always somethin' stark and cold about his pictures. I want this to be somethin' warm and homey."

Hawk's Shadow and Little Rain came to visit them one day. Blake went to the village whenever he had time, sometimes Corie went with him, but he had had a heavy, sad feeling that Hawk's Shadow might never visit him in his new home. On a bright, frozen winter day with heavy snow on the ground, Blake was nailing down the floor of his porch when Corie saw them coming and flung open the door, calling brightly, "Why, come in and get warm. Company's just what I've been wishin' for."

The house was filled with the rich warm smell of a cake she was baking.

Over the years, Little Rain had come to a fair grasp of

English and she and Corie sat by the kitchen table, talking. Hawk's Shadow would never speak the foreign language, though Blake felt certain he understood more of it than he wanted known. Blake had told Corie how to make coffee the way the People liked it and, when they held their cups, he said, "Sit down, Hawk's Shadow. Tell me how it goes in the village."

Looking dubiously at the cushion Corie had made for the chair Blake indicated, Hawk's Shadow said, "It would be better outside."

"It's cold," Blake said. "Let's wait at least until we've had dinner."

Hawk's Shadow sat down carefully, on the edge of the chair.

"Eagle Feather would not stop talking until I came here," he explained a little petulantly. "I told him that you come to see me, that sometimes your woman has come to see Little Rain, but he kept saying I must come here, that such a thing makes a difference to you."

"That's true," Blake said. "I'm glad you've come. How has the hunting been?"

"I have killed some good elk. This is the best time for elk."

"I know."

Hawk's Shadow grunted. "And still you do not hunt. You let Alec bring your meat."

"I've been busy."

He grunted again. "I think it is that this woman will not let you go away from her to hunt. Maybe she feels she needs you here to protect her from the People, to keep her from being scalped."

"No, it's only that I've been working."

"Yes." He waved his hand in a gesture that took in the house and all the place. "I wonder if you are still of the People."

"Some of the People have cabins and farms and herds that they must spend time on. *You* have a cabin."

"That is Little Rain's cabin, never mine. I only signed my white name, James Westfall, on the papers that time. I agreed to nothing else. Eagle Feather cut the trees and made the cabin for his mother. He plows in those fields like a woman, or like those oxen whites have. I never said

I would do more than make meat and do the things I have always done. Why do you have that fishing spear from the Spokanes hanging there?"

"It's good to look at."

"A fishing spear is for spearing fish, not for looking at. Your head has never healed from the time it was broken."

"Hawk's Shadow, I want a bow."

"You have a bow."

"But it's not one of the best ones. It was made hurriedly and it—"

"Is there something wrong with the shooting of it?"

"No. I haven't used it for a long time, but it used to shoot all right."

"If there is something wrong with that bow, it is that you never shot well in the first place. How can anyone aim an arrow truly with his left hand? There is nothing wrong with that bow. Anyway, you shoot game with a rifle, otherwise you do not hit it. Sometimes you do not hit it then."

"I want a bow to keep here in the cabin with these other things. Will you make one for me, in the old way? With much care and—"

"Any bow I make is made with much care, and it is made for shooting arrows, not for hanging on the wall of a cabin with a Spokane spear and a Snake blanket."

"I'd like some arrows, too; just one or two, with stone heads. Do you remember how to make stone arrowheads?"

"Red Sky my father taught me that when I was a small boy. Would I forget? Meat killed with a stone arrowhead always tastes better than that shot with iron, but it takes more time to make them of stone. Everything must be right and there is a medicine song that goes with the making. Why would I do all that to have those arrows hung on a wall? And I have no good sheephorn for the making of a good bow. Would I climb the high peaks in the snow, searching for a ram so that I must take the time and trouble of making a fine bow, only to have it hung on a wall and never used for shooting?"

"We could hunt a ram together, when the weather is better," Blake said mildly. "I want the finest bow I can get, to put with these other things, and you are the finest bowmaker the People, or any other people, have ever had."

"That's true," agreed Hawk's Shadow readily, "but I do not waste my time on foolishness. Even your woman must know by now that her husband is a crazy man. You are lucky, I think, to get any woman to live with you. Perhaps she will not stay."

"I think she will."

"Little Rain says she is a good woman, for a white." Hawk's Shadow moved restlessly. "Come outside now, Blake. I do not feel like myself in cabins."

They went out and sat on a log a little way from the house and Hawk's Shadow finally told him what was most heavily on his mind.

"Last night, Beaver Tooth came back. He has been to the council."

"The council was over a long time ago," Blake said, not wanting to talk about it.

"Beaver Tooth signed more papers there," Hawk's Shadow said wearily. "He says he is a very important man with the whites. He called a council of the People when he came back. He had brought some whiskey and he passed around a bottle while we smoked. That is not how it should be in a council.

"The reason he was away so long was that he was looking at land, reservation land to the west. He was finding a place to live."

Blake waited, looking up to the snowy mountain, a sinking, sick feeling inside him.

"These new papers he has signed say that no bands are to live away from the reservations anymore, that all must move there, where they are told. Beaver Tooth says he has found good land for all who will go. Eagle Feather is not here. He is with Alec in their horse business. I thought I should tell you what has happened."

Blake turned to study his face. There was no anger in it, no expression of struggling, only sadness.

Hawk's Shadow said, "I said nothing in the council and through the night I did not sleep. It has come to me that this may be the best thing. Since Beaver Tooth has been chief and all this paper-signing has happened, there have been argument and bad feeling in the village. They will go in the spring, Beaver Tooth and those who want to follow him, then maybe things will be more as they used to be in the Medicine Rock. He told the whites that some of the People have cabins and such things. Those who go will take their cattle and horses. They say the whites have said they will give them extra goods to pay for their cabins. Beaver Tooth believes this . . . . I have thought, Blake, that Beaver Tooth and those who think as he does were somehow born to be reservation Indians.

"When they are gone, I think Eagle Feather will be chief. He will be a strange chief. No chief of the People has ever built cabins or dug in the ground or spoken English so well that white men cannot tell it from their own. But he cares for the People as my father did, as Beaver Tooth never has. I don't know what he will say when he comes back and hears Beaver Tooth's talking. I cannot guess often what he will say about a thing, but I think it will be, as I say, that it is best for these others to go. Then those who could not live away from this valley will be left quietly alone. It will belong again, most of it, only to those who truly belong to it. We even have those papers with white names on them, to say, in a way that white men understand, that the land is ours.

"I think that for once Beaver Tooth may have done good to some of the People, without knowing it, while he thought only of himself. Some are eager to go. They say, with Beaver Tooth, that it will be good, living on that reservation. They can have more feasts and races and such things there, and whites will give them those allotments. They are fools. I think their ancestors were people who should never have followed Winter Thunder to the Medicine Rock in the first place. But when they are gone, we can have the Valley, those of us who truly want it."

His sharp eyes searched Blake's face, worried, pleading.

"Will the papers for those little bits of land mean enough to the whites? I see in your face, which always shows everything, that you think they will not."

"Did Beaver Tooth tell them about the claims?"

"He says he did not. He is still angry and jealous about those papers, that he did not think of making up white names and signing them . . . . An agent will come here in the spring, when it is time for them to move, to see how much the cabins and things are worth. We will tell that agent—you will tell him, or Eagle Feather will—that some of us will not go, that all the Medicine Rock People are no longer bound by the words of Chief Beaver Tooth. Should that agent be told, then, about those papers we have?"

"I suppose he'll have to be told."

"And will they go then and leave us in peace?"

"I'm afraid they won't, Hawk's Shadow, but all I know to do is wait until that time comes and see what happens, then we can decide what will have to be done.

"I will not go from this valley to live," Hawk's Shadow said quietly, his face and voice hard. "You know that I have never much liked war and battles, but I would rather fight the Snakes and the Blackfeet together, ten times over, than to just wait and wonder what these whites are going to do. It is not right that one man should believe he has control over another man's life, and it is even less right that one man *allows* another to think he can have such control. If people have a right to say which land belongs to which man, then I am a man and I have that right. This land is mine. I will never leave it willingly. If I ever leave it, it will be only because I am dead."

"We ought to have a party, Blake," Corie said enthusiastically.

It was beginning to be spring, muddy and dreary, but spring enough so that they could ride together to the upper valley to visit Katy. Alec had been away a good deal during the winter and Blake had gone up often. Both he and Corie had tried to persuade Katy to bring the baby and live with them during Alec's absences, but she had always refused, sweetly, adamantly.

Corie went on eagerly, "It could be a housewarmin' or somethin' like that. Would you mind?"

"No," he said easily.

He was thinking that there would be a good deal of flooding this year. The snow pack was heavier than normal.

She said, "Wyeth and the boys would come, of course. You know he's been sparkin' that Ethel Blackford."

Who?"

She made a sound of disgust and impatience. "That widow woman down at Harmony. *You* know. Her husband came out here prospectin' and got killed in a slide, left her with a little boy and girl. She's been cookin' at the Nugget Saloon these two years to raise the children. I swear to goodness, Blake Westfall, you won't try to keep track of anything but how much snow there is and such. I know what you're thinkin' . . . . Anyway, maybe Ethel would come with Wyeth, and there'd be Connall and Sally, Con, if he's around anywhere, Emmett and Amanda, Eli and Cricket, those Boyds that have just moved to the Camas, Eagle Feather and Snowbird. Do you think Hawk's Shadow would come?"

"I doubt he would. If you ask some of the People, you're likely to have the whole village."

"I know that," she said comfortably. "We'd manage somethin'. We could have an all-day barbecue, like we used to have back home. People from farther away could come the night before. The women and little children could sleep in the house and the men and older ones in the barn or outside. Would you mind all that?"

"No, not this once."

"I hope I can get Katy interested in comin' down to help me. She needs somethin' new to think about . . . . Do you think things are any better for them?"

"I don't know, Corie. It's hard to say how things are for other people."

"What you're really sayin' is 'Mind your own business, Corie.' "

"No, I just meant—"

"Well, I can't quit worrying about 'em. When they were down for Christmas, I thought she looked right thin and peaked."

"They don't say anything," Blake said. "I hope that when they're alone things are better now."

"Alone!" Corie snorted. *"She's* alone most of the time. But," she added quickly, "I haven't said any more to either one of them about each other than I've just absolutely had to, because I know how you feel about keepin' out of other people's affairs. I don't know. Maybe they will

425

work it out. Some marriages get started under some pretty strange circumstances and finally end up all right . . . . Blake?"

He raised his eyes from some otter tracks. She looked shy and hesitant.

"Katy's told me about that castle you carved up here. Would you—mind if I look at it?"

"No, Corie. I'd like you to see it—if you want to."

"Of course I want to," she said a little shortly, then wonderingly, "Do you know that you're an awful special man? If I live with you fifty years, I expect there'll still be things to find out. And I'll have to *find* out most of 'em. You're not just about to tell me. It don't always make for the simplest life in the world, not knowin' what you've done, or what you'll think or say or feel, but it does make things interestin'."

Sylvia was a beautiful little girl with her mother's big brown eyes and vivid coloring. Corie could hardly bear to let go of her, but it was Blake that the little girl wanted to follow.

Through the day, he tried to get some of the heavier work done for Katy while the women talked in the cabin, with their sewing and cooking. After dinner, while Katy put the baby down for her nap, Blake and Corie went up to look at the castle.

Corie said nothing for a long time. She walked slowly around the boulder, her face soft with awe and wonder while Blake looked up at Never Summer, feeling shy and a little afraid.

"It's beautiful," she murmured softly. "It's just the most beautiful thing. I've seen pictures in old books, but they weren't half so . . . . I just don't see how . . . ."

She came to him and put her arms around him. "I was wrong to make you go and live down below where you can't hardly ever look at it."

"I don't have to see it often," he said softly, beginning to relax. "I know it's here."

"Blake, I just don't know . . . . You're a wonder and I don't see why you ever married me. I don't have the sense or the learnin' or the *feelin'* to *know* you. Sometimes, you purely scare me."

426

"Corie, I love you. For me, it's the opposite. You're the one who—"

"Shoot!" she said and tried to wipe her eyes surreptitiously. Then briskly, "I'm glad it's not out in the middle of some place where a bunch of people would always be comin' around. The castle, I mean. Here, it really belongs to you and that's how it ought to be . . . . Look how much snow's gone off of Never Summer just today. Don't you think it's time we got my garden patch dug up?"

As they were leaving Katy in the afternoon, Corie gave her a hug that seemed particularly filled with warmth and love, even for Corie. She was quiet as they rode slowly down from the little valley. Finally she said flatly, "Katy's pregnant again."

"Oh, God," Blake groaned.

Corie flared. "Is that such an awful thing? People ought to be glad to hear news like that."

"I was thinking of Alec. You know that. You were thinking the same thing."

"Yes," she said, relenting. "I didn't mean to bite your head off. Only I was thinkin' more of Katy. She's worried sick. She wouldn't even have told me if I hadn't guessed it for myself. All she can think about is how mad Alec will be when he has to find out. I could knock that boy in the head, Blake. He makes her life a pure misery. If they have a baby, Lord knows it's no more her doin' than his. I can see how they wouldn't want more, things like they are between them, but such things *will* happen and he ought to try to make it a little easier for her when that can be done.

"When I finally got her to start talkin', she said things have been some better with them this winter, times when he's home, that he talks to her and sometimes acts like he knows she's there, for somethin' besides to wait on him and to sleep with. She didn't put it hardly like that. Those are my words. She says she's a little different, too, that she don't fall to pieces like she used to when he's around, but can stand up to him a little better. She said she was beginnin' to hope things would work out—not the way she'd dreamed they might—but somehow that they could maybe both live with and make a decent home for little Sylvia. Only now, with another baby comin'—well, she's just sick. She says the only good thing she can think of about it is that maybe this one will be a boy and that maybe that will mean somethin' to Alec. Do you think it will?"

"I don't know, Corie."

"I can see you think it won't, but most men set a lot of store by havin' a son. I never have seen why, really. Girls are so much less complicated and easier to deal with."

She sighed worriedly, trying to regain her normal exuberance and briskness. "Anyway, Katy will come and help about the party. We decided, she and I, that the last Saturday in May would be a good time to have it. That way, we'll have plenty of time to let people know, and I hope the weather will be decent by then."

"All right," he agreed absently.

"Blake," she said impatiently, "you do know that'll be your birthday, don't you?"

"No," he said with some consternation. "I hadn't thought about it."

Through supper, he kept thinking about Alec and Katy, and that the time must come, soon, when something would happen with the People and their homestead claims. When Corie had washed the dishes, she stood beside his chair and said, a little wistfully, "Let's go sit on the porch a little while."

"It's pretty cold out."

"I've got a sweater. Come on. There's a pretty moon. Just for a little while."

They sat on a split-log bench by the wall and she took his hand. The moon full and bright and there was a smell of green things, new from the earth. Never Summer stood up across the valley, great and majestic, silent, unchanging.

Corie said softly, "You've already got a son, but would it take your mind off other things for a minute to hear that you might be fixin' to have another one? or a daughter?"

"Corie!" A great joy and wonder welled up within him. "Why didn't you tell me before, if you thought—"

"I wanted to be certain, not to disappoint you. I thought it might have happened once before and it turned out I was wrong. Besides, I . . . ."

428

"What?"

"Well, I never have been right real sure how you'd feel about it, all the worry you've had with Alec and the way you . . . . It's a little hard to know how a man's goin' to think about somethin' as simple and ordinary as a baby—when he's in love with a mountain."

"I'm not," he said, surprised, a little defensive. "I'm in love with you and I couldn't be happier about anything."

"Of course you're in love with me," she said matter-of-factly, holding him close. "I know that and most of the time I'm not a bit jealous. I know the mountain's a part of you and I know that love's a stretchy thing that can take in any number of things and people. I just—wanted you to be pleased, about the baby."

"Pleased!" he said and could say no more, only hold her.

After a time, she laughed. "It took us a little while, but at least people can't count up on their fingers and say we had to get married."

Blake smiled, but then said worriedly, "You shouldn't have gone up to the valley today. That trail was slippery and your horse might have—"

"Now don't start that kind of thing, Blake Westfall," she said shortly, still leaning against him warmly. "I've always been as strong as an ox. There'll be times when I'll use this for all it's worth, makin' you wait on me and such like, but I don't aim to miss out on anything."

"Not even the party?" he said a little wistfully.

He wouldn't have minded the celebration as a house-warming, but the fact that it would fall on his birthday was somehow a little embarrassing and uncomfortable for him. No one, ever in his life, had done anything special about his birthday.

Corie was saying brusquely, "You're a sweet, silly thing. There won't be any kind of work that could hurt me in havin' the party, and the days are passin', especially around here, when a pregnant woman has to hide all through her time, like she's got somethin' to be ashamed of. Anyhow, I won't be showin' that soon and, even if I was, most men can't see what's right in front of their eyes.

"Wyeth told me when he was up here last week, while you and Hawk's Shadow were off huntin', that they're

429

talkin' about dividin' the territory up again, takin' off a big chunk to the south to make a new one. He says it's because those people that are goin' to put the railroad through down there want to have their own state one day. They'd call it Wyoming, Wyeth says, and they've already been havin' political meetings about it. But what I'm tryin' to tell is that they're talkin', down there, about lettin' women vote in that new territory. Wyeth says they're just doin' it to get publicity back east, but wouldn't it be the funniest thing if it was to happen somehow? A lot of things are changin' for women. Maybe we ought to move down to this Wyoming."

"Maybe you better just vote for going to bed," he said, smiling. "You're shivering."

"Just like a man," she said resignedly, "always makin' light of a woman's rights and thinkin' about nothin but goin' to bed."

"Corie," he said with exaggerated, teasing patience, "to make light means to light something, a candle or a fire or—"

"Oh, you just hush up," she said, laughing. "Look at those deer in the meadow. Look how close they've come to the house . . . . Blake, I'm just too happy to go in yet, for a little while."

Katy came down the day before the party and she and Corie cleaned and cooked, talking happily together, each of them enjoying the unaccustomed company of another woman. Alec was home again and he and Blake and others in the valley had been branding cattle. It was Alec's idea, and Eagle Feather's, because there were getting to be so many cattle. To Blake, it seemed a little wrong somehow. He kept hearing from Hawk's Shadow and thinking for himself how Red Sky would have felt about this marking and individual ownership.

Alec and Katy gave him a chess set for his birthday, all the pieces hand-carved by Alec over the winter, a beautiful job. They gave it to him at dinnertime on Saturday, before any guests arrived, because they knew how uncomfortable and reticent gifts made him. He had balked at having Corie tell any of the guests it was his birthday.

430

"Now you've got the chess set," she said, "why don't you and Alec just stay around the house this afternoon? We're goin' to need a little help with a few things and you can fool around with the game between times. Though how anybody could spend very much time with it, waitin' for somebody else to make one of those moves, I'll never understand."

Alec was not very enthusiastic about staying around the house, he was restless and had always been a little uneasy with Corie, but he did like playing chess. Blake found the boy's ease at winning a little appalling. He himself had not played chess since those long ago days in New Orleans with Etienne St. Croix.

Alec was quieter these days. Resigned was not a very pleasant word to apply to one's wife and family, but perhaps that was what he was becoming. He knew about the new baby that would be born in the fall, and he did not seem to be struggling too painfully against this established fact. The only mention he made of it was to say dryly to Blake that, between them, they seemed to be doing a fair job of building up the population of Montana Territory. Still, in his slightly bitter, cynical way, Alec seemed more willing to settle for things as they were than Blake had seen him before.

Toward late afternoon, Wyeth and the boys arrived, bringing Ethel Blackford and her children with them. Ethel was a small, pert woman in her middle thirties. Corie and Katy immediately drew her into their talk and activity. The children drifted away, down by the creek to look for frogs.

Connall came then. He had not brought Sally. Someone had to stay in town to mind the store and the little ones. Con was not with him; he spent most of his time in Helena and was looking forward to election time in the fall. There was still tension between Connall and Alec; Alec would have gone away from the group of men then if it had not been for Wyeth, who went on with his easy smile and talk, as if he had no idea that a rift had ever existed.

The men walked around the barn and corrals, talking, looking over the place. They went desultorily down to

431

look at Medicine Rock Creek, high with spring runoff. Finally, they came back to sit on the edge of the porch, smoking, waiting for supper.

"You're getting yourself quite a place here, lad," Connall said. "It's high time, too, that some proper use was made of this valley . . . . Have you heard that we're to have a school in Harmony, starting in the fall?"

"No, I hadn't."

"Aye, it'll be held in the same building where the church is. They've a teacher coming from the east. We were afraid, for a time there, that Harmony might die entirely, but it's picking up, getting some civilization at last, though I'm not so sure you can call that shouting Protestant church civilized."

Alec had a bottle of whiskey and they passed it among them. The boy had drunk from it occasionally through the afternoon and he was growing even quieter now, his eyes morose and brooding.

"And did you hear," Connall asked eagerly, "about what's been going on at Virginia City? The trial and all?"

They all shook their heads.

"I would have thought you'd know about it," Connall said irritably to Alec, "as much as you're always out and about the country."

"I've been west," Alec said coldly, "trading for horses. That's a little different from sitting in a store, listening to every rumor that passes through Harmony."

Connall looked angry but Wyeth said smoothly, "What trial was that, Connall?"

"It was for the man that killed Jesse Harris," he said, seemingly mollified.

"Jesse Harris!" Blake was startled.

"Aye. Jesse came down from out of the hills somewhere and was having himself a drink in a saloon over there. The way I heard the story, there was this greenhorn youngster, name of Stephens, a relative of that eastern woman Ellis Williams married. Ellis got himself some rich in-laws, but I suppose that was a foregone conclusion. Her brother and his boy have been out here for a while, looking over mining claims and land, and they say the young one thinks he's quite the man, with a gun and so forth. It seems the Stephens boy asked old Jesse something like what kind of breed he was, standing there at the bar, and if he thought they ought to be serving him whiskey.

"You know how Jesse was, Blake. He never said more than two dozen words a year. I've been out trapping with him several times, long years back. You could ask him a question in the fall and maybe by spring you'd get a grunt for an answer. When this easterner spoke to him, he didn't say anything. The dude got mad and it ended that he shot Jesse."

Blake's mouth had hardened and he felt sick. He remembered riding with Jesse to look for water that time, just after Henry Melton had died, and how it had been Jesse who did most of the work shepherding the Mormon band across the desert that time when he, Blake, had been so desperate to leave the country.

"And they've had a trial?" Wyeth asked.

Connall nodded. "The kid had to pay court costs because Jesse wasn't wearing a gun."

"That's all!" Blake cried.

Alec said bitterly, "It's a great stride toward law and order for this country if they even had a trial. You ought to see how things are getting west of here. There's not any discrimination against *Indians*. The Chinese get treated just as badly, and so do the Rebels or whoever happens not to be in power. If this goddam country gets much more civilized . . . ."

"You're a fine one to be talking," Connall began, and Wyeth drawled, "I wonder who that is coming now."

Five riders were coming up the valley. Blake recognized Hawk's Shadow and Eagle Feather. The other three were white and he could guess why they had come. As they drew nearer, he saw that one of the white men was Ellis Williams.

"These men," said Eagle Feather in his careful English, "came here to put a price on the cabins and things, and to tell Beaver Tooth and the People who will be moving with him to the reservation that it's time to go. Beaver Tooth has gone to Harmony today . . . . Mr. Williams you already know. This is his wife's brother, Mr. Stephens, who is looking for good ranch land, and this is Mr. Arthur, from the agency."

Eagle Feather's light voice was calm and steady, almost indifferent. There was uneasiness in his eyes, even a little fear, but it was so veiled that those who did not know him could not detect it. He said, "We have brought them here, my uncle, because you have kept our homesteading papers for us. They want to see those papers."

Hawk's Shadow said fiercely, in the language of the People, "The thing we should have done is to shoot them when they first came into the canyon."

"Will you get the claim papers?" Blake said to Alec.

Ellis Williams said, with a derisive smile, "I never heard such a bunch of shit. Indians with homestead claims! What kind of funny business is this, Blake? You've tricked these poor, stupid people."

Stephens, Ellis' brother-in-law, said smoothly, "This could be a pretty nice place you've got here, Westfall. From what I've seen, this valley's the best grazing land around. It will feed twice as many cattle, for the land, as most of the rest of this country. I plan to set my boy up with a good ranch, see if I can get him settled down and out of trouble for a while. He's had himself a little scrape over—"

"These are the deeds," Blake interrupted curtly, giving the deeds to Arthur, from the agency. "You'll find that they're in order and duly executed. These claims have all been proved on."

The women had come onto the porch behind them, to stand silently, worriedly, listening.

Wilbur Arthur, the government representative, was a nervous, harried little man, It seemed to him that all these westerners, even the women, had such sharp, direct eyes, and that everyone always felt so very strongly about everything. He was really only an appraiser and not supposed to have to handle other things, but they were short-handed at the agency and it seemed you could never guess what was going to come up with these people, Indians or whites. He took a long time looking at the papers, uncomfortably aware of the eyes upon him.

"These names," he said carefully, "these are not Indian names."

"How far do you think we'd have got with the deeds if they had been?" asked Alec, smiling coldly.

Ellis reached for the papers and Blake took them quickly from Arthur.

"This is the goddamned craziest thing I ever heard of," raged Ellis. "What in the hell makes you think you can get away with it? Didn't you ever hear of things like fraud and forgery? You could go to jail for the rest of your life for this."

"*You* ought to know about such things, Ellis," Blake said quietly. "I haven't signed anything for anyone, the way you did for White Water and those other people."

"He's basing his threats," Alec said caustically, "on the kind of justice this sovereign territory has—his kind."

"Mr. Westfall," said Arthur shakily, trying to be reasonable, "Indians can't own land like this. I'm sure you must have been trying to help these people, but I'm afraid all you've done is to give them false notions. I've been sent here to prepare them for moving to the reservation. These invalid papers only serve to make things more difficult, for all of us. I think the kindest thing you could do is just tell them the truth, that these papers are no good."

"They're bona fide deeds," Blake said. "Beaver Tooth and a lot of the People are ready to move where you tell them. Leave the others alone. They own the land and they—"

"Own the land, hell!" cried Ellis. "You're not about to get away with that. You want this valley for yourself and that breed bastard kid. Do you think I can't see through this bullshit? You're *using* these poor, stupid redskins."

Wyeth said quietly, "Blake, I've met a lawyer in Helena, name of Clay Morgan. He was a Yankee officer in the War, but he's all right and he's interested in Indian problems. We could talk to him about this."

"That would only be a waste of time, money, and effort, my friend," said Stephens condescendingly. "These Indians have to go to the reservation. It's in the treaties. They have no business on this land. Why make trouble for all of us by dragging the thing out?"

"I guess we'll drag it out," Blake said. "That seems to be what the courts are for."

"Courts!" Ellis spat. "Courts are not for *Indians*. You're a fool, Blake, a goddam troublemaker."

"I'll tell you what," said Stephens magnanimously. "I

had told Mr. Arthur that *I'll* pay for the improvements these Indians have made here, the cabins and fields and so forth. I've decided that the price the government has set, through Mr. Arthur, is a little less than I had figured on and I'll go ahead and pay that difference." He turned to Eagle Feather with a hearty, condescending smile. "We'll work out something very agreeable. Plenty of cash to buy fire water, huh?"

Eagle Feather said steadily, "This valley belongs to the People. Money cannot pay for it. There is nothing to pay; it is ours. The whites said we must have papers to show our rights here. There are those papers."

"Those deeds," said Mr. Arthur impatiently, "were obtained under false pretenses. The names on them are not legal names. For instance, I saw a James and a Patrick Westfall on two of them. I know there are no such people."

"I can't prove my name is Connall MacPheirson," said Connall a little unexpectedly. "Nobody was ever much for keeping such records in this country. We had no churches and things like that until a few years back."

"This is nothing but a bunch of crap and a waste of time," raged Ellis. "You know there's not a chance of—"

"We could adopt them," said Corie loudly, warmly.

The men turned to stare at her. Blake's lips moved into a half smile that showed her his gratitude. Finally Arthur said stiffly, "Ma'am, you can't adopt grown people, and Indians besides."

Grinning, Wyeth said, "Maybe the courts could declare them incompetent of handling their own affairs. God knows, that wouldn't be too farfetched if this is going to come to a long drawn-out legal battle."

"All we need in this country," said Stephens, finally angry, "is one more goddam Rebel, butting into what's none of his business."

"Yes," Alec agreed smoothly. "Everybody else tends so strictly to his own affairs."

Ellis said fiercely to Blake, "I'm warning you once more, you better do something about that kid's smart mouth if you don't want him carried home full of lead some day. He's stirring up trouble all over this part of the territory and people won't take only so much of his lip.

436

We're trying to make this a law-abiding, God-fearing place where decent white people can live."

Alec laughed and Ellis's face grew more deeply flushed with fury. He spluttered curses and Alec, still smiling broadly, said, "You'll have a stroke one day, *Mr.* Williams, getting so angry."

"Let's kill them now," Hawk's Shadow said impatiently. "We've always been able to hold the valley. These are not half the men the Blackfeet are."

"You're intruding here," Blake said to the three white men. "This is my land, and Alec's. You weren't invited. You go on, Mr. Arthur, and do your business with those of the People who are willing to go along with you. The rest of it, we'll see about in court. We have the deeds and, for now, they're legal. We'll just go on as we are until or unless some other decision is made."

"The law of the land—" began Arthur petulantly.

"Here's the land," Blake said, gesturing broadly, "and here *we* are, all of us. We'll see how valid the law is, whether there is such a thing as justice for all."

Stephens said fiercely, "Yes, I just guess we will. I tell you frankly, Westfall, that I want this valley and I intend to have it. This land is being wasted."

"Don't tell me," Blake said bitterly. "I know. You've got a God-given right to take it and do what's meant with it. Go ahead. Try."

"There can't be guards posted at the canyon anymore," Arthur said uneasily, after a little silence. "These claims you have, for what they're worth for the present, don't cover nearly all the valley and this never was reservation land. It's illegal to keep people from coming in here. I've explained that to the Indians. Those who are willing to see reason will be moving soon, and then the valley must be open to—"

Wyeth said, "But it won't be open to claim jumpers. The law is slow and far away, but there are enough of us right here who are crack shots with a rifle to see that this thing is done legal and proper for a change."

Ellis turned on Connall. "I hope you're not going to be a part of this crap, Mac. If you're thinking about it, just keep in mind that we could set up another store in

437

Harmony and run you right out of business. I hear, too, that *your* breed boy has got himself some high political notions. We could—"

"By God, Ellis," Connall said hotly, "don't you know I stopped worrying about what you can do years ago? It was about the time you ran and hid from the Blackfeet and then went to sleep without giving any warning to the others with you. You scare me just about as much as that porch post there."

"I do wish," Arthur tried lamely, "that we could reach some understanding here today. It would be so much simpler than—"

"We have reached an understanding," Blake said. "We're ready to take the matter to court. It'll take a lot of time but none of us is in that much of a hurry. We can wait. The valley will be here."

"And in the meantime," came Corie's firm, ominous voice, "you all can just get off this place and stay off. You've come where you're not wanted, buttin' into a celebration for family and friends where you've got no call to be. You've been asked to leave and now I expect you'd better just go."

Again, they turned to where the women stood. She was holding Blake's rifle and she cocked it deliberately in the silence.

XX

ALEC'S AND KATY'S SECOND DAUGHTER was born in October, in Blake's and Corie's house, a healthy little redhead. Alec was away, down in the Wyoming country, selling horses to the railroad builders. By the time he came back, it was Christmastime and Blake's and Corie's son had been born. The boy was named Richard Blake.

"Richard's a good strong name I've always liked," Corie said, "good and strong like Blake and he's got to have that name too, because I don't think there will be any more."

She had had a bad time having the baby and she said that both Amanda and Little Rain agreed with her that, because of various physical circumstances, she was not likely to become pregnant again.

"But, anyhow, we *have* got this one," she said and hugged the baby so warmly that he gave a forced grunt of protest.

Richard was a strong, good-natured baby, with Corie's light hair and brown eyes.

Katy named her daughter Sarah Ellen. Those had been the names of Blake's and Corie's mothers, and Katy said stoutly that the family ought to begin establishing its own tradition, that handing down names was a good beginning.

"But we could call her something else," she said to Alec on the first evening he was home again, "if you'd rather . . . ."

"No. That will be all right," he said absently.

Alec looked thin and tired and Corie kept pressing him

warmly to eat more supper. He said to Blake, "You ought to see the land they're giving away to the railroad, forty or fifty miles wide for right-of-way, all across the territory. People are coming in down there like crazy to work on the tracks and the railroad's promoting agriculture, towns, anything you can think of to get people to come and buy all that land. It's Indian land, goddam it to hell! Or it was once."

Alec's eyes were full of bitterness, misery, confusion.

Blake said lamely, "If they're all going into Wyoming Territory to work and settle, at least they're not coming here."

Alec shrugged, trying to veil his eyes. "Yes, I suppose if you have to find a good side to it . . . . But you ought to *see* what they're doing, to the woods, for instance, cutting timber for ties, just ruining everything. It would take centuries for the woods to come back the way they were, not that they'll ever be given the chance . . . . And their towns are as wild as any mining camp ever was. A lot of the people who are working on the railroad are ones who didn't find gold, either up here or to the south. Now that our governor's finally disbanded his mighty territorial militia, a lot of those people have gone to work on the railroad. They've also got Chinamen, Indians, I don't know what they haven't got—except law. Anybody can get away with just about anything he's big enough to try."

"Places always start out that way in this country, don't they?" Corie said mildly. "I mean, people get pretty extreme till they have the time to settle in and think about how things ought to be done. Lord! I remember how it was at Virginia City when we went there. Here, Alec, I want you to eat some more of this pie."

He shrugged away the pie, frowning. "The trouble is that most of the people who come out here never have any intention of staying. They're just out to get all they can as fast as they can, and then they mean to go back some place else and spend the rest of their lives living on the ruin of this country and bragging about how they did it. If settling new country attracts mostly the kind of people I've been seeing these past few months, maybe the place to go is somewhere where it's been settled for about three thousand years. If people are ever going to have any humanity, it might have started showing up by that time."

"People have humanity," Corie said placidly, gently. "There's some goodness in ever'body if you can see it."

"Hell!" Alec said wearily.

As the women were clearing away the dishes, he went to his packs and took out a bottle, from which he began drinking methodically, without pleasure.

Katy said, "Alec, do you want to go home tonight? If you do, we could . . . ."

"Let's stay here, if it's all right with Blake and Corie, until the storm's over. It would be hard now, getting up to the valley."

"You look so tired," she said tenderly.

He turned away and began talking to Blake about the ranch.

"Has everybody who's going left the village?" he asked after a time.

Blake nodded. "Most of the People went, even a few who had claims. The agents kept coming and talking to them, and Beaver Tooth talked, until they were worried enough to go. It's pretty empty down there."

Alec frowned at his pipe, which he couldn't seem to keep lighted. He put it down and drank from the bottle.

"This claim thing isn't going to work, Blake. You know it won't. We're going to spend a fortune, that we don't have, and everyone knows how it will come out."

"The lawyer, Morgan, thinks it'll make a good test case."

"I know what he thinks, but why should we and the People who are left be the test ingredients?"

"Somebody has to be, Alec, if anything's ever to be done. I keep thinking it's a little like a serious illness. If it can be lived with long enough, somebody may come up with a cure."

"You're getting damned sanguine since you've started another family."

"I guess some sanguinity is just about a necessity if a man's to keep on with living and bringing up kids."

Alec said dully, "I wish I could feel that way because it looks like that's what I'm in for, for a long while . . . . Has Stephens or Ellis Williams been back?"

"No, but they've bought land above here. I've heard they're having a big herd driven up from Texas next year."

"Goddam them. We ought to kill every cow of theirs that sets foot in the Medicine Rock."

"Hawk's Shadow's thought of that," Blake said dryly, "and it's a good thing to talk about, but, really, Alec, I don't see there's anything we can do. I don't want Stephens' people in the valley, or anybody else, but all we could do to keep them out is own the whole thing. That's not possible."

"I don't like seeing you resigned," Alec said sadly, then fiercely, "*I* don't like being helpless."

There was a silence and then he went on tiredly, "I ran into Stephens' boy down in one of the railroad camps. He was set up to be a kind of sheriff—Talmadge, his name is. He sees himself as a fast gun, besides being rich and having a powerful daddy and uncle and so on . . . . Some Snakes had killed a white railroad worker down there. The idiot had raped one of their girls. The young Stephens and his crowd captured a Snake boy. He hadn't had anything to do with the killing, but hell! one's as good —or bad—as another when it comes to Indians. They were ready to hang him. I had those Medicine Rock boys with me and we got him away from them."

"Was anyone shot?"

"No. That's what made it so hard for those whites to take. They were making a big town celebration of the hanging and we just walked in and took the boy. There were enough of us to get the drop on them. I even had leisure to make them a short speech."

Blake kept his worried eyes on the carving he was doing. He was making a wooden clock movement Corie wanted. It would take a long time.

Alec said, "I suppose you've heard about the new treaties?"

"Only that some more have been made. Since we don't have a chief who goes to councils anymore . . . ."

"Well, these are supposed to be awfully favorable to the tribes," he said bitterly. "Since the railroad will be in use soon, the government's agreed to close the Bozeman

442

Trail and the forts along it. The tribes are to have the Powder River country, for one thing, set aside as a communal hunting ground, henceforth and forever."

They were silent for a long time. The women were washing dishes in the kitchen. Gusts of wind came, occasionally, down the chimney and made the fire flare. Little Sylvia came, with her shy smile, and climbed on Blake's lap. He rubbed his cheek against her soft hair.

"And I suppose you've heard," Alec said scornfully, "that women can now vote in Wyoming. They introduced the bill just to get publicity for the territory. No one can quite explain how the damned thing got passed. It's funny, if you feel like laughing."

"I don't know," Blake said thoughtfully. "Things might be in better shape generally, if women had had a hand in making more decisions."

Alec shook his head in disgust. "Most women are more cruel than men. They're stubborn and tough and most of them can't see past their noses. The few there are in Wyoming are screaming their heads off for prohibition. My God! With all the wrongs that are being done! And all they can think of is outlawing whiskey!"

Katy had come in quietly to take Sylvia to bed and Alec said, trying to smile, "And it looks like women is what I'm going to be stuck with. It must run in the Mac-Pheirson family to have nothing but daughters."

The boy had truly meant, Blake thought, only to tease her, but Katy's eyes filled with tears as she turned away with the little girl in her arms.

Blake came down on a muddy, thawing day in the spring of 1868 to see Hawk's Shadow. Hawk's Shadow had been ill with chills and fever and finally, on this day of bright sunshine, he was feeling well enough to sit outside his lodge. Blake tied his horse to a tree. She was a young mare, skittish and frisky.

"Ho, Green Eyes," Hawk's Shadow greeted him weakly. "That is a fine-looking horse."

"She's Alec's, really."

"I could have guessed," said the other dryly. "You would have chosen a black or some such nonsense. I have

443

thought you were a bear, hibernating up there, that you did not come to see me."

"I've been here," Blake said. "It is only that you don't remember."

"Yes, I had fever dreams and times when I knew nothing around me. Still, I remember that your woman was here. Her medicines taste worse than those made by Little Rain."

They sat against Hawk's Shadow's lodge, put up near the cabin where Little Rain lived. She came out to offer food, but they preferred to smoke and be silent together for a time. Across the meadowland, on the other side of the creek, they could see the cabin of Eagle Feather and Snowbird, two of their children playing in its dooryard, Snowbird going in and out as she washed clothes.

Hawk's Shadow said sadly, "Nothing is left of our village now but lodge rings. It will take a long time before they can no longer be found."

Blake nodded and said nothing. His mind was being carried on a flood of memories: the first time he had struggled out to lie in spring sunshine at the Medicine Rock village and Hawk's Shadow had come and said he must get up and fight; the eagle-catching; the buffalo hunts; Shy Fawn; Red Sky; the village, noisy with dogs and children, quarreling and laughter.

Hawk's Shadow said, "I don't understand why so many of the young ones left. They said, finally, that living on the reservation would be better than staying here in the valley, that on the reservation they would be able to live more with their own kind, without whites always coming in, but it seems to me the young ones would want to stay and fight for what has been theirs since Winter Thunder led the People here."

"It's easier for the young ones to change," Blake said a little absently. "For some of them."

"And to be fools," Hawk's Shadow said hotly. "Except for Beaver Tooth who always stands with his hand out, nothing the whites have promised has come to the People. I am glad, at least, that Eagle Feather is no fool. Sometimes I say that he is, for digging in the ground and those things, but, even with that, he holds to the Valley and to some of the old ways. The People who are left have great

444

trust in him. He understands more of this differentness that comes than the rest of us do—far more than those like Beaver Tooth, who are so eager to change and don't know what they're doing . . . . I have been weak and ill and I could not help thinking during this time. I have thought that it is the ones like Eagle Feather who will keep the People alive. Those young ones who have gone to the reservations will learn enough of white ways to try to be whites, only they won't be, because they won't learn enough, and the whites won't allow them to be anything. They will forget that they are of the People and after a time they will be nothing at all."

Anger crossed his face, frustration, sadness. Finally his expression grew quieter, resigned, tinged with pride.

"I used to hope that Eagle Feather my son could become something like Red Sky my father. I think Red Sky would understand my meaning if I say that, in some ways, the boy is even better."

"I was just thinking," Blake said softly, "that you are very much like Red Sky today."

Hawk's Shadow looked away, shy and pleased. "I look like him, perhaps, but I am *not* like him. I care for the People, but I have always cared more for myself. Eagle Feather is both a dreamer and a practical man and, in him, the two things go together in just the right way. Dreams are good if a man makes them work for him. Red Sky was saddened by the changes he felt coming. He thought all we could do was to hide from them, but I think there is no longer a place to hide. Eagle Feather tries to find how they can be turned to our good, if they must come. *I* will not change. I am too old—Little Rain says I am too stupid—but because there are a few like Eagle Feather I think things may be better, easier, for my grandchildren."

Deliberately, Hawk's Shadow rid his face of its deep, thoughtful seriousness.

"Have you seen the butterflies, Blake?"

"I couldn't help seeing them. They're covering the valley."

"About once in every ten or fifteen springs, I have seen them come like this. They are like flowers on the bushes and grass. Perhaps they bring good news to us . . . . How

445

is it with your family? Corie has been here, torturing me, but what of the others? Is the new boy well?"

"He is."

Hawk's Shadow said dryly, "A child of that woman's would be very strong . . . . Alec has stayed in the high valley through the winter?"

"Most of the time."

"He was very sad when he came back from the south. It would be better for him, perhaps, if he did not go away so often. Alec takes things very hard, as you always have."

"I think he's better now, after the winter."

"Yes, winters here are good . . . . I wish Alec might have had a medicine dream when he was a boy. The sadness of not finding one stays in his eyes. Perhaps some day he can accept that medicine dreams are not given to everyone. Perhaps, too, some of his sadness and restlessness is because he has had only the two daughters. When a man can watch his son growing up, it makes many things different for him. If there are things that a man feels he has missed, he can hope that perhaps those things will come to his son."

Eagle Feather's oldest daughter, a girl of about six, came running across the meadow.

"Hello, my grandfather and my uncle," she said with a shy smile. "My mother has made these cookies and sent you some. We have many more in our house."

She was a beautiful child. Her long, heavy hair stirred a little in the breeze and one of the myriad butterflies had come to rest briefly on her shoulder. Hawk's Shadow gestured her close to him and whispered to her. She smiled conspiratorially and went into his lodge.

"Still," he said, trying to careless, "there are some points to daughters—and granddaughters."

The little girl came back and shyly offered Blake a bow.

"Grandfather has made this for you. He is the finest bowmaker of the tribe and this is his finest bow."

Blake took it and could say nothing. He studied the craftsmanship through blurred eyes.

"It's beautiful, Hawk's Shadow," he finally said huskily. "I never really thought you'd do it."

"It was a long winter," said Hawk's Shadow carelessly. "I had little else to do. I have only just finished it, now that I grow stronger. But it is made for shooting, Blake. It is a very fine bow and, if you had ever learned how to be a right kind of persōn, you would not just take it home and hang it on a wall . . . . I have made no stone arrowheads because I have no proper stone now. The best stone for that comes from that stinking country to the south. Perhaps we will go there again one day, when you are not too busy looking to the welfare of cows and horses . . . . That is a thing I do not understand. The horses of the People could always look after themselves for the most part, and I think they were finer, stronger animals than the ones you ranchers have now."

Eagle Feather's little daughter said importantly, "I must go now, to help my mother. Since I am the oldest, there is always much for me to do. Later in the day, Grandfather, I will come back and talk with you again."

They were silent for a time when she had gone. Blake's hand caressed the deer sinew covering of the bow.

"I am told," Hawk's Shadow said heavily, "that the buffalo are almost gone. Many have been killed for their skins only, and the meat left to rot. I would like some meat from a buffalo's hump now, and a large piece of the liver. That would make me strong much more quickly than this stuff of roots and bad-tasting herbs our wives dream up to force on a sick man . . . . Tell me, Blake, what will happen about this thing of the homestead claims?"

"I don't know, Hawk's Shadow. The lawyer, Mr. Morgan, will take it to the courts for us, but it will take a long time. The courts are far away and never in a hurry to make decisions."

"Eagle Feather tells me these courts are a kind of white man's council."

"Yes. Something like that."

Hawk's Shadow moved irritably. "I will never understand how white men's councils feel they have the right to decide whether or not we can have these little pieces of land in a valley that has always belonged to the People . . . . Still, we are here, those who truly belong to the val-

447

ley. Eagle Feather says that so long as they are playing with their laws and decisions, they are not trying to take the land . . . . What is that dust?"

They looked down the valley.

"It must be many riders or a large herd of animals," Hawk's Shadow said.

They at silently, waiting.

"It's cattle," Hawk's Shadow said finally, wearily.

Blake said, "It must be the herd Stephens is sending up here to put on the land he's bought."

There was another silence. The ugly, lean longhorns, hazed by a half dozen men, moved up along the creek, swinging their heads and bawling protestingly.

Hawk's Shadow said fiercely, "If I had arrows for that bow of yours, there would not be so many. Their meat would not be buffalo, but it would be very good for me to cook and eat it. Do you know, when the Stephens boy was here, what he asked Eagle Feather? He asked him who has climbed to the top of Never Summer. Eagle Feather told him that we all hunt on the mountain but that, so far as he knew, no one had followed game or had had any other reason to go to the top of the peak. That would be a very hard climb. A man could hardly even do it with ropes and another to help him. Why would a man want to?"

"It's a thing some whites like to do," Blake said heavily. "I suppose it makes them feel bigger, as important, in a way, as the mountain itself, if they can stand on the very top of it. It's a kind of conquering, maybe."

"Have you done it?"

"No."

Hawk's Shadow frowned at the passing cattle. "How can a man think he can conquer a mountain?" he said incredulously, expecting no answer.

Alec came into the barn where Blake was cleaning.

"That's not much of a job for a big rancher," he said, attempting lightness.

It was autumn again. Alec and Eagle Feather and others had been out branding cattle, cutting out and sorting the ones they would be driving down to the railroad. The men felt it necessary now that one of them be always within sight or call of the houses.

Young Talmadge Stephens and his half dozen riders had been making trouble for the people in the Valley, Indian and white, since the day they had driven in their cattle and begun building on the land up the creek. They had threatened and quarreled, broken fences, run off cattle, run cattle over fields, set fire to hay when it was cut and dried and ready for hauling, frightened women and children, kept the Valley in turmoil through the summer. Blake had managed to persuade the people not to do too much in the way of retaliation. The homestead claim case was pending and he kept reminding them doggedly that they must do nothing to damage their chances.

Then, a week ago, when Katy and Alec and the children were not at home, Stephens' men had burned the old cabin in the high valley to the ground. The need for reprisal was becoming a burning, festering thing in all of them. It had hurt Blake deeply, seeing only the charred stones of the cabin's chimney left standing above its rubble. A hardness had come into him, a determination that he and his family, and as many of the People as wanted to, would stay in the Valley, that a part of it would belong to them for as long as they wanted it, that they would *not* be driven out. He went away alone in the woods to think about it after looking at the burned cabin, and he came back, knowing still that the only way to hold onto what they had was to try to maintain their share of the peace, to protect, as best they could, what was theirs by legal right, to persevere in living.

"We ought to kill ever' sonofabitch that rides for Stephens," Eli had raged at a meeting they had held that evening. "Don't you know killin'll be *their* next step? They've already took pot shots at some of us."

"If we killed them," Blake said tiredly, "more would come. We can't kill everyone."

"What do they want with the whole valley?" raged Emmett. "They've got more than enough grazin' up there for the herd they've got."

"It's a matter of principle," Alec said grimly. "*They* know what this land was intended for—them—and, be-

449

sides, nobody has ever crossed a Stephens. They've always had enough money so that nobody's dared, or if anyone began to dare, he could be bought off. It's not in them to understand that people might get a feeling for land or that anyone would have the gall to stand up to them. Con MacPheirson says old man Stephens will be appointed territorial governor next time, and then God help us all."

"Even if he is," Eagle Feather said harshly, "they will not take our land. There are not kings in this country, as I have read about in other places, who can ignore the people's right."

Alec was about to say something caustic, but Blake frowned at him, his eyes pleading. As the men went on talking worriedly, Blake thought yearningly of all those years when he had had the high valley to run to for sanctuary. The valley was there, but there was no longer such escape for him. He was too deeply involved now with too many things, too many people.

That night, neither he nor Corie could sleep.

"Blake," she said tenderly, "it's more than bein' madder than fire and kind of helpless about that Stephens bunch. I know that. That cabin was a lot of your life."

"I have a life now," he said, "you and Richard, Alec's family, Hawk's Shadow and Eagle Feather and the rest. We'll work things out, with time."

"You never in your life meant or wanted to get this mixed up and responsible for other people," she said sympathetically. "All you've ever wanted is to be quiet and left alone."

"Still," he said, grateful for her understanding, "I wouldn't have anything changed, about us or . . . ."

"I went up there," she said almost shyly, "to see about your castle. It was just fine. Nobody had touched it. Thank the Lord it's a good way from the cabin and they didn't know about it. And, Blake . . . . the mountain's still there."

Except for Blake, the men had all started carrying pistols. He was afraid he could not trust himself not to use one if he had it, and he felt he might not come out of another experience of killing as a whole, sane man.

"We've got the steers sorted for shipping," Alec said

now, in the barn. "The others want to leave in the morning, to start them down toward the railroad. Why don't you go with them? It's been a long time since you've been anywhere."

"You go," Blake said, leaning on his pitchfork. "I want to stay here."

"The guardian of the valley," Alec said softly, without derision. Then, "That lawyer, Morgan, sent word by Con that we're to come and see him, you or me, with Eagle Feather. The case is supposed to come up during the winter and some of us may have to go to Washington."

"You go, Alec. If it's talking to the court he wants, you can do it a hell of a lot better than I can and Eagle Feather would rather have you with him. Besides, you ought to see Washington."

"However it comes out," Alec said, "I wish Hawk's Shadow would go, too. I'd like him to be able to hear Eagle Feather in court. It's Eagle Feather that Mr. Morgan is basing the whole case on. What an orator he is! When I listened to him in the territorial court, I could hardly believe he's the same man who hunts and plows and shovels manure around here."

"His grandfather was like that, *your* grandfather."

After a little silence, Alec said, "I've been trying to think what I ought to do now, about Katy and the girls. If I'm going down with the cattle, and then maybe to Helena and Washington, I was wondering if they could stay on with you."

"That seems like the best thing."

"After the old cabin was burned, I was thinking again of building down here somewhere, maybe just across the creek there, but with Katy pregnant again and all this trouble, I'd rather not leave them alone."

"They'll be welcome with us for the winter. Corie and I have talked about it."

Alec made a wry face. "I knew I could count on Corie to have the plans made before they occurred to anybody else." But there was no bitterness in his tone, only kind of satirical resignation.

"And how does Katy feel about staying with us?" Blake asked tentatively.

"I think you know how Katy feels about both of you.

451

She's been lonely, often, up there in the high valley and, even when I've been around, that hasn't been much help to her. Now there's going to be another kid . . . .

"I think maybe I understand, a little, how things are for you, Blake. You always liked being by yourself, keeping a little apart from other people's fights and all. Well, *I* never wanted a family. We both seem to be stuck in kind of the same way. I'd like to try some things I haven't tried before. Probably they'd turn out to be wrong and disappointing, but I guess I'll always wonder . . . . There's not much chance for experimenting when I've got a wife and three kids, but, at least, I think I've stopped blaming Katy. It's hell sometimes, looking back and seeing the things I've ignored until they've died.

"When we were first married, Katy was— We might have been happy, only I couldn't let it happen. Now, it's just sort of a marriage of mutual toleration and we keep adding kids to it, compounding the problems."

Alec had picked up a handful of new straw, letting it drop through his fingers. He crumbled what was left in a hard, tense fist, his eyes bleak and baffled.

"Maybe you could build something new," Blake said gently. "You're both older now, and smart enough to know how to make the most of what there is. Things can grow, Alec, even feelings can, when—"

"Only you have to want to try," Alec said heavily. "That's been the trouble all along. I've never wanted, enough, to try. I know how selfish I am. If I didn't know it for myself, Corie and Connall and others have damn well told me so often enough. I'm sorry about it. Often, looking at Katy and the girls, thinking about them, I hate myself for not feeling more than I do, but I just *can't,* and I've never been any good at faking. And when I try that, Katy always knows and it's no good.

"After this, though, there won't be any more babies. I've sworn that much to myself. I'm an injustice as a father and there are already three too many . . . . I think Katy keeps hoping, every time there's to be another one, that some miracle will happen. Hell, this kind of world is no place to bring kids into. There's nothing I can give them and there never have been any miracles."

"Life is a kind of miracle, Alec."

He shrugged that away impatiently. "If you can only teach a kid bitterness and cynicism, what's the point in its being alive? If you give it a bunch of sloppy falsehoods about innate goodness and such things, all that's going to happen to it is that it will be battered to death by disillusionment."

"What about some middle ground? A little of both."

"There isn't any, Blake, not that I've ever been able to believe in, and I couldn't lie to a kid. It would be a crime to give falseness. Kids know when you're acting, too."

"Alec, a lot of living with other people is a kind of acting. We do, often, what we need to, or what we think we ought to, or just what someone else wants. That kind of thing has never yet killed anybody."

"Since I can remember, you've told me how important it is to find out who I am and then be myself."

"But life isn't such a question of extremes," Blake insisted earnestly. "You don't have to give up being yourself to give in a little to what other people are . . . . Some of the things I taught you were a little wrong, or you took them in a little differently than I meant them. I stressed some things to you because I was only beginning to learn them myself. I was fascinated in those days with thinking, with finding out who *I* was. I hadn't done that kind of thing as a boy because it wasn't allowed. By the time you were old enough to talk to and to begin to understand a little, I was just getting the feel, for myself, of beginning to experiment with freedom of thought, and of trying to come to terms with myself. You had too many big doses of that kind of thought and talk when you were too young . . . . I'm sorry."

"It wasn't easy to try to think about things that way when I was a kid," Alec said slowly. "It's still not, and yet I wouldn't want to be the other way, just breathing and eating, like a cow, satisfied with nothing more than that, but I wish . . . . sometimes I wish there could be something that makes me really proud or really angry, or really happy. I think I just don't have the—capacity to let anything go very deep. I just don't know what it's like to feel I've truly achieved something."

"What do you want most to achieve?"

Alec walked restlessly around the small, dim barn. "I

don't know, Blake. Everything, I suppose. No matter what I manage, it always falls short. I know it's me. It's not the things I do or other people that make things come out seeming that way. If I had the nerve to blame circumstances or people, everything might be a lot simpler and easier. At least, if I could really believe it's the fault of something besides myself, I'd have somewhere to start trying to set it right. As it is, I just don't know . . . ."

"If you want to go east and live for a while—maybe study more painting or something like that—there'd be money enough from the ranch. We could—"

Alec laughed grimly. "I'm twenty-four years old. It's a little past the time for sending me off to school to be straightened out. Besides, haven't you read what the critics say? I'm a natural artist. Any more formal training might hamper my talent.

"No, I don't want to study painting. If I went east or anywhere else, I'd be taking *me* with me, the same problems and questions. Goddam it! Why can't I just settle down and be happy with what I've got?"

It was a plea, a cry of desperate helplessness. Alec's face was contorted as he turned away to look out the barn door. Blake was afraid of the responsibility the questions asked him to carry, afraid he would say the wrong thing, but he said slowly, "I was going to say, before, that life with other people is basically a series of little shiftings and adjustments. After you begin getting used to making them, they get easier. You begin to be able to take some pleasure in them and to see that you're not always the only one who can be right about how things ought to be done. It can be pleasant and it can get to be a habit."

"Is that how it is, for you and Corie?"

"Something like that, only most of the time, Corie has made it very easy for me. I'm afraid it's been worse for her, at times."

"The two of you are about as different as day and night."

"Still, I think we're a damned good combination."

"Well, maybe your second son won't give you so many gray hairs."

"Alec—" Blake began, but Alec interrupted.

"Somebody's coming."

454

Talmadge Stephens sat his horse and looked down at them disdainfully. He was a big blond man, handsome in a heavy-boned, pugnacious sort of way, perhaps thirty years old.

"I've come to warn you," he said without preamble, "to keep your goddam redskin pets off my land. We had our steers sorted and corralled and now some of those bastards have broken the fence."

"The cattle could have done that themselves," Blake pointed out, trying to keep his voice casual.

"Cattle, hell! Anybody is seen on that land up there, my men have got orders to shoot on sight."

"The same could go for this land," Alec said tautly.

"You'd just better mind what I say, if you don't want to start burying people—that is, if anybody wants to call those savages people. Just keep them away from my place till the goddam courts get through with this mess you've made. Then we won't have to worry about them, nor you either. Both you sonsofbitches'll rot in jail for fraud and forgery and this land'll be mine, free and clear."

"You've got a lot more land now than you're using," Blake pointed out, still trying to be calm and reasonable. "This country never has overtly operated under a feudal system, if it's a land baron you're trying to be. And we just may not go to jail. It could be that the courts will validate the claims."

Stephens gave a short explosion of unpleasant laughter.

"Shit! My family's got more money and influence back east than you could scrape up in this whole goddam lousy territory. If you think you've even got a prayer with this case, you're in for a mighty big disappointment and I'd just like hell to see you to have to suffer that. The very goddam cockeyed idea that those savages would be allowed to own land like white men! Homestead land! Or you two, either, you, a squaw man, and your breed bastard."

"You just can't get over it, can you?" Alec said smoothly. "How I took your Snake prisoner away from you that time down in Wyoming. Did people laugh a lot, Sheriff? My God! The kid didn't have a word of English. You tracked him down, in your great bravery, and caught him while he was taking a crap. You—"

455

Stephens moved but Alec's pistol was already in his hand. Alec spoke quickly, in a hard, harsh voice Blake had not heard before.

"There's little enough law in this country and I doubt there'll ever be justice, but you're not the dispenser or bringer of either, not on this land. You've burned and destroyed and disrupted about as much as you're going to. If it wasn't for Blake, you and everything in the upper valley would have been dead a long time ago. You'd better go home and round up your cattle and fix your fence. Any animal comes on this land, we run our brand on, and the same goes for people, starting in about ten seconds."

"You've lost one cabin, breed," said Stephens fiercely. "That leaves one to go, plus two women and God knows how many bastard kids. Me and the boys could find some use for that little redhead before we finished her off."

They stood silent, unmoving, not looking at each other until he was out of sight. Alec's hand shook as he reholstered the pistol.

"Goddam it to hell! Why didn't I just shoot the sonofabitch and have done with it?" he cried harshly.

"What would it have solved?" Blake said wearily. "Sit down, Alec."

The boy's face had flushed fiercely and now it was completely drained of color.

"I don't want to sit down, and for Christ's sake, don't start telling me how wrong it is to take life and—"

"Words are just—words, Alec. You're feeling exactly the way he intended you should."

Alec stared at him angrily. "How can you be so goddam calm? You *have* to be mad or—or . . . ."

Corie had come running out of the house.

"Was that Stephens I saw ridin' away? What did he—"

She stopped, looking from one of them to the other.

"Dinner'll be ready in a half hour," she said quietly to Blake and went back to the house, stumbling a little because her eyes had filled with tears.

"Of course I'm angry," Blake said a little unevenly, "but killing Stephens won't accomplish anything. He and his father and Ellis Williams have got some of the influence he thinks they have. A thing like that could be used in this case against us and the People. Don't you see? Any excuse—"

"The case can go to hell!" Alec cried. "It's hopeless anyway. It always has been. God, Blake! Surely you've always known that. I can't stand any more of being—"

"Alec, killing somebody is not hard to do at the time, if you're angry or hurt or scared enough, but after that, it can be a hard thing to have to live with. You may think, at the time, that the person you kill is not fit to live, but then you get to wondering. You wonder if there wasn't someone who loved him, if he didn't enjoy seeing the sun come up, things like that . . . ."

"You're talking about those Blackfeet now," Alec said more quietly, tiredly.

"Yes. I don't want anything like that to happen to you."

There was a silence and Alec said heavily, "All right, if you know so many answers, just how things ought to be handled, what are we going to do?"

"There's a sheriff at Harmony now," Blake said after a moment, trying to conceal the hurt. "I don't have any illusions that he'll be much good to us, but if you'll wait one more day to leave with the cattle, I'll ride down there and talk to him. I'll ask Wyeth to go with me and maybe Connall will come too, just to get as much weight as we can behind what we're saying. We'll get it on the record, what's been going on in the valley. That's about all I think we can expect of him, to record the fact that we have complaints. But that way, if anything more happens, we'll at least have the records to back us up."

"Records can be destroyed, especially when such a request is made by somebody with so goddam much influence as the Stephens bunch."

"Yes, but I'm doing what I can. That's all I know to do."

"I've heard you say, when I was a kid, to Connall and other people, that nobody ought to put any dependence on white men's laws."

"But the laws are here, Alec, to a degree. They're what there is to depend on in this kind of thing, and it seems we have to try to depend on something. The time is passing when every man could be his own law and had only to

457

worry about depending on himself. there are too many of us now; things are too complicated. The country's changing and if we're going to live here, we've got to try to work with what there is."

"I never thought I'd hear you say a thing like that and see you looking so—resigned to it."

"It comes as something of a shock to me," Blake said dryly. "But I love this country. It's one of the best things that's ever happened to me. I want you and Richard and your children to have what's best from it. It seems that arranging for that, trying to, means going along with several things that aren't just what I'd like them to be. In getting, it seems we always have to give something. It's taken me a long time to learn that, to come to be reconciled to it. It can be a frightening thing . . . . But since I've begun to see it, I've come to think, more and more, that it's, maybe, the most basic precept there is."

"You've changed," Alec said slowly, bleakly.

"Not so much. But what's wrong with *some* change? If a man stops changing altogether, stops growing and trying to revise himself a little, he just stultifies, doesn't he? He just becomes one of those you were talking about before, who's satisfied with just eating and breathing."

"You have to be awfully sure of yourself, to feel right about all that revision stuff."

"I'm not all that sure, Alec. I doubt that anyone is ever as sure as they may seem to someone else."

"Go ahead, with what you were saying."

Blake said slowly, "I used to think, when ideas that were new to me would come, that I'd discovered some great truth that no one else had ever thought about." He smiled ruefully. "That never was so. A lot of people in every generation as far back as Man goes have come upon those same truths. Only the beauty of it, that I've finally come to see, is that those things *are* new, they are a little different each time someone finds them for himself. Maybe that kind of—rebirth of thought is the thing that puts the drives in us, to love people, to own land, to raise children, just to—make the effort of being."

"To build castles," Alec said softly. "I always have envied you." Then he smiled. "You ought to write all this stuff down. You might come to be known as the philosopher of the Medicine Rock. People would beat a path to your door to glean pearls of wisdom."

Blake grinned. "God save us from anybody else beating paths."

XXI

IT WAS NEAR SUNDOWN when they left the Camas and turned up Medicine Rock Creek. There was a rutted, well-worn trail now, that the people in the valley had worked on from time to time as a community project, so that, in good weather, it could be traversed by a buckboard with reasonable ease. This was not good weather and Blake was having problems. There had not been as much snow as usual that winter, but it was melting now and the road was heavy with mud. From the looks of the sky, there would be rain before they reached home.

They had bought the buckboard in Helena and it was a joy to Corie. She was planning all sorts of outings.

"It's all right for you men to ride horseback ever'where," she said, "but I just ain't made for it anymore. This way, we can take Richard along, and Katy and the children, without havin' to worry somebody'll get their neck broke. Emmett's and Eli's families got buckboards a long time back and even Eagle Feather broke down and bought one. I'm glad you finally gave up for it."

Blake was not glad, not at this moment as he cursed to himself, helping the horses to get the thing unstuck again. His mind went back briefly to the time he had come west with Henry Melton and the missionaries. How old Henry could curse when the wagons were stuck!

But he could not be cross for long about the buckboard. It was a thing that so thoroughly pleased Corie and he liked seeing her pleased. Also, they were getting into sandier soil now; the mud should not be so bad the rest of the way home. And it was always good to be coming home. It seemed to him they had been away a long while. He looked up at Never Summer with the spring rain clouds moving fitfully around its peak and stopped caring much about the mud.

The hearing on the Medicine Rock homestead claims had been postponed again, but Clay Morgan, the attorney, had sent word that he wanted to talk to Blake. It seemed the government had some questions, perhaps even a proposition, and Morgan needed a consultation.

Blake had not wanted to go. He wanted to leave the Valley no more now than he ever had. There were Corie and Richard, Alec and his family, the ranch, the People. Periods of the old restlessness still came on him occasionally, but usually it was enough to go away in the mountains alone for a day or two. He was too busy, mostly too happy to be restless often.

Talmadge Stephens had left the Valley in the fall, when he took his cattle to the railroad. Two men had been left to look after his interests through the winter, but there had been no more trouble. Overall, it had been a good, quiet winter for all of them. Alec had been at home a good deal of the time and he and Blake had added two rooms to the crowded house. When the message came from Morgan, they were making plans to break and plant a big grain field. They needed more grain. Their horses were becoming finer, more sought after with each generation. Alec had offers for them as riding horses, cow horses, offers from enthusiasts of quarter-mile racing.

Blake tried earnestly to persuade Alec and Eagle Feather to go to Helena but they refused.

"You started this whole thing by coming to the Valley in the first place," Alec said.

They were sitting in the house after the noon meal because there was a heavy spring snowstorm outside. Hawk's Shadow and Eagle Feather had come because the weather was too bad for Eagle Feather to be working. Hawk's Shadow said, "He did not come to the Valley. He was carried here, dead."

"Anyhow," Alec continued adamantly to Blake, "you're the one with the stubborn faith that it can be worked out. It's you Morgan needs."

"And take Corie with you," added Katy, stacking dishes. "You can leave Richard here with us and have yourselves a nice trip."

"You don't need another young-un to take care of now," Corie told her.

Katy's third child was due and she had not been feeling well for some time.

"What difference will one more make?" she said lightly. "Sylvia's getting big enough to be some help and Rebecca's said she'll help out any time."

Rebecca was the youngest daughter of Storm Coming Out Of The East and she was making ready for her marriage to a white man. Frank Boyd had started a ranch on the upper Camas a few years ago and his wife had died, leaving him with four children. Katy and Corie had been helping Rebecca to make herself a "white" wardrobe.

It was clear to all of them that Corie wanted to go to Helena, and Blake wanted her to. She always took such chatty pleasure in everything that she made the trip worthwhile for him, almost.

They rode down to Harmony and took the new stage line. The roads were in deplorable condition and it took a long while getting to Helena. It was Blake's conviction that they would have done much better on their own, but he only said so once or twice. Corie enjoyed speculating about the stage driver, the other passengers, practically everything they passed.

In town, Blake talked with Morgan, and Corie looked through all the stores. She bought some necessities and complained about the prices of everything, but she thought it was becoming rather a nice place, as new, western towns went.

Blake bought the buckboard without her knowledge and she cried with pleasure when he showed it to her. He borrowed a team from Con MacPheirson to use with it and to be returned when that could be managed.

On the way back they had had to stop at Wyeth's. It was late in the evening when they arrived. Corie, Wyeth, and Ethel had all insisted they must not leave until after noonday dinner the following day. "So," Corie said thoughtfully now as they drove slowly through Medicine Rock Canyon, "Mr. Morgan don't know when the case may come up again?"

"Maybe it never will," Blake said. "It's happened before that a case has just been put away in the government files and more or less forgotten. They'd like very much to forget this one. It's getting to be a pretty sticky business, involving quite a lot more than just some questionable homestead claims. It turns out that more people than just the ones around here are interested. It's finally begun to occur to some, it seems, that the treatment of most Indians hasn't been exactly equitable, and some of the ones it's occurring to are people with a good bit of influence."

"More than Stephens and his bunch?"

"Clay Morgan thinks so. He knows some influential ones in Washington and he's kept things pretty well stirred up."

"So the gover'ment's kind of got its tail in a crack," she said with relish.

He grinned. "I guess you might put it that way."

"Well, what do *we* do now? I mean, what about costs and all that?"

"There won't be any more costs until something else happens. It's up to the government whether the case ever goes any farther. We certainly don't want to press for any kind of action. We have the deeds. Morgan has never charged us anything for his work. I don't like the man much but he's doing a damn good job for us and this kind of thing could jeopardize his whole career."

"Why don't you like him?"

"Oh, because he treats this like a charity matter, like he's doing a big favor for the poor, down-trodden savages, when all we and the People are asking for is justice."

"Now you sound like Alec," she said impatiently. "I declare, with both of you, when it comes to anything Indian, a body's damned if he does and damned if he don't. Did you ever think of it the other way? He might just *build* his career on a thing like this. Anyway, what difference does it make if he *does* think of it as a charity thing? You've just said he's doin' a good job. Maybe

463

thinkin' of it as charitable makes him work harder and feel good about himself. You know what the Bible says about charity."

"I know, Corie," he said resignedly, smiling.

After a little silence, she asked, frowning, "Do you reckon Talmadge Stephens or any of them will be comin' back up here soon?"

"Maybe they've found some new and better interests over the winter," Blake said, not feeling very hopeful.

"I've heard," she reported, "at Harmony and around, that Talmadge's tried nearly ever'thing and that he has never been able to do anything to please his daddy. Maybe that's how he come to be so mean."

It was growing dark and a few drops of rain were falling. The only cabin of the People's that was near the road seemed deserted as they passed.

"I wonder where White Bear's folks are at," Corie said idly, reaching down to pull up a buffalo robe. "That rain sure is cold."

"If we were riding horses," Blake reminded her ungraciously, "we'd have been home by now."

She laughed a little and touched his hand holding the reins.

"Blake, you wouldn't enjoy Heaven if they was to let you in . . . . Do you remember that it was rainin' the first time we came home here, when we were first married?"

"Yes, I remember," he said softly.

"I'm glad winter's about over," she said, after a moment. "I guess I never will quite get used to so much cold and snow . . . . Maybe the third grandchild will have been born while we were gone. Lord, I *do* hope it's a boy this time. Katy wants a boy so bad. You think they're gettin' on better, don't you, Katy and Alec?"

He said slowly, "I think they're settling into a kind of resignation to things as they are. It's not what either of them wanted."

She said tenderly, "Not many people are lucky enough to get just what they want, the way I have." Then with more gusto, "But it just seems to me like if Alec would do somethin' with himself. It's just a plain waste for a boy like him to spend his life horse tradin' and chasin' cows."

"What do you think he ought to do?"

464

"I don't know, Blake," she said impatiently. "He could be governor if he wanted to and could keep his smart mouth shut at the right times. With the talent he's got he could—I don't know—paint the White House or somethin'. Don't laugh. You know I don't know anything about what's to be done with that kind of talent. It just seems to me like a lot of his trouble comes from not *usin'* what he's got. He'll never be satisfied here, really . . . . You're the same way."

"You mean I ought to paint the White House?"

"Now, Blake, quit. I'm tryin' to say serious things. I mean there are so many other things you could have done. Only, thank the Lord you came here and stayed till I got here. I guess, I hope, you're about as content with the ranch and us as you'll ever let yourself be with anything, but I just don't believe it'll do for Alec."

"I love you, Corie."

"And I love you."

There was silence. Her hand on his was warm as the rain grew heavier. She said firmly, "And I'll tell you somethin', though you'll probably get a swelled head from it. You're a better lookin' man than I've ever seen, for one with three grandchildren. Sometimes I just wonder how you ever came to marry me, a smart, handsome man like you."

"Women were scarce," he said. "Besides, you told me to, didn't you?"

"Shoot!" she said, smiling. "You'd had nearly twenty years to look for a woman. It was time somebody told you somethin'."

"It was a long time," he said softly. "Sometimes, I thought you'd never come."

"Blake," she said tenderly and, after a moment, almost diffidently, "sometimes it scares me, how lucky I am to have got you and Richard. I know I don't deserve to be near so happy."

"You deserve a hell of a lot more than you've got," he said fervently and kissed her. Then he smiled. "When you say things like that, I begin to think you're crazy as a bedbug."

It was her expression and she smiled, giving him back his own.

"Why do you say a bedbug's crazy? You're just lookin' at it from a human point of view. Now if you was to see things the way another bedbug does . . . ."

People were standing on the porch when they drove up to the house. It was too dark to see faces, but something in their attitudes, the way they stood and shifted together to peer at the approaching buckboard, made Blake immediately uneasy. Corie, leaning lightly against him, stiffened and said in a tight, frightened voice, "Somethin's happened."

Eagle Feather moved reluctantly down the steps to meet them."

"Alec's hurt," he said tautly. "He's hurt badly, and Katy's in labor."

They pieced the story together in the midst of a quiet, frightened, worried turmoil. Rebecca, the Medicine Rock girl who had been helping Katy, had gone out to look for the cow for the evening's milking. She was a stupid, stubborn cow and rarely came home on her own. Rebecca had had to go a long way, looking for the cow, and she had been assaulted in the wooded pasture by three white men.

The men had then come down to the house, one of them carrying the battered, terrified girl before him across his saddle. Alec had just come in from the barn and was washing up for supper, his belt with its pistol hanging on the wall. The three men had wrecked the house, terrorized the women and children, and beaten and kicked Alec so severely that Corie, working over him with Little Rain, said through her tears, "He's bled so much I—I just don't see how he can last through the night."

Katy, in the throes of grinding labor, kept sobbing, "Two of them would hold him and the other would beat him. Oh, they said such awful, dirty things! They tried to make Alec say things and all he would do was curse them —with the blood running out of his mouth."

"You don't have any idea who they were?" Blake asked her, trying to gentle his roughened voice. He was trembling.

"I know Talmadge Stephens or some of those people sent them. They said the only reason they were leaving any of us alive was so that we could be an example to breeds and Indian lovers. They burned the one barn and started a fire in the kitchen, but Rebecca and I were able to get that one out. I couldn't do anything for Alec, not anything that helped him. He was bleeding so badly and I was so afraid . . . . The children couldn't stop screaming and then I started . . . . Rebecca had to go and get help and she's hurt herself . . . . Blake, if Alec—"

"Now, Katy," Corie said with what firmness she could muster, "You've got to quit talkin' and frettin'. You need your strength, honey. There's the baby to think about. We're seein' to Alec."

Blake found Hawk's Shadow and Storm Coming Out Of The East standing in the darkness of the porch, waiting silent and immobile. He said to Hawk's Shadow, his voice low and hard, "Can you track them in this rain?"

"I can track them."

Richard and the two little girls had finally gone to sleep under Snowbird's soothing; they were completely exhausted by terror. Some of the People had gone home. Alec lay on the bed in the front room, white and still. Eagle Feather sat beside him, his face dark with rage and helplessness. Corie and Little Rain passed in and out of the bedroom where Katy lay.

"We're going to find them," Blake said softly to Corie as she hurried toward the kitchen.

"Blake, please don't!" she cried in a low voice, her eyes frightened and pleading. "Let somebody go get the sheriff or—"

"I can't, Corie," he said harshly. "The sheriff's too far away and trouble in the Medicine Rock doesn't get him many votes. Surely, you see I can't just let them go."

"I do see, but . . . ."

"We'll be back when we can," he said and she held him close and let him go.

Saying nothing, Eagle Feather stood up from beside Alec's bed and followed Blake from the house.

Blake woke reluctantly. From the light at the bedroom window, he knew he had slept later than he should have. Dimly, he remembered the baby's crying a little earlier

467

and Corie's getting up to care for him. None of them had had enough sleep these past few weeks. He got up and dressed quickly, feeling stiff and unrested.

In the kitchen, Corie sat in a rocking chair, holding Katy's baby boy on one arm and churning with the other hand. Little Sylvia was folding diapers.

"I'm helping," the little girl told Blake proudly.

"You're a fine help," he said. "I don't know what we'd do without you."

"Daddy's up," said Sylvia. "He went to sit on the porch."

Corie nodded worriedly. "He oughtn't to be movin' around so much yet, but I couldn't get him to stay in bed. You ought to go out there with him, Blake. Maybe he'll talk to you. He looks to me like he's about as far down as he can go."

"You need some wood," he said, looking at the empty wood box.

"It can wait a while or I can cut it myself. Richard and Sarah Ellen are still asleep. I think maybe we'll have breakfast a little late this mornin'. It's Sunday, you know."

He hadn't known. The days had run together in a blur of sadness, worry, and exhaustion. He poured two cups of coffee and carried them to the porch. When Sylvia would have followed, Corie said gently, "You stay here, honey, and help me some more. I'm fixin' to put little brother down and I want you to stay and watch him, in case he wakes up again, while I go and milk the cow."

Alec sat looking out over the land. The sun had not come into the valley yet, but its light was well down on Never Summer, warm and bright. There was a soft, bright purity in the spring sky that was a tender poignance to look at. Alec was thin and haggard, his face and hands still showing the discoloration of deep bruising. The broken ribs he had suffered were far from being healed, so that he had to move with a careful, painful slowness. The deep cut on his temple, from which he had lost so much blood, was a fierce, ugly scar, though Corie had tried to give him some meager comfort by saying that it wouldn't show much later on, that Little Rain had done a good job of sewing the wound closed. His right arm was in a sling and he took the coffee cup awkwardly from Blake with his left hand.

"Corie tells me it's Sunday," Blake said.

"Corie told me quite a lot of things earlier," Alec said tiredly.

He turned his eyes to Blake for a moment. The misery and bewilderment in them were painful to see.

Blake said, "What I meant was that its being Sunday would be a good excuse to take some time off. Maybe you'd feel like a game of chess."

"You look like hell, Blake."

"I'm a little tired. It'll pass."

"Corie looks like hell, too. It's not anything like right, you with all the spring ranch work and Corie with four little kids to take care of . . . ."

"You'll be strong again soon, Alec."

"God, I hope so! I can't stand lying around much longer . . . . I'm afraid I hurt Corie's feelings this morning, by coming out here, but I had to. She's been good to me, to all of us and . . . ."

"She knows how it is."

They fell silent, each of them thinking back over the past few weeks.

Blake remembered the tense, defeated, fearful weariness as he had come back to the house with Hawk's Shadow, Eagle Feather, and Storm Coming Out Of The East on that damp windy morning. The rain had stopped briefly, but it would begin again. Corie came out onto the porch at the sound of their horses, her own fear and apprehension clear in her face.

"I'll take care of your horse," Eagle Feather said quietly, taking Blake's bridle from his hand.

"How are they?" Blake asked hoarsely.

"Alec's not come to yet," Corie said heavily. "I think he's a little stronger though. Katy's had her little boy but she's—awful bad, Blake. I'm afraid we'll lose her."

She began to cry. The tears made her impatient with herself and, in the midst of her anxiety and weariness, the impatience only made them flow faster.

Hawk's Shadow said, "We'll go home for a while. You send for me if . . . ."

He and Storm Coming Out Of The East rode away,

their tired horses at a walk, as heavy drops of rain began to fall again.

Corie said, sobbing, "Blake Westfall, do I have to drag out of you whatever else has happened? I've been scared so bad about you this whole night, I've not had half my senses about me."

"We found the men," he said heavily. "They tried to leave the valley by going over the shoulder of Never Summer to the upper Camas. They were caught in a snowslide. All three of them are dead."

For a moment Corie could not speak. Then she said chokingly, "Thank God you didn't have to shoot anybody. From the look on your face when you left here, I was so afraid . . . ."

"We stopped to have a talk with the two men at Stephens' place as we came back. They say they didn't know anything about this and I think they're telling the truth. They were fairly well frightened when they said it. Hawk's Shadow saw to that. They're going to leave the Valley this morning."

"Come in and get some dry clothes on and somethin' to eat," she said, trying hard to recapture her accustomed pragmatism.

Later in the morning, Katy roused a little.

"The baby?" she asked, her weak voice little more than a whisper.

"It's a boy, honey," Corie said, "a good strong, healthy little boy. He's asleep now."

"I remember you said before that it was a boy, but I thought I might have dreamed that . . . . I ought to feed him."

"After a while," Corie said soothingly, "when he wakes up again."

A shadow of terror crossed Katy's face as the previous night's horrors came back to her.

"Alec—" She struggled to get up.

Gently, Blake and Corie made her lie back again.

"Alec's doin' good," Corie said, "and Snowbird says Rebecca's feelin' a lot better this mornin'."

"What's wrong with me, Corie?" Katy asked, her eyes large with fear. "I never felt so weak and sick after the girls were born."

470

"They say ever' time is diff'rent and this has been a bad one. I want you just to be real still and rest."

"Does Alec know the baby's a boy?"

"He's real pleased about it."

Katy looked to Blake, trying to keep her mouth from trembling. "Corie's afraid to tell me. I know you won't lie. Is Alec dead?"

"He's still unconscious." Blake answered softly, "but he's stronger than he was last night. I think he's going to be all right."

She lay quiet for a time, her eyes closed, then she said softly, dreamily, "Let me see the baby."

Corie brought him and laid him beside her. Katy smiled sadly, looking into the wrinkled, sleeping little face.

"Do you think he'll look like Alec?"

"I think he's goin' to be the very picture of his daddy," Corie said and turned away abruptly to wipe her eyes.

"I'd like him to be named Alec," Katy said wistfully. "Alec has said he didn't want that but, please, ask him again."

The baby woke then and began crying. Corie took him up quickly and carried him into the kitchen where Snowbird was heating some milk. Little Rain had taken the other children home with her.

Katy said weakly, almost indifferently, "I always thought it would hurt to die. All I feel is—so tired."

"Katy—" Blake began and his voice broke.

"Don't," she said, trying to smile. "You never were any good at glossing things over. Everything shows in your face. Just . . . . do you remember that time just before Sylvia was born, when you held my hand and I fell asleep? Could you hold my hand again?"

Her hand was cold as he took it between both of his.

"I ought to see the girls," she said faintly. "That's what people are supposed to do at a time like this, isn't it? Only I don't want them to see me like this, to remember me this way. Alec . . . . oh, Blake, I couldn't do anything for him, not ever. I—I even stopped loving him the way I did in the beginning. About all we've done lately is—put up with each other. What's going to happen to him?"

"Try not to worry about any of that now," he said unevenly. "Just try to rest."

"Please don't ever tell him what I just said. I didn't stop loving him. It was just that he couldn't—let me love him in the only ways I knew."

Her eyes closed and she lapsed into unconsciousness. A few hours later, while rain still dripped morosely from a heavy sky, she died.

Now, as they sat together on the porch in the early June morning, Alec said painfully, "I wish I'd loved her, Blake. Anybody would have loved Katy. She deserved a million times more and better than she ever got . . . . What I understand least is why *she* was the one who died. Is there anything fair? Anything that makes sense?"

"There's time, Alec," Blake said heavily, "and trying to go on with living. I know you don't like to hear about it, but it's true. Time does make unbearable things easier, so that you can go on living with them."

"Does it make it so you can bear living—with yourself?"

"Alec—"

"Hell, I know I'm wallowing in self-pity and flagellation, but I can't seem to help it, or stop . . . . I don't think I *can* love anybody, Blake. What kind of way is that for a father to be thinking about his children—especially at a time when they've lost . . . ."

There was a long silence and then Blake began to tell him some things about the ranch work. He tried to talk in as much detail as he could, hoping to distract Alec's thoughts a little, knowing that he, himself, was still seeking to hide.

Finally, in a pause, Alec said, "When Wyeth was here yesterday, did he tell you Stephens has his land up for sale?"

"Yes. I want to see about buying some of it. I can get a loan from Connall."

"Maybe Connall won't want to lend you the money. He'll never forgive *me*."

"He will, Alec, with time. None of this was anyone's fault, except for those three men, and they're dead. Connall will be all right. I've known him a long, long time. At heart, he's a fair and reasonable man."

"Wyeth said the Stephenses have decided to invest in silver claims now," Alec said absently, then he looked at Blake briefly, his eyes again filled with misery. "They just came in here and . . . . tore everything apart and now they're going to invest in silver . . . . I ought to go after Talmadge when I can, and the old man, and Ellis Williams . . . ."

"No, son. It wouldn't change anything—not anything."

After another silence in which Alec made a painful effort to be more casual, the boy said, "Before Wyeth came out to find you yesterday, I asked him if he thought his boy George might come up here to work. Wyeth will have Courtney and Ethel's boy still at home. He said something could be worked out. George is just sixteen now, but he's a big, strong kid and a good worker . . . . Blake, I have to go away. As soon as I can, I have to go as far as I can. I'll send money to pay George's wages and to help out . . . . it's a hell of a thing to ask of you and Corie, to take the kids, but I just can't . . . ."

"They'll be fine, Alec."

"I've never believed it's any good, to run away, but, for now, I can't stay in the Valley."

"I know," Blake said quietly. "There was a time when I felt that way."

"I suppose it's true," Alec said wearily, "about history repeating itself. There are more such coincidences in this family than anyone would believe. Have you ever thought about it? Your father died, and your mother. My mother died, and now Katy . . . . And what do we do? We run. My God!"

"It may not be the way to handle things. I know it was wrong for me to leave you, but sometimes, there's just nothing else . . . ."

"Blake, why did you come back? I always have wondered."

"Because of you, and the country. I thought I could be of some use to you. I wanted to be."

"But which came first? Me or the country?"

"Alec—"

"No. Never mind. I've always known."

"I don't think you have. Let me try to tell you . . . . I guess it *was* the country that drew me back, chiefly. This

473

country, this valley, have been home to me since the first spring I spent here. I've been afraid of a lot of things, Alec, all my life. Mostly, I suppose I've been afraid of being insecure. This place gave me security. I don't know how to explain it. It's just the way I've always felt . . . .

"Do you remember that first year I was back, when it was beginning to be winter and you came up to the high valley? After that, it was more you that I was here for. I don't know how things came to be confused between us the way they are, but it was my fault. I didn't have the strength, the courage, the unselfishness to *give* you enough while you were growing up. I gave you theories, hypotheses, a lot of things that did nothing but add to your confusion. I couldn't give myself. I'm sorry, Alec. I can't begin to tell you how sorry I am. Now, I just don't know . . . . unless you and I could . . . ."

"Yes," Alec said tiredly, "I think I can see how it was—a little—because I can think of what I might do with the kids, if I stayed here. It's really true—isn't it?—that there's nothing new under the sun."

Blake shook his head sadly. "But we're all new," he said softly. "Every person that's born, everything that grows and is alive is individual enough to be new. All we have to be able to do is recognize the newness, the differentness, for everything it's worth. Just look at the mountain. You won't see it looking the same for any two minutes together."

"The mountain's not alive."

"It always has been, for me."

"And you'll always have the mountain," Alec said dully.

"Everyone has something," Blake said earnestly. "We have to have something. You've got whatever's inside yourself, and you've got the kids. If you don't and can't feel love for them now, that doesn't mean they stop existing. Let yourself depend on them and on us a little. Your responsibility to the children could keep you going for now. I don't mean you should stay here, not for a while, if you don't want to. Going away seems cowardly to you, I know, because of what I did and the way you've always hated that, but I truly think it may be the best thing you can do for now, for the kids and for yourself. But think

474

about them. Remember them. Know that they'll be counting on you, one way and another."

"You and Corie will be better for them as parents . . . ."

"Still, they're yours. We'll do all we can for them, you know that, but nothing will change the fact that you're their father. Let that help you to reconcile things. It can be a beginning, Alec . . . . Do you know where you want to go?"

"I—I'd like to find some place where I belong, like you found the Medicine Rock."

"You don't feel you belong here?"

"It's home but . . . . I've never been content just to stay here for long at a time. It seems that here, more than anywhere else, I have to be always trying to sort out the Indian and the white, trying to understand . . . ."

"Alec, when you were ten years old, you went up on Never Summer and you had a medicine dream. Don't say anything until I've finished. You had more of an experience up there than most boys ever dream of having. I should have told you this at the time."

"No!" he said harshly.

"Why?" Blake cried. "Accept what there is. You've got more, in that way, than most people ever even think of hoping for. What do you want?"

"I—I want enough to—please you."

"Alec, for God's sake," Blake said brokenly and could say no more.

"I've never felt—good enough to be your son."

"I don't see how you could ever have thought that way," Blake said brokenly.

"While you were away, I remember how the People talked about you. Hawk's Shadow, Owl Woman, all of them . . . . they acted as if there was something magic about you."

"They never have—"

"Oh, I know how they *seem* to feel, always saying you're strange and crazy and things like that, but you never saw into them. I've begun to think lately that maybe you never really saw into people, how they feel and such things, because you, maybe, haven't thought highly enough of yourself to be able to believe what other people think of you. The People have, underneath, always had great re-

475

spect and admiration for you and I—have always been afraid of you, that I wouldn't please you, wouldn't measure up . . . ."

Blake's hand was on his shoulder, gripping it tightly, feeling the thinness, the trembling. He said hoarsely, "I never imagined anything like that. I've always thought it was the other way around. That I couldn't . . . . but what I was trying to tell you about the medicine dream is . . . . why expect the world to shift and tremble? Just how much are you going to go on expecting, demanding of yourself? Why have you always had to be . . . ."

"You're my father," the boy said painfully. "I've expected myself to be a good son to you, and I never have been. At first, I thought it would please you if I was just a good Medicine Rock boy. That didn't seem to work out, so I decided to be a white son to you. The People all kept saying I was wrong about that and I thought it didn't please you much either. I just can't be . . . ."

"Alec, you *are*. You're my son. I've always loved you and been proud of your being my son. You're a good Medicine Rock boy and a good white. I've let you go on struggling all these years because of my lack of courage and because I've thought it was your prerogative to want the moon and to expect yourself to be able to get it. Whenever you began thinking this way, you were too young to be able to understand things properly for yourself. I guess grown-ups don't know, often, what's going to count most heavily with their children, what concepts they're going to take up and not be able to let go of. I've been grossly unfair to you, son, and selfish. I'll tell you now, because I can't go back and tell you earlier, that you're not going to have the moon. You've been far too hard on yourself all these years. Please—try to begin easing up a little. Everything you do—almost everything—you're the very best at. If you can't be best, you say the hell with it and then tear yourself apart because you're not best and because you quit . . . . This thing of being a father is an example. Come home again, some day, and try it. You could begin by just being a dutiful father, if that's all you feel. Who knows what could grow out of that? For God's sake, Alec, don't go away just to look for more things that you can't have and do and be."

Alec said softly, "Blake, do you really believe it was a medicine dream?"

"Yes. I know it was."

Alec looked at him briefly and turned his blurred eyes up to Never Summer.

He said, his voice uneven and awed, "I've just remembered . . . . when I fell asleep up there, after the storm, and dreamed of my mother . . . . I've always thought she said nothing, just stood and looked at me . . . . but just now, something has come back to me. Nearly sixteen years and I never remembered it. Do you think I'm inventing now, just to make things—"

"Don't do that, Alec. Don't take it apart and analyze it. Just let it be, please, son. What did she say?"

"She said, 'You've come from the midst of a storm.' " He was speaking in the language of the People. "She said, 'Your life will be storm, but sometimes . . . . there will be sunshine.' "

Alec covered his face with trembling hands and began to cry.

XXII

"I NEVER HAVE CARED MUCH for winter, but I like this kind of day," Corie said with a happy sigh as she came in from the kitchen and sat down at her spinning wheel.

It was January and snowing heavily outside. They were all together in the front room, the children studying, Blake reading a not-too-old newspaper. Corie took note, as she seemed to be doing so often these days, with pride and nostalgia, of how the children were growing up.

Sarah Ellen said, "Couldn't we make some snow ice cream? Just look at all that snow out there, waiting for us to use it."

"There's two feet of it," Corie said placidly, "with this new stuff fallin' on top of that. You just go ahead and do your lessons. We'll see about the ice cream for supper."

Blake was reading about the preserves or national parks they were calling Yellowstone and Grand Teton. It was 1877 now. The areas had been set aside several years ago to be "preserved for posterity." He had been asked, as the plans for preservation were being implemented, to take a part in the mapping and surveying of that Stinking Country where he and Hawk's Shadow and so many others had gone to collect tool stone and to marvel at the geysers and glaciers, the lakes and mountains, the magic, mystical beauty of the country. Blake couldn't put much credence in the part of the proclamation that said "in perpetuity," but it was a beginning, a concrete gesture that might indicate that the country as a whole was coming to have some respect for its western heritage. The eastern tourists who came out to gaze and wonder made him feel irritable and uneasy, but some of them *did* gaze and wonder with something of the awe he had felt and that countless generations of Indians had felt for the place. That gave him hope.

"The thing is," Corie had pointed out, "if they come out to see those parks, they can't help lookin', a little, at the country and people around them. Maybe they'll get to thinkin' some about westerners that way, Indians and whites, that we're just more people pretty much like them, who want safe, secure homes and all the rest of it."

Blake worried that gold would be found in the parks, or silver or copper or something else that someone could make big money from, that the part about perpetuity in the proclamations would go the way of those many henceforths and forevers in the Indian treaties.

Just now, he was reading a glowing report of a big new hotel planned for Yellowstone. If he could have, as Corie said, his "druthers," he would have preferred that the easterners stay back east. Still, it was their country, too, and perhaps they were entitled to the chance to come to know it. So long as they stayed in their tourist hotels and did their clumsy, aching horseback riding on the planned trails, the country was far better off than if they came in wild, exploitative stampedes to look for gold or to erode the land with abortive attempts at plowing and irrigation.

"Why are all these stories so silly?" asked Richard, looking up restlessly from his reader. "Who ever heard of a crow with sense enough to drop pebbles into a pitcher till the water came up to where he could get a drink? And why do they have to say pebbles anyway? It must have been just plain old rocks."

"It's like a fable, Richard," murmured Sylvia with a kind of absent patience, scarcely glancing up from her own book. "It's supposed to teach you a lesson."

"If I want a drink," he said, exasperated, "I wouldn't have to drop rocks in a pitcher. There's the pump and the creek and all that snow."

Richard was Corie's son. He looked like her and he *was* like her, with Corie's easy terms on life and Corie's unimaginative, beautiful pragmatism that went on being a joy and a marvel to his father, like a fresh summer wind coming down off the peaks. He was a sturdy, robust boy, who took great, animal pleasure in anything physical, from eating to fighting. His light brown hair—he had escaped, somehow, his mother's last haircutting session—kept falling over his eyes as he sat frowning over the didactic reader.

Blake went back to his own thinking, a kind of review of the past decade. There had been more new Indian treaties and, before that, more trouble. There had been many small incidents and there had been the massacre at Meeker's Agency, down in Colorado, and the ghastly, ridiculous debacle of Custer's men with the Sioux on the Little Bighorn. America seemed to feel it was finally getting such problems solved to everyone's best interest, though. The Indians, of course, were not considered by many to be a part of Everyone. Confinement to reservations was much more stringent now and many tribes had been moved to territory that was completely alien to them, leaving them bruised and bewildered, capable of doing nothing more than trying to survive. Some tribes and bands from the interior northwest had been set as far away as the so-called Indian Territory, and even that land, set aside forever, was now being opened under the intense pressure of encroaching white settlers.

"I have to go out to the toilet," announced Sarah Ellen, a little defiantly, glancing petulantly at Blake.

"You've already been," he said calmly. "Just write the sentences and have them done."

She grimaced and moved the candle. It was growing darker, though it was only mid-afternoon. It looked as if this would be a long, heavy storm.

"I never will be any good at penmanship anyway," Sarah Ellen said fretfully. She was the MacPheirson of Katy's and Alec's children, with the red hair, the vivid coloring, the restless need for activity, and the reluctance to sit still long for anything that had to do with books—Connall's granddaughter. She had gone to school for two years in Helena, living with her uncle Con and his family. Sarah Ellen had liked that, not because of the schooling but for the opportunities living in town gave her for seeing new people and varied things. She was not there this year because there had been an outbreak of serious illness and the school authorities had felt it best to close the school for the rest of the winter. Sarah Ellen was finding Blake a harder taskmaster than her teachers had been.

"Girls don't need to know things like penmanship and how to add up figures," she would point out petulantly.

"Everybody," he would reply, "needs to know all they can—about everything."

There was a school in Harmony but it was very small and ill-equipped, its teacher having, perhaps, a sixth-grade education of his own. Connall had suggested once or twice, rather half-heartedly, that the children could stay with him in order to attend this school, but Blake had said to Corie that it would be worse than no schooling at all.

"All they would learn is recitation, no thinking at all."

And Connall already had a houseful of children, his second family. He was in his late sixties now and sorely troubled with rheumatism. He spent most of his time sitting on the porch or by the stove, talking with whoever happened to come in, while Sally and the children looked after his store.

Sadly, Connall had never quite got over Alec's and Katy's marriage. Nancy, the youngest daughter from his first family, had married a wealthy cattle buyer, and young Con's wife was the daughter of a man who owned large blocks of silver stock. But Connall couldn't help thinking, more often it seemed as he grew older, that Katy, his darling red-haired girl, and whatever children she might have had could have done so much better than Alec Westfall. Not that he had anything against Blake, he had tried rather pathetically to explain once. Blake, he said, had always been like a son to him, though he still couldn't help considering the "lad" a little incompetent, dreamy, with too many idealistic, romantic notions. Connall sometimes sighed and brooded briefly over what might become of poor little Katy's children, but he had so many grandchildren, and so many more children in this second family of his, that there was not a great deal of time and thought to be spared.

Sarah Ellen said, with restless defiance, "When I get big, I'll have a store like Grandpa Connall's, and just sell things."

"You'll have to be able to write out orders and things so other people can read them," Sylvia told her.

"No, I'll just sell things. Somebody else can do the books."

"Girls don't have stores," Richard said scornfully.

"Girls have anything they want to," stated Sarah Ellen irately.

And Sylvia said, "I wish you'd both just be quiet. I can't think about what I'm reading when you keep talking all the time."

Strangely enough, the room fell silent. There was only the busy, businesslike whirring of Corie's wheel and, during pauses in its activity, the ticking of the clock, the faint hiss of blown snow against the windows, the pleasant, complacent chuckling of the fire.

Sylvia, Corie said, was like Blake. She always had to go off and think about everything. For the most part, she was quiet and serious, a beautiful child at eleven, with large sober dark eyes. She liked to wear her heavy black hair in severe braids that made her look older than she was. She had had a year of schooling in Helena, living with Con's family, and then she had asked to stay at home.

"When they teach us things like history," she had reported soberly to Blake, "it's all George Washington and Thomas Jefferson and Benjamin Franklin and people like that. I know they're important but, at school, nobody has ever mentioned people like Jim Bridger and Winter Thunder and Brigham Young. They're part of it too . . . . Anybody can learn to read and write. You can help us with Latin and math and such. Corie teaches us to cook and sew and all. The best thing about studying at home is talking about things, trying to figure out how they came to be the way they are. They don't do that at school. They just try to get through the lessons. Nobody wants to think about things."

When the children were small, it had been confusing that Blake and Corie were parents to Richard and grandparents to the rest of them, and so eventually everyone used first names.

"I never heard the like," Corie had worried in the beginning. "*I* never thought you ought to have let Alec call you Blake. It's not a bit respectful."

482

"I could call a man 'sir' or 'your honor,'" Blake pointed out, "and still think he's a sonofabitch. What do titles mean, really?"

She had smirked at him disapprovingly. "I don't have to listen to that kind of language, Blake Westfall. The things I put up with around this place would turn most women's toenails."

He looked at her now fondly in the candlelight. She was graying and her face had taken on the gaunt, harried look that seemed to be the stamp of pioneer women, but her brown eyes were sharp and bright, her tongue as quick as it had ever been, she smiled often and liked to sing old hymns at her endless work.

Blake himself was beginning to show age. Why not? he thought a little resignedly. He would be fifty-eight in the spring. His brown hair was liberally streaked with gray and he seemed to get tired sooner than he used to. Still, he and Hawk's Shadow and Eagle Feather were the best and most successful hunters in the Camas country and he was making a reasonable success of the ranch.

He still had George Hamilton, Wyeth's boy, working with him most of the time and, if things were especially busy, he could usually get one or two of the Medicine Rock boys to help. George was grown and married now, with a baby son of his own. He lived farther up the valley in the house the Stephenses had built and then abandoned. Wyeth had helped George to buy some of their land and Blake had bought all the rest of it he could, so that they were what Corie called land poor.

"You wouldn't care if you had a cow or horse to graze on it," she had said tolerantly. "All you want is to look at it and to see a big figure of acres on a deed."

"That's true," Blake had agreed readily. "It seems the only way I can keep the valley the way I like to see it."

New people had come in occasionally over the past years, but none had stayed more than a season or two, so that only the old settlers were there now. Emmett Price had died two years ago, leaving sons to run his place. His farm and Eli's, with their irrigated fields, provided more than enough food for their families.

Out along the Camas, there were two well-established ranches besides Wyeth's between the Medicine Rock and

Harmony, and there was the Boyd place on the upper Camas. Cattle prices fluctuated wildly, but few of the people who came to stay had ever had much hope of getting rich. They managed, as Corie said, to keep body and soul together. They kept holding on, through good years and bad, because the land had a hold on them.

A few of the Medicine Rock People with claims had decided over the years to join the ones on the reservation. As they left, Eagle Feather had managed to buy their deeds. During the past few years, he had been investing all he could in sheep. This was a sore point with some of his neighbors, but he went on quietly and soberly about his business, making more money, comparatively, from the sale of wool than the cattlemen did from beef, convincing some others of the People, by his example, to try sheep-raising.

"Maybe sheep are what the land was meant for," he had said to Blake once, with that clever foxy grin.

Hawk's Shadow had not heard that. He was out hunting elk at the time.

The question of the People's homestead claims had been settled anticlimactically and with as little publicity as possible when Clay Morgan, the Helena attorney, became a territorial representative. He had won that election by a huge margin over Ellis Williams, who had died of heart trouble soon afterward. When Morgan went to live in Washington, he and some of the influential people he knew from the days of the War Between the States moved, in the complicated and mysterious ways of politicians, to make things warm and uncomfortable for various government agencies, bureaus, and officials. Finally, to keep things quiet, they had settled the matter by unobtrusively validating the Medicine Rock claims. The whole affair was not quite legal under various statutes and several high officials huffed pompously—but privately— that nothing like it must be allowed to happen again, but, as Morgan told Blake later, "What they want most is to have the thing hushed up so they can begin convincing themselves it never happened. Their excuse is that these people have been living on their claims for so long now. There aren't many of them, they say, so an exception can be made this once, even though they are Indians who used illegal names."

"The land belonged to the People a long time before that," Blake had repeated, dissatisfied, "to all of them."

Morgan had sighed, a little crestfallen. "My God, man! Try to be satisfied with this much for now. Can't you see this as a beginning, a kind of hole in the dike?"

Blake got up now to replenish the fire and Sylvia looked up at him, sighing discontentedly.

"This new history book isn't any better than the old ones," she said. "All it tells about west of the Mississippi are the Louisiana Purchase, Lewis and Clark, and gold in California. Don't the people that write these books know how long people like us have been here and that things happen to us, too? You can tell all about trappers and miners and Indians and ranchers. Corie knows all about slaves and plantations, the War Between the States and how it was to come west. I think people like you *live* history and it's a waste of time to read about the Boston Tea Party."

"Still, you need to know things about the rest of the world," Blake said almost automatically, sitting down again and taking up the newspaper that he had long since stopped reading.

"Throwing tea into Boston Harbor is not nearly as interesting and exciting as things like when Hawk's Shadow brought you here that time after you'd been hurt so bad and you were the first white man ever allowed to live in the Valley."

Richard had pushed his slate away eagerly, glad of any excuse. He said with gusto, "I want Corie to tell about in the war when all those people were starving to death in Vicksburg and they ate rats."

After a little persuasion, Corie obliged, digressing into some details about her girlhood life.

Blake saw that young Alec went on with what he was doing while he listened. The others had all stopped their work. The little boy had been laboring over some math problems. Math did not come very easily to him and a part of the reason was that he could never seem to overcome the temptation to keep drawing little pictures on the margins of his papers.

485

Almost seven, this Alec was a serious child who tended to spend more time alone than Corie thought good for him. He looked as his father had at that age, with the chiseled, handsome, faintly Indian features, and his eyes were green. He was left-handed, the only one of the children to inherit that characteristic, and Blake had told Corie that he dared anyone to so much as mention the phenomenon to the boy. Young Alec was also the only one who had inherited the pixylike smile of Red Sky's children. It did not come as often as they wished it might, but, when it did, it wrought a striking transformation in the sober, intent little face.

The children sat enthralled by Corie's account of what Sylvia called "living history." Blake, also listening, glanced idly back at his paper, to see that the country's financial situation seemed to be gaining a more stable footing.

There had been an economic panic in 1873 and speculators in metals and western land had sustained heavy losses. It had caused the exodus of a good many people from the west, mostly those who had never intended staying anyway, but it had also brought a new influx of easterners, trying to make a living for their families, seeking the Promised Land.

The railroads had done a great deal of heavy promoting of towns, farm and ranch land, looking for nothing more than a quick return on all the government land they had been given for putting the tracks through. Once the railroad work was done and most of the trains did no more than pass through, many of the towns had dwindled away to little more than a water tank and perhaps a weathered depot. Dry land farming in the high plains and mountain country was proving, in great part, to be a dismal failure, disastrous for the settlers and the land alike. Some ranchers had managed to stay, proclaiming smugly that God had meant the country for ranching and nothing else. And there was the mining.

Some years ago, a few prospectors had come into the Medicine Rock to do some desultory panning and haphazard digging. They had found color in two or three small streams of the valley, including the one that drained

Blake's little cirque and that was now being called West-fall Creek, but there had not been enough to do much for their feverish hopes and aspirations. Then word had reached them of silver and copper strikes east of the Divide and they had left in a frenetic rush, stopping long enough to ask Blake as he shod a horse in the corral if he knew what copper ore might look like.

Silver and copper and other valuable minerals were being taken from the ground in places all along the mountains, but the Medicine Rock, all the Camas country, seemed to be settling back into a quiet routine of simply existing, moving through the seasons, dealing with what came.

Perhaps, Blake thought, the West as a whole was destined always to be more or less in some state of boom or bust. It was that kind of country and it attracted that kind of people. It was, and he hoped always would be, a land of extremes and rather violent variety.

Corie had finished her story, and Richard was chattering enthusiastically about what he would have done had he been living in Vicksburg during the war. Young Alec asked rather incongruously, "What do they mean when they say 'Uncle Sam'? I heard Uncle Wyeth say 'Uncle Sam is going to take more money in taxes.'"

"It's just another name for the country," Sylvia told him. "You know, those pictures you see of that nice old man? It's a symbol for the country and the government."

"But not for the Confederacy," said Richard proudly.

"There's not any Confederacy anymore," said Sylvia a little absently, looking back at her history book.

"Richard's an uncle!" exclaimed Sarah Ellen, having just come upon the discovery. "He's the uncle of all the rest of us. Uncle Richard!" She laughed delightedly.

"Shut your mouth," said Richard hotly.

"That's no way to talk, Richard Blake Westfall," said Corie severely.

"Well, I'm not any uncle. Uncles are old people."

"You are an uncle and there's not a thing in the world you can do to change it. Now, I don't ever want to hear you sayin' 'shut your mouth' like that to anybody."

"I don't *want* to be an uncle, so what *can* I say to Sarah Ellen then, to make her quit talkin' about it?"

Sylvia suggested sweetly, "Say, I do not care to discuss the subject further at this time."

Richard snorted. "You think *that* would shut up Sarah Ellen? It takes a bash in the mouth to keep her quiet."

"It doesn't, either," said Sarah Ellen. "I don't think you're even proud to be our uncle."

Richard was ready to agree with that, but Corie said sternly, "There's entirely too much smart talk around here and I want it stopped, right now."

She looked at Blake who had his eyes on the paper and was smiling.

"That's what comes of all this free-thinkin' and liberalism. In my day, kids behaved."

"Yes," he agreed blithely, "In mine, too. Now it's hardly anything but recalcitrance and iconoclasm."

She frowned, shrugged resignedly and went back to her work.

After a while, looking up from the paper, he said, "This barbed wire is quite an invention. Eli and Eagle Feather have both ordered a lot of it."

"What is it?" asked Corie. She was carding more wool now and not much interested in barbed wire, but it was so good having them all here in the house together like this.

"It's just strands of wire twisted together with a sharp barb put in every so often. You can make a tight fence that will hold almost any stock, with just three or four strands of it."

"I'll bet it wouldn't hold elk." said Richard. "They'd lean against it like they do our fences now, and manage to break it down."

"That's the stuff I heard Wyeth talkin' about," Corie said. "He says most ever'body's against it."

"Most cattle ranchers," Blake agreed. "They're afraid of being fenced away from all the free, open range they've been using all these years."

"Well, why shouldn't they use it?" she demanded absently. "The good Lord put the land here to be used, didn't he?"

"I guess He did," Blake said quietly.

Sarah Ellen said restlessly, "I wish it was about to be Christmas again."

488

"We just got through havin' Christmas last month," said Corie.

"But it's the *best* time," said the girl dreamily.

"And if it was Christmas again," said Sylvia wistfully, "maybe we'd get another letter from Daddy."

Alec was in Paris, had been there five years. He was teaching art classes and not very happy about that, but he was also doing his own painting. "The native western American artist," said the newspaper clippings he sometimes sent them, "with a talent for truth and realism in art which is, perhaps unfortunately, beyond his time and not readily acceptable to his fellow artists or the buying public." But he was selling some work and had been able to raise his prices gradually.

He had been back to the Medicine Rock twice in nearly eight years, for periods of several months at a time, but each time he had eventually grown restless and dissatisfied, nervous and irritable. His children, their growth and mental acuities, left Alec bewildered, saddened, more than a little frightened.

"When I'm rich and famous enough to sell paintings from here," he had told Blake the last time, "I'll come home to work. I've lost most of my chances with the kids, if I ever had any, but maybe I can get to know some grandchildren one day. Maybe I could build in the upper valley and live there again. It would beat hell out of any city."

He had spent a good deal of time during his visits making plans about the horses. Horses from the Westfall ranch were now considered the best quarter-horse stock in the territory, and Alec was still searching for Indian stock, later to be known as Appaloosa, for breeding and strengthening of their lines.

"He spends a lot more thought and energy on those horses than he does on his own children," Corie had complained in consternation.

"Horses are so much simpler," Blake had replied almost curtly.

"Well, *Alec's* not simple," she said impatiently. "Why can't he just—"

"That's the whole problem, Corie," he said. "Please,

just try to be patient and let him work things out as he can."

Alec sent the children gifts and he sent money to provide for them. Two or three times a year he wrote long letters to the family, faintly cynical and humorous, about what he had been doing, places, things, and people with whom he had come in contact. He wrote practically nothing about himself, what he might be thinking or feeling; but trying to read between the lines, Blake thought that perhaps the self-derision and bitterness, the impossible expectations were being leeched out of Alec, little by little with the passing of the years. Perhaps one day he truly would be able to come home, if not to the Medicine Rock, then to wherever was right for him.

"Anne and Bonnie want Sylvia and me to spend the night with them tomorrow," reported Sarah Ellen.

Anne and Bonnie were daughters of Eagle Feather and Snowbird.

"If we do," said Sylvia eagerly, "we can go over to Hawk's Shadow's lodge and get him to tell us stories before bedtime."

"Why does he just keep livin' in that old lodge?" Richard wondered. "Little Rain's cabin is right there, next to it, and it's a lot warmer and everything."

"Because Hawk's Shadow likes the old ways best," Blake said, folding the paper. It was time they got the evening work done.

"Maybe you can't understand that, Richard," Sylvia said, a little condescendingly, "because you're not Indian."

My God! Blake thought dryly, a little incredulously. Discrimination begins at home.

"Well," said Richard, only slightly perturbed, "I can shoot with a bow better than anybody in the valley my age. If the girls get to go and stay with Anne and Bonnie, then Jim ought to get to come up here. We could go hunting or something."

"I'll tell you one thing," said Corie critically, "there's not been much lesson-gettin' around this place today. Look at that clock! It's time to start supper."

"Let me see what you're doing, Alec," Blake said.

The boy brought the papers and stood by his chair.

"This is the math here," he said in shy apology.

He had a front tooth missing and he stood waiting while Blake looked at the papers, poking his tongue through the hole in his teeth.

The pages were covered, for the most part, with sketches—of horses and dogs, of Hawk's Shadow chipping at a stone, of Corie at her spinning wheel, looking harried and proud and loving. What the boy could do with faces, at his age, was a miracle to Blake.

"You've not done much math," he said mildly. "If you're going to be a painter, you'll have to know enough math to be able to add up the money you make."

Alec gave him the shy, pixy smile, his green eyes sparkling.

"I don't care about making any money. Look at this."

He turned one of the papers to show Blake a sketch of the boulder castle up in the high valley.

"Some day, I'll make something like that. I want to go up there next summer, all by myself, and draw it real good with those new kind of paints Daddy sent. Could I use them?"

"Yes."

"Maybe," said the boy dreamily, "there's not another boy in the whole world with a grandpa that's made a castle."

After a moment, Corie got up, saying brusquely, "Come on, girls, let's see what we can do about supper. Sarah Ellen, you peel some potatoes and, Sylvia, you wrap up good and go see if there's any eggs. Somebody ought to have gathered them before this. They're likely frozen. You can't put a thing down in this country in the wintertime without it freezes. Richard, quit playin' in the fire. You've poked at it now till you've nearly put it out."

Blake and the boys went out to do the chores around the barn. Richard energetically forked down hay. Young Alec brought oats to a brood mare they were keeping up because she was due to foal. The boy stayed on in the stall, caressing the mare's head. Sylvia dashed in, her black hair almost white with snow. She had got away, somehow, without wearing any covering on her head.

"It's going to be really cold tonight," she reported happily.

491

"It's January," said Richard. "What do you expect?"

Blake found the ointment for which he had been searching and began treating a sore on the milk cow's flank. She had evidently snagged herself somehow on some brush.

"I got three eggs and they're not frozen," Sylvia said.

Richard said, "You all remember about the snow ice cream for supper."

"I love it when it storms," Sylvia said fervently. "It's so nice when we're all home together and it's snowing. The only thing I don't like is that you can't see Never Summer. When I think about that, it makes me feel sort of— lost somehow."

"You don't have to see him," Alec said soberly, leaning his cheek against the mare's lowered muzzle. "You can *feel* Never Summer standing there. *I* can feel him, even in Harmony or Helena. I'll bet you can feel him any place in the world if you know how. Never Summer'll never go away."

To the Reader

GEOGRAPHY DRAWS MY INTEREST because I like the feeling of being a part of the country, wherever I am, and so a part of the world, of knowing about things that have happened in any particular place and imagining what the people involved in these happenings had to go through to accomplish what they did. There are also comforts and reassurances for me in being in touch with the topography of an area.

THIS LAND IS MINE is fiction. It is very firmly grounded in real history and geography, but I have taken many liberties, shifting dates and places a bit to fit in with the story. There are, obviously, some real places and people mentioned: William Clark, Brigham Young, Jim Bridger did exist. There were forts Laramie, Hall, Union, and Vancouver. There are, of course, rivers called the Missouri, Platte, Snake, Clark Fork. There is not, so far as I have been able to ascertain, a mountain called Never Summer in western Montana, and there is no Camas River nor any actual locations such as Medicine Rock Valley, Camas Post, St. Denis Mission, or the town of Crownsville. I have made free use of western Montana's Bitterroot Valley, changing its topography somewhat and calling it Camas Valley. None of the characters who appear in this book are meant to represent any real persons.

Basically, events did take place in the interior northwest along the lines I have laid down here. First the fur trappers and traders came into the country, then missionaries and some settlers. Military posts were established;

then came the miners, the railroads, and, always, more settlers.

I have taken liberties with actual dates and events not only because the book is basically fiction, but as a form of self-protection. Some of the research work was hard to certify absolutely, and I felt that suiting events to my own purposes, and saying so, would prevent other and far better students of the period, some of whom I hope will read this book, from the temptation of catching me up on all the small details.

Should any reader care to study the history of this period further, I highly recommend David Lavender's book, *The Rockies,* and a book called *Across the Wide Missouri,* by Bernard De Voto, as a good beginning. There are also some good books on the Indian tribes of the area such as *Flathead Indian Nation,* by Peter Ronan, and *The Nez Percés,* by Francis Haines, and a book called *Wilderness Journey,* written as a diary in the 1840's by Father Nicolas Point but only recently published. My most informative sources of information about Indian life came from reports to the Department of the Interior and ethnographic commentaries. I would like to thank the staff of the Western History Department, Denver Public Library, for helping me to locate and obtain access to these reports.

What struck me most strongly and regrettably all through my research was that through all the "development, civilization, and progress" of the West, the Indians always came out the losers. I have not played down or excused this disgraceful fact. On the other hand, I do not mean to vilify the whites who came west. Most of them were fine, honest, even heroic people who entirely believed that they were in the right and who did not have the advantage of the perspective and hindsight we have today.

THE BEST OF THE BESTSELLERS
FROM WARNER BOOKS!

THE KINGDOM by Ron Joseph   **(81-467, $2.50)**
The saga of a passionate and powerful family who carves out of
the wilderness the largest cattle ranch in the world. Filled with
both adventure and romance, hard-bitten empire building and
tender moments of intimate love, **The Kingdom** is a book for all
readers.

BLUE SKIES, NO CANDY by Gael Greene   **(81-368, $2.50)**
"How in the world were they able to print **Blue Skies, No Candy**
without some special paper that resists Fahrenheit 451? (That's
the burning point of paper!) This sizzling sexual odyssey ele-
vates Ms. Greene from her place at the head of the food-writing
list into the Erica Jong pantheon of sexually liberated fiction-
alists."—**Liz Smith, New York Daily News**

THESE GOLDEN PLEASURES   **(82-416, $2.25)**
by Valerie Sherwood
From the stately mansions of the east to the freezing hell of the
Klondike, beautiful Roxanne Rossiter went after what she wanted—
and got it all! By the author of the phenomenally successful **This
Loving Torment**.

THE OTHER SIDE OF THE MOUNTAIN 2   **(82-463, $2.25)**
by E.G. Valens
Part 2 of the inspirational story of a young Olympic contender's
courageous climb from paralysis and total helplessness to a useful
life and meaningful marriage. An NBC-TV movie and serialized
in **Family Circle** magazine.

 A Warner Communications Company

Please send me the books I have checked.

Enclose check or money order only, no cash please. Plus 50¢ per
copy to cover postage and handling. N.Y. State residents add
applicable sales tax.

Please allow 2 weeks for delivery.

WARNER BOOKS
P.O. Box 690
New York, N.Y. 10019

Name ....

Address ....

City .... State .... Zip ....

_____ Please send me your free mail order catalog